THE HOUSE THAT BJ BUILT

THE HOUSE THAT BJ BUILT

Anuja Chauhan

𝓌

westland ltd

61, II Floor, Silverline, Alapakkam Main Road, Maduravoyal, Chennai 600095
93, 1 Floor, Sham Lal Road, Daryaganj, New Delhi 110002

First published in India by westland ltd 2015

Copyright © Anuja Chauhan 2015

10 9 8 7 6 5 4 3 2 1

ISBN: 978-93-85152-18-4

Typeset in Electra LT Regular by SÜRYA, New Delhi
Printed at Thomson Press (India) Ltd.

The author asserts her moral right to be identified as the author of this work.

For Niranjan Alva,
father, FIL, feminist
amazing lyricist
loyal, vocal cheering squad
stress-swallowing lightning rod
giver of solid talking-tos
industrial strength family glue

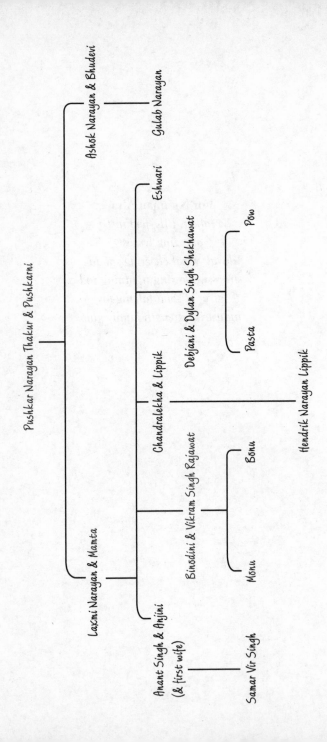

Pushkar Narayan Thakur & Pushkarni

Laxmi Narayan & Mamta

Ashok Narayan & Bhudevi

Anant Singh & Anjini
(& first wife)

Chandralekha & Lippik

Eshwari

Gulab Narayan

Samar Vir Singh

Binodini & Vikram Singh Rajawat

Hendrik Narayan Lippik

Debjani & Dylan Singh Shekhawat

Monu

Bonu

Pasta

Pou

PROLOGUE

'What the hell?' Samar Vir Singh rears up in bed, looking around dazedly for the source of the cacophony, his head throbbing fit to burst. His phone glows green in the gloom and he lunges for it, thumb jabbing downwards to shut the damn thing up.

There are sixteen missed calls from Zeeshan. But Zee never wakes up before noon. Is it that late already?

Also, sixteen?

Samar calls him back.

'Hello?'

'What *hello-hello*, bastard,' laments Zeeshan Khan hoarsely, his famous baritone barely recognizable. 'Here our balls are on the chopping block and you're saying hello? We're fucked. We're finished. We're dead. Where the hell are you?'

'At home,' Samar replies. 'Stop being so dramatic, Zee. What happened?'

Zeeshan makes a weird gibbering sound.

Samar stretches and shakes his head. 'I didn't get that. Speak slowly.'

'Get online and Google our names. Then call me back.'

'But—'

But Zeeshan has already hung up.

Samar drops the phone onto the bed and looks about blearily

for his iPad. It is nowhere in sight. The dark fitted suit he had worn last night is lying crumpled inside-out at the foot of the bed, along with the tight shoes his stylist insisted 'went' with it. Samar shudders. God, that outfit was uncomfortable. He walks over to the window and yanks open the curtains, wincing at the glare. Ah, *there's* the iPad.

The early Mumbai sunshine illuminates a lean, muscular figure, clad only in white low-slung drawstring pyjamas. His hair is dark, his skin-tone warm, his feet well-shaped and sinewy as they grip the wooden floor. His prominent aquiline nose and strong, stubbled jaw combine to create a harsh effect, but he also possesses a sudden little-boy-smile which, when it flashes, makes nonsense of the harshness and puts even the rawest of Bollywood newcomers totally at ease.

He isn't smiling now, though.

* *Upstart duo badmouth industry bigwigs.*

* *'My dick can direct better than the moron who won Best Director,' declares Samar Vir Singh.*

* *'Chutiyon ki baraat' is how gen-now superstar Zeeshan Khan and edgy young director Samar Vir Singh summed up the sight of the Bombay film industry stepping onto the red carpet for the Sparkler Awards tonight.*

Watch the video of the disgruntled nominees, who won nothing last night and ended up at the Oregano Bar and Kitchen for a late night bitch-fest, here.

Samar rubs his scummy eyes and clicks on the link. Zeeshan and he, dishevelled and disorderly in their awards night finery, bloom into sight, standing atop the deserted bar at Oregano, waving about bottles of Jack Daniels while singing a bawdy version of the classic song from *Yaadon ki Baraat*.

Samar swears and reaches for his phone. Zeeshan answers at the first ring.

'You saw?' he demands.

'Yeah,' Samar replies. 'D'you have any idea who recorded it?'

'That fat smirky waiter—Desmond. I'm sure it was him. He spits into the food and waters down the alcohol. I never tip him.'

'Did we actually say all this stuff?'

'We must have,' Zeeshan replies morosely. 'I remember you ranting on about how sycophantic directors are Bollywood's biggest bane, and how the slippery slope of tiny, tiny compromises leads inexorably to a shit-pit full of glittering, diamond-encrusted, 100-crore turds. But it gets a little hazy after that.'

'How mad is everybody?'

'Seething. AK, the older Khans, the studio heads. There's been abso *no* reply to the sorry-sorry smses I've been sending out all morning. Hell, they aren't even taking my dad's calls. He woke me up with the bad news, by the way, raving with crazy eyes about The Chawl.'

Samar holds his pounding head. 'What chawl, fucker? We didn't go to any chawl last night.'

'*The* Chawl, man. You know, where my dad grew up. When me and my sis were little, we were always made to listen to Legends-Of-The-Chawl. "You are growing up in superstar Zaffar Khan's sea-facing bungalow—but I grew up in a CHAWL. I shared a room with thirty people and a bathroom with four hundred people blah blah blah." It was a nightmare, dude. If we dared ask for Hubba Babba chewing gum instead of bloody Boomer, we got a lecture on The Chawl, if we asked for a second scoop of ice cream, we got a lecture on The Chawl. Anyway, he thinks yesterday's fiasco is going to send our family straight back to The Chawl.'

'So the Khans are actually *Chawl*as?' Samar can't help grinning.

Zeeshan's voice climbs an octave.

'Don't joke, bastard! We've attacked *legends*, and we've been recorded doing it. My dad's shut himself up in his study with his lawyers. I think he's trying to disown me.'

'Sonix is calling,' Samar says abruptly. 'Gotta go.'

He hangs up on the still-talking Zeeshan and takes the incoming call.

'What is this, yaar Samar,' says the mild, conversational voice of Cougar Malhotra, the massively fat head of Mumbai's biggest film production house. 'What is this?'

Samar sighs and ploughs his hair off his forehead. 'Yeah, I know. Major shitkrieg. Sorry.'

'Sorry se kuch nahi hoga,' Cougar breathes heavily down the line. 'You must understand, you're an outsider. Not like Zeeshan, whose dad will grovel for him and get him off the hook by pinning all the blame on *your* bad influence.'

Samar's jaw sets.

'Look, Cougar, whatever we said last night was completely justified. The awards were a travesty. They were—'

'Samar, baby.' Cougar's voice grows even softer, which is never a good sign. 'This film has been too long in the making. Two red-hot new directors have been hatched since you started it. You're not hot anymore, you're lukewarm, and there are lots of eager, lukewarm directors in Bombay. Lots.'

'Stop pressing my buttons with that not-hot bullshit.' Samar begins to pace the wooden floor, eyes blazing. 'It's a goddamn golden shackle anyway, being hot. If I hadn't been so *hot*, as you put it, my film wouldn't have had such an obscenely swollen budget and I wouldn't have been forced to stuff it full of needy egomaniacs who can't act for arse.'

'Such ingratitude,' Cougar sighs. 'We've given you India's biggest stars and a budget indie directors can only dream of.'

'Fuck off. AK is a senile and obnoxious know-it-all.'

Cougar clicks his tongue. 'The film is delayed and way over budget and the buck stops with you. Stop blaming others.'

'I'm not blaming others,' Samar snaps. 'It's entirely my fault. I was in too much of a hurry to make this film. I started shooting without completing my homework, and now that stupid, *inexcusable* decision has come back to bite me in the butt.'

'AK thinks there's nothing wrong with the film a good item song can't fix,' Cougar says. 'Something sexy and catchy, maybe by that rap artist everybody's nuts about. All of us at Sonix think it's a good suggestion.'

In one graphic, concise, and feelingly uttered sentence, Samar Vir Singh tells his producer what he can do with his good suggestion.

'We're issuing an official apology on your behalf,' is Cougar's unfazed response. 'Now for heaven's sake, lie low and don't talk to anyone.'

He hangs up. Samar curses and throws his phone down upon the bed, where it starts to throb and gleam as notifications—probing, salacious, insistent—pour in from what feels like every publication in the country.

SAMAR STORM at AFTERPARTY?

He was hashtagged as #Raw #Rare #SearinglyHonest and hailed as Indian cinema's new hope less than three years ago, when he wrote and directed two brilliant films back to back, won a slew of awards, and rocked the box office.

Superstar AK famously said of him that, 'Samar Vir Singh is a director who genuinely provides *direction*. Never have I seen such clarity, such rock-solid vision, and such sureness of touch in one so young.'

However, recent reports reveal that the young director's much-lauded 'clarity' and 'vision' are now being talked of as stubbornness, cockiness, and even full-blown megalomania.

Certainly it is no secret that his third film, an untitled 125-crore rupee project for Sonix Entertainment, has been stuck in post-production for nearly six months now.

While the studio claims this is because the film requires a lot of special effects, insiders at After Animation talk of blazing rows in the edit suites, with the director almost coming to blows with Sonix top management.

'Samar was fine through the shooting but now suddenly he doesn't like how the film has shaped up,' said an editor at After. 'He's talking of rewriting and reshooting some portions. Naturally, the producers are reeling.'

'He's lost his sense of judgement,' our source at Sonix agreed. 'In fact, he's lost the plot entirely. Last night's behaviour proves it.'

Beyond doubt, the director's drunken, blistering critique of the industry that welcomed him with open arms can only be described as the own-goal of the decade.

'People don't like being made fun of,' rued an industry insider. 'Especially film people. There is talk of the movie being shelved.'

With his partner in crime Zeeshan Khan having conveniently fled the city to 'shoot in Canada' and Samar himself 'out of town on personal business', we can't help but wonder if this is the end of the road for Samar Vir Singh, a maverick who was always out of place in the incestuous, highly hierarchical Mumbai film industry.

1

Twenty times the amaltas trees along Hailey Road have burst into glorious yellow flower since the day Dylan Singh Shekhawat threw himself off a terrace six stories high (ripping his shirt in four aesthetically-pleasing places as he fell) and saved the life of the puggish, gimlet-eyed Mrs Bhudevi Thakur, thus securing for himself the hand and heart of her pretty niece Debjani, the fourth of the five famed, alphabetically-named Thakur sisters of 16 Hailey Road.

Nothing quite as sensational has happened to mar the serenity of Hailey Road since. It continues to be a dreamy, secluded quarter, unaffected in the most part by the changes that have wracked the city of Delhi—the transition from petrol to CNG, the granting of statehood and the creation of NCR, the arrival of low-calorie Coke and high-waisted Levi's, the influx of 30 million rural immigrants, the rise in crime, the awakening of public conscience, and the random, worm-like mud excavations caused by the busily burrowing steel termite that is the Delhi Metro.

Today, as the watery winter sunshine filters in through the grilled windows of number 16, it sparkles upon the tiny diamond nose stud of the lone Thakur girl in residence: deliciously curvy Bonita Singh Rajawat, clad in black harem pants, a clingy fuchsia ganji and a turquoise pashmina shawl, warming her hands on an electric blower and chatting cosily with her team of ladies tailors, as sewing machines whir around her in the fabrication workshop she has set up on the first floor.

This workshop is Bonu's pride and joy. Smelling strongly of Mangaldeep Agarbatti and plastered a cheery yellow, it is equipped with eight shiny Brother machines and twenty-five locally made Dutta sewing machines. There is a whole separate embroidery section with ten massive Friend work-stations, capable of performing the most intricate needlework quickly and delicately. A Neelam Threads colour chart hangs on one wall, while a painstakingly organized rickrack-buttons-threads-and-ribbon station is ranged along another. Massive bales of cloth, stacked colour- and material-wise, line the back. In the middle of the room is a huge cutting table, opposite which, in pride of place, hangs a remarkably hi-tech fifty-inch LCD TV.

'She *hates* me. I know it.'

Bonu sits up, her vivid black brows snapping together impatiently.

'Uff, of course she doesn't hate you, Parveen! So what if her first word was Pup-pa? You know it's only because he's always hanging about the house like a bad smell, boozing and watching TV and spending all the money you earn. It doesn't mean she loves him more than she loves *you*.'

But Parveen, a delicate-featured mother of four girls, refuses to be comforted. Her heart and her ego have taken too much of a beating. Fat teardrops plop onto the off-white chiffon placket she is embroidering with tiny pink (Neelam Thread number 2 by 22) rosebuds. Bonu watches them fall and hopes they won't stain—her dry-cleaner has just upped his rates again.

'My ammi says your first words define who you are.' Parveen wipes her tears on her bony forearm. 'My youngest is going to be a Pup-pa's girl, and this when he doesn't even like her. How much he grumbled when we found out the fourth one was also a daughter!'

'Your ammi could be right,' Bonu admits, cupping her chin thoughtfully, waves of thick black hair falling about her face. 'My Anjini mausi's first words were I-sabse-pretty. And she grew up to be *very* vain.'

'And what were your first words, didi?' asks one of the other lady tailors.

But this Bonu doesn't want to reveal. Because her first word—spoken when she saw a packet of table tennis balls burst open, sending them bouncing and rolling everywhere—had been a loud, clearly enunciated and gurglingly gleeful: 'Balls.'

Some versions of this story claim that there had been no table tennis ball packet at all, and that Bonu's grandmother had made up this tale to appease the shocked neighbours. Apparently, the true story is that Bonu had been a papa's girl too, and had only been trying to articulate her beloved father's favourite word.

'I don't remember,' she tells her tailors. 'Uff, who's knocking now? Get it, somebody.'

But before they can, the door bursts open. A wild-eyed lady, attired in an over-embroidered phiran and badly in need of a roots-touch-up, practically falls into the room.

'My silk kaftan!' she shouts. 'Copied from the Cavilli Aishwarya wore in Cannes after she became fat. For my grandson's first birthday party—happening at a five-star hotel! Hai hai, Bonu bitiya, ready toh hai na?'

'Cavilli kaftan!' Bonu's voice is sharp. 'Masterji!'

A slithery blue and black silk garment lands on the counter almost immediately. The lady pounces upon it, her expression changing instantly from panicked to purring.

'Haaaiiii Bonu bitiya, tu toh dolly hai, dolly!'

'Auntieji, try it on. Then we'll see ki who is the real dolly!' Bonu smiles.

Auntieji dives into Bonu's bedroom, which doubles as a trial room, and emerges minutes later, walking with shoulders thrown back, pinched features softly flushed, hair draped over one shoulder foxily. Everyone applauds.

'Looks a bit goddy, na?' Parveen murmurs critically to Bonu.

'I think she looks lovely,' Bonu whispers back.

Auntieji goes off, all flushed and excited, and the tailoring unit heaves a sigh of relief. It is vitally important to keep Auntieji happy—to keep *all* the Hailey Road auntiejis happy. Running a business of this size in a residential area is technically against the law, but Bonu keeps the housewives well-supplied with the latest fashions at very reasonable prices. In return they all keep mum about Vicky's Secret.

'Good job, Masterji,' she says to her head tailor.

This worthy is sitting half hidden behind a growing pile of detachable, poly-fill-stuffed bust-boosting pads, churning them out at a feverish rate. They are the last little detailing left to be added to the complicated twenty-six-panel anarkali consignment bound for Dubai tonight. Tiny acrylic shell-shaped buttons are now being hand-stitched onto the first of the finished garments.

Everything seems to be proceeding smoothly. The ladies tailors chat and stitch, the LCD TV plays a happy medley of Hindi movie songs, and all is busy, peaceful industriousness. Suddenly Bonu gives a bellow of such fury that the needles stop plying and blood curdles in the hunched-over head tailor's veins.

He stands up.

'K...kya hua, maidumbji?'

He cuts an unimpressive figure. Ancient, diminutive and foul-smelling, Daulat Master—or Do-laat Master, as his disrespectful crew of ladies tailors has privately dubbed him because he never gets anything done until Bonu administers two figurative kicks in his bony backside—is notoriously unreliable. He is also extremely combative—he gets drunk and picks fights with people four times his size on a regular basis, and then swaggers into work the next day, proudly sporting the most magnificent of shiners.

Bonu snatches up a bust-pad, points at a spray of tiny orange dots along it, and says in a trembling voice, 'Paan ka stain, Masterji. Bright orange paan ka stain. Yeh kaise hua?'

Daulat gives a little yelp, swallows with a massive gulp and sits down with a thump.

'It's on all of them,' Bonu begins to panic as she scoops up a handful of pads from the pile heaped in front of his machine. 'One, two, thre—shit!' She turns one over. 'It's on the reverse side also! How did this happen?'

'From his mouth only,' Parveen mutters. 'He is all the time chewing and chewing, sometimes dribbling also. In summers at least he goes outside to spit. Nowadays, everything is happening yahin par.'

Daulat Master immediately launches into a loud, incoherent denial of this monstrous accusation. The ladies hiss and smirk.

'Hush, Parveen,' Bonu frowns. Parveen, a long-time vier for Daulat Master's job, is always happy to see him in trouble. But it can't be denied that he's the only one who eats paan in the unit. Bonu tells him as much.

'She should spend more time with her daughters,' is Daulat Master's illogical, whining reply, 'instead of coming here and making trouble. Her one-year-old girl can't even say her name... It's un-Islamic, the amount of time she spends here.'

Parveen lets out an outraged shriek. Do-laat cowers over his stool, sending up a strong smell of fear and Tiger bidi.

Bonu stands with arms crossed against her chest, considering the evidence. Finally she speaks. 'Masterji, please. This is a Susan Adams anarkali. *Susan Adams*. Do you know what that means?'

He shakes his head miserably while Parveen pipes up, 'Susan Adams has the best finish in the industry. Sab kuch tip-top. You can wear her clothes inside out if you want. Sometimes the backside is better than the front side. Crikkits have compared it to Kundan jewellery, which have Meenakaari work on the backside.'

'Thank you, Parveen.' Bonu glares at Daulat. 'That is what we are trying to achieve here. A Susan Adams finish! And you have dribbled paan on it. How will we get these clean by evening?'

Do-laat mutters incomprehensibly, his tone aggrieved.

'What!' Bonu thunders.

He speaks again, and this time Bonu manages to decipher the burden of his song.

'It's not paan ka peek, it's the exact colour of the orange bar Parveen's daughter eats when she comes here for lunch every day.'

'*You* were the one who stitched up all the pads,' Bonu says severely, ignoring Parveen's gasp of protest. 'You always want to stitch up the bustline pads, God alone knows why. So please pick up the whole pile, apply the bleaching chemical and spread them out in the garden. Luckily they're only poly-fill and satin, so they should dry quickly.'

Soon countless puffy little poly-filled mounds are lying on cotton sheets, drying in the weak sun like batches of homemade papad. As she watches the gnome-like figure straighten up and slink off to steal a beedi in the back garden, Bonu feels a twinge of guilt.

Maybe I'm too hard on him, she muses. After all, he is a fantastic master-cutter—it's largely thanks to him that I've realized my dream of running a successful business…

'You need *balls* to do business!' Bonu's small, fiery father used to say over dinner every night, spraying slightly in his eagerness to emphasize the importance of this point. 'Remember Bonu beta, any incomepoop can work in an office, but setting up your own dukaan, being your own boss—*that* takes real balls!'

He had been holding forth on the same theme to his wife as he drove the family down from Bhopal to Delhi, his children eating sandwiches in the backseat, when a speeding Madhya Pradesh Roadways Bus had come out of nowhere, lifted their old Maruti Esteem clean off the road and flung it off a sheer cliff, thus ridding the earth, in one fell swoop, of entrepreneur Vikram Singh Rajawat, his devoted wife Binni, their stolid little son Monu, and their scrawny daughter Bonu's carefree laughter.

The stunned ten-year-old had been scooped up by her heartbroken grandparents, Justice Laxmi Narayan Thakur and his wife Mamta, less than a day later. Sleeping cuddled between them by night and shamelessly spoilt by day, she had soon healed and smiled again. Over the years her scrawniness slowly filled out, thanks to her grandmother's fabled cooking, and she grew to be five-feet-six inches tall, black-haired, full-lipped and bold-eyed in the style of her mother Binni and her aunt Eshwari. Laughingly nicknamed Bonus when she was born unexpectedly, three minutes after her twin brother Monu, her bottom and bosom blossomed out so generously as she grew, that all of

Hailey Road agreed that this indeed was a lush bumper bonus that any man, anywhere would be very, very happy to receive.

Binni, perhaps trying to compensate for the fact that she was the only one of her sisters who had received a Hindi-medium education, had named her daughter Bonita. This international-sounding tag had caused Bonu many cringing moments through her school years in Bhopal and at Modern School, Barakhamba Road *(Are you a foreigner? Can we call you Bournvita?)*, but by the time she was twenty-one she was sorted enough to look people straight in the eye, smile and confirm, 'Yes, Bonita. It's Spanish for beautiful, you know.'

At this point, Justice Laxmi Narayan Thakur, perhaps in a bid to cover those bountiful curves in sober black robes, had suggested she become a lawyer, but Bonu had been quite clear. The arguments her parents had when she was a child and the babble of careless whispers she overheard after they died had revealed to her that every one of her beloved father's many business ventures had flopped. So she wanted to start one of her own, name it after him, and make it a huge success.

'But what sort of business, beta?' her grandparents had asked worriedly, to which Bonu confidently replied as she wolfed down her breakfast paranthas, 'I'm going to copy high fashion garments from the movies—you know, the ones designed by Manish Malhotra and Sabyasachi and Susan Adams which cost like five lakhs each? Those. I'm going to make them available to all the auntiejis of Hailey Road for a fraction of the price.'

When her bemused grandfather had enquired if this was possible and even legal, she had leaned in and passionately explained that the right to be fashionable belonged to everybody, not just the rich ladies, and that she had already put together some outfits for her grand-aunt Bhudevi, copied from her favourite movies.

'She loved them, BJ!' Bonu had said earnestly. 'She was so happy. Fashion is such a rip-off, everything is overpriced, and for *every* fancy embellishment there is a cheaper, sturdier alternative available in the marketplace if one just looks properly. I'll make a solid profit, wait and see!'

All those early years of frugal living with that failure Vicky have turned my granddaughter into a baniya, the Judge had thought resignedly. Well, thrift is a virtue, I suppose, though certainly unusual in us Thakurs.

Bonu had been true to her word. Her carefully selected and trained team of tailors, led by Daulat Master, studied every glitzy new Bollywood release with the earnestness of art students sketching the Mona Lisa, then trotted back to the workshop and replicated the ensembles faithfully. In case they forgot any details, Bonu would replay the film on pirated DVDs on the massive LCD TV. In less than twenty-four hours, outfits worn by Deepika/ Priyanka/ Sonam/ Katrina/ Kareena would be hanging in her show window in sizes from XS to XXL, with a queue snaking halfway to Connaught Place outside.

'I don't think we need to worry about the Bonus anymore, Mamtaji,' the Judge had said with satisfaction as he watched this phenomenon repeat itself week on week. 'She's become a real B for blooming businesswoman!'

But Mrs Mamta hadn't been so sure. Bonu's self-sufficiency worried her a little. She feared it was making her too hard too fast.

'A girl ought to be girlish,' she had fretted. 'Sometimes Bonu is too grown up. And she's rude to her aunts. I don't think she even likes them, LN!'

'You're imagining things,' her husband had replied. 'It's just that this generation is different. There's nothing diffident about them. They're very assertive. They don't wait till thirty to bloom. They're —'

'Born with pubic hair on,' Mrs Mamta had sniffed. 'Look at that Samar, for instance. Changing girlfriends practically every day.'

But the Judge, who wouldn't hear a *word* against his darling step-grandson, counselled her not to believe everything she read in the *Delhi Times*. 'Besides, our time here is toh almost up, Mamtaji,' he had added. 'The fact of the matter is that we are all seated in the departure lounge with our boarding passes in our hands and our destination unknown. Who knows whose flight will be announced first, eh?'

It was with thoughts like these running through his mind, that he'd had the house neatly partitioned on paper, ten years ago. The upstairs portion was divided between his two eldest daughters, Anjini and Binni, the annexe was allotted to the third, Chandralekha, while the downstairs was split between Debjani and Eshwari. The Judge and his wife continued to live in the downstairs portion belonging to their two youngest girls.

A few years later, when the Celestial Control Tower decreed that it was Mrs Mamta Thakur's flight that would depart first, the Judge had been terribly put out. He kept telling the mourners at the funeral that he'd been ten years ahead of her chronologically and one letter ahead of her alphabetically. His family handled the situation as best they could, hiding their own grief, chattering brightly, playing endless games of cards with BJ. The sisters made it a point to visit every month in those days, spending hours with the old man, walking in the garden, listening to music with him late into the night. There was chatter and intellectual stimulation and determined laughter all around, but still BJ sat — bathed, changed and exuding Brut

33 to be sure, but also exuding a constant, heartbreaking confusion.

He never quite recovered. He would have good days, when he would scan the newspapers keenly, harangue the luckless gardener and make waspish remarks about Eshwari's continued spinster status; and bad days, when he would chat garrulously with people long gone—like his beloved wife, his troublesome daughter Binni and his gentle grandson Monu. His eyes grew hazier and his movements slowed. The doctors pulled long faces and muttered to one another about Alzheimer's and Huntington's disease and vascular dementia but couldn't quite agree on anything. The family took him to the US for treatment but it didn't take, and he became scarily vague in the unfamiliar surroundings. After a few abortive trips to Bombay and Allahabad that were enjoyable for nobody, they re-installed him at Hailey Road, upon which familiar turf he did much better. Resigning themselves to the inevitable, they brought in Lachhman, a trained male nurse, worked out a sort of roster system, phoned every day, and visited as often as they could.

But it is Bonita, living and working out of her mother's hissa upstairs, who really holds the fort at Number 16 Hailey Road.

Now, she wraps her pashmina tighter around her and exits the warm space, making her way to her grandmother's floral-themed drawing room downstairs where BJ will be waiting for their afternoon ritual of tea, snacks and a chat. It's that supremely depressing time of year, the post-new-year's-eve slump, when all the festivals and the partying is over and a cranky, hungover Delhi hunkers down to just somehow, grimly, survive the cold, the fog and the sleet. BJ never does well in this weather. Lately, he has been lacking the concentration required to play cards, even a simple game of seven-eights.

She finds him sitting in state, flanked by his bulldoggy sister-in-law Bhudevi, glowering at the chicken sandwich the Doberman-faced Lachhu has set before him.

What a soft, insipid-looking thing, the Judge thinks irritably. Such a far cry from the devilled Maggi with chopped chillies and crunchy baked beans on fried toast I feasted upon at teatime in my heyday! Then again, I'm a soft insipid thing myself these days. He reaches for a sandwich resignedly.

'Hi, Chachiji, whassup? Did you miss me, BJ?'

The Judge perks up immediately at the sound of Bonu's cheerful young voice. He drops the despicable sandwich, looks up twinklingly, and recites, his voice quavering slightly:

'Did you miss me?
Come and kiss me.
Never mind my bruises,
Hug me, kiss me, suck my juices...'

'Hai hai, what is he saying!' Bhudevi Thakur hides her face in her hands, hot with embarrassment.

'It's Christina Rossetti, Chachiji,' Bonu explains. 'Very high-level poetry.'

'Call me Naniji,' says her grand-aunt. 'Not chachiji.'

'But everybody calls you chachiji,' says Bonu. Then she links hands with the old man and grandfather and granddaughter finish the verse with a flourish.

'Hug me, kiss me, suck my juices
Squeezed from goblin fruits for you,
Goblin pulp and goblin dew!'

He chuckles, she claps and perches herself on the arm of his chair and picks up a sandwich. As she bites in, Chachiji leans forward and says cosily, 'Woh paanch number ka suna?'

The years have been kind to Bhudevi Thakur. Her iron-grey curls have brightened to white and her eyes are softer, more peaceful. Her need for constant politicking well nourished by the torturous daytime TV serials she watches so avidly, she has become almost mellow. Besides, her philandering husband Ashok Narayan Thakur has recently been operated for prostate cancer and is currently out of sexual commission, thus giving her a break from her constant, agonized husband-guarding. Still, she keeps up with the dramatic happenings on Hailey Road, just to keep her hand in, so to speak.

Now she tilts her eyebrows at her niece inquiringly.

'No,' Bonu responds, mouth full. 'What happened at number 5, Chachiji?'

Bhudevi Thakur blows out her cheeks and assumes a lugubrious expression. 'Bhai, it is very sad. The brothers were fighting—over the property, of course—the case has been going on for fourteen years—and this morning the younger brother took out a pistol, put it inside his elder brother's mouth and pressed the trigger. I heard there's a hole in the back of his head like a sambar vada. All soggy and uneven.'

Bonu puts down her sandwich. 'Ugh.'

Chachiji continues, 'Of course, some are saying it wasn't just the property. Apparently the older fellow—a bachelor, you know—was carrying on with the younger one's wife. She's lucky her husband didn't shoot her too—really lucky, because now one is dead and the other will go to jail and she will end up inheriting everything!'

'Wow.' Bonu looks impressed. 'You think she *planned* it, Chachiji?'

'Maybe.' Chachiji lowers her voice into a confidential whisper. 'She's as chunnt as they come. Does yoga the whole day so she's as supple as a snake. They say she can twist herself into any position, that's why all the men are mad after her. Now, of course, she will swallow the whole property like a python and digest it so completely that there won't even be any shit left to fight over.'

The Judge and Bonu consider this, stunned.

Chachiji continues, 'And at number 4 toh you know what is happening. Such a close family they used to be, mother-father, two brothers and one sister. But today there is an ad in the newspaper saying ki please, we want to make it very clear ki there is no sister-shister! This woman was an orphan we kept in the house out of kindness and now she is getting ideas above her station and demanding a hissa! The brothers have burnt her birth certificate and told the old parents ki khabardaar! She has no hissa! If you open your mouth we will borrow the next-door-ka-pistol and sambar vada you both. Imagine!'

What drivel this infernal woman talks, the Judge thinks as he munches drearily through his soggy sandwich. Always going on about hissas. Hisssssas! He's not very sure what the word means anymore, but it makes him think of a cobra, all flickering tongue and flared hood, hissing and swaying, ready to strike. Why does she visit so often, anyway? He has no idea who she is. Lachhu's wife perhaps? Or the cook? If she's the cook, he's got a thing or two to say to her about these insipid sandwiches. Or is she one of those pushy ladies who keep coming around seeking donations?

He prods Bonu in the ribs. 'Give her a hundred chips and tell her to git.'

Bonu hushes him. Just then, the curtains fly up as a massive gust of breeze sweeps through the room. 'Oh God, is it *raining?*' Bonu groans. 'Please let it be just breeze but not too much breeze—*shit!*'

She puts down her tea, grabs her shawl, and rushes out to the lawn just as another gust of wind sweeps in, tossing the treetops, scattering champa flowers over the grass and, as Bonu watches horrified, hurling all the buttercup yellow, Dubai-bound boobie-padding into the air and sending them tumbling and spinning in the misty wind, towards the front gate.

With a collective agonized wail, the entire tailoring unit gives chase. Bonu leads the charge, hitching up her black pyjamas, and kicking off her shoes.

'It's okay,' she calls out pantingly to her little crew. 'They'll hit the gate and stop. Thank God the gate is shut. If it wasn't, they would have blown right out into the stree—'

And even as she says this, the gate opens, the wind surges, and just like that, the entire consignment of feather-light falsies is loose and whirling on Hailey Road.

'Oh no!' groans Bonu, doubling up in dismay. 'Go, Masterji! Run! Why are you staring at my face? I don't have my shoes! Catch them! This is all your fault! Go!'

The miserable Daulat and the rest of the unit caper out, leaping and lunging after the wildly whirling pads. Bonu, meanwhile, squares her shoulders and turns to face the person who has opened the gate at that exact, inopportune moment.

'Your sense of timing,' she says with exaggerated politeness, her heart thumping hard and not just because she's been running, 'is perfect.'

The new arrival, tall, brown, scruffy, and attached to a bulging backpack, looks down at her sardonically.

'Lovely to see you too,' he says politely. 'What are those poor unfortunates being yelled at for now?'

'You're the one I should be yelling at,' she says shortly, not quite meeting his eyes. Her step-cousin Samar's eyes have always been hard for her to meet. Looking straight into them, for some reason, feels like looking straight into the sun. 'If the gate had been shut we'd have caught them in time.'

'What's "them"?' he enquires, looking out onto the road interestedly.

'Boobie padding,' she replies shortly. Let him make of that what he wants.

'How, uh, *uplifting*,' he murmurs, then bends to kiss her carelessly on the cheek. 'How've you been, little Bonu Singh?'

'Fine,' she manages to reply nonchalantly. 'It's been a while since you visited.' (It's been almost three years, actually, but God forbid he ever find out she's been counting.) 'Is that your only bag?'

'Yes,' he says. 'It's been a while, yes, but I've been busy...'

He trails off, looking about the property, which appears rather shabby. The grass is both overlong and patchy, the trees need pruning, the house needs a coat of paint, one of the lights at the front gate is busted. The only person who's looking in the pink of health, glowing like an exotic bloom in this muck, in fact, is his brat of a step-cousin.

'But you're free now?' she asks.

It might be an innocent question, but it makes Samar wince. She must have read about the Sparkler Awards incident. Damn.

'Sort of. But like I said, I've been busy. I know I should've called before I showed up, but I won't be any trouble. I'll stay upstairs.'

Bonu Singh gulps, then quickly recovers.

'Uh...upstairs? You want to live upstairs? But your hissa's all locked up and I don't have the key, and it's probably filthy.'

Samar grimaces. 'Ugh. I didn't think of that. So maybe I can just shack up in one of the bedrooms downstairs?'

'Good idea,' she agrees instantly.

His gaze grows speculative. 'What are you looking so happy about, suddenly?'

'Oh, just happy to see you,' she assures him demurely. 'BJ will be happy too.'

'I've been busy,' Samar repeats defensively. 'The film and so on... But we've been talking on the phone. Well, I've been talking—he just tends to say a loud and cheerful hello and then zone out till it's time to say a loud and cheerful goodbye. How is he?'

Her lips tighten.

'See for yourself.'

Saying which she whirls around and starts to walk back to the house, her turquoise shawl billowing behind her like a super-heroine's robe.

Samar follows at a leisurely pace, taking in the generally run-down state of the house, and also, it must be admitted, the voluptuous figure of the girl in front of him.

Quite the local hottie, he thinks, amused. Nothing hot about her walk, unfortunately. Whatever devil's brew she'd sold her soul to buy, drink and thus transform herself from a scrawny brat into this luscious avatar, it clearly hadn't been potent enough to alter her barrelling strut. She has retained that aggressive, outta-my-way swagger which used to make his stepmother shudder and say, 'This girl walks like a rapist. Kuch karo iska.'

He also notices that, because of her nose pin, the tiny ghungroos swinging at the end of her ridiculous gypsy belt, and the stack of jingly bangles around one wrist, she gives the impression of being lightly sprinkled with oxidized silver. There is a slight chhamchhamming quality to the whole package. A chhamchhamming rapist, Samar thinks to himself as they reach the house and she announces him. God help us.

2

The Judge recognizes Samar almost immediately.

'*Director saab!*'

He smiles sweetly after Bonu mutters a sulky, 'Look who's here, BJ,' and holds out his hands to his tall, strapping grandson. Then he looks around the room and quaveringly asks Lachhu why he hasn't served the boy some raw green guavas as yet.

Samar sinks to his knees in front of the wheelchair, a lump rising in his throat, and says, his voice shaking very slightly, 'Hello BJ, how distinguished you look.'

The Judge's eyes twinkle in response, softening the shock of how frail he looks.

'*O come ye in peace or come ye in war, or to dance at our bridal, young lord Lochinvar?*'

Chachiji, too awed to speak in front of somebody who has directed two-and-a-half Bollywood movies, stumps off to her flat at Hailey Court next door, to inform the world of the glamorous visitor.

Samar and the Judge talk all through dinner, covering a wide range of subjects. BJ is unusually lucid, speaking well, listening intently, his gaze focused, his questions pertinent. Bonu is torn between feeling happy that he seems so well, and sulking because she feels so excluded. Sulkiness prevails.

As they polish off bowls of cool ilaichi phirni, BJ points to himself with a drippy spoon and says, his eyes gleaming with quite their old vim, 'Great-grandfather.'

'Excuse me?'

'Make me one.'

'It's not my job to fulfil your every ambition, BJ,' Samar returns firmly and changes the subject.

After dinner, the Judge aggravates Bonu further by taking Samar into his bedroom where they remain cloistered for the next few hours. She sits at the dining table for a while, then springs to her feet, carries her plate to the kitchen sink and flounces off to her bedroom upstairs.

Why the hell did he have to come? she thinks fiercely as she brushes her teeth, glaring at her reflection in the mirror. I'm happy, I'm sorted, the business is rocking—and now *he* shows up.

Her mind flips back to those mortifying days when she was so obsessed with him that she used to call the May-June holidays the Samar vacation and wait like a loser, with bated breath, for him to come back from Mayo. She even used to go to Depaul's and ask them to put more 'mayo' on her sandwich and would get a little thrill every time she said the word 'mayo'.

God, I was pathetic, she thinks as she spits and rinses. And I'm still pathetic, my heart was totally thumping when I was talking to him!

She decides she might as well shower while she's at it, and impulsively makes it a cold shower. Stop acting like a fool, she tells herself, teeth chattering, as the rusty old shower fixture spurts down water like a tap upon her head. And focus on what's important. Samar Vir Singh is here—back at 16 Hailey Road. And he's not stupid, or obsessed with BJ like the mausis, or too lazy to climb up a flight of stairs. He's sure to want to go all over the house. What am I going to do if he comes nosing about upstairs?

Eight hours later, Samar wakes up in the bedroom Dabbu and Eshu used to share decades ago, to find the rough leafy branches of the harshringar tree squashed up against the glass panes, trying to get a peep at how big Anjini's boy has grown. He gets out of bed and opens the window.

It is a miserable, chilly morning. Green guavas lie scattered, almost hidden in the overgrown grass, speckled white with parrot droppings. Little brown anthill bumps meander through the grass interrupted by the fleshy gleam of toadstools. There are squelchy puddles all along the driveway, some late cannas lie with their orange faces flat in the dirt, a colony of large black ants marches busily towards the rotting guavas, and a few bedraggled crows caw in the champas overhead.

This place is going to the dogs, Samar thinks in disgust and jumps out of the window to find the lawn mower.

He is making good headway, going around the lawn in concentric circles, bits of grass flying past his face, a line of crows pecking the ground in his wake, when Bonu appears at the upstairs window, dressed in pyjamas, sipping a cup of tea. Her vivid black brows snap together when she sees what he is up to. Samar, striding along steadily below, feels her eyes boring holes into his grey cabled sweater, so baleful is her glare.

He stops and turns to stare up at her.

'What?' he calls, his tone slightly bored.

She sniffs and looks away.

'Say it!' he shouts.

She sets down her teacup, winds her hair into a messy top knot, skewering it into place with a pencil, and vanishes from the window. Two minutes later, she chhamchhams through the verandah and walks out to the lawn to scoop up the soggy newspaper.

As she goes past him, she says, 'It's amusing how you think you can randomly show up, cut some grass and make up for almost three years of gross neglect.'

He resists the urge to advance upon her with the lawn-mower and see her jump out of his path. How she would squawk, he thinks wistfully.

Instead, he rests his elbows on top of the mower.

'Are you mad because I neglected BJ, or the house, or you?'

She rests her hands on her hips.

'BJ, *obviously*!'

Samar doesn't see what's so obvious about this. The brat's nursed a not-very-well-hidden crush on him for years (she seems to have gotten over it in recent times, thankfully), and she's always loved the house like it was a person, not a thing.

'He's been pining for you,' she continues.

Samar, who already has an unquiet conscience about this, finds himself snapping, 'Well, I'm here, aren't I? And he's happy to see me.'

'But he'll be miserable when you go. So the net effect of your visit will, eventually, be negative. That's why I don't like it when the family visits.'

He stares at her, perplexed. 'Then why are you complaining about my not visiting?'

She shrugs. 'Anyway, you're only here because you and your bestie abused the Sparkler jury and all the winners in a bar and they kicked you out of Bollywood and you need a quiet place to lick your wounds.'

His lips tighten. 'That's pretty much it, yes,' he says lightly, feeling rather proud of himself for not rising to her bait.

Bonu looks slightly cheated at this low-powered response.

'How long will you stay?' she asks.

'I don't see how that is any of your business, but whatever. I'll stay a few days. I want to catch up with BJ.'

'Haven't you caught up enough?' she says. 'You kept him up way past his bedtime last night.'

Samar stares at her, amused, almost sympathetic. 'You're just jealous 'coz BJ welcomed me like a prodigal son and ordered the servants to kill the fatted guava. Poor Bonu Singh. Is he the only man in your life, then?'

Since she responds to this with a smug toss of the head (which causes her hair to tumble out of its top knot and mantle her shoulders, by the way), he assumes the answer to his question is no.

'I don't care about men,' she says loftily. 'I'm *wayyy* too busy with my business.'

'Ah yes, how *is* that crystal meth cooking lab you've got going upstairs?' he asks politely.

She flushes. This is a mean dig about something that happened a few years ago, when Bonu's unit was still new and finding its feet. She had attempted to dye some material in-house and it hadn't gone well, and the chemicals had stained and stunk up the driveway for days.

'It's a state-of-the-art garment fabrication unit,' she informs him. 'And it's doing *very* well now.'

This is not a lie. The business *is* doing well. Of course she's not doing one-tenth as well as he is, BJ's darling grandson with the Sparkler Award for debut director and Page 3 appearances and the *10 Most Important Thinkers of the Year* listing in

Outlook magazine. But then, she reminds herself, he is six years older than she is. She'll be exporting all over the world by the time she's thirty-two.

'That's nice,' he replies peaceably. 'Can I come and have a look?'

Shit. Shit. Shit. No way can she let him come upstairs.

'I don't want my tailors bedazzled by Bollywood stardust,' she says coolly.

'That's a good point.' Very white teeth flash in an aggravating smile. 'I'll come up when they've gone for the day then.'

Bonu's heart bounds up into her mouth. She swallows manfully, 'Why are you being so *nosy*, suddenly?'

Samar's eyebrows rise. 'I'm being friendly,' he says mildly. 'Besides, Ma called me and said I should open up our hissa and clean it out a bit—no one's been up there for over a year.'

Bonu coughs loudly. 'Ermmm…yeah!' she says. 'Maybe in a couple of days, okay? I've got stuff spread out all over the floor in my half that I don't want to move. Embroidery panels and all, you know.'

'Cool,' Samar nods, getting ready to start pushing the lawn mower again. 'I'm fine with that. Take your time. Like I said, I'm here for a few days.'

'Just stay out of my hair,' she mutters ungraciously.

'But you have such pretty hair.'

Bonu Singh's head jerks up in surprise. 'Thank you,' she says blankly, then quickly looks away. Samar looks away too, his lean cheeks flushed.

Awkward silence.

'I, uh, just shot a shampoo commercial,' he says eventually. 'It was a lousy script, but the money was really good—anyway, that's why I'm, sort of, noticing hair nowadays.'

'Right.'

'And I will,' he assures her, fiddling with the handle of the lawn mower. 'Stay out of it, I mean. Your hair, that is. Er, figuratively speaking. Also, physically speaking.'

'Good,' she says, red of cheek, and hurries away.

Breathing hard and moving fast, Bonu chhamchhams up the stairs to the first floor, bursts through the double wooden doors into the tailoring unit, and secures the door behind her, pushing up the old iron bolt and smartly turning it to the right.

The ladies tailors, bent over their machines, look up and smile.

'Good morning, didi!'

'Morning,' Bonu pants. 'Brrrr! What a cold wind, na? That's why I have shut the door. Consignment ready, Masterji?'

Daulat jumps forward, his knobbly little face wreathed in obsequious smiles. 'Haan maidumbji, haan—all the bust-line padding has dried ekdum clean. Check any piece and see.'

Quickly she inspects the sumptuous Dubai-bound consignment, impossibly decadent anarkali confections in buttercup yellow mulmul, each featuring twenty-six tapering panels heavy with embroidery, foam, lace and shimmer in sizes M, L, XL, XXL and XXXL.

'Keep one for yourself, didi,' Parveen sighs. 'So pretty they would look on you.'

'Where will I go wearing this yellow shuttlecock?' Bonu demands. 'To Mother Dairy to buy milk? Chalo, let's pack them… Masterji, tell the courier wala to come up.' Then she mounts a stool and claps her hands. 'And now listen, everyone. Listen to me!'

The entire team, busy bagging the anarkalis, looks up at her trustingly.

'What I am about to say is very *very* important, okay?'

Everybody nods.

'You have to keep the main door locked ALL the time. NEVER leave it open. NEVER! Not even for a minute. Is that clear?'

'Yes, didi.'

'Don't let any outsiders into the unit. NOBODY. NEVER.'

She glares around at everybody, her big black eyes seeking an individual 'yes' from each one.

'*Especially* that bhaiyya who has just come from Bombay!'

They look a little disappointed. 'The big director? But he's famous! Why not?'

Bonu stamps her foot.

'Just *promise!*'

Everybody promises obediently, looking a little confused.

Satisfied, Bonu jumps off the stool.

'Good. I've got an important call with Dubai now. Lock up after me.'

And they do.

When Samar walks into the kitchen a while later, he finds Bonu sitting at the table eating toast and talking loudly, her cell-phone on speaker mode propped up against a bottle of Maggi tomato ketchup.

'He is requesting *what*?'

'He is *requesting*, madam,' says a patient Middle-Eastern voice, 'for the monogramming on the jacket pocket to be included, FOC.'

Bonu tilts her head, chewing busily. 'Sorry, to be included, what?'

The voice on the phone rises a little. '*FOC*, madam.'

Bonu's nostrils flare, she leans forward. 'In *your* business parlance, Mrs Suleiman, FOC might stand for free of charge, but here in India it stands for fuck off cheapskate. The monogramming will cost two US dollars more, per piece.'

'There is no requirement to be offensive.' Mrs Suleiman's voice is pained.

'You're the one who's being offensive,' Bonu snaps. 'The monogramming is a lot of work—'

'We'll get back to you,' says the lady snootily and cuts the call.

Bonu shoves a savage middle finger into the air and chews her toast moodily.

Samar clears his throat.

'Er…is there more of that toast?'

'Help yourself,' she says shortly.

He sits down next to her and reaches for the bread loaf.

'Work problems?' he asks.

She nods.

'Negotiating can be a bitch.'

'Tell me about it.' She rolls her eyes. 'She was asking for freebies and calling *me* rude. Was I rude?'

'Oh no,' he shakes his head. 'You said fuck off, *cheapskate*. If you were rude, you would've said chutiye.'

She chuckles. 'But she doesn't know Hindi.'

'Ah.' He grins. 'You know your shit.'

She raises her chin. 'Yes,' she says proudly. 'Vicky's Secret is a world class unit. I filed an income tax return of Rs 2 crore last year.'

'Impressive. As in Victoria's Secret?'

'As in Vikram Singh Rajawat. My late father.'

His eyes soften. 'Of course. Stupid of me not to make the connection.'

He smiles.

Bonu looks away. First that random comment about her hair, and now that smile. It is more than she can handle. If he would just stay away for many years at a *go*, she thinks, frustrated, she would be able to get over him. Or if he got married or something. Or made a truly awful film, or became fat, or best yet, lost all his hair. But the lovely films, the random visits, and the continued singleness and hotness and non-baldness render it impossible for her to get him out of her head. Especially since all the other guys she knows are just...*not* Samar Vir Singh.

She pushes away her plate and stands up to get some tea.

Samar walks up to the toaster, standing far too close to her for her liking, and slides in two slices of bread.

'Butter?' He looks around.

'Go for it,' Bonu mumbles, pushing it towards him.

'So did you study design or something?' he asks as he warms his hands over the toaster. 'I've no clue what you did after school, sorry.'

'I did a B.Com,' Bonu answers, sipping her tea.

Samar looks at her, confused.

'And the designs?' he asks. 'Matlab, who does the designing? You?'

She doesn't reply. Just plays with her hair and sips her tea.

Samar doesn't get the hint. 'I mean, I've recently started seeing a designer so I know designing stuff is serious shit.'

Bonu chokes, spluttering tea, and puts down her cup. As he watches in concern, she wipes her chin, hits herself twice in the chest and asks, her voice a little squeaky, 'Whi...whi...which designer are you seeing?'

'Susan,' Samar replies as his toasts pop up. 'Adams. Are you okay?'

Bonu gives a strangled little gasp. 'Susan Adams! Of course I've heard of her. Good for you. Are you going to get married?'

Samar was buttering his toast, but at this he sets the knife down.

'And the Bonster strikes again. Hasn't anybody ever taught you to mind your own business?'

'I *am* minding my own business!' Bonu makes a quick recovery. 'It's called Vicky's Secret! And that's what I was talking about when you show-offily dragged your so-famous designer girlfriend into the conversation!'

He bites into his toast unconcernedly. 'I was not showing off. If I were showing off, I could have mentioned more impressive stuff than that, you know.'

Bonu, who is guilty of stalking him fairly obsessively in her younger years, knows this only too well.

'So what's Vicky's Secret busy with right now?'

Bonu improvises glibly, her palms clammy with panic. What if he'd seen the Susan Adams anarkali and recognized it? She could've been facing legal action—again. This has happened twice before, a fact she omitted to mention when she gave him her little two-crore-turnover speech. Bollywood designers had complained that their designs were being lifted and they were losing serious business, especially in the Dubai market. Bonu had to shut down her website twice and relaunch it under a new name, the first being Vikram&Binni and the second Fashion Vickypedia. Vicky's Secret is the third avatar of the same business venture and she doesn't want to go through the tiresome process of shutting shop, lying low, and then going onto GoDaddy.com all over again to see which domain names are still available for her to buy. It's too exhausting.

Samar, meanwhile, is studying her face. She is clearly very proud of her business, at the same time strangely reticent about it. But then, so am I, he thinks wryly. I bite off people's heads if they start going on and on about my movies.

He ends up doing exactly this when he talks to his stepmother on the phone, later that evening. Anjini Singh has read about the fiasco at the Sparklers and is worried Samar's getting all cranky and snappy because his movie isn't shaping up well. She tells him as much.

'The film's going fine, Ma,' he snaps. 'Can we please talk about something else?'

'Okay,' Anjini says peaceably. 'How's BJ? What's Chachiji up to? And how's Bonu Singh?'

'She's about to make the *Forbes* list of richest Indians, I think,' Samar replies wryly. 'Her business is doing really well.'

'Well, I'm all for girls being financially independent!' Anji declares energetically, and Samar rolls his eyes. Anjini has recently been appointed editor of *Allahabad Buzz*, a gossipy Page-3-type supplement to *India Post*, Allahabad's biggest newspaper. The fact that her stepson is a successful Bollywood director has nothing to do with this appointment, of course. It all happened because, 'I'm considered such a style leader in Allahabad, na, and everybody says I should compete in Mrs India but I can't because you need to have a biological child to do that and my darling Samar is not really mine, and all the jewellery stores love me and they toh sponsor everything, and I also have such a talent for writing—I was just about to start my MA in Literature when BJ got me married off. I cried for three nights.'

Now she continues, untroubled by the fact that she is contradicting her little homily on the essentialness of financial independence for women, 'How come she isn't married yet?'

'Ma, I can't ask her stuff like that.'

'Let's just hope she has more business sense than her father,' Anjini continues with a sniff. 'Thankfully, she hasn't inherited his looks.'

'Yes, she *is* pretty,' Samar allows after a pause. 'Her hair eats food, though.'

'What?' Anjini sounds confused.

Samar explains. 'Well, it's so long and wriggly and all over the place that when she sits down to eat—she doesn't even sit, actually, she sort of sprawls out—it gets into the plate and laps at the raita.'

'Well, thank God all she got from that ugly Vickyji is curly hair,' Anjini says candidly. 'What is she like, but? Matlab, as a person.'

'But Ma, you know her.'

'She barely talks to me,' Anjini sniffs. 'Keeps to herself, upstairs, in that unit of hers.'

'Well, she is rather prickly,' Samar allows. 'I overheard her chattering away merrily to her tailors, so it's not like she doesn't talk. And BJ just lights up when she's around.'

'Hmm.' Anjini is noncommittal.

'She doesn't talk to you at all? When you're here?'

'No.' Anjini's bright voice has gone rather flat. 'She's a snob—or maybe she's insecure because We all did so well in life and her mother was such a Fail. She didn't even accept my Facebook friend request.'

Samar sighs. 'Ma, FB isn't as popular with younger people as it is with your generation. Besides she seems really busy. The sewing machines upstairs are always whirring away.'

'That reminds me, Samar, I want you to get out Ma's old sewing machine for me. We're doing a feature on unusual hobbies of celebrities—like Amanda Seyfried knits sweaters and Richard Branson flies in hot air balloons? Ya, so I happen to be an excellent seamstress and the *Buzz* wants to shoot me stitching.'

'Oh! Of course.' He clears his throat. 'Uh, Ma, isn't it unethical of your paper to feature you so often?'

Anjini gives a guilty, girlish little giggle.

'Yes, it is!' she admits. 'But I'm the editor, I get to call the shots, and I like to see myself in the news! Achha, you still have to get me a big star to come for our annual awards night, by the way. If you keep behaving badly and making fun of all of them, how will it happen?'

'I'll get you someone, don't worry,' Samar assures her. 'Okay, I've gotta go—'

'No, wait,' Anjini says. 'Ma's machine…it's lying in our hissa upstairs getting rusty. Make Bonu's tailors give it a good servicing.'

Samar groans.

'What is this? I barely know her, I can't just ask her to…'

'Arrey, I'm her aunt! And it's right there only, behind the Lion-the-Witch-and-the-Wardrobe wallah wardrobe.'

'I'm not staying in our rooms.'

'What?' she demands, her voice suddenly sharp. 'Why?'

'Bonu Singh said our rooms are really rundown and dusty. Plus, she doesn't know where the keys are. So I'm staying downstairs, in Mausi D and Mausi E's old room.'

Anjini clicks her tongue. 'She told me that the last time I visited too. My God, it's been over a year since those rooms were aired. It must be so musty in there, ugh! You have to track down the keys, Samar. Get the rooms cleaned, and the machine too. I want to be photographed sitting behind it. Your new girlfriend's not the only designer in the family, you know.'

And so Anjini Singh's desire to have her hidden talents showcased leads to Samar Vir Singh breaching the barricade of tailors and insisting on opening the door to his hissa. An incident that unleashes a Mega Kaand in the house, of the scale and type those venerable walls have not witnessed in decades...

3

Crouching like a giant toad beside the bed as she does the morning jhaadu-ponchha, Mrs Bhudevi Thakur's cleaning lady informs her that Samar bhaiyya and Bonu didi have been sighted in the garden of number 16, setting up BJ's ancient green baize table and laying out a pack of cards. It doesn't take Chachiji long to wrap a bright pink bandhani sari around her busy body and waddle across to number 16, brimming over with enthusiasm and curiosity.

'Hai, this is just like old days!' she exclaims. 'That day I was too shy of you, Samar, plus-also I did not want to introod. But today, you and I will be partners and have a nice talk!'

Samar seems ridiculously touched, Bonu notes with some disgust. His harsh features soften as he beams into Chachiji's pug-like face, clasps her gnarled little hands and laps up the guff she gives him about how he exhibited signs of rare genius even in his childhood and how she'd always known he would become this big, block-busting film-maker.

'Remember all the stories I used to tell you?' she asks, nudging him coyly. 'You *loved* jumping into bed with me!'

Samar chokes. Bonu doesn't bother suppressing a grin.

'Er, yes,' Samar manages to say. 'Tell me, does the Pushkarni still haunt the houses?'

Chachiji gives a delighted cackle of laughter. 'He

remembers!' she crows. 'Suna, Bonu, Samar ko Pushkarni waali story yaad hai!'

'Even *I* remember it, Chachiji,' Bonu rolls her eyes. 'You scared us to death with that one!'

The story, a grisly gothic saga involving the Judge's dead parents, had held Samar, Bonu and her twin Monu enthralled when they were children.

'She was a simple, pure woman and her husband, old Pushkar Narayan Thakur, was a drunken lech,' Samar recites now. 'He wanted to kill her because she was rationing his alcohol and not letting him gamble away his houses and lands. One day when she was on the terrace, shouting his name, Pushkar...Pushkar...!'

'He came up from behind her...' Bonu takes up the narrative.

'Giggled wetly...' continues Samar.

'Said, "*You* only said Pushkar!" and pushed her off the terrace!' Bonu finishes with relish.

There is a satisfied silence.

'Was that story true, Chachiji?' Samar asks.

Chachiji looks a little trapped. 'Arrey nahi nahi, beta. Ekchully, I was going through my meenupause those days na, so I had become little bit mental. Of course nobody pushed my mother-in-law! Anyway, my father-in-law was standing downstairs when she fell, not upstairs behind her. She was cremated with all the proper ceremonies, poor thing!'

Samar leans forward, his dark eyes intent on Chachiji's jowly face. So keen is his interest that Bonu looks at him curiously.

'But the bare bones of the story? The unhappy marriage and the many affairs? The fact that he lost four houses like this one in the gambling dens? What about all that, Chachiji?'

Another little silence. Then Chachiji says constrictedly,

'Bhai, I don't know, it was all before my time. I had not even come to live in this house then. You had better talk to your uncle or Laxmi bhaisaab!'

Samar looks dissatisfied, but just then BJ appears on the verandah, the long-faced Lachhu pushing his wheelchair. Samar leaps to his feet and strides across to them.

Chachiji relaxes, takes a big swig from a glass of Pepsi, and smacks her lips. Then she leans towards Bonu, eyes gleaming beadily over the rim of the fizzing glass, and asks in a lowered voice, 'He's not yet shaadi-shuda, no? No chup-chaap civil marriage ceremony or anything like that? What about living girlfriends?'

'He has a "living" girlfriend,' Bonu replies sourly. 'Though, frankly, if I were his girlfriend, I'd rather be dead.'

'She *lives* with him?'

'Why don't you ask him only, Chachiji,' Bonu snaps. 'I neither know nor care.'

Meanwhile Justice Laxmi Narayan Thakur dodders slowly into the lawn and eyes Chachiji with open disfavour.

I hope he isn't going to insult her again, Bonu worries. Thankfully, the old man ignores his sister-in-law, sits down and addresses Bonu, his voice querulous, 'Mamtaji, where is the Maggi?'

Samar, looking at Bonu, sees her animated expression falter. Then she smiles with determined cheerfulness. 'No Maggi for you, BJ! And I'm Bonu, Binni's daughter.'

'Where's Dabbu?' is her grandfather's reply. 'And Balkishen? Late, I suppose. That bugger Balkishen is always late.'

'Balkishen Bau departed for his heavenly abode over twenty years ago,' Bonu tells him firmly. 'And Dabbu mausi lives in Mumbai. All you've got today is me, Samar and Bhudevi chachi.'

'Here are the cards,' Samar says. 'Won't you shuffle them?'

The Judge glares at him aggressively, his faded brandy-brown eyes seeming to bulge from their sockets. Samar holds his gaze steadily. After a while, the older man's eyes grow more placid and he takes the cards. He doesn't shuffle them though, just looks down at them, his expression lost.

'*I grow old, I grow old,*' he murmurs. '*I shall wear the bottom of my trousers rolled.*'

'BJ, you have to deal.' Bonu's voice is gentler now. 'I'm your partner. Let's play.'

The old man glances at the insipid chicken sandwiches set before him and says,

'*Do I dare to eat a peach?*

Should I wear white flannel trousers and walk upon the beach?'

'*I have heard the mermaids calling, each to each,*' Bonu completes the verse with an encouraging smile. 'Now c'mon, BJ, less Eliot, more kot-piece.'

The Judge looks up, snorts, and starts to deal, very correctly and precisely.

'Got to settle everything,' he mutters as he weaves around, setting down the cards. 'Got to *do* it! Mamtaji said so. Or it'll create problems for the princesses.'

'Both are mad,' Chachiji whispers to Samar in a resigned aside. 'Whole day reciting poetry-shoetry to each other. This girl needs a man. Are you married?'

'Uh, ummm, no,' Samar responds. 'I'm not married. Chachiji, is BJ often like this?'

Bhudevi Thakur's pug-like face sags wearily at the jowls. 'Yes, beta,' she says. 'He is like Bijli now.'

'Bijli?' Samar repeats, rather at a loss.

'Electricity,' Chachiji clarifies in a loud whisper, reaching for her Pepsi. 'Some days he is bright and some days he is dim. He has voltage fluctuations all the time, and Bonu is his stabilizer.'

She sips her drink and returns to her cards while Samar studies grandfather and granddaughter sitting opposite each other at the table, impressed despite himself. Who would've thought that snively little Bonu Singh, always playing the Poor-Orphaned-Me card, would grow up to be so sympathetic and enterprising?

'Play, Dylan, play!' the Judge urges, his eyes on his cards.

'I'm Samar,' he says gently.

'Oh?' The Judge's eyes twinkle. He looks from Bonu to Samar. 'To me, this whole scene smells strongly of D for Déjà vu.'

He chuckles to himself while the younger people look at each other, mystified.

He's really wandering now, Bonu thinks, her heart sinking.

'Uh, how's everything at home, Chachiji?' she asks.

'AN is still not fully recovered,' Chachiji reports brightly. 'He can only lie in bed and follow me with his eyes. I have to do everything for him. So sad.'

Good, Bonu thinks privately. If I had a husband as goatishly philandering as Ashok Narayan Thakur and he ended up sick and totally in my power, I would do horrible, unmentionable things to him in the privacy of my bedroom. She wonders if Chachiji is doing any of these things, and if that is the reason for her jaunty air and pink cheeks, then decides she's being too fanciful.

'Come and meet AN,' Chachiji entreats Samar. 'Seeing you will cheer him up, he really enjoyed your fillums.'

'AN,' mutters the Judge, gnawing on his sandwich. 'AN, BN, CN, DN! EN, FN, GN, HN!'

'AN is Chachiji's husband,' Bonu explains to him gently. 'He's your younger brother. He lives next door, remember?'

The Judge responds to this by poking Bonu between the ribs with the back of his fork.

'Give the ruddy beggar woman a hundred chips and tell her to *git*,' he whispers urgently. 'Tell her it's a family-only party. Then we can play two-threes-and-fives.'

He waits imperiously for her to do his bidding, but his nitwit of a granddaughter just pats his hand placatingly and smiles vaguely around the table.

Meanwhile, Samar is asking Chachiji what exactly the problem with Ashok Chacha is. Bhudevi Thakur puts down her glass and heaves a gusty sigh.

'First toh he got a Happytietis B,' she recounts sorrowfully. 'I thought it would make him little bit happy, but no, it made him so sick and fereved and septick! Then the doctors said he had cancers in his prostate and we had to do radio and keemo, aur kya kya. Uff, beta, what with all the moaning and balding and diaper changing, I felt like I was looking after a small baby only. And after that, just when he was getting little better, something even *more* bad happened!'

'What?' asks Samar, concerned. What could possibly be worse than hepatitis B and cancer?

'The Bail's Pelsy got him!'

Nodding sympathetically, even as he does some discreet Googling, Samar discovers that Bell's palsy is a sort of facial paralysis, not very serious.

'I got up one morning and found half his face sagging,' Chachiji continues tragically. 'Like a phussss balloon from which the air has leaked. The corner of his eye, the corner of his mouth! But only on one side—the other remained nice and tight. So ugly it was, so disfiguring. Hai hai, this was the worst blow yet! I immediately got to my knees and asked God why he had done this to me!'

But this extremely lookist lament has reminded Samar of his stepmother. He pats Chachiji reassuringly on the arm and turns to BJ.

'BJ, Ma said to ask you for the keys to our half of the upstairs. She wants your tailors to service Naniji's old sewing machine, Bonu. She'll be happy to pay, of course. Possible?'

BJ nods serenely enough and beckons to Lachhu, but Bonu makes an odd, gulping noise. Samar stares at her curiously. What is *up* with the girl? Why is she always so jumpy?

'Shuh…shuh…*sure!*' Bonu smiles. 'Except that all my tailors are on leave. And old Ekramuddin, the machine mechanic? He just died. His sons died too, all six of them, and their workshop has shut down. Forever.'

'*Really.*' Samar's voice is now silky with speculation. 'How tragic. Thank you, Lachhu.' He accepts the key from the manservant, who has already loped up with it, Doberman-like. 'In that case, I'll just clean the machine myself. Shall we go upstairs?'

Bonu jumps to her feet. 'You can't clean a sewing machine! It's a very specialized skill. Tell you what, let *me* do it for you! It'll be such a lark. Ha ha.'

But Samar's large hand has clamped down on her wrist. 'Oh, no you don't,' he says gently. 'We'll all go up and clean it together. Ha ha.'

They go upstairs in a little procession, lanky Lachhu in the lead, with the key in his hand, followed by Samar, smiling blandly, then Chachiji, huffing and puffing, and finally Bonu, pale, clammy-palmed, and wringing her hands.

The main door to the upstairs, common to both portions, is locked—Bonu's workers are anything but disobedient. With a quailing heart she bids them open. They do.

'Naaice,' drawls Samar as he looks about the unit. 'Truly world-class. Namaste, everybody. Bonita, I thought your workers weren't here today?'

But Bonu is beyond answering. Samar Vir Singh strides through the workshop, ignoring the stunned tailors, seeming to move (at least to the numb Bonu) like a panther zooming in on its prey, and stops at the large wooden door which marks the beginning of his portion.

'Open,' he tells Lachhu.

Lachhu steps forward, the dull brass key in his hand poised to enter the keyhole. But as he grasps the door, it gives under his hands and swings open smoothly, on remarkably well-oiled hinges.

'It's unlocked,' Lachhu says, bemused.

'No shit,' says Samar softly. 'And what do we have here?'

What they have there is the newest, most state-of the-art section of Vicky's Secret. Ten large Friend work-stations, behind which sit ten more ladies tailors, all busily embroidering a vibrant pink lotus motif onto a consignment of turquoise chiffon harem pants, in sizes M, L, XL, XXL and XXXL, as the song *Achha sila diya tune mere pyaar ka* plays melodiously on a radio set to Mirchi 98.3. A banner is strung along the back wall.

HEALTHY CHILDREN = HAPPY MOTHERS!

IF YOUR BABY IS UNDER FIVE YEARS, DON'T

FORGET TO BRING IT HERE FOR PULSE POLIO DROPS
ON SUNDAY, 3rd FEBRUARY

Beyond this is a large, well-stocked kitchenette, from which
the fragile, sweet-faced Parveen now emerges, bearing a massive
tray loaded down with about forty cups of tea. She blinks up at
the little contingent and gives them a very hospitable smile.

'Aadaab ji. Chai? Mera matlab, tea. You vant tea?'

There is stunned silence for almost a minute. And then,
predictably enough, Chachiji is the first to react. She had
scuttled ahead once they reached the first floor, sniffing tension
in the air, and now she whirls around, beating her hands upon
her bosom, her voice rising in shrill reprimand.

'Hai hai, Bonu-ki-bachhi, you have ghussoed into Anjini's
hissa? Chhheee chhheee chheeee! How could you do this, you
ungrateful girl? After all the family has done for you!'

Bonu's pale face turns even whiter at this reproach but she
doesn't flinch. Her shoulders are thrown back, her stance
unrepentant, her eyes on Samar.

Chachiji's voice spirals higher. 'Your grandfather trusted
you! Your aunts trusted you! Samar trusted you!'

'Hush, Chachiji,' Samar says finally. 'You're freaking out
her workers.'

Then he turns to look at Bonu, his expression inscrutable.
'Is there some place we can discuss this privately?'

Now he wants to be private, Bonu thinks bitterly. After
making such a big hoo-haa, leading a bloody procession up the
stairs. Hypocrite.

'Sure,' she says tightly. 'Come to my room.'

Inside her little lair, he stands before her with long legs spread wide, hands crossed across his chest, his entire attitude, at least to Bonu, extremely judgemental.

'Ya, so?' she says, not quite looking him in the eye. 'Okay, I know, strictly speaking, it wasn't the legally correct thing to do, but we're family! And with the business getting bigger, I couldn't cram all the workers into my hissa. You saw for yourself how much space those machines take up. It's so stupid to lock up half the house like this, and deprive women, *desperate* to feed their families, of employment! Makes no financial sense whatsoever! Especially when anarkalis are all the rage and they contain up to fifty panels and have to be spread out on the floor to assemble. I know BJ is really strict about everybody sticking to their own portions, but he can't climb the stairs anymore, so I just got the Trings to um…fiddle with the locks a little.'

Samar, who, truth be told, has started to feel hopelessly out of his depth, holds up his hands.

'Whoa, go slower please. Who are the Trings? And why do they know how to pick locks?'

'They live in the annexe,' she says sulkily. 'Biren Tringji and Namgay Tringji. Don't you remember?'

'Vaguely,' replies the harassed Samar, raking his hand through his hair. Why is the girl being so brazen about everything? She could at least offer some bullshit story as her excuse—that the locks got rusted and broke by themselves or termites ate up the door. Clearly, she's too shameless for that. Or too honest. Which?

'You could've called my mother and asked for her permission,' he suggests.

'As if!' Bonu tosses her head contemptuously.

Samar's eyes narrow. 'What's that supposed to mean?'

She shakes her head. 'Nothing,' she mutters. 'So what are you going to do now? Sue me? File an FIR?'

He throws up his hands in exasperation. 'Look, this is none of my biz. It's Ma's. She'll have to know, and then the two of you can figure it out.'

'Oh God.' She scrambles up, stricken. 'Samar, don't tell her. Please don't! She'll tell BJ and he'll get all worked up and make himself more sick than he already is—please!'

'Unbelievable.' Samar shakes his head in disbelief. 'Are you *threatening* me?'

'No!'

The anguish in her voice seems real enough.

Samar sighs. 'Look, brat, I have to keep Ma in the loop, okay? And I suggest we drag out Naniji's old machine. Maybe if you service it lovingly enough, she won't be so mad at you.'

Bonu's mobile features go through a series of convulsions as he speaks, before settling into an expression of mutinous martyrdom.

'Everybody always gets mad at me. I don't care.'

'BJ will find out in any case,' Samar says. 'Chachiji was there, and Lachhu. They'll tell him—in fact, he probably knows already.'

'That's your fault,' Bonu says bitterly. 'Chachiji hasn't been up these steps in years—her knees give her too much trouble. But you got her antenna up with all your insinuations, so up she waddled, sniffing scandal. She'll spread the story up and down Hailey Road now and everybody will despise me.'

'Well, you did encroach on somebody else's property,' Samar tells her, losing patience. 'You're in the wrong here. Stop blaming other people! And learn to face up to the consequences of your actions.'

'Don't lecture me!' Bonu snarls tearfully. 'Get out of my room!'

'Oh no, Bonita,' he leans in and says, very gently but very firmly. '*You* get out of my rooms—and make it fast.'

Samar gets drawn into a long conference call with his producers that afternoon. When he emerges, it is evening and Bonu Singh, that two-faced, encroaching toad, is talking earnestly to a pink-faced young man in natty clothes, in the pillared verandah outside the Judge's room.

'Yes of course,' she nods vigorously. 'No no, I'm not over-tired… Yes, yes, I won't neglect myself! Thank you *so* much.'

As Samar watches she reaches out for the pink young man's hands and squeezes them hard. He blushes even pinker and stammers incoherently.

'I don't know *what* I'd do without you!' Bonu practically coos. Her bosom leans in confidingly towards the pink-faced stranger's chest and Samar is strongly reminded of his own stepmother, Anjini, operating at the top of her game.

Practically incandescent now, the stranger takes his leave. Bonu stands in the verandah, looking after him, her expression dreamily satisfied.

'Who's the Pinky?' Samar inquires as he steps out from behind a pillar.

'Hmm? Oh, that's Dr Bharadwaj, BJ's GP.'

'Ah,' Samar remarks. 'The *doctor*. Why were you flirting with him?'

'Huh?' She seems to have something else on her mind. 'Oh, because when I flirt with him, he doesn't charge for house visits.'

'You pay BJ's medical bills?' Samar is surprised.

'Obviously not! The mausis do.'

'Then why do you care how much it costs?'

Bonu looks confused. 'But money is money, no? Why should anybody spend extra?'

'Or maybe you just fancy the doctor. What are you looking so happy about, anyway?'

Bonu beams. 'You were right. While you and I were yelling at each other upstairs, Lachhu glided up to BJ and gave him a comprehensive account of my encroaching.'

'And that's why you're so happy?'

She gives a little wriggle of excitement. 'Samar, the news *galvanized* BJ! I haven't seen him so sharp or so animated in years! He called me in and blasted me thoroughly, and used all these big-big legal words and he was *perfectly* coherent!'

'O…kay,' Samar says slowly.

'Dr Bharadwaj says his vital signs are looking great,' she continues, all glowing cheeks and shining eyes. 'He even recognized Chachiji, which he hasn't done in over a year! Asked her if Gulgul had finally got his law degree—which means he's still confused about which year we're in, but still, at least he didn't poke me in the ribs and tell me to slip her a hundred chips so she'd *git*! She was so touched I thought she'd start crying. And now he's in there organizing a family Skype concall!'

What a strange, strange girl, Samar thinks, staring at her as she burbles on with excitement at being in so much trouble. But before he can say anything, a voice rings out from behind them, so clear and commanding that they both jump.

'Bonita. Samar. My chambers. *Now.*'

'Just listen to him!' Bonu chortles. 'Summoning us to his chambers, indeed. Well, come *on*, you've got to see this!'

They walk into the study, Samar striding ahead, Bonu, for once, chhamchhamming docilely behind him.

The Judge is sitting erect on his green leather-upholstered swivel chair. His frail figure is girthed in a dressing gown, and his hair is rakishly disarrayed. His computer, a 52-inch Mac, a gift from his youngest daughter, is open behind him on the desk. Upon a split screen are the faces of his four daughters, Anjini, Chandralekha, Debjani and Eshwari.

'And it's the Newshour with Arnab Goswami!' Samar says lightly. 'Ma, Mausi C, Mausi D and Mausi E! What are we discussing?'

'Hurry up, you two,' the Judge replies irritably, swinging his chair around to face the computer screen. 'I don't have all day.'

'Hello, kids!' Anjini Singh exclaims gushingly as Samar and Bonu move closer to the screen. Fifty-year-old Anjini mausi's first words — 'I sabse pretty' — weren't entirely untrue. Her glossy curls, as stiffly set as ever, frame a girlish, pouting face that clearly has no clue that it is now fifty. A delicate pair of glasses are perched on the tip of her perfect nose for extra IQ points. She leans forward, flashing just the slightest hint of cupcakey décolletage. '*Hi* Summerwine… Oh baby, you have dark circles! You must drink two litres of water as soon as you wake up in the morning! Bonu beta, step forward, we all want to look at you…'

Bonu steps forward, her hair already up in its militant top knot and secured with her trusty Natraj pencil. 'Hi mausis,' she mutters.

Bonu's mother's first words had been 'Not fair!' and they pretty much summed up her time on the planet. She would have been forty-seven if she were alive today.

'Haiiiii!' responds Anji with full enthusiasm and then runs out of anything more to say.

Awkward silence.

'Well, look who it is,' Anjini sniffs finally. 'The elusive Chandralekha—we haven't seen you for at least ten years. Still looking like a besan ka laddoo, I see. When are you going to get over this silly phase?'

Forty-four-year-old Chandralekha, who is shaved bald and dressed in the banana yellow robes of her order—Redemption Is God's Immortal Design or RIGID—looks at her eldest sister out of cold, untroubled eyes. 'Please be as accepting of my choices as I am of yours.'

Nobody knows what Chandu mausi's first words were because she didn't speak much.

Anjini bridles. 'What's wrong with my choices?'

'Nothing,' Chandu says, making it sound like everything is wrong with them.

Anjini tosses her head.

'Well, I think it's stupid of them to make you shave your head but not allow you to thread your upper lip,' she says bluntly. 'Hair is hair, na.'

'Earthly vanity hampers our quest for the eternal,' Chandu replies. 'How are all of you? Well?'

'Oh, you just think the shape of your head is pretty,' Anji says dismissively. 'And it is, thank God. We're all well, I suppose. And you?'

'I am well too,' Chandu replies stiffly. 'I pray for all of you every day.'

'Ya, well, you could phone us more often instead,' Anjini retorts and turns to Debjani. 'And you look like Vaitaal from Vikram and Vaitaal. So much long, lanky grey hair!'

Dabbu mausi, simple and silvery, grins her attractive lopsided street urchin grin. 'I don't think mutton should dress as lamb,' she says, her amber eyes twinkling.

Anjini, whose hair is a lustrous L'oreal #05 streaked with a luminous L'oreal #13, flushes at this.

Forty-three-year-old Dabbu mausi's first words had been 'My turn, my turn!' Being the fourth of five sisters isn't easy, but she has handled it remarkably well and is now a media person of note, anchoring a daily primetime show on India's most watched news network, and a senior vice-president there, besides.

'You're vegetarian,' is all Anjini can come up with in response.

'We are all vegetarian in RIGID,' Chandu volunteers. 'We believe cows are our sisters.'

'And we believe our sisters are cows,' Eshwari says with an inelegant snort of laughter. 'Stop scrapping, you guys! *Hiii*, BJ! Lookin' so dapper! But could you back up a little? All I can see are your nostrils. Children, show yourselves—hello young Bonu, hello Samruddin—how are you hotties?'

Thirty-seven-year-old Eshu mausi's first words, uttered whenever she was told to eat or bathe or play or sleep, were 'Eshu, eat!' Now a chic, athletic New Yorker who works hard and parties harder, her appetite for life remains largely unchanged.

The Judge makes an exasperated noise and leans forward, unmindful of his nostrils, which now loom even larger on the Skype screen. His daughters cower at the sight.

'If you have all quite finished with the social niceties, can we talk?' he demands.

'Wow, BJ, you're in good form,' Eshwari says admiringly. 'Acting so bossy and all!'

'Stop drivelling, you!' thunders the Judge. 'This is a serious matter. A VERY serious matter!'

There is total silence. Bonu's heart starts to thump. Yeah sure, it's cool that he's so articulate and everything, but what is he going to do with her?

How handsome BJ looks, thinks Dabbu, meanwhile. That lovely grey hair, the royal blue robe and (I'm sure) the scent of Brut 33. His eyes hold a sort of grim confusion, though. Last week he had confessed to her that, nowadays, the words he wants to say wobble before his eyes in jumbled letters, like alphabet soup, and that he has to struggle to nail them into place. They're slippery buggers, he complained.

'Um, has he gone to sleep?' Anjini ventures as the silence lengthens.

Samar steps closer to his grandfather and puts his hand on his shoulder.

'Aaye!' says the Judge, coming alive with a start.

He pauses.

'...*I* have allowed things to...'

They wait. He continues:

'...*drift* for too long. I have always been organized...and methodical...and...'

'And?' Bonu can't help urging.

'And I *will not leave behind a mess!*'

He roars this out suddenly and with great emphasis, glaring balefully around the room. Everybody squirms, immediately wondering if they are the mess he is referring to.

The Judge looks around, scanning every face. Dabbu looks serene, he notes with satisfaction. Anjini likewise. Chandu, placid. Eshwari, distracted. Bonu, his youngest, most urgent responsibility is looking confused...and hurt. Her big black eyes (*so much like my Mamta's*) meet his, wide with apprehension. How much he loves this girl. But can he trust her? She idolizes her father too much, and the less said about that bugger the better.

She is speaking now, her young voice chastened. 'I...I didn't realize that what I did was so serious, BJ.'

'Wha'd she do?' Eshwari inquires.

'No clue,' whispers back Dabbu.

'It is serious.' The old man's voice is stern. 'Because, you see, the thing you did is how it *always* begins. I thought you would realize that, Bonu.'

Bonu flushes. 'That part of the house is empty anyway. What's the big deal if I opened up the rooms and—'

'You did *what?*' Eshwari's voice is sharp. 'Man, you're *impossible*, Bonu Singh! Such a little brat! BJ, how can you possibly condone this?'

Cow, thinks Bonu. How mean she used to be to me when she lived here, always telling BJ and Naniji that carrying me around was going to give them spondylosis. She used to deworm me with such gusto too, and comb out my lice, and come to school and gossip about me to my teachers. And Samar had a crush on her! How? Why?

Chandralekha clicks her tongue disapprovingly. 'Very wrong. This girl must be removed from the house immediately. It is both cruel and irresponsible to allow her to be tempted with free access to all our portions.'

'Ya, well, it's just my portion at the moment, so I'll do the yelling, if any is required.' Anjini's sweet voice is steely. 'Bonu, BJ's already filled me in on the details. You'll have to pay me one year's rent with retrospective effect. Market rates. Also, please get your stuff out of there immediately.'

'Um, I've only been in there five-and-a-half months actually...' Bonu starts to say.

'Pay what she says!' BJ snaps. 'And you're getting off cheap!'

Well, it was worth a try, Bonu tells herself philosophically. I've been in there for sixteen months actually, but like he said, pay what *she* says.

'Okay,' she says, very docile. Then adds, clearly as an afterthought, 'Sorry.'

A little silence falls again, broken by the Judge repeating, more mildly this time, 'I will not leave behind a mess!'

'But BJ,' Dabbu sounds rather bewildered. 'The house has already been partitioned into five pieces. It's all clearly written down and legally approved. So why would you be leaving behind a mess?'

The Judge's eyes swivel to her. D for Dreamer, this one, he thinks with resigned fondness. Some people might even say D for Dumb, especially when it comes to worldly matters. Good thing she's married to that savvy fellow, Shekhawat's son.

'BJ?' Dabbu repeats. 'Why would you be leaving behind a mess?'

The Judge blinks. 'Because of that...' His eyes glaze over as he hunts for the right word. 'Case,' he says finally.

'*What* case?' Anjini asks.

The old man blinks again.

'I've been talking to this big builder,' he says, switching subjects and becoming eloquent again. 'Very big builder! He came over to see me. Made a good offer...a damn good offer.'

Bonu stares at him, surprised. 'When? Who?'

BJ chuckles. 'Think you know everything, don't you? Well, he came. And he said that if we all sell together, we can get a good price. I want you all to take the offer, sell the house and divvy up the money while I'm still around to make sure you all don't...'

He pauses. 'Silt,' he says experimentally, then shakes his head. '*Still.*' He shakes his head again, growing frustrated. '*List...*'

'Slit?' Samar's voice is dry.

The Judge looks at him gratefully and nods. '*Slit* each other's throats.'

Everybody soaks this in soberly.

'But he's a believer in…' The old man waves his hands about in the air disgustedly, 'in…religious mumbo-jumbo and he wants to start construction on Akshaya Tritiya.'

'What's Akshaya Thimgumia?' Bonu asks.

'The most auspicious day of the year to buy something or start a new venture,' Anji supplies. '*Allahabad Buzz* gets lots of ads on Akshaya Tritiya.'

'Silly superstition,' Chandu murmurs. 'Oh well, one must be tolerant.'

'When is it?' asks Eshwari.

'April–May-ish,' the Judge says irritably. 'Is that all you have to say?'

'Money is mael,' says Chandu. 'Dirt. Anybody who comes in contact with dirt gets dirty. I will immediately donate my hissa to the needy.'

'I'm needy,' Eshwari grins. 'BJ, just how much money are we talking about here?'

'Two hundred—crores.'

Silence again. Longer this time.

Two hundred crores, Bonu thinks faintly. That's like, *insane*. Surreal. I knew the house was worth a lot but I never thought it would be as much as that! What-what I could do with my slice of two hundred crores!

'Uh, and he just came home and had a chat with you, this builder?' Debjani asks gently. 'Did he bring any lawyers with him?'

The Judge shakes his head. 'He came alone. Brought me chocolates.'

Bonu looks scandalized. 'You've been eating chocolates!'

Anjini clicks her tongue in disapproval. 'How can you not know about all this, Bonu? People are just walking in and talking to him! Supposing they poisoned him? Or made him sign something? You didn't sign anything, did you, BJ?'

Talk about ungrateful, Bonu thinks, stung to the core. I stay here looking after their father for them, and this is the thanks I get. Accusations that he got poisoned on my watch. Ma was right, they're all cows.

'Didn't know about the case,' the Judge chuckles.

'*What* case?' everyone wants to know but BJ responds with another silence. He seems to have gone to sleep again. The family look at one another.

'So what could this builder's plans for the house be?' Dabbu asks.

'To build an apartment block, I suppose,' says Anjini. 'Like Hailey Court.'

'Only fancier,' nods the Judge, coming to life again. 'Schindler's lifts. Central ACs.'

There is a long pause.

'Well, I can't pretend that this wouldn't be a total godsend,' Dabbu says finally. 'The network could actually get by without corporate funding, which always tries to mess around with editorial. We could stay unbiased and independent, this way.'

'It would help Samar too,' chimes in his fond stepmother. 'He wants to set up his own production house and make the films he really wants to.'

'Ma.' Samar looks hassled. 'I don't need BJ's money—I'm *fine*.'

'I've read what's going on in Bombay,' his stepmother says fiercely. 'They're trying to control your creative process. Well, they won't be able to now.'

Everybody else, very delicately, makes no mention of the splash Samar has recently made in the news.

'Um, yes, well, it'll come at a great time for me too,' Eshwari changes the subject. 'And what about you, Bonu-the-brat? Will so much money be good news for you?'

Eshu's voice is affectionate, she's trying to make up, Bonu can tell, but Bonu isn't ready to make up yet.

'What of the tenants?' she asks instead. 'You know, the Tring Trings?'

'They're still around?' Debjani is surprised. 'I thought you threw them out, BJ.'

'No, they live in the annexe,' Bonu replies. 'They're very nice people.' Her tone is challenging, daring anyone to contradict her.

'Well clearly, as they pick locks at your command, they must love you, Bonu Singh,' Samar says sarcastically, 'but the rest of us may not be as fond of them.'

'They eat the pigeons.' Debjani's voice has a slight tremble. 'I *know* they do. They make a sort of biryani stew... I've seen Namgay Tring walking around under the verandah pillars laying traps for them. I think they ate up Moti's puppies, and grand puppies too.'

Debjani's love for animals has intensified over the years. She is an official RSPCA ambassador and quite manic on the subject of vegetarianism.

'Yes, well, pigeons *are* a pest, you know, Dabbu...' Eshwari ventures hesitantly. 'And Namgay Tringji is really sweet. He rigged up this hoop for me in the garage so I could practise dunk shots.'

'They're horrible people!' Dabbu says hotly. 'We have to get them out of the house!'

'They live in *my* portion,' Chandu says placidly. 'And I need the rent. I'm sure they'll vacate amicably enough when the time comes.'

'I thought you were all animal lovers in RIGID,' Debjani flashes. 'Not when it means money, clearly!'

Chandu's face twists, and she sits back abruptly. Debjani looks shame-faced.

'So our childhood home will become a block of fancy flats,' Anjini sighs. 'Oh well, you stay in Mumbai, Samar, you're used to living in buildings.'

But *I'm* not, the Judge thinks gloomily. Still, Mamtaji always said it was better to demolish the house and keep the family together than demolish the family and keep the house together. And she was right. His intense rush of energy is ebbing, but he feels at peace now, rather like he's snatched his family from the jaws of some terrible fate. These disputes always start with something small, like Bonu's encroaching, and before you even know it, you're bang in the middle of a full-scale war, sides chosen, battle lines drawn, everybody pillaging and murdering and looting madly, and glibly quoting verses from the Bhagwad Gita to justify the fratricide.

But my girls are grounded, he comforts himself. Mamtaji has done a good, solid job. They love each other and they have an innate sense of justice and fair play. There's something niggling at the back of his mind, though, what is it?

'That damn-fool case,' he mutters.

'*What* damn-fool case?' Anjini prods. 'That's the third time you've mentioned it.'

The Judge looks foggy.

'The 1993 document—I have to do something about that 1993 document!'

Everybody looks at a loss.

BJ sits forward, suddenly animated, his eyes bulging as he glares at Anjini.

'You know what I'm talking about?'

Anjini leans in. 'Bauji, you're shifting subjects. You were talking about a damn-fool case, and then some document.'

Debjani pipes up, 'Oh, the 1993 document. I know what you mean, Bauji. Don't worry about it.'

'It's been destroyed?'

Anjini nods. 'Yes.'

'All the copies?' the Judge presses.

'Yes, yes,' Anjini says. 'Girls, tell him we destroyed all copies of the 1993 document.'

'Ya,' says Debjani.

'Yo,' says Eshwari.

'Of course,' smiles Chandu.

And the old man sits back in his chair, relieved.

'So who's this builder?' Eshwari asks. 'What has he built before?'

The Judge's eyes narrow. He surveys her with dissatisfaction, his forehead furrowed.

'Still not...married,' he mutters. 'Single.'

Eshwari rolls her eyes. 'So are *you*, BJ. Chachiji called me today with a rishtaa for you, by the way. A very jolly widow— sixty years old, but looks a nubile fifty-three—plays kot-piece— and knows seventeen different ways in which to cook Maggi. Should we set up a blind date?'

'Shut up, Eshu. BJ, you didn't answer. Who's the builder? The same person who bought Ashok chacha's house?'

'No-no,' the Judge says, his fluency suddenly restored, the words flowing easily, tripping off his tongue in a carefully-casual rush. 'It's that bugger from next door—that tall, troubled fellow. He's made a big name for himself in the construction business, he says.'

'Not *Steesh*?' Eshwari's voice is practically a squeak.

'Yes, him only.' The Judge swivels to smile at her. 'Your South Indian admirer. E for Engineer. *He* brought the chocolates. *And* the offer. Satish Sridhar.'

'Did you see Eshu mausi's face?'

'Yes, of course I did,' Samar replies. 'But as it was just one face in a split screen of four and BJ was hogging the screen, I couldn't see much, and I doubt you could either. What's your point?'

Bonu jumps up and down, her face bright with excitement. 'When BJ said Satish Sridhar, she went absolutely white!'

'She's a fair-complexioned girl,' Samar maintains fair-mindedly.

'Uff!' Bonu whirls to point a finger straight to his nose. 'You just don't want to admit she may like him, because *you*…' She waggles the finger and comes to a taunting, suggestive halt.

'…used to like her yourself,' he completes the sentence calmly. 'God, how old are you? Twelve?'

Bonu turns pink, irritated that he's made her look like some giggly teenager. *Why* is she incapable of talking naturally in front of him? Either she gets all snarly and taloned, or she gets all flaky and feather-brained. This has to stop.

'Twenty-six,' she replies.

'Really?' He looks faintly surprised. 'Wow, in my head you're still some little kid running around, threatening me with jars full of susu.'

She ignores this.

'You *really* don't fancy Eshu mausi anymore?'

Samar gives an incredulous, mirthless laugh. 'You don't give up, do you?'

'Really?' she presses. 'Like, not even a bit?'

'No.'

'But you were madly in love with her!'

Which, Samar reflects, is not entirely untrue. He had certainly nursed his crush on Eshwari to epic, reverential proportions in the hothouse atmosphere of the all-boys Mayo College hostel. When he'd arrived at Hailey Road for the holidays after his class twelve boards, finally eighteen, and eight whole inches taller than the twenty-four-year-old Eshu, he'd felt the time was ripe to declare his passion. Bonu, lurking about the house, a scrawny, undersized twelve-year-old, had egged him on for dark reasons of her own, assuring him that Eshu liked him and that his advances would not be rebuffed.

It had ended badly. Eshwari had dismissed him as a silly boy. Then, when he tried to take her in his arms and 'be masterful', as Bonu had advised, she boxed his ears sharply and ordered him out of her room. He had found Bonu holding her sides and guffawing herself sick just outside the door when he exited, red-faced. He had shaken her shoulders very hard, stormed out of the house, and sworn never to trust her again. He still doesn't.

'Why'd you tell me she liked me?' he asks her now. 'Sheer bloody-mindedness?'

Bonu looks away.

She remembers that afternoon well. She'd been so excited that Samar was coming home. She had combed out her ratty little crop of hair, put cream on her skinny knees, and worn her frilly new Benetton blouse, the one that made her look like she had a little boobage. And then he had bounced in, so tan and lean and heart-breakingly hot, and confided in her that he was in love…with Eshu mausi. The cow who kept telling BJ that Bonu was spoilt, that she needed to study more and watch less TV! The cow who was in some weird, complicated relationship with the only other hot guy on the road, Satish Sridhar.

She shrugs.

'You know why I did it, Samar. You're not that dumb.'

At least he has the decency not to look clueless.

'No, I'm not,' he says simply. 'I'm sorry I was so nasty to you, Bonu Singh.'

'Yeah, whatever.' She glances at him briefly before looking away. 'I still find it hard to believe you're over her. Like, completely.'

'Why?' he asks, amused. 'After all, you're completely over me, aren't you?'

And Bonu can feel her face turn red, bright red, right there, under his gaze.

'Oh, yes,' she replies airily.

The Skype session has exhausted BJ. He goes to bed early, and Samar finds himself at a loose end. Hoping distance has lent him detachment, he pulls out his laptop and sits down to watch the edit of his film. He is about a quarter of the way through, thoroughly dissatisfied and frowning moodily, when the sound of somebody banging hard on his door makes him start. The room is dark and disorienting, and he stumbles several times before he can switch on the light and yank open the curtains in front of the glass doors.

Bonu stands on the other side, dressed to party, her mouth even redder than usual, jumping from foot to foot and jingling urgently in a black gypsy skirt and scarlet sweater. He eyes her warily.

'What?' he demands. 'Dammit, I'm working. Go away, Bonu Singh.'

She pulls crazy faces at him, pressing her face against the glass. He sighs, slides the bolt open and lets her in.

'Can you drive?' she pants, half-falling into the room.

'What?'

'Uff, can you drive a car? The old Ambassador? 'Coz I need to get somewhere quick.'

'Now?' Samar reels. 'Where? And why can't you drive yourself?'

She leans on the door-jamb, eyes wide open, pupils huge. 'Drrrrunk!' she declares. She points at herself to make things clearer. 'Me. I'm drunk. And the Trings are drunk too, so they can't drive me either.'

'Celebrating the news of your inheritance?' Samar asks, somewhat snidely.

But Bonu has started jumping from foot to foot again. 'Please! It's an emergency! A matter of life and death! I can't drive, I tell you—it's foggy and I'll bang into things.'

'Take a cab.'

She sucks in a shocked breath. 'That's so expensive! Why would I take a cab when we have a car and you can drive?'

Samar looks at her in disgust. 'You're so cheap.'

'Yes.' She smiles proudly.

He starts to shut the door on her.

'I'm going back to bed. Whatever it is can wait till morning.'

Now she grabs his arm, hanging off it, fixing huge, appealing black eyes on him till he feels quite hypnotized.

'Quit looking at me like Ka from *The Jungle Book*.'

'Please. *Emergency*.'

Ten minutes later, he is nosing the ancient Ambassador out of the rusty green gate onto misty Hailey Road.

'So who is this Parveen again?' he asks. 'And what is her problem?'

'She's one of my tailors,' Bonu replies tersely, her hands gripping the dash, her eyes on the road. 'A good, capable girl. Her husband is a chut.'

Samar cocks an eyebrow. 'Could you elaborate?'

'He's an alcoholic.'

'I see. Wife-beater?'

Bonu nods grimly. 'Because she's had four girls. That's the official reason anyway. Not that he needs a reason.'

'Big guy?'

'Huge. She comes to work with blackened eyes quite often. Or nasty bruises. Once there were strangulation marks around her neck. The time that happened, I went to their place and threatened to have him put in jail. He backed off a little, especially when she got pregnant again, but now that the baby girl is out, he's gone back to his old ways. Bastard.'

He looks at her curiously. 'You really look after your crew, don't you?'

She hiccups, blinks, and crosses her arms. 'Yes.'

After a while, she adds, clearly feeling this admission requires some explanation, 'I can't afford to have key people miss work because of crap at home, na. It affects my deadlines.'

'Ah.' He nods. 'I knew there'd have to be a good, practical reason for your concern.'

Bonu glares at him suspiciously, then gives a little snort and goes back to scanning the road ahead.

'So is she hurt very badly?' Samar asks. 'Did she call you?'

'No. Yes. Shit! We've overshot the turn. Left! Take that left! I mean, make a u-turn and then take a right!'

'Okay, okay,' he says as he manoeuvres the venerable vehicle. 'Damn, this steering's stiff.'

Bonu ignores him. She is sitting at the edge of her seat, nose to the glass, one leg jigging up and down impatiently, clearly not in the mood to answer questions.

Samar continues driving, following her directions.

Thankfully, damsel in distress Parveen is revealed to live fairly close by, in the maze of narrow lanes that interconnect the big Lutyens boulevards. Bonu shoots out of the car before Samar can even switch off the engine, barrelling down a lane lined with seepage-stained, triple-storied housing blocks and chhamchhamming aggressively up to a second-floor landing. Samar swears, slams the doors shut, locks the car and races after her, concerned that the abusive husband might materialize any moment and grab his inebriated step-cousin by her interfering throat.

Reaching the second-floor landing, he gets hold of her bangled wrist and shoves her back.

'Lemme handle this,' he growls. 'It could get ugly.'

Making sure she's well behind him, he knocks authoritatively at the painted wooden door. 'Open up! Darwaaza kholiye.'

An eerie silence.

Bonu clutches his shoulders hard.

'Suppose she's dead!'

'Shhush! Are you sure this is the right house?'

She nods several times, her chin digging into his shoulder.

Samar bangs the door again, harder.

'I said, open the door!'

The sound of slow, dragging footsteps slowly approaching…

Bonu sucks in her breath.

The battered wooden door opens with a keening creak, straight out of a horror movie—and reveals a sight that makes Samar's hair stand on end.

A fair, fragile girl is standing there, head and shoulders shrouded in a white lace dupatta. There is a pair of large golden-handled scissors in her hand, horridly stained with something dark and gooey. Slumped on the floor behind her is a massive man in a checked tehmet, caked in coagulated blood. Small whimpering noises emerge sporadically from his throat.

'I told him the rest of the mutton pieces were for the girls,' Parveen tells Samar tearfully. 'These are their growing years, they need good food. I told him to be an unselfish father and to eat just the rice. I told him and told him, but he didn't listen. So I *made* him listen.'

Saying which she stumbles straight into Bonu's outstretched arms.

'I thought she'd bobbitized him,' Samar grins on their way back home a few hours later. 'Really, when I saw him lying there caked in blood, I thought the fair Parveen had severed his manhood.'

Bonu laughs. It is a gleeful, carefree sound, a sound Samar remembers from childhood.

'No chance,' she says. 'She likes sex with him too much.'

Parveen's husband had to have eleven stitches in his side, and was spending the night in the hospital. Parveen was staying with him, her mother having come over to look after the girls. Samar and Bonu had left her sitting next to his bed, waiting for him to emerge from the general anaesthesia, eyes huge with love and anxiety, looking as delicate and angelic as ever.

'Although I *did* tell her,' Bonu continues, lowering her voice slightly, 'that while they had him under general anaesthesia, she should quickly get his vasectomy done.'

'*What?*'

She nods serenely. She is completely sober now, having consumed about a gallon of cold water and two hot samosas at the hospital canteen.

'What?'

'That's *illegal.*'

She shrugs. 'The doctors here know Parveen well. She's been brought in, beaten up, quite a few times. They'll do it if she tells them to.'

'But that's evil!' Samar is horrified. 'You can't mess with a man's plumbing against his will! Tell me you're joking.'

She looks inscrutable. 'I'm joking.'

Samar eyes her uncertainly. 'Bonu Singh, you should really mind your own business!'

She throws back her head indignantly. 'But he beats her! And he keeps getting her pregnant. She's had four girls in five years, and two miscarriages.'

Samar isn't listening. 'The poor sucker!'

'He'll never know.' She pats him on the back reassuringly. 'By the time he's well enough to notice a scar, there will be nothing left to notice. It's a very non-invasive procedure.'

Not knowing what to say to this, Samar shakes his head dazedly and continues driving.

She adds, her tone conciliatory, 'Besides, she may not have taken my advice.'

Which, actually, does make him feel just a little better.

When they reach 16 Hailey Road she jumps out of the car to open the gate for him, and he trundles the old Ambassador into the ramshackle garage. As they walk towards the house, shivering in the intense cold, Bonu gives a happy little cry.

'Hey, listen, the party's still on!'

'What party?' Samar asks warily. Sounds of drunken voices, singing very badly, waft down the driveway. 'There's a party in the *annexe*?'

The annexe, a small independent two-floored gatehouse meant to house the domestic staff, stands at the end of the driveway, facing the kitchen garden.

'The Trings were having a bonfire,' says Bonu. 'That's where I was when the call came. *Come on.*'

And grabbing him by the hand she walks him down and pulls him through the old wooden door, into a tiny courtyard.

Samar emerges into what at first appears to be an exotic forest bistro. It is only when his eyes have adjusted to the gloom that he realizes that he is in the presence of grinding, backbreaking poverty.

The annexe hasn't been painted in so long that the walls are bare red brick with strips of plaster clinging on, damp and flaky. A large peepul tree is growing straight out of one crumbly wall. The ancient tiling on the floor is cracked and worn. There is a strong smell of bathroom pipes and an equally strong one of wood smoke and frying onions. Two naked yellow bulbs hang from exposed wires, a blazing bonfire holds centre stage, and sitting around it in a circle of camping chairs and moodhas, are a group of people, swaying and singing, not very melodiously.

'Meet the Tring brothers—Namgay Tringji and Biren Tringji!' Bonu Singh glows with pride, as though she is introducing her children. 'Yeh Anjini mausi ke bete hain. Samar Vir Singh.'

A pair of wiry, wrinkled old pahadis, clad in worn sweaters and faded jeans, immediately get to their feet, slapping their knuckles to their forehead, and flash gummy gap-toothed grins at Samar.

Samar smiles politely at the alleged puppy-eaters while a glass of whiskey-water is pushed into his hands. 'How nice to meet you.'

He can't help thinking of Chachiji's dark mutterings— that Bonu and her grandfather are crazy to let these pahadis live here. Then he puts the thought firmly out of his head. Besides, Biren Tring has a pronounced limp and Namgay Tring clearly can't see out of one eye. If it ever comes to a fight, he reckons Bonu Singh can take them on.

'They're my guardian angels,' Bonu shouts sentimentally over the music. 'They watch over me so well!'

Privately, Samar can't imagine anything less angelic than these two leathery old lock-pickers, but he decides to let it go. After all, the only thing he's seen them picking so far is their noses.

'Do *all* these people live here?' he shouts back.

She nods, eyes bright and happy, clearly back in party mode. She knocks back her drink. 'Yes! There are the two old brothers, their wives, kids and grandkids. It's a big brood. They all work for the school. Some of the kids are very smart—state topper types!'

Samar nods, recalling now that back in the early sixties, old Pushkar Narayan Thakur, frantic for more funds to finance his debaucheries, had rented out the upstairs of the house to a highly respected freedom fighter and educationist called Mustafa Khan, who ran a school called the Muskaan School for Challenged Children out of there. His stepmother, going through a violently virtuous phase, had even taught there in the eighties. Sometime in the nineties, the school moved to a more spacious campus on nearby Kasturba Gandhi Road. Mustafa Khan had continued to rent out the annexe for some of his support staff, which must've consisted of these two bandy-legged individuals and their families.

'So are you a regular at these little soirees?' he turns to ask her and discovers that she has already been pulled to her feet and is dancing to a gentle folk melody, hands swaying above her head, hair swinging from side to side.

'Wow,' murmurs Samar, tilting back his chair and taking a long sip of his drink. '*Okay*.'

The flames of the fire leap higher, the music grows more insistent. Bonu kicks off her shoes, laughing, swaying, whirling faster. Her sweater rises slightly, flashing a delicious indent of soft belly button, her bangles jingle, her skin glows golden with a fine sheen of sweat. Thankful for the cover of semi-darkness, Samar finds that he is unable to look away from her. And he isn't the only one—everyone is cheering and clapping, and the dirty, apple-cheeked children are staring at her quite worshipfully.

They walk back to the main house about an hour later, carrying a tasla of hot, glowing coals from the big fire between them—to warm our hands before going to bed, she explains as they set it down in the verandah.

'Aren't you going to miss this place once it's sold?' he asks her once they've made themselves comfortable. 'The whole set-up here—your work, your pals—I mean, it's your whole life, isn't it?'

An odd, closed expression crosses her mobile face. She frowns, wrapping an emerald green shaneel razai tighter around her, and sips on the bottle of rather foul raspberry-flavoured vodka she has carried back from the party.

'I don't know,' she shrugs. 'I mean, the sale of the house seems so unreal…and far away. Maybe it won't happen.'

She makes floaty, witchy-fingered gestures in the air as she says this, like she's wishing the whole situation away.

Samar doesn't quite agree with this view of things but decides it is better not to argue. He looks at her sitting swathed in her razai and gazing into the coals like some weird, omniscient medicine woman, her dark hair rippling, her nose stud gleaming in the firelight. She's had such an odd life, he muses, living in this rattling mansion with only old people for company. It's made her very childlike in some ways, and horribly ancient in some.

'So how's your new film coming along?' she turns to ask him suddenly, taking him by surprise. 'I mean, I read somewhere that you were happy with it, and then I read that you weren't at all happy with it—so what's the sitch now?'

She tilts her head inquiringly, her huge eyes meeting his fully for once, without skittering away, and somehow, Samar, for whom this is a sore topic, a *very* sore topic—one that his friends and colleagues would have advised Bonu Singh not to raise for fear of getting her head bitten off—finds that he's good to talk about it. That he *wants* to talk about it. That he's relieved, even.

Eyes on the glowing embers, he says, 'It's a long story. Are you up for it?'

She laughs, hugging her knees, bangles tinkling mutedly under her quilt. 'Sure! Stories by the fireside are my favourite thing.'

Samar sits back comfortably, folds his arms across his chest and says, his voice velvet-deep in the darkness, 'You may not recall, but I spent a lot of time here last time, hanging out with BJ. He used to talk a lot more those days, and he was pretty upset about the way people on Hailey Road spoke of old man Pushkar and the Pushkarni.'

'He murdered her,' Bonu says, resting her chin upon her knees, "Coz she wouldn't let him booze in peace.'

Samar glances down at her, controlling an inexplicable urge to stretch out a hand and stroke her rippling hair, so easily within his reach.

'Exactly. That's Chachiji's version, the one she told me, you and Monu when we were kids, the only one we've ever heard. But BJ has a different take.'

Bonu looks impressed. 'You brought up the Pushkarni story with BJ? I'd never have the guts.'

Samar nods and takes the vodka bottle from her for a quick, stinging swig.

'BJ is deeply convinced that his parents loved each other. That's the impression he received when he was a child, and nothing that happened later could shake it. Sure, Pushkar was a total wastrel, he inherited six houses on Hailey Road and gambled away four—he was left with only two by the time he got married. But his wife was a good, strong woman and she fixed him. He stopped drugging and debauching and gambling, and was determined to bequeath the last of the houses to one son each.

But the gambling sharks got worried because he stopped visiting their dens, so they bribed this dude Zulfi—a young boy who worked in the house—to loosen the railing from where the Pushkarni used to lean out every day to throw grain to her pigeons. The next morning she leaned on it, it broke, and she fell and died.'

'Shit.' Bonu's eyes are huge. 'That is *so* sad.'

'But their plan backfired, because instead of running back into the arms of alcohol, the kothas, and the gambling dens, Pushkar reformed. He got the entire red-light district shut down, retained his two houses, and made sure the shark who'd planned his wife's murder died a quiet, horrible death.'

'Good for Pushkar.' Bonu pokes at the embers with gloomy relish. 'I *much* prefer BJ's version!'

Samar nods. 'Yeah, well, he wanted me to write it all down for him—so that when you and the other grandkids heard the nasty rumours, you'd know the truth. But when I started writing it down, I thought, why not make a film on their story instead? I was looking for a period romance anyway, and it would serve his purpose much better. I would shoot the film, dedicate it to him, invite him to the premiere and give him the surprise of his life!'

Bonu looks at him, open-mouthed. 'So this movie you're making—the one you've been fighting with your producers about, the one starring AK and Zeeshan Khan—is the story of Pushkar and the Pushkarni?'

'Yeah.' Samar looks at her uncertainly, not sure how she is taking this revelation. 'But it's well disguised, don't worry. All the names, and the location, have been changed. But the story's the same.'

He needn't have worried. Bonu Singh's eyes are shining.

'Cool!' she breathes. 'Am I in it?'

'No,' comes the dampening response. 'It's set in the 1930s.'

'Damn. Still, Preetali Shah's playing the Pushkarni! Oh my god, Samar, that's *awesome*.'

His face darkens, a lock of hair falls across his broad forehead. 'Not really. I've been working like an indentured mule on this project for the last sixteen months, wanting to get it ready for BJ to see, and now…'

He pauses, shaking his head, his eyes vulnerable. She reaches out and squeezes his hand.

'You'll get it ready in time,' she says comfortingly. 'I know seeing how much he's deteriorated must have been a shock but he does have time, Samar. On a good day, he understands everything. I mean, look at today, he was on fire! He'll come to your premiere, wait and see, and watch your film and…oh!' she gasps, enchanted by the prospect: 'I can be his date, pushing his chair in a strapless gown!'

But Samar isn't listening. 'It's not just that,' he says bitterly, swigging back the vodka at a pace Bonu finds seriously impressive. 'There's more to it.' He turns to look at her, his gaze intense. 'Look, can you keep a secret, Bonu Singh?'

'Totally,' she assures him at once, sitting up straight and staring at him, all ears.

Samar stares into the big hypnotic eyes, not at all sure he's doing the right thing, and says, 'I did a lot of research for this film. And the story BJ told me fully checked out. But after we wrapped up the shoot, and I was halfway through my edit feeling very pleased with myself, this thin, green-eyed old man came to see me—and said he was Zulfi. Remember Zulfi?' He looks at her questioningly.

'The guy who had been bribed to loosen the railing,' Bonu says immediately.

He squeezes her hand.

'Correct. Well, he'd been a young lad those days, a sort of happy puppy, raised by old man Pushkar. *He* said...' He pauses, shakes his head. 'I *still* don't believe it!'

Bonu leans in.

'What?'

Samar looks up, his eyes haunted.

'He said he'd found out I was making this movie, and could I please hear his version of events because he wanted to set the record straight, once and for all.'

'And what was that?'

'He said he'd loved the Pushkarni like a mother and that no amount of money could've tempted him to touch a hair upon her head.'

Bonu frowns. 'What the hell. So he didn't do it?'

Samar's gaze grows even grimmer. 'Oh, he did it, all right. But he did it not for money but for love.'

Bonu's brow wrinkles. 'Matlab?'

His hand grip hers even harder, the knuckles white. 'He said...' He pauses to take another swig of vodka and then decides against it. 'He said that the *only* reason he did it was because the man he idolized, venerated like a god, asked him to do so.'

'What?' Bonu falters.

Samar drops her hands and stares moodily into the fire.

'Yeah.'

'Pushkar?' she says blankly.

'Yes!' Samar gets to his feet and strides about the verandah. 'Bloody Pushkar! He really did bump her off, after all, and everything that BJ believes, that he thinks is true—and that I've spent sixteen months of my goddamn life transferring lyrically onto celluloid—is a bloody lie.'

His words echo savagely in the quiet, misty verandah, and all is quiet for a while.

'Maybe he was lying?' Bonu suggests finally. 'Isn't that a possibility?'

Samar makes a hasty, violent movement.

'I asked him the same question. He replied, quite simply, that if the bribing story was true, Pushkar Narayan would have had him killed too. But here he was, still alive, living on a little piece of land bequeathed to him by Pushkar himself. And you know where that leaves me? It leaves me wondering whether BJ's a fool living in a fool's paradise, or if he knows the truth and is using me to launder it, which just makes me some kind of Nazi propaganda machine, whitewashing the sins of my murderous, whoremongering family!'

With that he chucks the empty vodka bottle across the verandah. It bounces harmlessly upon the dewy grass and comes to rest, intact. Samar stares at it in disbelief.

Bonu gets to her feet.

'Samar, it's okay,' she says, distressed. 'I mean, it's just a film, so many bio-pics take creative liberties—look at Milkha Singh. You think Milkha really got it on with a hot blonde Aussie chick the night before his big race? *Samar!*'

This, because, with a bellow of rage, the man has pounced upon the vodka bottle and hurled it across the grass again.

Fuck, thinks Bonu, feeling drunk and harassed, shaking back her hair. This is turning into one crazy night. Wrapping her razai tighter around her, she steps onto the frosty lawn.

'Stop being so filmi,' she says firmly. 'Is *this* why you've been so screwed up lately, fighting with your producers, saying you want to reshoot half your film, and abusing all the stars at award functions?'

He has been hunting about for the bottle but now he stops to glare up at her balefully. 'Aren't you too busy and important to Google me?'

She waves his comment away. 'Is that why?' she repeats.

'Sort of.'

'It's cold. Come back inside.'

'Where's that bottle?' he snarls, looking around distractedly.

Bonu has already spotted it and, very sensibly, is standing right in front of it. 'Look, it's still a good movie, right? You're happy with the way it turned out? It'll make three hundred crores or whatever films like this are supposed to make?'

'Yeah, but it's a *lie*.' Samar's voice is savage. 'When I think back to all those scenes we shot—especially the scene where she dies in his arms, the scene Zeeshan says has clinched next year's Sparkler for both him and Pree—it makes my gorge rise with self-loathing. Hah, *there's* the bottle!'

He lunges for it gleefully, scoops it up and makes to hurl it at the verandah wall but Bonu grabs his arm.

'Don't be idiotic,' she says sternly. 'Somebody could cut their feet. Besides, I can sell that bottle to the raddiwallah for ten rupees.'

'Cheapskate.'

She pulls at it, he pulls back even harder. The luckless bottle goes flying and suddenly, Samar's arms are full of Bonu. Her face hits his chest with a *whooomph*, her nose bumps against his cabled grey sweater before she pulls back, lips parted in soft surprise. He stares down at her, startled, seeing with random heightened clarity the creamy skin, the lushness of her lashes, the witchery of her tiny nose pin.

'Sorry,' she mutters confusedly, dropping her gaze, her hands rising to his chest to push him away. 'Tripped.'

'That's okay,' he replies, rather stunned.

She tries to draw away but he stops her, his hands coming up to cradle her face.

'Why d'you never look at me?'

She looks up, surprised. 'But I do.'

'Only when you're very drunk. Not otherwise.'

'I do, too!'

'No.' He shakes his head, very sure of his facts. 'You look — and then, *immediately*, you look away. See, you did it again.'

Bonu swallows.

'I have better things to look at.'

Which, even to her ears, sounds like defensive, empty bluster.

He laughs, 'Really?'

Her chin rises. 'Really.'

But clearly Samar doesn't have better things to look at. He continues to stand there, in the middle of that cold, wet lawn, staring down raptly at the girl in his arms, watching her breath quicken and her cheeks redden beneath his gaze.

And then, moving as naturally as though he has been doing this all his life, he grasps the corners of her shaneel razai, pulls her even closer and kisses her gently on her upturned mouth.

The kiss that lands on Bonu's lips is as warm and soft as a puff of poly-fill. It draws from her an involuntary little sigh before her fingers curl into the back of his neck, pulling him closer. His hands slide smoothly down her body in response, raising her higher. There is a moment of hesitant, questioning eye-contact, and then his dark lashes blink and he comes in for a longer, more demanding kiss, a casting-anchor kiss, a pulling-off-your-shoes-and-getting-comfy kiss, like he intends to do nothing but kiss her all night.

What the hell was I thinking, Samar tells himself, striding up and down in his bedroom half an hour later. That crazy girl, her messy hair, that pushy, cushy lower lip, that talk-to-me bosom. Oh god, I'm raving. I've been cooped up in this dusty old house for too long. I'm losing my mind. And all perspective.

He pulls out his phone and scrolls through his contacts list, pausing guiltily at Susan's name. He doesn't want to talk to her. Zee, then? It's probably three in the morning where he is, but that's the only time one can get Zeeshan's undivided attention.

'What, fucker?' Zeeshan's voice is grainy and sleepy. 'Who died?'

'Nobody. I just wanted to talk.'

'So talk.'

But now Samar finds he doesn't quite know what to say.

'How's the shoot going?'

'You're calling me at three in the morning to find out how my shoot is going?'

'Yeah.'

'It's *freezing*, fucker, that's how it's going. It's minus 34 degrees. When you pee, the stream of piss freezes right there in mid-air before it even hits the pot. You get a long, thin icicle of pale yellow susu, which you have to break off carefully at the tip of your dick and chuck into the john. That's my big news. What's yours?'

'I'm lying low at my grandfather's.'

'Oh.' Zeeshan digests this. Then, rather delicately, he inquires, 'Did you…uh, tell him about…you know, what that Zulfi said?'

'No.' Samar scowls. 'He's not been keeping too well.'

'That sucks,' Zeeshan says soberly. 'You'd better stay put then. In any case, my dad thinks we shouldn't come home for at least a month. Everybody's still mad at us.'

Samar brushes this aside impatiently. 'Whatever.'

'So...why'd you call then?'

'There's a...girl, Zee,' Samar says hesitantly.

'Girl? Which girl? Adam?'

'No.'

'Then which girl? You never bother with girls. You notice them only after they've hit you on the head and dragged you into a cave to have their way with you.'

Samar chokes. 'What crap!'

'It's true. Anyway, who is she?'

'My cousin.'

'Your *cousin*? You incestuous little fuck.'

'Shut up, Zee, my *step*-cousin. '

'Is she hot?'

Samar stares straight ahead of him, feeling both blank and bewildered. Why is he even talking about this?

'Her hotness is immaterial. I have a *girlfriend*.'

Zeeshan makes an impolite sniggering noise.

'Anyway, she's not supposed to be hot,' Samar continues, talking more to himself. 'She's supposed to be pathetic. And by the way, I've had an insane night. A man almost got murdered by his wife, then there was this crazy party full of pot-smoking pahadis, plus, my grandfather thinks the family's on the verge of civil war. He wants to sell the house, like tomorrow, so that we don't start squabbling murderously over it.'

Zeeshan displays the single-minded focus that makes him such a superb actor. 'So is she hot?'

Samar shakes his head in confusion.

'That isn't important.'

'Then why are you making transatlantic calls to discuss the issue, fucker?'

'I don't know,' Samar says honestly. 'She used to have a crush on me when she was a kid, but she's over it now...'

He pauses, remembering how her fingers had curled into his neck, how her eyes had closed, how her body had snuggled into his so...*exactly*.

'Fuck,' he says feelingly, pacing the room. 'Crap. Damn. *Fuck*!'

Zeeshan is saying something.

'Who kissed who?'

Samar blinks. 'Me, I think. I kissed her.'

'Are you sure? Sometimes you know, you think you made the first move but actually *they* made it. They're smart that way, chicks.'

'Thank you for your expert insight,' Samar says drily. 'However—'

'Had you been drinking on an empty stomach?'

Samar frowns. 'Maybe. Actually, come to think of it, yeah.'

'So it was just the booze then,' Zeeshan concludes knowledgeably. 'And if you're still not sure, just have sex with her. The moment you're done, you'll know.'

This, of course, is Samar's cue to mention that, as Bonu had ended the kissing session by pushing him away really hard and then run off muttering *shit shit shit*, trying to get her to have sex with him might not be a very good idea.

But for some reason, Samar doesn't want to tell Zee this. So he draws himself up with great dignity and says instead, 'You, *Chawla*, are a sick, perverted bastard.'

And ignoring the outraged squawks at the other end, he hangs up.

It is with a strong sense of déjà vu that Samar sits up in the darkness once again, half an hour later that night, and stares in disbelief at the door.

'Christ, who the hell is it now?'

He stumbles to the door, yanks aside the curtain, and comes face to face with Lachhu's dour countenance.

'Saab is asking for you,' he says laconically.

With a nasty sense of foreboding, Samar strides down the verandah towards the master bedroom, to bump into a panicked-looking Bonu at the door.

'But he was doing so well today!' she says. 'Better than he's been in months!'

Samar says, as steadily as he can, 'Let's go in, shall we?'

'I don't get it…' Bonu mutters as they enter the bedroom. 'It could be just an attack of insomnia—or gas—he gets those often in the middle of the night. Then I just sit by the bed and let him ramble, and in the morning he's fine.'

This seems a little too sanguine to Samar, but all he says is, 'Yes, that's probably it. He'll be fine.'

She barrels ahead of him, flying to BJ's bedside.

'*Well met by moonlight, proud Titania,*' she says gaily. And then Samar sees her face go strangely white, almost as white as the sheets on the Judge's bed.

Laxmi Narayan Thakur is half-sitting, half-lying against his pillows. His face is grey, his brow sweaty, his eyes bulging out of his sockets as he glares around the room, seeing things Bonu and Samar cannot.

'Enough!' he thunders. 'I want that document destroyed!'

Bonu's breath catches in a little sob.

'BJ, lie back!' she says. 'Lachhu! Where are you? He's trying to get up. Uff, lie back, *please*, BJ!'

Lachhu moves smoothly to the Judge's side, murmuring, readjusting the slipping blanket around his body. Slowly, the old man raises a bony finger and points it at people only he can see.

'No grumblings or buts-buts!' he says. His voice is strong, without a quaver. 'Absolutely *no* backtalk, madam!'

'Of course, BJ,' Bonu manages to say. 'Lie back now.'

Finally, he registers her presence. He's been fighting Lachhu's hands, which are trying to coax him back onto his pillows, but now he stops struggling. A sweet, childlike smile lights up his face as he reaches up for Bonu's chin. '*One kiss, my Bonu sweetheart, I'm after a prize tonight...*'

As Samar watches, strangely touched, Bonu lays her hand over the wrinkled old one, calming the shaky fingers.

'*But I shall be back with the yellow gold before the morning light,*' she says softly.

His brow puckers. '*But if they tarry me...*' He falters, then tries again. 'H...*harry me...?*' His face grows confused, his hand drops, he coughs weakly and falls silent.

Bonu starts to cry, silently, steadily.

Laxmi Narayan Thakur's laboured breathing is the only sound in the room for a while. Then he coughs again, and starts to mutter, thrashing about the bed before sitting upright, eyes wide open and staring.

'That damn-fool case! If he *dares* bring it up again, *quash* it, do you hear me? S for Quash!'

'Like a fly,' Samar reassures him, moving to his side. 'Gotcha.'

The Judge's bulging eyes swivel towards him. Later, Bonu will swear that he had really been looking for *her*, that his eyesight had been failing for months, and that it just so happened that he made eye contact with Samar at that moment.

But Samar remembers differently. He remembers the clammy, specific urgency with which the old man's hand had gripped his own, the way the veins on his neck had stuck out, and the total conviction he'd had that generation upon generation of Thakur patriarchs—gamblers, extortionists, patriots, war-heroes, contract killers, womanizers and pimps—were staring at him through his step-grandfather's level, rheumy eyes.

'You,' breathes the Judge. 'I trust you. Don't let me down!'

'I won't,' Samar tells him steadily. 'Everything will happen just the way you want it to.'

'Sell the house,' the Judge commands, his voice a compelling whisper. 'Divide the money into five equal hissas...and make sure all the prin...princ...'

'Princesses.' Bonu's voice is a choked whisper.

The old man nods. 'All the princesses get one.'

Samar swallows the lump in his throat.

'I promise,' he says. 'I will.'

4

The thirteenth day ceremony for the late Justice Laxmi Narayan Thakur (retd) is extremely well attended. The list of mourners is long and varied, ranging from ayahs, peons and stenographers from the Judge's reign in Delhi High Court, several top celebrity lawyers, a sprinkling of Supreme Court Judges, the presidents of three different Rajput Mahasabhas, some card-playing cronies, a contingent of long-faced rustics, and one convicted murderer who has served out his life sentence and become a social worker.

And, of course, there is that seldom-seen-together band of sisters whom the old-timers on Hailey Road still refer to as Those Pricey Thakur Girls.

The Judge's daughters have all been given tasks to perform through the havan, as has Bonu, representing her mother. Samar, watching from across the fire with a director's critical eye, can't help thinking what an aesthetically pleasing picture they make through the spiralling smoke—Anjini, haggard today, but still undoubtedly the most beautiful; Chandu, striking and serene, lips moving in a constant, inaudible chant; Dabbu, silver-haired and huge-eyed; Eshwari, with her heart-stoppingly direct gaze and clean sportiness intact; and finally Bonita, wavy black hair lapping at her feet as she sits cross-legged upon the white gadda, eyes down, chin up, bundled in a white dupatta but still alarmingly curvy, her usual aggravating mix of vulnerability and pugnacity.

'What were you thinking as you sat there across the fire?' Samar's stepmother asks him in the verandah, once the havan wraps up and most of the mourners go off to eat. 'You looked so sombre and slit-eyed. Like the Marlboro Man in Lucknowi chikan. Only you don't smoke, thank God.'

'I was thinking that the five of you should form an all-girl band,' Samar tells her lightly. 'The Spicy Sisters or Mamta's Girls or, wait, how about Hailey Road Hotties?'

Anjini makes a face. 'Sounds like a flop IPL team. So what were you *really* thinking?'

'How nice you all look together. And how proud BJ must've been of all of you.

Anjini replies to this with a weary hand gesture. Then she looks restlessly about the shamiana'd compound, thick with lunching mourners. 'Oh God, baby, I just want to crawl back home and sleep now.'

Samar pulls her into a warm hug. It has been a tough two weeks for everybody. They've all been crammed into the downstairs of the house, sniffling and reminiscing and circling each other warily, queuing up for the bathrooms and trying to get comfortable around each other again.

'What's Chandu mausi doing?' he asks, nodding discreetly towards that lady, sitting cross-legged in the grass and muttering solemnly under her breath.

'Praying in chants, whatever that means,' Anjini says gloomily. 'She keeps muttering *yelli yelli yelli, eliyo shaka laka boom boom* under her breath. It's so irritating. Why can't she pray in English or Hindi? God knows those too.'

'You guys should keep in touch more,' says Samar. 'Then it wouldn't be so emotionally draining to meet like this.'

Anjini sniffs. 'Hello, I've always wanted to keep in touch! But ever since Ma died…it's been hard. Dabbu's so busy with her kids and the dog shelter, and she has to be on the news desk every evening, and her in-laws are so bloody needy they gobble up every holiday she gets—and Eshu has become this hard-nosed, New York singleton with a busy social life and no time for her boring big sister—and Chandu…well, I can't talk to Chandu! She's turned into one of those big plain women Gandhiji was always leaning on and never having sex with. Basically, my sisters have become strangers to me. What to do?'

'I love you,' her stepson replies, which is a disconnected response but perhaps the right one. Anjini smiles and pats his cheek.

'I love you too, baby. But you're too thin and bony. If you were a fish, nobody would eat you. Come home more often.'

'To be told I'm thin and bony and nobody would eat me? No, thanks.'

'Except women on no-fat diets,' Anjini says tartly. 'Models and actresses and designing women.'

'Designers,' he corrects her. 'You look really tired, Ma.'

Anjini *is* tired. Her lovely skin looks lined and greyish today, and her hands are shaking with exhaustion as they grip her teacup. Besides, there is a heaviness in her heart, a depressed stone-in-the-stomach feeling she just can't shake off. Over the years, she's heard a lot of her contemporaries gush glowingly of the closure and peace that descended on them after they performed their parents' last rites—but Anjini, having done it twice, thinks this so-called 'closure and peace' is highly overrated.

She holds on to her boy, tousling his hair. 'Who are all those hopeful looking people over there? The ones you were talking to during the havan?'

'Bonu Singh's admirers,' Samar returns briefly. 'The pinkly blushing dude is BJ's doctor, the guys-in-ties are her chartered accountants, the old pahadis are her pals from the annexe, the surma-eyes are her fabric suppliers from old Delhi, the greasy older man is her dry-cleaner, and that gaggle of over-muscled boys are her "friends" from Gulgul mama's gym.'

'Not bad,' says Anjini with grudging respect. 'They all look quite smitten, no?'

'Yes.' Samar's voice is dry.

Silence. Then, 'I'm an orphan now,' Anjini says abruptly. 'Just like Bonu. It feels awful.'

Samar replies, his deep voice gentle, 'Ma, the word orphan only applies to kids. There's no such thing as a sixty-year-old orphan. You're being silly.'

'Fifty, you horrible boy. Where is the girl, anyway? Why doesn't she talk to anyone?'

Good question, thinks Samar wryly. Bonu Singh has been avoiding him, too. For two whole weeks, in a very crowded house, which means she's doing it on purpose. Which shouldn't matter but somehow does.

Hugging his mother, he thinks back to that crazy night in February. And how, once they'd done everything that needed to be done—notified the family, activated the process for the death certificate, called the cremation ground and organized the priest—he had collapsed onto the floral sofa in the drawing room, curiously numb and very exhausted.

'Drink this,' Bonu had said, appearing behind him with a mug of hot adrak-ki-chai. 'It's got lots of cheeni. C'mon.'

Samar had sat up and glugged the tea back without argument. She had sat stiffly beside him as he drank, patting his back in a manner he had found oddly maternal.

'It's all fine, you know,' she had said in a high, tight voice. 'He was so old. This is a release, really.' Then she'd given a little snort of laughter. 'I bet Mamtaji and he are Getting It On in some celestial honeymoon suite right about now, huh?'

Samar had nodded, thinking what a tough little nut this Bonu Singh was.

'He'll see your movie from…up there.' She had gestured vaguely into the air, smiling a twisted, lopsided smile. 'Balcony seats! He'll love it, don't worry.'

And again that awkward patting of his back.

Samar had felt the oddest wrench at his heart. She's consoling me, he had thought. This girl, who's just lost the last person on earth she ever loved, is worrying about *me*. He had pulled her to him, and hugged her tight, murmuring words of comfort. Bonu Singh had sat stiff and silent for a moment, and then, suddenly, with an almighty shake, her tears had gushed forth. Steady, stunned, unstaunchable.

'It's all my fault…' she had hiccupped half an hour later, her head pillowed against his chest. 'I encroached onto your hissa and got him all worked up…and he over-exerted himself…and *died*!' Her back had shuddered against his chest and snot had fallen freely onto his jacket sleeves.

'You're giving yourself way too much importance,' Samar had whispered sternly. 'He'd been ill for ages. And what about me, and how much I neglected him? I didn't visit for almost three years. Who does that?'

'But you were making a movie for him,' she had said, blowing her nose. Then her face had crumpled again. 'Oh, it would've been such an awesome surprise, Samar! What a horrible waste!'

'Screw all that,' he had grated, his voice thick with regret.

'But I'll make up for not visiting him now, I really will, I made him a promise, and I mean to keep it.'

Bonu had pulled back, blinking.

'What...what promise?'

'To sell the house, of course—before Akshaya Tritiya—and divide the money amongst all five heirs equally.'

'Oh.'

She hadn't spoken to him again. They had sat quietly on the sofa for a while, his arms around her waist, her cheek against his chest. Samar had felt warmed, comforted, peaceful. Then she had given a long, shuddering sigh, stood up, picked up the teacups and chhamchhammed off mutedly. And now she wasn't talking to him.

'I don't know why she doesn't speak to anyone,' he says now, rather curtly, to Anjini. 'She's complicated, that kid.'

'Just like her mother,' Anjini says tiredly. 'Well, I'm going to lie down for bit...you see off the last of the stragglers, Samar.'

❧

Over at Hailey Court, Chachiji is trading tea for sympathy. The news of his elder brother's demise, delivered without preamble by his loving wife, has so excited A.N. Thakur that it has brought about a relapse of Bell's palsy. One side of his face is now drooping alarmingly. Chachiji, well aware of the essentially non-serious nature of the disease, is holding forth to Debjani and Eshwari with gloomy relish.

'Just see, girls, AN's Bail's Pelsy is back. So sad he was to hear that Laxmi bhaisaab is no more. How much he had loved his brother!'

The sisters, still red-nosed and subdued from their father's terveen ceremony, receive this statement without comment. The relationship between the brothers, always rocky, had deteriorated entirely since Mamtaji died. BJ hadn't either met or spoken to Ashok since, as far as they can remember.

Perhaps even Chachiji isn't convinced that grief is the chief cause of her husband's relapse. She continues, 'Khair, this is what happens when you don't accept your old age and act like that old humped Bail in the story—the one who sawed off his horns to go wooing with the calves. So sad, na? Come and cheer him up, girls.'

The sisters peep into Ashok chacha's sick room warily. It smells of Volini and urine. A.N. Thakur's once thick hair is arranged in a dirty white combover. His skin is slack, his vest grey. He smiles at them in greeting and Dabbu suppresses a gasp. His weak, handsome face is certainly sagging strangely. He attempts a rakish wink. Eshwari smiles encouragingly and winks back. Then Chachiji sweeps them out of his room.

'More chai? Fanta? Cold coffee? Such a sad day. Your poor father! Such a good! Such a kind! So much generous! So much patient! Religious, God-fearing, duty-doing! No bad habbits and no tom-fooling! So lucky Mamta bhabhiji was to have him!'

Clearly, her elder brother-in-law, not a person she particularly cared about when he was alive, has been elevated, by the act of his physical passing, into some sort of plaster saint.

Her nieces adjust to this slowly.

Chachiji continues with grim gusto, 'Not a word of reproach to his wife for producing girl after girl—that too, in those olden days—when men took one look at second daughter and immediately went off and married a second wife!' She changes gear, her voice growing fretful. 'My Gulgul is the only Thakur boy now...but I'm so worried about him!' She looks up, her eyes hopeful. 'Hai hai ladkiyon, find him a nice, first-hand girl na—you both are so rich and connected!'

Dabbu pats her hand and makes soothing noises. Rich and connected, indeed. If Chachiji only knew! Network News is in dire straits and the money from the sale of her father's house will be extremely providential in saving it—both Dylan and she regard the timing as nothing short of a miracle.

She tells Eshwari as much as they walk back to number 16, her voice shaking with emotion.

'It's good news for me too,' Eshwari replies soberly. 'I've been having some...financial issues lately.'

'Arrey!' Dabbu turns to look at her, concerned. 'Why didn't you tell me?'

Eshwari shakes her head. 'Oh, it's no biggie, but still, I could do with some ready cash, and this sale will give me just that. In the nick of time too. So woo hoo, I guess.'

'And *Satish Sridhar* is saving your bacon,' Dabbu smiles. 'Imagine that.'

Eshwari's back stiffens. She looks away, her eyes very cool. 'Well, our house is clearly a good investment,' she says. 'It's not like he's doing us a favour or anything.'

'True,' Dabbu agrees. 'Bit weird that he's become so obsessed with vaastu and numerology, no? He used to play the drums and listen to heavy metal!'

'His Tam-Bram genes must've reasserted themselves,' Eshwari shrugs. 'He probably wears a sacred thread under his shirt now, and puts a chandan ka teeka on his forehead every morning and has a nice, well-rounded, idli-fed paunch.'

Dabbu turns towards her impulsively. 'Hey, maybe we'll meet him to sign the papers and all! Won't that be fun?'

'No,' Eshwari says with finality, and that is the end of the conversation.

Bonu is holed up in her grandfather's study, feet on his desk, swivel chair tipped back, playing moodily with the Judge's glass bubble paperweights.

So her business is to be disrupted and the gorgeous rambling old house that is her only home is to be sold—all so that, in BJ's words, 'the family won't fight'.

Why hadn't he applied this precious logic when her mother had wanted to sell, all those years ago? Didn't that qualify as the family fighting? Why had he gone quiet on her increasingly hysterical calls, when she had told him that if she didn't get her hissa, her husband would be disgraced, bankrupted, thrown into prison for tax evasion? Why had he eventually stopped taking her calls, with the result that Binni had packed up her family and driven to Delhi in the old car with the bald tyres, in the freaking monsoon, for heaven's sake, to plead with him?

'It's not BJ,' Binni had sniffed in the car that thundery day, handing out boiled egg sandwiches to Monu-Bonu. 'He loves me—and you—and the children—it's those cows, my sisters. They're the ones who don't want to sell.'

Evil Aunts, the child Bonu had thought as she chewed. Two-faced aunts, hugging me and loving me but being mean to my mummy.

'I'll manao them, but,' Binni had continued, 'they are my sisters, after all, and blood is thicker than water.'

Not so Evil Aunts then, Bonu had thought in relief. Which was a good thing, because she was rather fond of them.

'Except for that Anjini—she's jay of me because she has no children, only that sautela Samar, and I had the twins within nine months of our wedding...'

Ah, so *Anji* mausi's the bad one, little Bonu had told herself. God gave her no children, which proves that she's evil...

At this point Vickyji had murmured something about the children listening and Binni had quietened down for a bit—but presently, she had started up again, her voice shrill and carrying to the backseat, even above the sound of the rain pelting down on the roof of the car.

'But if Anji makes them all say no, I'll be patient. A day will come when she will want to sell—when they will all want to sell—and that day, *I* won't maano. No, you don't laugh and shake your head, Vickyji, and tell me ki I am just cutting off my nose to spice my face. I swear, when they're desperate to sell, because they're the ones going broke or in need of money, then *I* won't sign!'

Her husband had continued to chuckle, saying her nose was her best feature—it was better than Anjini's nose, or Chandu's nose, or Dabbu's nose, and definitely better than Eshu's nose, and she would look mighty odd without it, and where would she wear her pretty diamond nose stud then?

But he hadn't been able to cajole her out of her dark mood.

The four sentences she had spoken next have played in Bonu's head several times since, like a looped recording, like the future foretold, like destiny cast in reinforced concrete.

'I'll make them squirm like well-salted earthworms. I *won't* sell. Even my jutti won't sell. And if I die na, then even my *gosht* won't sell.'

'Why are you sitting in the dark, young Bonita?'

Quickly, she wipes her eyes and looks up. It's the great

Samar, of course. The Man with the Mission. Whom BJ trusted well enough—even though Bonu is the one who looked after him all these years—to Finish his Unfinished Business. Why does he always come up to her when she's feeling all fragile and fucked up and disadvantaged?

'I didn't realize it had become so dark,' she replies, pushing back her hair and looking up at him, her gaze unfriendly. 'Sorry, did you want to say goodbye?'

His jaw tautens. Why is this girl so eager to see him leave?

'Yes,' he replies steadily. 'I've decided to escort my mother home to Allahabad. Are you going to be okay by yourself?'

Oh, please. What conversational platitudes. As if he really cares. Except that the concern in his voice sounds genuine. A weird lump gathers in Bonu's throat.

'I'll be fine,' she says politely. 'It's time I got back to work, anyway. Lots of consignments to deliver. Things have got disrupted enough.'

Fine, be like that, he thinks in exasperation, folding his arms across his chest and leaning against the wall. She is clearly sorted and there's no reason at all for him to feel guilty. Which is good, because he's got a lot of work to do too.

'The aunts are going to be fanning out here and there for about a month, when we congregate again to sign the builder's sale deed,' he informs her.

'Mmmhm,' she nods.

'You sure you'll be good? No weeping jags? No hitting the vodka in the wee hours?'

Why is he bringing up the wretched vodka *now*? To remind her of the kisses that followed? She looks up at his face and quickly looks away.

'Oh, stop making me sound so pathetic!' she says impatiently.

'I'm not some poor dependent relative anymore, you know. I have good sense—and good friends!'

He laughs, not very pleasantly.

'Oh, I know. The pink doctor's been extremely attentive. He's married, isn't he? Maybe his wife can look after you.'

'Would you please shut up about the pink doctor?' Bonu flares up. 'I've managed for years without you. I'll manage again.'

Samar has difficulty reconciling this pugnacious creature sitting there with her chin up and elbows out with the soft, yielding bundle he had cradled in his arms just two weeks ago.

Good for her, he tells himself sternly. And shame on me for being a vain bastard—getting hassled because the child is over her silly crush.

'Okay,' he says.

Then he proceeds to slide his hands into his pockets and just stand there looking at her.

'Gulgul mama will be back soon,' she says without looking at him. 'He'll hang out with me. And there's always B. Tringji and N. Tringji.'

'Breaking ji and Entering ji,' he says lightly. 'What would you do without them?'

'Not much,' Bonu replies idiotically, feeling distinctly weirded out. The conversation is banal and Samar's gaze is anything but. She can't meet it.

As her voice trails away, there is silence in BJ's darkened study until Samar breaks it, slowly, reluctantly, his voice deep.

'So...goodbye then, Bonu Singh. We've had some memorable times.'

Bonu's hands close into fists, her nails digging into her palms.

'Yes.'

'It was really nice meeting you again.'

She closes her eyes.

'Yes,' she answers tightly.

'Bye.'

'Bye.'

As she senses him turning away, leaving for good, she blurts out before she can stop herself, 'Give my love to Susan Adams.'

Samar turns back. 'Aha,' he drawls.

Even in the dark she can see triumph glinting in his dark eyes. And laughter. And cockiness. *Bastard*.

She blushes bright red.

'What?' she shrugs airily. 'You mentioned the doctor, I mentioned your girlfriend. What's the big deal? I mean, I'm just being polite! And anyway, I happen to be a great admirer of her work and—'

She is still babbling when Samar pulls her roughly into his arms, crushing her body to his, and holding her there for a long long minute before finally, reluctantly, letting her go.

'Be good, brat,' he murmurs into her hair. 'I'll be back.'

5

'I told him to his face—he was the biggest producer in those days, mind you, but still I told him ki, Zaveri bhai, things have changed. I won't demand a full script, that much trust and respect I have for you, but you have to at least tell me the *basic story* of the film before I say yes and assign you my dates. Don't mind, but everybody is saying ki aap mujhe For Granted lete ho!'

'Imagine that,' says Samar politely.

'So then he said ki arrey AK saab, of course I will tell you story of the fillum, I will tell you *full* story of the fillum! He used to say fillum, you know, instead of film, poor chap, had absolutely no class, bless his soul!'

'And the story?' Samar prompts dutifully.

'Story is quite simple, he said. Bilkul James Bond type. Basically, right through the fillum, you have one hand on your gun and one hand on your lund.'

Samar, who is sipping water, chokes.

'When the villain comes, you whip out your gun, *dhish-kiyaaooooon!* When the heroine comes, you whip out your lund, *dhish-kiyaaooooon!*'

'Superb,' manages Samar. 'Just brilliant.'

AK collapses into gales of happy laughter. '*That's* how we made cinema in the old days! We kept it strong and simple.

Now look at you chaps, dithering and waffling and tying yourself into knots over *nuance* and *motivation* and *character graphs*! RRRRRubbish! All a film needs is heart.'

'Maybe you're right, sir,' is Samar's response. 'Uh, where's Zeeshan?'

'Must be at the gym. Speaking of strong and simple, that's a perfect description of young Zeeshan. Chalo, nice talking to you, Samar—and *do* take my advice—stick in a catchy item song and put this film out in the market, phataphat. People will lap it up. G'night.'

'Goodnight, sir.'

AK exits the dubbing studio even as Zeeshan Khan makes an entry, a vision made radiant with eagerness, facials and hair gel. His hair is short and spiky for a film in which he's playing second lieutenant in the Indian Army, his clothes fit his chiselled body like a glove, and enough of his chest is visible for oglers to note that it is freshly waxed and gleaming. He strides up to Samar and embraces him soberly.

'So sorry, bro.'

'Thanks,' is Samar's terse response. 'It was...quick and painless. He's in a good place now.'

'I wish you could've shown him the film, though.'

'Yeah, well. Guess it wasn't to be. '

Zeeshan sits down, grabs three seaweed-covered bundles from the sushi platter that's been waiting for him, and wolfs them down, all at once

'So, like, what's the plan now? We carry on dubbing on the same edit?'

'I guess.'

Zeeshan chews, eyeing Samar assessingly.

'You okay?'

'Yeah,' Samar shrugs. 'AK just spent the last hour telling me I'm over-thinking the film.'

'AK's a chutiya.' And thus Zeeshan dismisses the industry's most senior star. Then he adds, with a tentative sideways glance at Samar, 'Though Dad says Indians *love* stories where the hero reforms because of the heroine's good influence. The whole love-of-a-good-woman-reforms-the-rake syndrome. He thinks we have a perfect film. He says you're just wanking around for no reason.'

Samar's eyes smoulder but he doesn't say anything.

'But then,' Zeeshan continues quickly, 'unlike me, neither he nor AK knows how personal this whole story is for you. So you can't expect him to be sympathetic.'

Samar turns on him, bristling. 'Bastard, you want brownie points for being sympathetic?'

'No-no,' Zeeshan denies this hastily. 'Of course not. I just...hey, I just want some more details on the hot cousin, that's all. Give!'

Samar glowers. 'You're a one-track minded dog.'

'Yeah, but it's the *best* track, so why get off it?' is Zeeshan's reasonable reply. 'Gimme deets, bro.'

'There's nothing to give,' his friend growls reluctantly. 'She's my stepmom's niece, that's all. And she's...' He pauses before admitting softly, 'interesting.'

'Sweet!' Zeeshan slaps his muscled thigh, looking extremely pleased. 'But what will Adam say?'

Samar winces. 'Don't call her Adam.'

'But she's got a dick!' Zeeshan protests. 'I swear it! You just have to look at her face to know. One of these nights she's gonna haul it out and put it on the bed between the two of you and then whatchu-gonna-do, Mr I'm-too-nice-to-dump-anybody, huh, whatchu-gonna-*do*?'

'You're crass and disgusting. Goodnight.'

Zeeshan looks indignant. 'Fucker, *you* kissed another girl while having a girlfriend and *I'm* disgusting? Arrey, what the hell, Samar! Sunn toh yaar—you can't just lea—!'

But Samar has already slapped him on the back, stalked out of Tamasha, the quaintly named studio at Bandstand, and made for home.

Traffic, the greatest leveller in Mumbai, ensures that he reaches his apartment a good hour later and in a foul mood. Mind solely focused on a cold shower and a long drink of water, he opens the front door, only to be hit by the scent of Thierry Mugler's Angel.

Samar freezes.

It was just a kiss, he tells himself. Okay, a few kisses. These things happen.

For one craven moment, he thinks of turning around and walking out of the apartment again. Then he takes a deep breath, squares his shoulders, flat-palms the door to his large, wooden-floored bedroom, and enters smilingly.

'Hi, babe,' he says.

Susan Adams, clad in champagne satin pyjamas of her own design, is draped across the bed, talking on her BlackBerry, her helmet of sleek black hair half obscuring her face. She looks up at the sound of his voice, beams, blows him a kiss, and then points to her phone and makes a *wrapping-it-up* gesture. Samar gives her a wave and strolls into the loo to shower.

When he returns, she is sitting cross-legged upon the bed, her phone put away, her arms outstretched, her wine-red toes contrasting prettily with his pale cream sheets. 'Hiiii, stranger!' she beams. 'All my friends think I should stop seeing you!'

He has just sat down on a leather lounger to towel his head

but at this he looks up guiltily. Her busybody friends are a right pain and always super well-informed, but they couldn't possibly know he's been kissing Bonu Singh in Delhi.

'Why?' he asks.

'Oh, they're fans of your work and they think I'm distracting you, not letting you finish your film. They're desperate to see it, you know.'

'I want to see it too,' Samar says whimsically.

'Oh, but so much has been going on in your life, Samar. Cut yourself some slack. How's things at your grandfather's?'

'Okay, I suppose. I have to go back to Delhi next week to wrap up some of his paperwork.'

'I'm so sorry—it's a cliché, I know, but it really is a blessed release. And at least you got to say goodbye to him. It's almost like he was waiting to meet you.'

'Oh, that he was,' Samar agrees. 'He was worried about the house—he's put me in-charge of the selling and division of it.'

'You were his favourite grandson?'

'Oh no,' the denial comes quickly. 'I think he just trusted me more than my slightly dodgy cousin Bonu Singh, who was the only other relative in the room when BJ died.'

'How old is he?'

Samar looks at her blankly.

'Who?'

'Arrey, your cousin Bonu!'

There's the oddest little pause. Then Samar mutters, 'Twenty-six.'

'So you're the eldest. And the house is on Hailey Road, right? That must be worth a lot today.'

'A lot,' Samar says briefly.

'How many square yards is it?'

He shrugs. 'I'm not sure.'

'How's the rewriting going?'

'What's with the inquisition?' he demands.

'It's called catching up with your loved ones,' she says, her voice trembling a little.

Samar immediately feels like a jerk.

He sinks down onto the bed and pulls her close. 'I'm sorry,' he says, resting his chin on her shoulder. 'The re-scripting's going fine. Well, actually, it's not, but I'll figure it out. I just want it to be authentic, you know.'

Susan's eyes brighten. Authentic is one of her favourite words. She is all for authenticity. She sources all her materials scrupulously; her weaves, motifs and materials are all one hundred per cent pure. She never settles for shortcuts or fakes. Her competition suggests snidely that this is because she is rigid and lacks imagination, but that is just routine bitchiness. Her obsession with authenticity is mostly the reason her clothes are so expensive.

'And it's not authentic?'

Samar sighs. 'Let's just drop it.' He pulls her closer. 'How were the shows in Milan?'

Susan purses her lips and shakes her head.

'Derivative. No new ideas—they were all recycling the same-old same-old.'

'Really?'

'Really!' She rolls her eyes. 'It's just so lazy of creative people—especially the ones supposed to be at the cutting edge of design—to do stuff that's already been done! I mean, they have a responsibility to the rest of the industry! We look to them to provide excitement and inspiration. Every single thing they put up on the ramp could've been hashtagged "done before".'

Samar has started to zone out. He tends to, when she talks shop. Clothes, unlike cinematography and writing and direction, are just not his thing—that's part of the reason he'd been so relieved to have her as the designer on this film. The stars had been terribly fussy about their 'look', and Susan handled them brilliantly. Even Zeeshan, who doesn't like her personally, admitted that she knew her job.

Now she is dimming the lights. The scent of Angel—pretty, sparkling, a bouquet of dancing, dew-kissed wildflowers—is everywhere. It was what had attracted him to her in the first place.

'I missed you,' she whispers, reaching for him.

Samar gives her a quick hug, then sits up, brightening the lights.

'Are you sure you want to do me?' he grins, getting out of bed and gently chucking a pillow at her. 'After all, I can also be hashtagged "done before".'

She stares at him for a moment, then laughs.

'Idiot!' she says. 'Come back here.'

But he blows her a kiss and walks out backwards towards the study. 'Later, babe,' he says, his deep voice laced with regret. 'Gotta prepare for the big meeting tomorrow. You cuddle down and sleep well.'

He arrives at the glass-walled conference room on the seventh floor of the massive Sonix office at nine o'clock the next morning to find them all grim-faced and dark-suited, sipping the green tea that is so good for their acid reflux. Random whispers waft into his ears as he pushes back the heavy double doors.

'Prima donna…'

'Unhinged…'

'Overrated.'

'Pressure of the spotlight…'

'Bloody idiot…'

The combined blast of their aftershave and their hostility is almost enough to knock him right off his feet. But he squares his shoulders and slides his hands deep into the pockets of his jeans, even as the expression on his face changes to decidedly sardonic. Lord, what had he been thinking, getting involved with this bunch of bitchy, fretful old women?

'Morning,' he says lightly. 'I'd like a bottle of cold water, please.'

Cougar Malhotra gets creakily to his feet.

'Hullo hullo,' he says before turning to address the room in his soft, rasping voice. 'Gentlemen, ladies, all stake-holders are finally in the house! We can now begin. I'd just like to lay down a few ground rules. This meeting is meant to be constructive. So no blame-gaming or I-told-you-so-ing. Is that clear?'

'Well, thank *you*, Cougar, for putting ideas in their heads that perhaps weren't even there yet,' Samar says lazily. 'Now that we've clearly laid down what this session *isn't* about, could we please get it over with?'

Cougar blinks his hard little eyes several times and begins.

'*Tharki Thakur* is delayed—and it's way over-budget. Fact.'

Samar chokes on his water.

'Excuse me, did you just say *Tharki Thakur*?'

'Well, as you haven't come up with a name yet, we've started calling it TT internally,' Cougar replies mildly. 'It's a working title, an affectionate nickname. But that isn't important—what's important is that it's, like I already mentioned, delayed and over-budget. Has there been any progress on the rewrites?'

Samar shakes his head. 'No.'

'But I don't understand...' a brown, podgy individual breaks in querulously. 'Ki why we are not sticking to thee ending detailed in thee virginal bound script? It was cunceived as an Epic Human Drama, narrated to everybody as a potential Sparkler Award winner—they all signed their contracts on basis of that virginal cuncept and ending—now how can we change it?'

Samar leans forward. 'Nobody's talking of changing anything. I am only requesting you to let me *think* over this a little—and then maybe reshoot a tiny chunk. I'm concerned that the Thakur's character is so evil that his repentance in the end is unconvincing. Both Zeeshan and AK have had so much fun playing the asshole to the hilt that when he becomes all goody-goody at the end, it looks fake.'

'You wrote it,' Cougar points out.

'I know,' Samar scowls. 'And you approved it. But we're mortals—not gods. We could be wrong.'

Silence.

Samar gets to his feet and starts to pace, then swivels to face the room.

'Look, you guys trusted me because you liked my previous work. So trust me now.'

They sit there in their fancy chairs and look at him, their faces blank. A feeling of hopelessness starts to steal over Samar.

'Earlier,' Cougar wheezes, 'you had given us to understand that Zeeshan Khan was supportive of this...*rethinking*—and that he refused to dub till you fixed it. But he has since communicated to us that he too is satisfied with the current film and *you* are the one causing the delay.'

Et tu, Zee, Samar thinks wryly. Then again, what else could he have expected? Zee's contemporaries all have big releases this year, and if *Tharki Thakur* (what a name!) doesn't release, his price, his ranking and his endorsements will all take a pounding.

'You have deceived us!' a cadaverous lady with a face like a sucked-up mango says shrilly. 'Cinema is not an art, Mr Singh, with all this wishing-washing and back-tracking and moaning that the climax is fake. Cinematics is actually mathematics, and creative people are, let's just say, not strong in maths.'

Cougar holds up one meaty arm, shaking his head and smiling benignly. Not that Samar is fooled. He knows that the bad cops at these meetings operate with Cougar's full blessing.

'People, people, *please*. We have huge respect for your talent and your instinct, Samar, but the film *must* be released asap. The money's been tied up for too long.'

Everybody nods, sips green tea and avoids eye contact with Samar. Remembering how they'd all wrung his hand and sucked up to him when they green-lit the project makes him want to burst out laughing.

'Had your say?' he says pleasantly. 'Now please hear me out. I've made a film on a two-crore budget that earned fifteen on the market. I've made another on a ten-crore budget that earned seventy. So I am not,' he makes quote marks in the air, '"a fail" at math. You're welcome to take the film away from me, assign one of your tame directors to finish the edit, slap on some music, stick in an item song, and put it out there before Diwali. But I won't put my name on it as writer-director.'

Silence.

'This film has cost too much,' rues the cadaver finally, deftly deviating to another pet theme. 'That original gold zari embroidery on Preetali Shroff's lehengas for instance, three lakh rupees per running metre...'

Samar throws up his hands. 'I didn't ask for bloody gold zari! I don't even know what it is!'

'And the ruby buttons on the Thakur's jacket.'

'Those were *real* rubies?' Even Samar is shocked.

'The designer's your girlfriend,' points out Podgy.

'Who was appointed by the star directly,' Samar replies.

Silence. And then the mutters start again, growing louder. Do they think he's deaf?

'Better a tame director than a wild director.'

'Let's just pay him his fee and get somebody else.'

'But *why* are we deviating from the virginal cuncept?'

'Doesn't realize that if we throw him out, no hero will work with him again. He'll be making female-oriented comeback films for ageing heroines for the rest of his life.'

'Please, this is getting too nasty,' implores a Zen-like lady with large, tragic eyes. 'Let's keep it positive!'

'I *am* positive,' Samar says, getting to his feet. 'Positive that I need a little more time! *Support* me.'

The intensity in his voice quietens the room. The suits subside, looking here and there, sipping tea and shaking their heads.

Cougar sighs and spreads out his hands.

'Let nobody say that Sonix Studios does not back its directors. We'll hold off the release for a month. But it can't be longer, or we'll clash with other big releases. This is your last chance, Samar baby. Go do your rethinking, reshoot a little, tinker with your climax if you will. I don't need to tell you what a blow it will be to your reputation if you blow it.'

'Then don't tell me,' Samar says curtly and turns to leave.

'The item number's non-negotiable, though,' Cougar calls out even as the doors swing shut. 'You'll have to shoot it.'

Samar swears and strides away.

6

In a bid to recreate 'family feeling', the Thakur sisters, now regrouped at number 16, gamely surrender phones, clothes and cares to spend the day together at a highly recommended 'organic' beauty salon in Malcha Marg Market. It is Anjini's idea, of course.

'Nothing like stripping down to tiny disposable pink chaddis to bond with your sisters, I say,' she declares happily as they lie on four parallel massage beds, tended to by one sturdy, impassive lady attendant each.

Nobody replies.

Stealing a look in the baroque gilted mirror, Anjini confirms that what she'd suspected last month, when they were all swathed in their winter wear, is correct. Nobody else's body is as firm or as smoothly exfoliated as her own. Sighing happily, she tries again.

'Should we take a sisters picture? I was thinking of doing a sisters special for *AB*—about how some sisters are more famous than others, and some prettier, and how they may all live far apart but how they're still always there for each other, no matter what. I thought I could do Kareena and Karisma, Katrina and her six sisters—and just for a laugh, us also! Because Dabbu is quite well known na, and Chandu is bald, and I of course am very popular in Allahabad.'

'Anji di, you can't keep printing pics of yourself in that paper,' Eshu tells her sternly. 'You'll lose your job.'

Anji pulls a face. 'Maybe you're right,' she admits. Then she brightens up. 'Ooh, let's take before and after pics, at least— before our beauty treatments and after. We can post them on FB, c'mon!'

'No,' Dabbu says crossly. Hanging out with Anjini is having its usual effect on her. She is starting to feel both flabby and frumpy. 'Let's just…bond, okay? Isn't that why we're doing this?'

Anjini nods quickly. She doesn't want them to start getting cranky. They hardly ever have time for her.

'Okay, okay. So, tell me your secrets, girls! But only sexy ones or spiritual ones. I'm in the mood for something deep.'

But nobody else is in the mood to talk. Dabbu is enjoying her massage too much, Eshwari is tensing in advance for the point at which the conversation will inevitably deteriorate into a let's-find-a-boy-for-Eshu mission, and as for Chandu, Chandu's Spartan soul has gone into shock, faced with so much luxury. Her tall, gaunt body is stiff and goose-pimpled, and she is battling with her massage lady for a fluffy pink towel to preserve her modesty.

'Chandu, let the towel go. You're not Chanduben from Sabarmati,' Anjini snaps. 'Relax, okay?'

'Yeah, it's your treat,' Eshu says slyly. 'You should at least enjoy it.'

Chandu rears up in panic, like a zombie rising from the dead, spilling soapy water everywhere. '*My* treat? I'm paying for *everyone*? How much does it cost?'

'But money is mael,' Eshu murmurs.

Chandu looks so alarmed that Dabbu quickly speaks up, 'It was a joke, Chandu didi, chill. We'll split the bill equally.'

Chandu's face flushes an unbecoming red.

'I don't like jokes,' she mutters disjointedly and lies back again.

The other sisters exchange glances. Chandu's frugality is almost pathological. Nobody knows quite what to make of it.

Meanwhile, the massage lady is tsk-tsking over her general state of disrepair.

'Madam has no hairs on her head! Kitna dead skin hai! Aur face pe so much dryness and dark spots and blackheads! Meri maano, aap straightaway laser karwalo! We have a good offer— two full legs ke saath, one full crotch area free.'

'Beautification is forbidden in my Faith,' Chandu says, warding her off. 'We believe in glowing from the *inside*.'

'A hairy upper lip gets you to heaven faster?' Eshwari marvels. 'Who knew?'

'Madam is a saadhvi,' Debjani explains to the massage lady. 'A sanyasan. Please understand.'

'But madam is not a dead!' the massage lady replies stoutly. 'God wants us to be beautiful.'

'Hush,' Anjini frowns. Then she turns to Chandu. 'Achha, tell us all about Redemption Is God's whatsiz, na. Your church. What's it like, how does it work?'

'Is this for *Allahabad Buzz*?' Chandralekha asks warily. 'I don't want to be featured in your magazine. It's against our rules.'

'No no, this is just for us,' Debjani assures her. 'We want Redemption too, you know!'

'Oh!'

From the patronizing way Chandu enunciates that one little word, her sisters get the uneasy feeling that Redemption, somehow, is out of their league. Like we have two hundred rupees in our pockets and we want to eat at a five star, Anjini thinks, stung. Or we're India, dreaming of winning the football world cup.

'My church believes that the way to be redeemed is to do good works, sacrifice and charity,' she continues, 'because *only* good works, sacrifice and charity can earn you a place in heaven. It's all explained in *Poor Is the New Rich.*'

Poor Is the New Rich is the title of the runaway *New York Times* bestseller written by the founder of RIGID. It was swiftly followed by a second blockbuster, *Giving Is the New Receiving.*

The sisters consider this.

'So your good deeds, sacrifice and charity are a sort of EMI?' Eshwari asks. 'With which you buy a bit of real estate in heaven?'

'What about love?' Dabbu wants to know. 'And faith? Jesus said we must—'

Chandu waggles an indulgent finger. 'Dabbu, Dabbu, marrying a Christian doesn't make you an expert on the Bible!'

'So love isn't important?' Anjini demands.

'Of course it is,' Chandu says seriously. 'But love without good works is empty. That is why, when I joined RIGID, I immediately gave away all my savings to charity.'

(And borrowed five lakhs from me two years later, Eshwari thinks privately. I never caught a whiff of that money again. Well, she did say she'd pay me back when we sell the house...strange she hasn't mentioned it, though.)

'I think good works without love are empty,' Dabbu says stubbornly.

'Besides, isn't it impractical?' asks Anjini. 'I mean, suppose you needed money, suppose there's an emergency or something?'

'God is my only insurance policy,' Chandu says simply. 'And it is enough.'

'You mean *He* is enough,' says Dabbu.

'Or She,' puts in Eshu.

Well, not *really* enough, Anjini thinks privately. *I* supported her family when her husband lost his job. Not that she asked me for money directly—she just called and sounded so stricken that I sent her one lakh every month for two whole years. Strange she hasn't mentioned that—well, she did say she'd pay me back when we sell the house…so it's okay, I guess.

'Cool,' says Debjani. 'Uh, what do your husband and son have to say to all this?'

Chandu frowns down at her fingers which are being massaged with cuticle cream. 'They live in Chicago. My son's not so little now, you know—he's finishing university.'

And I put him through college, thinks Dabbu privately. I paid all his fees because Chandu had nothing. Oh well, he's a sweet boy, and she did say she'd pay me back one day.

'But I pray for both of them, every day,' Chandu continues. 'And for all of you, too. For health, for peace of mind, and for a nice man for Eshu.'

Immediately, all eyes swivel to Eshwari.

'Thank you,' she says, her tone sarcastic. 'If I find him, I'll know who to thank—the God of RIGID things.'

Chandu looks hurt. Dabbu frowns.

'You've become too cynical,' she says severely, 'and selfish. That's what happens when you don't have anybody to look after. You should get a dog.'

'Too much responsibility,' Eshwari responds. 'Where will I leave it when I go walkabout?'

Because this is Eshu's life. She works hard at her corporate job in the big city and spends a whole month having a blissful holiday in a new country every year. She did the obvious ones first—Europe, Brazil, Australia—but now her choice of destination is getting (according to Dabbu) rather too exotic, if not downright dangerous. Last year, she went trekking in Afghanistan.

'Then stop going walkabout,' Dabbu tells her. 'Pick one country. And one man.'

'It must be nice to be single,' Anjini says dreamily. 'I think about it sometimes, how life would've been if I hadn't been married off to Antu so quickly…How many boyfriends have you had, Eshu?'

'A few,' Eshwari says shortly, 'I don't recommend it, though.'

'Why why?' Anjini sits up. 'I thought variety added spice?'

'Okay.' Eshwari sits up too, and even though her massage lady looks pained, starts to talk in earnest. 'Remember when you changed your darzi? You complained the new man put darts in your cholis and stitched your salwars all baggy, and the kurtas he made tore under the armpits?'

'Ya,' Anjini nods. 'So?'

'And when you got a new driver he didn't know your regular haunts and stunk up the car by smoking beedis inside it?'

'What's your point?'

'Change is a pain. Drivers *or* lovers. It's hard enough to find somebody good—and it's a real wrench to lose them, especially after you've got them trained just right.'

'So the next time you find a good "driver"—don't let him go,' is Dabbu's prosaic advice.

'I haven't been driven in *ages*,' Eshu confides gloomily. 'I've sunk to driving myself now.'

Everybody giggles, a little guiltily.

'Well, we all have to drive ourselves now and then!' Anji concludes. 'It's only healthy. But I envy you your experiences— I've only ever seen one man's in my whole life.'

'I've seen two,' Dabbu says. 'Counting Pow's.'

'Two whats?' asks Eshu, confused.

'Son's penises don't count!' Anjini shakes a stern finger. 'Chandu, you?'

'One, then,' Chandu reveals, her face very red.

'Oh!' Eshwari screws up her eyes in thought. 'Four, five…no, wait, does just seeing and holding count or does it have to be a penis one has actually had sex with?'

Seeing and holding counts, decree her sisters, their eyes wide in awe. Eshu wrinkles her pretty forehead.

'Seven,' she says with a decisive little nod and everybody gasps. 'What? Uff, you guys, it's not that big a deal—it's actually like less than one in three years since the time I became sexually active. C'mon.'

Now, of course, the sisters want her to tell them about all these penises and the men they came attached to. But Eshwari shakes her head. 'Nope. Let's not have a penis retrospective, please. I'd rather look ahead.' She lies back, much to her massage lady's relief. Silence reigns for a while.

'I don't like Samar's girlfriend,' Anjini says presently. 'There's something not quite right about her.'

'She's bhainga,' Chandu declares unexpectedly.

'Cock-eyed?' Debjani is surprised. 'No!'

'Yes,' Chandu insists. 'One eye is sort of *glassy*. I'm telling you!'

'Maybe there's something wrong with your TV,' Dabbu says. 'I've met her, face to face—and her eyes seem just fine.'

'*Cock*-eyed only,' Anjini says gloomily. 'Man-mad. Boy-crazy. And my son is stuck with her.'

'Stop talking about private parts,' Eshwari sits up. 'Shall I tell you my favourite daydream? I want to start up an international trekkers and explorers company with my share of BJ's money. Make My Trek, I'll call it. The website's all done, and I have all the contacts—I've trekked in so many countries, I could take people there, see it all afresh through their eyes, embrace the planet...'

'But what about your job?' Dabbu asks. 'It's a good steady job!'

Eshwari's face falls slightly.

'I could chuck it,' she mutters tentatively.

'Don't!' is Dabbu's instinctive reply.

'But she'll have the money from the house,' Chandu points out. 'So technically, she can.'

'I think Chandu's right,' Anjini chimes in and Eshwari smiles at her, a little surprised. 'Susan *is* a bit bhainga. I don't like her—and her clothes are unnecessarily fussy.'

Eshwari rolls her eyes and lies back resignedly.

'But why d'you want to chuck up your perfectly good job?' Dabbu asks again. 'It's so tough to get a job with the US economy being what it is...'

'She'll have BJ's millions,' Anji points out.

'Only if the sale goes through,' Chandu cautions.

'There should be no problem with that,' Anji waves a hand about airily. 'Eshu's boy will see to that!'

Everybody giggles. Eshwari sits up again, looking harassed. 'Look he's *not* my boy. And behave yourselves tomorrow—all of you, please. I'm off men, I tell you, they're just...pathetic. Whiny and self-obsessed and oozing slick charm.'

'You used to like slick charm,' Debjani says. 'It was your criterion number one.'

Eshwari widens her big bold eyes. 'No, my criterion number one was a cute butt. It still is. It's a necessary but not sufficient criterion, though. I mean, if we're talking marriage, which I'm *not*.'

'Why buy a whole pig when you can get the sausage for free?' her massage lady joins in jovially, making them all jump. Seeing their expressions, she adds, feeling an explanation is due, 'A foreigner lady told me that when I asked her if she was married.'

'I'm vegetarian,' Dabbu says automatically.

'Then don't buy the mandi when you can get the shakkarkandi for free,' Anjini giggles, and Debjani snorts so hard some of the floral detoxicating goop on her face flies across the room and hits the pastel wallpaper.

'You know what, Eshu?' she says when she comes up for air. 'I've just had a good idea—why not do some trekking while you're here? You've been all over the world, ab kuch desi bhi dekhlo.'

'Speaking of which,' Anjini says. 'Have you ever been with a foreigner? Gora penises must be pretty *eww*, right? Like boiled arbi, with a hairy chhilka.'

Debjani stares at her in horror. The fact that Chandralekha's husband is a 'gora' has clearly slipped her mind. Or has it? Looking at Anjini's beautiful, serene face, it is hard to tell. Fortunately, Chandu is too busy being rinsed off to hear what was said.

'No comments,' Eshwari says, studying herself earnestly in the mirror. Her hair is sheeny-shiny black, her full mouth scrubbed to peony pink. 'Phew! I look half-human now.'

'Good enough for Satish, who we're meeting tomorrow,' Anjini says slyly.

'Oh, please.' Eshwari shudders. 'Can't I skip?'

'If you don't come he'll think you're avoiding him,' Anjini points out, reasonably enough. 'Do you really want to give him that much bhaav?'

'No,' Eshu scowls. 'I'll come.'

Anjini smiles to herself, satisfied. Dabbu looks at her with grudging respect.

Then she grins. 'Hey, I just thought of something!'

'What?' they all want to know.

'Sat-*eshwari*,' she says. 'Get it? *Sateesh*-wari. Their names are like a Venn diagram, with "eesh" in the middle. It's a sign.'

Major excitement. Everybody sits up, eyes glowing, much to Eshu's disgust.

'BJ would've approved!'

'Why'd we never think of this before?'

'Look, I'd really appreciate it if you people would just lay off this whole Satish-used-to-like-Eshu bit of ancient history, please,' Eshwari says, clearly upset. 'Especially now that he's made good and become so rich and all.'

'We're rich too,' Anjini objects. 'Our house is worth two hundred crores. And you're an NRI.'

Eshwari ignores her. 'It's just soo immature and it will make things awkward between us for no reason.'

'Okay,' Chandu nods.

'My bad,' Dabbu apologizes.

'He isn't married, you know,' Anjini contributes.

Eshwari glares at her.

'Okay fine, we'll behave ourselves,' Anjini sighs. 'We'll act like there's no history at all. No physics—no chemistry. Like Salman Khan never even *met* Aishwarya, okay?'

'Deepest condolences for your loss.' His hand is massive—practically engulfing hers—yet gentle. 'I was travelling, otherwise I would definitely have attended the funeral. He was a great man.'

'Thank you,' Eshwari replies steadily. 'It's nice to see you agai—'

But he has already moved on, repeating the same set of words as he looks deep into Dabbu's eyes.

Hrrummmph, thinks Eshwari, miffed. She tucks a shiny bit of hair behind her ear, lifts her chin and looks around the conference room composedly.

The corporate offices of SteelBird Builders in Connaught Place can only be described as smug, superior and spread out. Set between a Starbucks Coffee outlet and an Ajanta Curios in the inner circle, their gleaming glass front displays impressive images of projects all over India: malls, theme parks, gated communities and the sprawling campus of an international baccalaureate school. There is also an altar to Balaji, in front of which stand three three-tiered brass lamps lit with fragrant oil. In the massive conference room there are orthopaedically correct chairs, a glass-topped table and chrome finishings. A row of well-polished awards line the back wall.

Against this impressive set-up, Satish Sridhar—once a gawky, shaggy-haired lad who used to ask Eshwari to 'be his chick' repeatedly and had been deservedly spurned for using such ineloquent language—is now leaning over Chandu's hand solicitously, repeating his offer of deepest condolences for the third time, in the glibbest of language.

He sounds like he's swallowed a *Roget's Thesaurus*, Eshwari thinks, flustered, as she hears 'heartfelt' and 'tremendous loss' and 'commiserate' roll off his tongue in a voice that is much deeper than she remembers. The Kindle version clearly, because it hasn't given him a paunch. Damn, he looks good. But that's okay—so does she. Not that this is a competition.

Finally Satish finishes with Anjini and turns to face them. He is looking at her, she realizes with a start, his expression bland, a half smile playing on his rather (sexily) full lips.

'Coffee? The Starbucks is just next door.'

'Huh? Yeah, sure.'

They place their orders and a distinguished grey-haired gent, who looks more like the CEO of SteelBird Builders than Satish does, is dispatched to fetch it.

Satish turns to Eshwari. She looks chic today, dressed in trendy, long-sleeved black, with a chunky silver bracelet and red lipstick.

'So…Bihari, it's been, what, fifteen years?'

And the sound of that old nickname on his lips, that stupid, entirely-without-logic nickname, makes Eshwari suddenly want to burst into tears.

'About that much,' she nods.

He continues to look at her and Eshwari realizes, much to her disgust, that her heartbeat has quickened. Her sisters, the cows, have started talking to each other; clearly they feel they should give her and this *person* time to catch up.

'You look just the same,' he smiles, showing very white teeth. She remembers that she used to think of his smile as having a distinctly wolf-puppy quality. Well, he's fully wolf now. All smooth jaw and sleek, backcombed hair, dressed in a linen summer suit and radiating expensive aftershave. A slick city beast.

'You don't,' she replies bluntly. 'You look…*smooth*.'

He raises an eyebrow, a faint gleam of amusement in his eyes.

'You were expecting a ruffian, clearly.'

'I'm stunned at the width of your vocabulary, yes.'

'I got that studying for the CAT,' he grins. 'After your time.'

Clearly a lot has happened 'after her time'. Whatever.

'You've done very well,' Debjani beams at him approvingly. 'Such a big, fancy office!'

Uff, why is Dabbu going all proud, maternal mummy-ji on him, Eshwari thinks, irritated. He's smug enough already.

'Thank you,' Satish's eyes light up. 'It's so nice to see you again…Dabbu.'

Debjani gives him her street urchin grin. Anjini leans forward.

'Eshwari heads recruitments for a big company in New York,' she says importantly, which immediately makes Eshwari slide lower into her seat in embarrassment.

'Yes, of course,' Satish smiles at Eshwari, not at all patronizingly. 'How nice.'

'She is also setting up an international trekkers and explorers company,' Anjini goes on.

Eshwari starts to seriously consider sliding *all* the way till she's safely under the big polished table.

'Wow!' His smile is more genuine this time.

Anjini beams and opens her mouth again. Eshwari, suddenly, irrationally convinced that Anji is about to say 'and she's seen seven penises!', butts in smoothly.

'It's just an idea at the moment, but I'm pretty keen on it.'

'Cool,' he says.

'Forgive me for asking, Satish, but are you married?' Debjani inquires. 'No, na?'

Unbelievable, thinks Eshwari. You can't take these women anywhere.

'No,' he shakes his head, entirely unoffended. 'After the accident—you know about my accident, right?'

They nod. Of course they know. All of Hailey Road knows about Satish Sridhar's turbulent adolescence. He'd done brilliantly in class twelve and pleased his parents no end by getting into IIT Delhi. But three years later, shortly after Eshwari left for the US, he got heavily into substances, was caught cheating on a paper and sent home in disgrace. He had spent the next few months brooding around the house by day and taking his father's car out for long drives by night, and ended up hitting a drunk pedestrian. He had stopped the car immediately and taken the victim to AIIMS—but the injuries were serious and the man died. Hailey Road shunned him—and he has shunned Eshwari since.

'Yeah, so after the accident I spent six months in Tihar. Word spread through the Tam-Bram network that I was a substance-abuser and undesirable. So, even though I cleaned up my act and got my degree,' he spreads out his large hands self-deprecatingly, 'nobody wants to marry me.'

Debjani thinks this is a highly convenient and far too glib explanation but she lets it go.

'What are substances?' Anjini wants to know.

'Drugs,' supplies Chandu grimly, speaking for the first time. Everybody jumps a little. 'The hard stuff.'

'Oh!'

'Turn to the one true God,' Chandu continues seriously, the lights in the conference room bouncing off her shiny bald head. 'Then you will not require crutches like drugs.'

'Yeah, well, he's fine now, he just said so,' Eshwari snaps. 'He's cleaned up.'

Why the hell am I defending him?

'Well, we did hear about all that,' Debjani says calmly, 'and good for *you* for beating your demons and being so frank and open about it—well done!'

The affectionate approval in her voice makes Satish's lean cheeks flush.

'Thanks,' he says gruffly.

Anjini is looking accusingly at Eshwari, the thought in her head so clear it might as well have been written across her face.

You dumped him and drove him to drugs.

I did *not*, Eshwari stares back at her fiercely.

Anjini's eyes widen.

It's actually quite romantic. And you heard, na, he still isn't married. And he's so rich and all now! Hai, maybe he's buying the house just so he gets to meet you again!

Eshwari rolls her eyes and turns to accept the coffee the CEO-type is handing out.

'So when did you meet BJ?' Dabbu asks Satish. 'Did he recognize you?'

Satish takes a sip of coffee and nods. 'Oh yes, he placed me at once—though he found it hard to grasp that I actually headed a construction company. He kept telling me, quite kindly, to send my father round to meet him.'

'And you just walked into the house?' Anjini sounds worried. 'Just like that?'

'Oh no,' Satish replies. 'I mailed him first—and he responded. He used to check his mail every day. And then we fixed a time and everything, and Lachhu opened the gate and escorted me in. His fort was quite well guarded, if that's what you're worried about.'

'BJ was clearly quite lucid when he wanted to be,' Debjani says thoughtfully.

Eshwari laughs. 'Oh, that he was. He used to call me Shweta Rani sometimes, which worried me at first, but then I realized he only did that when he was mad at me. Quite deliberately.'

Anjini smiles. 'And he'd call me Khadija Bai. *Only* when I called and said I couldn't visit.'

Everyone sips their coffee in silence.

'When did you become so religious?' Debjani asks, putting down her paper cup. 'During your, um, troubled phase? All this vaastu and Akshaya Tritiya?'

What *is* this? Eshwari thinks, harassed. *Koffee with Karan?* Why do they want to know every detail of his stupid little life?

'Oh, that!' Satish laughs and tilts his chair back. 'That's because of my crew. Construction is a superstitious business. The workers are mostly uneducated and they take their pujas very seriously.'

'Really?' Eshwari tries to sound polite but ends up sounding ungracious, even to her own ears.

Satish purses his lips, his expression serious.

'I started a project on an inauspicious date once, and ten days into the job, a worker died. He fell from a scaffolding because the safety harness broke—and the union went on strike. We lost a *lot* of money. So now I respect the Hindu calendar. I may not believe in it, but I do adhere to it quite strictly.'

There is silence.

'Well, luckily there should be no problem at our end,' Debjani says brightly. 'Our family is quite united in its decision to sell! And all the paperwork is in order. You should meet your deadline quite easily.'

A peculiar look crosses Satish's face. He looks up at the hovering CEO-type (who wrings his hands, but says nothing), then back to the little line-up of calmly coffee-drinking Thakur sisters. Seeming to come to a decision of some sort, he leans forward abruptly and says, his tone changing from his smooth, formal drawl to something more familiar: 'Ladies, what's up with Bonu Singh?'

'Huh?' Anjini almost drops her coffee.

'Yeah, where the hell *is* Bonu?' Eshwari looks around with a start. 'Why isn't she here yet?'

Satish nods grimly. 'Exactly. I've been trying to be subtle, waiting for you to broach it to me. But you're all clearly unaware of her state of mind.'

'W…what state of mind?' Debjani has started to get a Very Bad Feeling.

'She called me yesterday,' Satish tells them. 'She was very polite but told me, quite unequivocally, that she has no intention of selling her portion of the house, and that her decision is final.'

'Last price, sister, best-I-can-do.'

'Balls,' Bonu snaps, hot and bothered. 'Arrey, what last-price last-price? Regular client hoon mein tumhaare! I need five hundred metres of this rani-colour kundan border—so mangwao two Pepsis and two plates of aloo ki tikki, turn the fan towards us, sit down and bargain properly.'

'*Last* price, sister! You want five metres or five hundred metres, rate will stay the same!'

'Shame on you, calling me sister and then cheating me. Do you think I am some foreigner? Come here to take photos? Or some big madam doing wedding shopping?'

The undernourished shopkeeper passes a hand across his harassed brow. 'Sister, why you joking? You are bigger than the biggest madam!'

'Bigger than the biggest? Oho, now you're calling me fat? I look fat to you?'

'Last price, sister!'

There is a genuine edge of desperation to his voice. Bonu relents.

'Okay fine. Just check it before you give it to me—open it all out, yahan, where I can see it.'

Looking much perkier now, the shopkeeper obliges, unspooling the gorgeous pink and gold border and measuring it out by the metre. As the glittering pile grows at their feet, Parveen turns huge eyes to Bonu.

'Didi,' she whispers reproachfully. 'What are you *doing*?'

'Oh, never mind,' Bonu mutters crossly, sucking on the 'pipe' of her Pepsi. 'I know he's ripping me off, but I just don't have the bandwidth to haggle.'

It is only early March but the wholesale lace, ribbon and borders market of Kinari Bazaar is already suffocatingly warm this afternoon. Shop No. 137 feels particularly still and hot, a lone fan rotating in a demoralized sort of way and the walls, against which every kind of precious stone and gota-patti edgings is piled all higgedly-piggedly, seem to be closing in on Bonu. There is a weird smell lurking about, like burning rubber, which always reminds her of the road accident in which her family perished, and makes her mildly panicky. She wonders what would happen if a fire were to break out in this narrow, mile-long, over-crowded street, stuffed to bursting with highly flammable nylon, silk, satin and lace borders. I'd probably slip on a pile of fresh cow dung as I make a run for it, and get trampled to death by screaming hordes before I get asphyxiated, she thinks. God, how long is he taking? If he would just give me the damn border, I'd go pick up the sequins and the pompoms, rattle home on the metro, hand the stuff to the tailors, and go to sleep for like four years.

She puts down her empty Pepsi bottle and checks her phone. The aunts' meeting with Satish Sridhar would've finished about three hours ago. Presumably, he has told them she doesn't intend to sell. Things have been ominously quiet so far and Bonu is starting to feel a bit miffed. Why aren't her horrible aunts contacting her? When will they start grovelling? Don't they want to sell the house? *Isn't he done with the damn border yet?*

She demands as much and the shopkeeper reassures her that he is just a few metres short and he's sent off a boy to get it from the godown.

'Typical,' mutters Bonu. Her eyes are starting to close. She sits back in her stool and fans herself with a Manish Malhotra catalogue. The outfit they are replicating is one of his, a particularly tricky one with lots of poofy layers and satin and tissue and embroidery borders—but nothing Vicky's Secret can't pull off with ease.

The little shop shakes on its flimsy wooden foundation just then, and Bonu's eyes fly open, hoping the boy has returned from the godown, bearing the last of the border. But he hasn't.

Dressed in his trademark scruffy jeans and a dark v-necked sweatshirt, Samar Vir Singh is standing in the rickety aluminium doorway, the top of his head grazing the torpidly rotating fan above. Numbly, she notices that his forearms look extremely sinewy and that the expression on his face is extremely nasty.

'Hello, Parveen,' he says politely, not looking at Bonu. 'How nice to see you again. Why don't you and this gentleman step out for lunch and leave me to talk to my...*cousin* alone, okay? Order whatever you like, I'll pay—I'm told the paranthas at Wah Ji Wah are awesome.'

And such the force of his personality that Parveen and the shopkeeper slink off immediately, but not before grasping the folded thousand-rupee note he holds out between his fingers. Bonu, betrayed, can only gasp in outrage.

'What are you doing here?' she asks him.

'Chasing turn-coating rats,' he replies coolly. 'You?'

'I'm...I'm shopping for material,' she says.

'Yes, of course. So you can rip off some poor sod designer's designs and sell them on the cheap.'

'How...how d'you know that?'

She is wearing a salwar kameez in a muted floral print today, with a mint-green dupatta. The kohl in her eyes is slightly messy and her skin glows with a sheen of sweat in the stuffy room. She looks tired but still manages to radiate more energy than most people he knows.

'Well, it wasn't very hard to piece together. I went to your workshop to look for you, and that bow-legged little minion who runs your shop—'

'Fabrication unit.'

'Whatever. He was very chatty. He said you'd be here, either at shop number 137 or 59, sourcing kinaris to embellish a Manish Malhotra anarkali. So I hopped onto the metro and came.'

'You took the metro?' She sounds impressed. 'Surely you're too posh for that.'

'Stop changing the subject!'

Bonu twists her heavy hair into a messy top knot, and drives a red and black Natraj pencil through it.

'What's the subject?' she says, squaring her shoulders.

He leans against the counter and folds his arms across his chest.

'The house. Its sale. Your little chat with Satish Sridhar.'

She looks surprised.

'You were there too?'

'No. But Ma called and said you'd pulled a no-show, and asked me to track you down. Would you care to tell me why you think two hundred crores is not a good enough price for our property?'

'We can get better,' she mutters.

'Bullshit. It's an excellent price—what d'you think BJ was doing all those months before he died? He checked it all out thoroughly. So have we.'

'BJ was hardly fit enough to do thorough research in his last days,' she says calmly. 'Besides, I don't owe you any explanations—I'm just not in the mood to sell, period.'

Samar throws up his hands.

'But the mausis need the money! And so do you!'

'Speak for yourself.' Bonu's voice is very cool. '*I* wasn't waiting for my grandfather to die so I could immediately sell his home for millions. Maybe *you* were.'

Samar's hands clench. 'I promised BJ I'd oversee the sale. I did wonder then, why he picked me and not you—it's because you're an incorrigible troublemaker!'

'That's not true!'

'You were a twisted kid and now you're a twisted adult.'

Bonu finds that her throat is painfully constricted. She forces herself to speak calmly.

'Nobody asked me. It was just high-handedly assumed that I would fall in line with my great mausis. Well, I won't. It's my house too, and I don't. Want. To. Sell!'

Samar leans in very close.

'Just suppose,' he says, his voice low, 'that I go to my designer friends—and I've got many—and tell them exactly what you're up to in your little fabrication unit upstairs? They could order a raid and close you down.'

Bonu swallows. 'You wouldn't.'

'Maybe not,' he agrees. 'A better idea would be to drop into Minto Bridge police station and inform the cops that you're running a commercial enterprise in a residential area. They'll confiscate your shiny machines, and all your sweet, husband-stabbing employees will be without a job.'

Bonu gasps. Her hair slips out of its militant top-knot. 'You wouldn't!'

'Try me.'

'But that's just *mean*.' Her voice is despairing.

Samar rocks back on his heels and hardens his heart.

'Grow up, Bonu Singh. Your playing party-pooper on the sale is mean, too.'

'But that's not—I mean, you can't just—*dammit*!'

'Yeah,' he nods. 'Exactly.'

Silence. She sits before him, her expression mutinous.

'You'll thank me later,' Samar says in a gentler voice. 'It's a very good price—you'll get a gorgeous apartment in the heart of town, and crores in cash, right at the start of your adult life. Hell, it's a dream come true! What's going on in that twisted head of yours, anyway—why don't you want to sell?'

Her head comes up. 'I don't want to lose my home, or shift my workplace. I don't want to throw the Trings out. I love living there. You people all live so far away that you have no feeling for the house. I do.'

'But it was BJ's last wish. Surely you loved him more than you love his house?'

For a moment her eyes grow soft. But then she raises her chin and says, 'You're just playing with words. I'd rather sit tight for now. The prices are still climbing in the area. And I'm much younger than my aunts. I can afford to wait.'

'But some of them really need the money!' He throws up his hands in exasperation.

Her face is inscrutable. 'I'm not going to sell, Samar,' she says. 'My mind is quite made up.'

'D'you want more money?' he asks, not even sure of what he's saying anymore. 'Is that it? Is this some kind of, I don't know, mild extortion racket?'

'It's anything but mild,' she assures him, her eyes flashing.

Their eyes lock. The tension grows.

'Okay,' he nods finally, dismissively, and turns on his heel and stalks out, leaving the cheap aluminium door rattling on its hinges behind him.

Samar comes back to his hotel to find that his stepmother and her sisters have taken over his suite—one of them is drying her hair in the loo, the second has ordered room service, a third is out on the little verandah meditating in the lotus position, and the fourth is on her knees on the floor, scrabbling about inside the mini-bar.

'Having fun, ladies?' he asks politely and Anjini and Debjani spin around to look at him.

'Hai, what happened? Did you talk to her?'

'I can't believe my son can afford to stay in The Imperial!'

'Only because I shot a bunch of scenes here for my second film,' he replies. 'So they give me a discounted rate—but not on alcohol.'

'Twoo bad,' Eshwari mumbles, pulling out two miniature bottles of Jim Beam from the minibar and knocking them back neat. 'You can 'fford to buy your poor bachelor aunt a coupla dwink.'

'She met Satish,' Debjani explains in answer to Samar's raised brows. 'He was looking hot.'

'But not as hot as my hot Mausi E, surely,' Samar says gallantly as he sinks to his knees beside Eshwari. 'This gorgeous, cruel New Yorker who slapped me roundly when I offered her my hand and heart at the tender age of eighteen!'

Eshwari puts down the bottles and glares at him. 'Don' you dare hu…hu…*humour* me!' Her body sways forward.

'I didn't know you liked Jim Beam,' he says, steadying her.

'I don't,' Eshwari chuckles. 'Onny thing left.'

'O-kay…' Samar hands her a bottle of water from the minibar and makes sure she knocks it back.

'Really, Eshu, this is very self-centred of you,' scolds Anjini. 'Going on and on about Satish Sridhar when we are in the midst of a genuine crisis!'

'Chandoosh out on the balcony,' Eshwari points to the meditating Chandralekha. 'Nobodish calling her shelf-shentered!'

Chandu is rocking back and forth in the balcony, lips moving inaudibly.

'Some sort of prayer-chant,' Anjini says. 'I'm sick of it.'

Debjani sighs.

'Samar, what did Bonu say?'

'She refused to sell,' he replies grimly after giving Eshwari a hug and getting to his feet. He looks around the messy suite, frowning. 'Has anybody seen my iPad? It's in a leather case.'

'Arrey, never mind your iPad!' Anjini snaps. 'Tell us properly, what did she say?'

Samar looks distinctly harassed. 'Ma, I told you, she says she doesn't want to sell—and that all of you are old but she's young and time is on her side and she'd rather wait because prices are still rising on Hailey Road.'

Debjani looks sceptical. 'There's got to be more to it than that.'

'Yeah, maybe...' Samar's gaze wanders. 'It's a dark brown case. It's got all my notes in it—I had it with me when I was chatting with Chachiji in the afternoon...'

'You and your chats with Chachiji!' Anjini sniffs disdainfully. 'You're fonder of her than of us! Here's your stupid iPad. I was sitting on it.'

'Thank you!' Samar lunges for it. 'I just want to read back the notes I...'

He starts to sink back on the bed and bumps against Eshwari, passed out cold, mouth slightly open, shiny hair spread out all over his pillow.

'Whoops,' he says. 'Er, what do I do now?'

'Let her sleep it off, I suppose,' Anjini says. 'Come and spend the night at the house—why have you checked into a hotel, anyway?'

'Because I wanted to *work*.' He pushes his hair off his forehead in exasperation, glances out of the French window and sees Chandu mausi doing a headstand. 'Christ, what a looney bin.'

Debjani chuckles. 'Anjini's right. Go stay at the house.'

And so Samar finds himself back inside the musty, girly bedroom at Hailey Road. It's much hotter now, though, and the ancient air-conditioner makes weird wheezy sounds that refuse to let him sleep. He tosses and turns and discovers, much to his disgust, that his mind, instead of focusing on the problem with his film, has circled back towards the encounter he'd had with his aggravating step-cousin in the afternoon.

He had been irrationally happy to see her, he admits that now. When his mother had called him and told him to go find her, he'd leapt at the excuse. He hadn't been able to put that surreal night they spent together out of his head, try as he might. So he had jumped onto the metro and tracked her down in that teeming hot bazaar. When he saw her through the shop window, sipping her Pepsi, her hair trailing everywhere, a pile of pink tinsel glowing at her feet, he felt like a lucky mortal who had been granted a vision of a goddess. Who, instead of granting him a boon, had calmly kicked him in the guts.

He wonders briefly why he feels such a strong protective instinct towards somebody who is clearly in no need of protection.

I'll talk to her again, he resolves as he gets up to switch off the wheezing AC. Without getting mad, and without letting her get mad. I'll make her understand that what she's saying is stupid and self-destructive—and that BJ only wanted what was best for all of us.

He strips off to just his pyjamas, lugs a bucket of water from the bathroom, chucks it over the stone floor, lies down upon it, and reaches for his iPad. Frowning down at it, he is finally able to grapple with his edit.

Bonu is holed up in her lair in the upstairs, avoiding Samar and the mausis, when Gulab Thakur shows up. He looms up behind her while she is sipping her morning cup of chai, a *Being Hanuman* t-shirt stretched across his husky muscular chest and biceps, his reed thin hips and thighs encased in tight red cycling shorts.

'Hullo, Bonu bete. I'm so sorry about Tauji. I tried to get back earlier but there were snowstorms everywhere and full road blocks.'

Bonu takes one look at the concern in his soft gulab-jamun eyes and flings her arms around his neck and hugs him wordlessly. Gulgul mama, top-heavy already, rocks backwards, his bouffant grey thatch of hair wobbling a little, then steadies himself and awkwardly pats his niece's back.

'Don't cry, don't cry. He was eighty-five plus and he lived a good life. I wish I had been here for you, but.'

She gulps and pulls away, smiling now though still precariously close to tears. Gulab Thakur looks around the overcrowded room.

'You bought more sewing machines?'

She shakes her head. 'No, they're the same old machines— just stuffed into a smaller place.'

'Oho.' He purses his lips. 'So Anjini didi found out, eh? Who told her?'

'Samar,' Bonu replies bitterly. 'It's a long story—d'you want some tea?'

'No no, I just-now had my protein shake. And she made you vacate?'

Bonu nods. 'Yes.'

'Oh.'

Gulgul squeezes her shoulders. Sympathetically, then critically. His hands move to the flesh of her upper arms and massage there for a while. Then he punches her, not too hard, in the stomach, and pulls a long face.

'You've become soft, Bonu Singh,' he announces, disappointed. 'Muscle tone is all gone. Not been working out?'

Bonu snatches her arm away.

'Gulgul mama, so much has been happening! BJ, then the funeral, all the aunts, and now look at this place—there's no space to exercise!'

'Excuses,' he snorts. 'That's the trouble with your generation! You people have no discipline! We discussed this on the trip also.'

'What?' she asks, not really listening. She is too busy feeling her upper arms—they do feel rather pulpy.

'That we live in morally corrupt times. Kalyug. Our young people have no discipline, no healthy outdoor habits! They are fully in the grip of pornography! Whole day sitting with one hand on the computer's mouse and one hand on their own mouse, looking at dirty fillums on the internet. Chheee.'

'Excuse me, I have not been watching *porn!*' Bonu says indignantly. 'My grandfather died!'

'No no, but boys from your generation watch all the time…'

'*Girls* also watch porn,' Bonu asserts, with slightly twisted feminism.

'Ya, anyway, my friends and I have come up with a good way to bring these poor sex-addicts back on the right path!'

'How?' asks Bonu, intrigued, despite herself.

Gulgul mama chuckles fatly. 'You take any good, clean, five-minute-long video clip of some famous actress or socialite lady, dressed up nicely, going to a function or red carpet event. Then you upload it on YouTube.'

'How does that help?'

'Suno toh! If it is a clip of Katrina Kapoor you must caption it *Katrina Kapoor wardrobe malfunction—whole boob showing*. If it is Safina Mirza, you must caption it *Tennis for your penis, full panty showing*. You upload the clips in the night, and by morning each clip will have more than five lakh hits each! And in the comments, all the tharki perverts will be so angry—panting and cursing and shouting ki saale, where's the panty, where's the panty?'

'Er, that sounds like a lot of fun, Gulgul mama,' Bonu says. 'But how does it reform them?'

'Because you end the clip with a message saying: SHAME! You are the future of the nation! Stop this dirty habit, go outside, exercise, and pray to Hanumanji!'

Bonu stares at him. 'I hope you don't put your name or email id on these clips,' she warns. 'The tharkis might come looking for you.'

But Gulab Thakur is no longer listening. Nose pressed to her grilled windows, he is peering down at the garden. 'Samar looks quite fit. And not at all proud—I thought he would not bother to remember his humble uncle, but he met me very nicely.'

'You're not a humble uncle,' Bonu says staunchly. 'You're great. I don't know what I'd do without you, Gulgul mama!'

Gulgul turns pink. 'Arrey, Bonu, you and I, our parents are from the simple side of the family—but Samar, he is *Anji didi's* son, and his father is a big banker, and he himself is doing so good!'

'What's so great about Anji didi?' Bonu demands. 'My mother was every bit as hot as Anji didi. And only boring people work in banks—everybody knows that. Because you need balls to do business.'

'Ya ya, of course Binni didi was also beautiful,' Gulgul says hastily. 'You also na, just climb on top of me every time I open my mouth! What is the problem—don't you like Samar?'

In reply, his niece bangs her cup down on the table, picks

up the newspaper and starts leafing through it agitatedly. Gulab Thakur blinks, starts to say something, then thinks better of it. Resting his arms comfortably on the table, he goes back to gazing placidly out of the window at Samar, who is deep in conversation with his grand-aunt downstairs.

Chachiji is talking about old times—the day of her engagement, how much in awe she had been of all the Thakurs, her beautiful sister-in-law, her distinguished vakil brother-in-law Laxmi Narayan, her larger-than-life father-in-law Pushkar Narayan, and his quiet, docile wife.

'Was she always so quiet?' Samar is asking. 'Didn't she ever let her hair down, hang out with you ladies, chill, party?'

Chachiji shoots Samar a dissatisfied glance. Her jowls have started to sag. This Samar is a big man, she has seen his name written in large letters at the beginning of two of her favourite movies, so she is delighted to be talking to him in the garden, easily visible from the windows of all the flats in Hailey Court. But instead of telling her about movie stars and their scandalous lives, he seems to be obsessed with making *her* talk, that too about her boring, dead family.

'Haan, we joked-shoked sometimes,' she says vaguely. 'Like all saas-bahus do. But vegetarian jokes only.' She leans forward eagerly. 'Aishwarya and Jayaji must be joking-shoking also, no? D'you know them?'

But the boring fellow just shakes his head.

'Did she have any friends in the neighbourhood? Are any of them still alive?'

'They are all dead,' Chachiji snaps. 'But you, Samar Vir Singh, are still alive! Act like it!'

And she glowers at him with such beady disgust that he has no option but to smile charmingly and put his iPad away.

'You're right, Chachiji,' he says. 'Here, have some tea—and yes, of course I know Aishwarya...'

Thus Samar embarks upon an entirely invented exchange between him and Bollywood's most beautiful bahu, a personage he has never even met.

Upstairs, Bonu pretends to pursue the papers as she digests the fact that Samar is back in the house. He is clearly hot on his mission to 'fulfil BJ's last wish and command'. Damn. She is still recovering from the encounter they had yesterday—she is not confrontational by nature, and going toe-to-toe with him has taken its toll. She had planned to lie low for a few days, supervise the latest consignment, and pad around the house in BJ's old shirts. Maybe go out on a low-demand date with one of the Hailey Court boys. But his return has upset all that. The last thing she needs is Samar hanging around, sizing up her date and making snide remarks.

She skims through the *India Post*, her mind on the aggravating man downstairs. Page 1 is devoted to a massive ad for a new model of family car. On page 2, the Prime Minister has started sporting a new style in churidaar pants. On page 4 auto-rickshaw drivers are on strike. And on page 6, Mustaq Khan, ex-MP and director of the Muskaan School for Challenged Children, is railing at the cruel hearts and small minds of the people of Delhi.

'Everyday there are new cases of violence against people with disabilities. Just pick up the paper and see! And every day, people from the North-East face humiliation and discrimination from locals who themselves came to Delhi from Punjab only sixty-five years ago!'

The educationist was speaking at a dharna he had organized to protest against the impending eviction of disabled chowkidars Biren Tring and Namgay Tring from their quarters at Delhi's high-end Hailey Road.

'These two brothers have been working at my school for over forty years now. They are peace-loving and law-abiding citizens. But now they are being thrown out of their family home just because they are poor, disabled people from the North-East.'

The Trings had this to say:

'Our landlords are intolerant racists who keep telling us to go back to China. They call us drunkards and thieves. They say we trap pigeons and dogs, mince them and stuff them into momos. They say our women are prostitutes. When we showed them this childhood photo, which proves we have lived here for forty years, they said, this is not you, this is some other chinkie. All you chinkies look alike. And then they laughed.'

When asked what he hoped to achieve by starting this agitation, Mustaq Khan said:

'We will sit here and not eat or drink anything until the heirs of Justice Laxmi Narayan Thakur relent. All the disabled peoples and all the peoples from the North-East and friends of peoples from the North-East will come and join us. We will bring the Thakurs to their knees.'

Picture caption (from left to right): Visually challenged Namgay Tring and physically challenged Biren Tring (aged fourteen and thirteen respectively) sitting in front of the barred windows of the 16 Hailey Road annexe with their ex-landlord, Pushkar Narayan Thakur. The calendar of Hanumanji carrying Mount Dron indicates that the year is 1964.

'Why are you laughing, Bonu Singh?' Gulgul mama asks uncertainly. 'You *are* laughing, aren't you? Not crying? What is so funny?'

7

'My father was a great, great man,' says Mustaq Khan wistfully in his high nasal voice. 'A patriot. An educationist. He set up this school in the sixties—in the upstairs of your house, as you must know. Twenty years later he vacated it, the *moment* your grandfather requested he do so, and moved here. So it is not that we are difficult people, Mr Samar.'

Samar gives a curt nod. He is sitting in the office of the Director of the Muskaan School for Challenged Children. A gleaming black marble plaque outside proclaims the school's mission: 'To provide physical, emotional and spiritual succour to challenged orphans of every caste, creed and region. Inshallah.' It also mentions that the foundation stone of this campus had been laid by the Hon'ble Mr Mustaq Khan, ex-sportsman, ex-MP and s/o freedom fighter Mustafa Khan—in other words, the worthy now rocking gently in a pista green metal chair before Samar, dressed in a crisp white kurta pyjama, to be sure, but still managing to convey the impression that life has somehow, magically, been breathed into a massive, oily, extremely well-browned shami kebab.

Samar sips his glass full of sweet red Rooh Afza and wishes the thuggish Mustaq would come to the point.

'But we couldn't accommodate our two chowkidars and their large families in the new campus, so they continued to live in your annexe. Now we hear the house is to be sold! Naturally, they are upset—they have to be accommodated somewhere, no, Mr Samar?'

Samar nods moodily. He'd gone looking for Biren Tring and Namgay Tring the moment he read their poignant story in the *India Post*, and they had both smiled gummily at him and acted like their 'challenges' were not being lame and one-eyed respectively, but being totally deaf-mute. The only sentence he'd gotten out of them was: 'You talk Mustaq bhai.' Clearly they were just a pair of warm bodies the slimy Mustaq had placed in the annexe to keep his long-term tenancy rights alive. A sleeper unit of sorts, which had been activated as news of an impending sale leaked out.

'Accommodate them here. This place is huge,' Samar says testily.

'Oh no no no no no.' Mustaq Khan's tiny, kohl-lined eyes glint beadily. 'We are choke-full here, choke-full! Of course, if you compensate them so that they can purchase a small place somewhere in this area only, they would be happy... What do you say, eh?'

'I say no,' Samar says pleasantly. 'That is extortion, pure and simple.'

Mustaq Khan spreads out his hands. 'Words are just words. It is much less than the money you will end up losing if this case goes to court. Possession is nine-tenths of the law—and our school has been a tenant of your grandfather's, and *his* father's, for over forty years. Rest is up to you.'

Samar leans in, curious to know how big the shami kebab will open its maw. 'So, how much money were you thinking, Mustaq bhai?'

Mustaq's nasal whine voice drops to an almost inaudible murmur.

'Well, this is Lutyens' Delhi, you know, even the smallest room here will cost a lot. So let us say five crores. Per tenant?'

'I still don't believe it,' Samar tells Satish Sridhar on the phone a little later. 'D'you have to deal with this kind of thing often?'

'All the time,' Satish tells him. 'The trick is to beat him down to the bare minimum and keep the thing out of court.'

Samar digests this. 'Okay, but he knows he has me in a bind. How do I bargain with him?'

'Oh, there are all kinds of ways,' Satish replies breezily. 'You could send in thugs and throw them out, but that won't work in this case because Mustaq will match you thug for thug, besides making this out to be a discrimination case. The local press is in his pocket, and it's no accident that he's picked tenants who are blind and lame. You're lucky he hasn't parked children with serious challenges in your annexe.'

Samar can't help thinking that Eshwari's old admirer seems extremely up-to-date on all things dodgy.

'What else?' he asks.

Satish clears his throat.

'Well, there's your stepmother,' he says delicately.

'What?'

'Uh, yeah. She could weave quite a spell around young Mustaq, back in the day. He used to drive by your main gate on his little orange moped every evening, at least six or seven times, and if she looked at him and smiled, he would do cartwheels.'

'On the *moped*?' Samar says in disbelief. 'That shami kebab?'

'Yes. The seventies were pretty wild and he was thinner then. Just like his voice. I was just a child those days, but it made quite a deep impression on me, so I remembered. Maybe if she came along for one of these meetings…?'

'Out of the question,' Samar growls. 'Isn't there something else we can do?'

'You could go to the MCD, ask them to conduct an inspection and have the annexe declared unsafe. They'd issue an eviction notice and the chowkidars would *have* to move out.'

'That sounds like a good plan,' Samar says, relieved. 'Thanks, Satish.'

'No worries,' Satish replies. 'It's a long shot but it may pay off. Let me know how it goes. And Samar…any news on Bonu Singh?'

'What kind of news are you after, exactly?' he asks, hackles rising slightly.

'Well, I was hoping you people had spoken to her, explained that it would make sense to sell together. I did tell her that but she's a bull-headed kid. I don't think she got it.'

'I'll talk to her today,' Samar says shortly and hangs up.

When Samar reaches the old green gate of number 16, he glimpses Bonu's crew, hard at work on the first floor, sewing machines whirring busily, but the ballsy businesswoman herself is nowhere in sight. Tightening his lips, he crosses the lawn, strides upstairs to the unit, turns a sharp left into the corridor that leads to her bedroom, and pushes the door open.

She isn't here, he thinks at first, but when he turns to leave he catches sight of her on the floor, clad in skimpy black gym gear, face down in a position he recognizes as the 'plank'. Her toes and forearms are on the ground while everything else hovers a foot above, gleaming with sweat and straining with the effort. She has obviously been holding the position for a while.

Samar's irate gaze travels over her taut golden calves, over the abundance of her lycra-encased butt, to settle with a sigh on her breasts, pushed together by her propped-up arms and somewhat inadequately contained in a black racerback vest. He allows himself a lingering look (made possible because her eyes are closed and she is muttering her favourite incantation of *shit shit shit* under her breath) before he speaks, his voice low and vibrating with resentment.

'Bonita? A word with you, please.'

Bonu's eyes fly open. She sees Samar leaning comfortably against the door jamb like he's been watching her for a long long time. Her muscles give a shocked little jump and she flops to the floor.

'Are you okay?' he asks, concerned. From where he is standing, it looks like her nose has hit the pink yoga mat.

'I could've held it for one more whole minute if you hadn't interrupted me,' she huffs, sitting up and dealing with the humiliating fact that she is stupidly happy to see him.

He raises a sceptical eyebrow. 'You looked about done-in to me.'

She flushes, tosses her head, gets to her feet and bolts the door in his face.

Samar stands in the little alcove outside her room, very conscious of the fact that the tailors in the unit behind him are eying him curiously.

'Hey, um, Bonu Singh?'

'Showering!' she shouts from inside, which makes him shake his head and grit his teeth. He could've done without that mental image.

When she lets him in five minutes later, she has reverted to her usual loose pyjamas and tee. She has also got back her composure, and is grinning from ear to ear.

'You look pretty fed up,' she says smirkily. 'Dealing with the Tring Trings?'

He reminds himself of the resolution he made two nights ago to be nice to her.

'Yes,' he replies. 'I thought carrying out BJ's last wishes would be simple, but I guess not. First *you* happened, and now the tenants. BJ must be getting uneasy up above.'

She sniffs. '*I* think he must be making some long, extremely overdue explanations to my mother.'

However, a slightly haunted look does steal into her big black eyes.

'Really?' says Samar interestedly. 'Is that how you see this? So your decision not to sell has to do with your mum?'

'My reasons are my business,' she flashes, tossing her head. 'Besides, why shouldn't the Trings protest? I mean, is it fair to just ask them to vacate and give them nothing? Did you really think they were going to slink off quietly?'

'Listen, Bonita, we are not talking small amounts here,' Samar says, exasperated. 'Breaking and Entering are just a front for that extremely slimy operator Mustaq Khan. The tenancy is in his school's name and he's just asked me for ten crores to vacate the annexe.'

Bonu's jaw drops. '*What?*'

'Five crores per tenant.'

She sinks down on the bed, looking rather awed. 'Wow.'

Samar, watching various expressions chase each other across her face, gets a nasty feeling. 'Now *you* please don't start getting any ideas!' he says sternly. 'I can only deal with one extortionist at a time.'

She smirks and leans back into her pillows. 'Frankly, the harder the time you have flogging this old house, the happier I'll be.'

'Oh, I'm well aware of that,' he assures her. 'God alone knows why, though.'

Her face grows inscrutable. She grabs a bit of her hair and starts looking for split ends in the slanting sunlight. Samar's exasperation spirals.

'Look, Mausi D's channel is going to shut down. It's the only TV channel one can trust today. Mausi E's really on edge. Doesn't that mean jackshit to you?'

It's like a rocket has been lit below the girl's bottom. She stops playing with her hair and lunges to her feet, eyes blazing, her breath fast and ragged, her every word a bullet.

'My father went bankrupt. He was disgraced. My entire family died in a car crash, driving on bald tyres in the freaking monsoon to Delhi to beg these same women to sell, and they didn't. Doesn't *that* mean jackshit to *you*?'

Whoa.

Slowly, Samar backs away and sits down on a chair by the window.

Bonu sits down too, rather heavily, upon the unmade bed.

There is a long silence.

Outside, the sewing machines continue to whirr soothingly.

Finally he says, his voice gentle, 'I'm sorry.'

She hunches her shoulders defensively. 'Whatever.'

How little we know, he thinks, watching the sunshine catch on her diamond nose stud, of what goes on inside the heads of people, even those we've known since childhood, even those we've held in our arms and rocked to sleep.

Leaning back, he says lightly, 'You know what, brat, I may have directed two-and-a-half Hindi movies, but you're much more Bollywoody than me. So you're driven by some deep, dark notion of rrrevenge, are you?'

'Don't make fun of me.' Her voice is trembling.

Samar shakes his head in denial of this charge. Then he walks over to kneel at the foot of her bed, puts a finger under her chin and tips up her face until their eyes are level.

'Listen.'

Bonu tries to look away—his eyes, as always, are too intense. But she can't avert her face, his fingers are holding her too firmly. The only option she has is to shut her eyes, but that would be childish.

'What?' she asks, feeling perilously close to tears.

I want to kiss her, he realizes. Christ, what is this?

Aloud, he says, 'I'm not making fun of you. You are a brave, independent, and slightly messed-up person—'

'I don't need a character certificate from bloody you!'

'—and I just want you to understand that there are two sides to every narrative. "Those women" aren't necessarily evil. They probably have their own version of the events leading up to your parents' and brother's deaths. Have you ever talked to them about it?'

She closes her eyes and shakes her head.

'Well, I think you should, whenever you feel ready. Will you?'

He is kneeling at her feet, his elbows resting lightly on her knees. She wishes he would back off—she wishes he would close in. Memories of that cold night on the lawn course back to her, sweet and strong. Abruptly, she sits up, pushing him away.

'I'll think about it,' she says.

An uneasy truce has been declared between the upstairs and downstairs factions of 16 Hailey Road. Samar has definitely told the aunts *something*, because they all start being warily nice to Bonu. Debjani keeps hugging her randomly, Chandu shoots her strained, encouraging smiles from across the garden, and even Eshwari has made several gruff little speeches about what a solid kid the 'Bonster' used to be.

Bonu herself is feeling much sunnier since her outburst.

'It's like I've got this massive weight off my chest,' she confides in Samar as they clean out the musty wardrobe in his hissa together. 'Like I was carrying something toxic inside and now it's gone, you know?'

'Pamela Anderson said something similar when she got her silicone implants removed and went back to *au naturel*,' he tells her, grinning. 'I imagine it must feel nice.'

For a moment Bonu looks blank. Then she bursts out laughing.

He sits back on his heels, enjoying looking at her. 'How did you find out all this stuff, anyway? Surely your mother wouldn't have told a little kid about bankruptcy?'

'Oh, Mummy told us everything,' Bonu replies comfortably. 'Full disclosure. She said we were a team, the Rajawats against the world. Of course, a lot of it didn't really make sense to me when I was a kid, her venting was just a comforting noise in the background, but as I grew older, I started to tune in and pick up stuff.'

'Like what?'

'Everything. Like how my dad's businesses always flopped. How Chandu mausi was so weird and secretive even before she ran off with the Estonian. How Ashok chacha was always getting it on with his cooks. How everybody was turning BJ against

Mummy. And how Anjini mausi was so jealous of Mummy because Mummy had us twins and all poor Anji mausi had was—'

She comes to an abrupt halt.

'Me,' Samar completes evenly. 'I see.'

'Sorry,' Bonu mutters, her cheeks very red, and goes back to sorting out the dusty shelves.

It is in this atmosphere of fragile peace that a many-sheafed letter, drafted somewhat inexpertly by part-time advocate Gulab Thakur at the behest of his father Ashok Narayan Thakur, explodes inside 16 Hailey Road with all the clatter and clang of a bomb in a stainless steel bartan shop.

Or rather, several bombs. Because many copies of the letter arrive all at once, each addressed to a different one of Laxmi Narayan Thakur's heirs.

FOR YOUR KIND INFORMATION

To the Honourable District Court,
Shah Alami Road,
New Delhi
Respected Sirs,

This is to put before you the sad case of myself, Ashok Narayan Thakur, who, being the ONLY biological son of late Pushkar Narayan Thakur am still having to spend my old age homeless and penniless, having being done out of my rightful inheritance in the matter of my late father's ancestral property, 16 Hailey Road, New Delhi, due to the machinations of my illegitimate half-brother Laxmi Narayan Thakur (henceforth referred to as the Pretender) and his heirs.

It is with great shame and utmost reluctance that I reveal to you that this Pretender was the base born son of my mother and her paramour, and was smuggled into my family fold in the form of a two-month-old foetus at the time of my mother's marriage to my father, late Pushkar Narayan Thakur. My mother succeeded in this deceptive act because the Pretender was a two-pound weakling when he was born and could therefore be passed off as premature. My father, blinded by his love for his beautiful wife, accepted this fabrication as fact.

Six years later, I was born and cemented the bond between my mother and father. I was my father's favourite and my half-brother the Pretender resented this, going out of his way to poison my mother against me and thus depriving me of her love.

Gradually as the Pretender grew, doubt started stealing over my father, for he looked nothing like the macho Thakurs of our noble line and proved to be a weakling in all things manly, besides being addicted to thick books and all. Everybody started saying that Pushkar Narayan Thakur had been fooled, that a buy-mum-get-son trick had been played on him. He was very much humiliated. And all his doubts crystaled into belief when, after his marriage, the Pretender proceeded to produce daughter after daughter without even one diamond of a son to brighten the long dreary strand of drab girl pearls. This was unheard of in the Thakur family where, generation after generation, only sons have been born.

And so my father decided to disinherit the Pretender. He did so and made a new will, leaving all his property to Me, his rightful son and heir. But my mother, being unhealthily fond of the only momento she had of her Paramour, moved like a Shakespearean Villainess to suppress this will.

Thanks to Divine Justice, and the presence of my father late Pushkar Narayan Thakur in God's Celestial Durbar, I was able to place before the courts this long suppressed document for the first time in the year 1989.

Sadly for me, my half-brother turned out to be not just my mother's favourite, but Fortune's favourite as well. The case went backwards and forwards in the court for years, till finally I ran out of funds and let it lasp.

But now the Pretender's heirs are planning to sell the property and so I have had to come forward for Justice once again.

On the basis of this last will and testament of Late Pushkar Narayan Thakur, I hereby seek immediate injunction on the sale of 16 Hailey Road, which is in the process of being finalized with one SteelBird Builders of Connaught Place, New Delhi. I pray, urge and beseech your Lordships to throw out the Pretender's heirs, who have no Lowcut Standi in this affair. I put before your Lordships the plea that if these five females, heirs of the foetus who came to cheat us, inherit my father's property it would be a Hideous Miscarriage of Justice and Lady Justice herself would weep in sorrow.

Thanking you
Ashok Narayan Thakur
Drafted in the office of Gulab Thakur
(ADVOCATE)

'This must be the "case" BJ kept referring to that day,' Eshwari says dazedly, putting down the vodka bottle. 'Shit.'

Dabbu reaches for it.

'But I thought Ashok chacha was sick!'

'Well, he's clearly made a swift recovery,' Anjini says soberly.

Chandu spreads out her hands. 'Why don't we *know* about this?'

'Ma and BJ must've kept it quiet,' Anjini shrugs. 'Because it said such crude things about his mother, I suppose. No wonder they stopped talking to Ashok chacha.'

'But Chachiji came over all the time!' Eshwari says. 'She still waddles over, like, thrice a week!'

Bonu looks up. 'But BJ never spoke to her. Or even *recognized* her. He'd keep telling me to give the beggar woman hundred rupees and throw her out. I used to feel so bad for her!'

A stumped silence rules the room for a while.

'This is a sick, sick family,' Dabbu says finally, in slow, stunned tones. 'A *seriously* sick family.'

Bonu thinks back to how Chachiji ruthlessly combed lice out of her hair when she was little, laughing gleefully each time she squashed a particularly fat one. She remembers the many Diwalis she spent at the Hailey Court apartment, gorging on kheel batasha while Ashok chacha let her win at cards. She sees herself and Gulgul mama working out at his gym together—the way his hair would bounce every time he struggled to do a sit-up while she held his knees. Then she imagines Chachaji, Chachiji and Gulgul huddled together cosily, laughing and chatting and plotting how to snatch away her birthright.

'It's all balls,' she says gloomily.

'Do you think Satish knows that this case is in court?' Chandu asks. 'We might lose his offer if he finds out.'

Obsessed with money, as usual, thinks Anjini, shooting her ascetic sister an irritated glance. She does have a point, though.

'I don't think Satish knows,' she says, 'otherwise he would have mentioned it that day in his office. I think BJ was so traumatized about it that he sort of blanked it out. Or maybe,' she looks hopeful, 'the case is *so* laughable that it just faded from BJ's mind. We'll have to tell Satish about it, of course, and get his opinion.'

'I never thought we would fight with each other over something as sordid as property,' says Debjani. 'Matlab, I know our family's been up to shady shit like this for centuries. Thakurs whored and gambled and fought and died, that was their life. Those days they warred over entire kingdoms, now, they squabble over per square foot built-up area on Hailey Road. But I thought *we* were different. I like Gulgul. We used to wax his chest, Eshu, remember?'

'Ugh,' Eshu shudders and gropes about for the vodka bottle. 'And how two-faced is Chachiji—always telling us not to miss our mother because she's like our second mother only?'

'We're like any other squabbling family on the road,' Debjani continues. 'Like that man who shot a hole in his brother's head the size of a sambar-vada. Or the lady who fed her daughter pills and had her declared insane. How humiliating.'

'It is just pride to think one is better than one's peers,' Chandu murmurs. 'Far, far better to have no such illusions.'

Bonu's head comes up at once.

'I'm better than Ashok chacha,' she says hotly. 'I have more integrity. I *know* I am.'

'I wouldn't be so sure,' Chandu gives a mystic smile. 'Now that money has entered the picture. You see, money is mael. Dirt. It soils the hands and it soils the mind.'

'Ya okay,' Anjini replies crankily. 'You've been saying that for years, Chandu, but that hasn't stopped you from coming running to grab your slice of Hailey Road cake, has it?'

Chandu throws up her shiny bald head. 'My hissa will go to the needy,' she informs her. She closes her eyes and starts to murmur, her lips moving silently.

'And how he's made old Pushkar Narayan sound like a cuckolded saint!' Eshwari marvels. 'When we all know that he could get turned on if he looked too long at the cleft on a fuzzy peach!'

'We belong to a sick family,' Dabbu repeats.

'Actually, we *don't.*' Bonu brightens up. 'That's the silver lining. If Chachaji's allegation is true, none of us is related to that old sleazebag Pushkar Narayan!'

'Oh, please,' Eshwari dismisses this. 'I've *definitely* got Pushkar Narayan Thakur's village-belle-ravishing genes sloshing about inside my body.'

'How can you be so sure?' Bonu demands.

Eshu leans in, her eyes serious.

'Haven't you ever fantasized about plucking muscular cycle-rickshaw puller boys from the road, taking them home, making them brush their teeth and bathe, and using them as sex toys?'

Their eyeballs lock in a moment of total connect. Then Bonu sits back, relieved.

'Phew,' she says. 'So I *am* a Thakur, after all. Thank God.'

'What's this about cycle-rickshaw boys?' asks Samar, walking into the verandah.

'They're cute,' Bonu replies wistfully. 'So tan, you know, and without an *ounce* of fat…just pure muscle and sinew.'

'Like you,' Eshu twinkles at Samar.

'I look like a cycle-rickshaw puller?'

'You're richer,' Eshu allows. 'And you're English-speaking and all. But basically yes. No, Bonu?'

'Of course *not,*' denies Bonu at once.

'Stop talking rubbish,' Anjini frowns. 'You're both drunk! Take that bottle away from them, Dabbu.'

Dabbu takes the bottle away, to be sure, but only to swig deeply from it.

'I'm not into cycle-rickshaw pullers, per se,' she says. 'But I do tend to ogle carpenters. Leching at the working classes is a Thakur thing, clearly.'

Bonu tucks her hair behind her ears. 'I'm not saying we're a sick family because our great-grandmother might have had an affair. I'm saying we're a sick family because Ashok chacha made that absolutely foul accusation. Even if he believes it—how can he call his own mother a villainess in court? And try and rob his own nieces? After all BJ did for him!'

'Whatever.' Eshwari looks up. 'Girls, we need to get a legal opinion on this—fast.'

'I've just been around to see Satish,' Samar says. 'Gulgul mama's office sent a copy of this letter to the SteelBird office too. For Satish's *kind information*. He is seriously perturbed.'

Eshwari gives a strangled laugh. 'Satish freakin' Sridhar is using words like perturbed? What is *wrong* with the world?'

Samar frowns. 'Focus, Mausi E. Please. The SteelBird lawyers have already gone through the will Ashok chacha has supplied and they seem to think it's not gonna stand up in court. So that's goodish news. Still, he sounded quite rattled. He wants to meet us and assess the situation.'

'I'm not meeting him,' Eshwari says immediately.

'Nobody volunteered your name,' Chandu gives a tinkling laugh. 'Relax. Really, Eshwari, you've got to stop behaving like you're fifteen.'

Anjini looks around the little group, her expression harassed.

'There are too many complications now!' she says. 'One, Bonu doesn't want to sell, two, the tenants are refusing to vacate, and three, Chachaji says we don't own this house only! Where's that vodka bottle?'

'Yes, well, let's get cracking on the tenants and Ashok chachaji first,' Samar says quickly. 'Bones, we'll need your help there, especially with the tenants, as they're your buddies. We'll come to your own objections last.'

'Why last? Let's bell the Bonu cat right now,' says Anjini, who's just knocked back a swig of vodka. 'We've been pussy-footing around this child too long. What is your objection, Bonita? Why don't you want to sell? Huh?'

This is the cue for all four aunts to turn and look at her, their faces frustrated and accusing.

Faced with their combined aggression, Bonu feels her palms grow clammy. They're so much older than me, she thinks. This isn't fair. How can I possibly take them on?

I'll make them squirm like well-salted earthworms.

I won't sell. Even my jutti won't sell.

And if I die na, then even my gosht won't sell!'

'It's quite simple,' she says composedly, her hands reaching up to secure her hair with her red and black Nataraj pencil. 'None of you wanted to sell when my mother wanted to sell. So I don't see why I should be in a hurry now just because you are. Besides, you were all mean to Mummy—and you laughed at Papa.'

There's a stunned silence as the aunts absorb this defiant little speech.

Chandu is the first to speak.

'Oh, for heaven's sake, we're reeling from a lawsuit here and you're whining on about your mummy-papa? Who filled your head with this petty childish rubbish? Not BJ surely! Chachiji?'

Bonu flushes. There is truth in what Chandu mausi is saying—faced with the lawsuit, her objections to the sale do seem a little childish.

'Umm, her mum told her everything,' Samar puts in. 'She didn't believe in secrets.'

'*You're* very well-informed,' Anjini snaps. 'When was the last time you spoke to your girlfriend?'

'Ma.' Samar's voice is a growled warning. '*Behave.*'

'Ya ya, *I'm* the one who's always misbehaving!' Anjini's sweet voice is close to hysterical. '*I* treated Binni badly, *I* flirted with that pimply class eight boy she had a crush on and made him fall in love with me! *I* was jealous because she had twins, *I* was the one who didn't want to sell the house! *I* instigated Dabbu-Eshu because they're far too stupid to have brains of their own! I even sang Raag Malhar and made it rain and caused your parents' car to skid that day, I suppose! I am personally responsible for murdering them. What else did she tell you?'

'Okay, that's enough, Ma.' Samar is furious. 'You're upset about the letter and you're taking it out on Bonu. Stop.'

'You flirted with Binni didi's crush and made him fall in love with you?' Eshwari repeats. 'In class *eight*?'

Anjini hunches a shoulder pettishly. 'I was bored. Summer holidays in the village with Chachiji. There was nothing to do.'

'Dabbu, I love you.' Eshu turns to Debjani. 'Thank you for never flirting with my crushes.'

Bonu swallows, suddenly looking very young and very vulnerable. 'You don't have to explain anything to me, Anji mausi,' she addresses her eldest aunt. 'All I'm saying is that I'm not in a hurry to sell the house. I'll sign the papers when I'm good and ready and not a day before.'

Anjini shrugs, sniffs and looks away.

'Oh God, baby!' Dabbu exclaims, rushing up to the pale-faced girl. 'You don't have to sign anything you don't want to. Please, just relax. And listen, I know Binni resented the fact that I chose Samar to be sarbanna at my wedding instead of your brother, but little Samar...' she glances apologetically at the large, thirty-two-year-old man in front of her, 'was feeling so excluded, you know, and not quite one of the family, so I picked him instead of Monu and I know Monu was *very* upset!'

'I made you do that too, I suppose,' Anjini says bitterly. 'Emotionally blackmailed you into it!'

'Well, you did, actually,' Debjani fires up. 'Samar definitely didn't give a damn about it, either way.' She turns back to Bonu. 'But I *did* make Monu the ring-bearer at the church wedding!'

'Which was wimpy,' Samar can't help saying. 'The poor kid—he wanted a sword and a horse and he got a bow-tie and a satin cushion instead.'

'Yeah, well, it wouldn't have been such a big deal if Monu hadn't died two years later,' Bonu mutters, her nose very red. 'He was *so* looking forward to being sarbanna at Eshu's wedding...'

'Which *still* hasn't happened,' Eshwari says ruefully. 'I'm sorry too, Bonu Singh...'

'It wasn't like he was her *boyfriend*,' Anjini mutters defensively, now off on another tangent. 'He didn't even know she existed. She just used to sigh after him, dur-dur se. I didn't know she cared so much...'

'Anyway, I'm just glad we're having an honest talk about this,' Debjani tells Bonu. 'We love you and we loved Binni didi—I miss her every day!'

'You put up a picture of her on your FB page on every anniversary of her death,' Bonu says gruffly. 'A different one each year. I've seen them.'

And thought how hypocritical you were.

Tears rise to Dabbu's eyes as she hugs her niece. Bonu

doesn't hug her back—but she doesn't push her away either. What incredible boobage she has, thinks Dabbu with somewhat incoherent pride as she pulls back and gives the girl a misty smile.

'And now that we're all *slightly* easier with each other,' Samar says lightly, 'can we please focus on the crisis at hand? Bones, will you please help me break the ice with Biren Tring and Namgay Tring?'

Bonita blows her nose hard and then turns to face all of them.

'Look, you guys, I'll pitch in and help with the tenant situation. I don't see why this Mustaq should get any little bit of our house—Mummy sure as hell wouldn't have wanted him to have it! And if I can help in any way with Ashok chacha's case, I'd be happy to do that too. But I'm still not committing to selling my hissa just because you all want to. *You* took your own sweet time making up your mind last time and my parents died in the meantime. Okay?'

'That's not exactly how it happ…' Eshwari starts to say, then stops. 'Fine, whatever, okay.'

Anjini nods. 'Fine. Let's deal with the outsiders first—then we'll all sit round a table and discuss our internal issues. Fair?'

'Fair,' Bonu agrees.

'Fair,' Chandu echoes.

'Okay,' says Debjani. 'There are just two fronts to handle, then. Bonu and Samar can deal with the Muskaan school people for now. Is that doable, you two?'

Samar and Bonu look at each other.

'No more threats,' she tells him. 'You tell on me to the cops or your designer friends and I'll fully chaavi the Trings to never vacate.'

He folds his arms across his chest.

'Truce, for now,' he replies.

Debjani looks satisfied. 'Good. Now what about Chachaji? What should we do about *him*? Should we try the same thing as with Mustaq? Offer to pay him off?'

'Pay him off, over my dead body!' Anjini snorts, getting to her feet, eyes flashing. 'Ashok chacha can't cheat us by calling my father an alien foetus. We'll throw him out of court so hard he'll break all his bones. Let's *do* this.'

8

'He just said it right out?' Bonu asks. 'Like, gimme ten crores or I won't vacate?'

'Pretty much.'

'And what did *you* say?'

'I gave an incredulous laugh, got to my feet and left.'

'Weak,' she frowns, beetling her vivid brows. 'Very weak.'

Samar glowers. '*You* would have handled it much better, I suppose.'

She grins. 'Perhaps.'

They are sitting in the flowery drawing room, AC running full blast. She is wearing a light cotton salwar kameez with a net dupatta embroidered all over with tiny pastel roses, a relic from the eighties, which Dabbu mausi found in some old trunk yesterday and bestowed upon her with many hugs and kisses.

'I embroidered it myself,' she'd said. 'The year I met Dylan— it took *ages*. Oh, how pretty you look in it, Bonu Singh!'

Looking at her now, Samar has to agree.

'What would you do?' he asks. 'Give me an example of your low Delhi cunning.'

She shrugs. 'Well, I think Steesh has been advising you well. Hopefully the MCD will declare the place hazardous and we'll soon get an eviction notice.'

'That's Satish's idea. What's *yours*?'

Bonu starts fiddling with her hair, a faraway look entering her eyes.

'We could release snakes into the annexe?' she suggests. 'Poisonous ones? When the kids have gone off to school, of course. B. Tringji and N. Tringji might run out screaming...'

'More likely they'll eat the snakes for lunch,' Samar replies. 'Lightly fried, with bamboo shoot.'

'Racist pig,' Bonu retorts. 'Where is the Pushkarni when we need her? One would think she'd be haunting up a storm, what with Ashok besmirching her character.' She stops. 'Hey, hasn't this whole new angle about her paramour and the bastard-baby and all got you even more confused about your script?'

Samar rakes his fingers through his hair. 'It's not a script, Bonita, it's a film, and it's all been shot. I can't randomly give her a lover now—that would involve extensive amounts of re-shooting.'

'Oh.' She looks sympathetic. 'And that costs a lot of money?'

'Yes,' he says curtly.

She eyes him curiously. 'What are you planning to do, then? Change the ending so that he kills her after all? But why?' Her eyes widen. 'Oh, because he finds out about the foetus she sneaked into their marriage. But why would he wait twenty years? Besides, Ashok's tale is so obviously false! God, it's confusing. I think you'd better just leave it as it is.'

'Thus allowing Pushkar to get away with it—*again.*'

His voice is so harsh that she looks up. 'Don't get so snappy, I just—'

But he cuts her off.

'Just look at it from her point of view for a moment, would you? She married an asshole, got murdered by him, and now her son is calling her a loose woman.'

'Aren't you a little obsessed?'

'I don't want to talk about work!' he explodes.

Silence.

Then she says peaceably, 'Okay, what d'you wanna do about the Trings?'

'Thank you!' Samar gets up and starts to pace the room. 'See, Satish explained it to me. The important thing is to just get them out. Possession is nine-tenths of the law. Once they're out, they can't get back in. But they have to leave voluntarily, and with bag, baggage and everything—or we could end up in jail. Mustaq has contacts *everywhere*.'

'Hmmmm.' Bonu stares at the table for a while. Then looks up impulsively, 'How about we walk over to the annexe tonight and invite ourselves to dinner? It's Friday—they'll be partying.'

'But they're just his stooges,' Samar says restlessly. 'We should be concentrating on Mustaq.'

'They might give us some dirt on him,' Bonu says. 'Dirt we could use. Let's get them all drunk and chatty, then pump them for info?'

He stares at her, sitting there swathed in her soft, rosebud-festooned dupatta, radiating so much cocky optimism. The last time she took him partying at the Trings, they'd ended up kissing. He still can't get that kiss out of his head.

'Okay,' he shrugs finally. 'Now git. I have to make some important calls.'

'Oh, I'm busy too,' is her instant reply. 'Be ready by nine.'

The We-Want-Item-Number cry grows shriller through the day, culminating in Cougar Malhotra calling Samar in the evening and telling him to please just shut the fuck up and shoot the damn thing already. Swearing, cursing and snarling that he will never consent, Samar has had to consent. His mood is consequently black.

When Bonu comes looking for him, a bottle of imported whiskey tucked under her arm, she cocks her head to one side and whistles in sympathy.

'Wow, you look fried.'

'I'm fine,' he replies, his tone surly. 'Let's go.'

The oppressive weather has dampened the party spirit in the annexe somewhat, and they find the Brothers Tring in the central courtyard, lounging torpidly in the warm damp breeze of a large desert cooler, dressed in tatty Lux Cosy vests and baggy undershorts. They are in pretty good shape, physically, Samar is amused to note, and when he mentions this, they tell him that Gulgul Thakur lets them work out in his gym for free. They coyly stump off to change, however, seeing as they have female company, leaving their angel-faced grandchildren to play host to the guests. Samar and Bonu sit down, accept glasses of water, and inhale the annexe bouquet of bathroom and frying onions, while the children squat on the floor and survey them solemnly.

Presently Namgay Tring and Biren Tring reappear, dressed in bush shirts and long pants, and the little party sits down to chat in a rather self-conscious little circle.

The brothers rue the passing of the Judge, bemoaning those golden days when he reigned at number 16 with his serenely smiling consort Mamtaji by his side, recalling the regal tableau they made in the garden when they sat at the cards table with their children about them, electric fans whirring on either side like handmaidens serving a revered deity. They skirt delicately around the issue of how they've been complaining loudly to the press about those very children and quickly move on to praise Samar's two films. The imported whiskey starts to do its job, and slowly, the atmosphere grows convivial.

'So where are you guys from, exactly?' Samar asks, reaching for the salted channas drizzled with pungent mustard oil. 'Bhutan?'

'O ya,' Namgay Tring replies. 'Our father is vir-ginally from Chongza village, he used to grow cucumbers and corn.'

'Have you ever thought about going back there?'

Biren Tring chuckles sadly. 'We can't.'

'Why?' Bonu asks.

Namgay Tring turns to look at his brother out of one bright, canny eye. 'Shall I tell?'

Biren Tring nods.

'Because when my father left his village, he swore he wouldn't come back till he became both rich and famous. He died a nameless pauper, and we are not much better off, so we cannot return.'

'But why did he make such a strange vow?' asks Samar, the film-maker in him immediately sensing a good story. 'To become rich and famous? Was there a girl involved?'

Namgay Tring nods. 'He had a Fancy.'

'Fancy?' Samar says blankly.

Bonu digs him in the ribs and leans forward.

'He was engaged?' she asks, smiling.

Namgay Tring turns towards her and nods.

'Yes, he had a Fancy. They were fancied for two years. But then she left him to marry the richest man in Chongza. So my father left the village—after making his vow in full public hearing—and now we can't go back because though he is dead, she is still alive, and still the richest woman there, and will laugh at us and make bharta of the family izzat.'

'She must be really old now, no?' Samar probes hopefully. 'Fading, about to die, perhaps?'

The brothers shake their heads. 'Women live long in the hills,' Biren Tring says. 'Easily cross hundurd, hundurd-ten years. This lady is only now starting to lose her teeth.'

'But you don't even want to go back, right?' Bonu says brightly. 'I mean, look where you live, in the heart of the biggest city in Asia! Why would you want to go back to Bhutan?'

Namgay Tring rubs his empty eye socket. 'Home is home,' he says with lugubrious finality.

Everybody sips their whiskey pensively.

'Namgay Tringji and Biren Tringji,' Samar says, after a pause, 'we were very sorry to read that some sections of our family have been maligning you...'

Namgay Tring snorts, a loud, honking sound. Biren Tring turns to Bonu.

'All of them except *you*, Bonu didi!' he says emphatically. 'Especially that Dabbu didi—she thinks we are murderers! Always worrying about those shitting pigeons but never worrying that humans also have needs! If chicken is out of my budget, should I feed my grandchildren only kaddoo-cabbage? How will they grow strong?'

Privately Bonu thinks Biren Tring's grandchildren look extremely strong but she just nods and murmurs sympathetically.

Namgay Tring chimes in, 'Vegetarians are like pseudo-secularists! So worried about the minority that they don't care about the majority. Arrey, for hundreds of centuries, animals have abused *us*, now it's our turn to abuse them little bit!'

Samar ignores this unique simile. 'Yes, but you two are

intelligent people, surely you can see that Dabbu mausi is a little crack? She has a mental problem, poor thing—the worms and pesticides from all the cabbage leaves she eats have got into her brain. Mental disease is terrible, you know, so much harder to bear than the physical challenges you have… But what is your plan, exactly? Because, let's be realistic, this house is going to be sold.'

A sly look creeps across the faces of the two pahadis. 'Mustaq bhai is going to pay us,' they say with simple pride, 'a *lot* of money for leaving the annixee!'

'One?' Samar murmurs knowledgeably. His solitary meeting with Mustaq Khan has given him a fair idea of the kind of largesse the man might spread around.

The pahadis nod. 'One lakh each.'

Bonu chokes on her drink. The difference is so huge it's obscene.

'It's too little!' she tells them sternly, putting down her glass. 'Are you mad? Do you know how much this annexe is worth? Ask for more money!'

The Trings giggle nervously. 'No no, Bonu didi! Besides, Mustaq bhai will give us quarters in the new school campus also! We will each get a room to live in, same size as this one.'

The smallness of this offer, and their seeming satisfaction with it, depresses Bonu so utterly that she falls silent.

And then Samar speaks out in the semi-darkness, his voice carefully casual, 'How about if we just cut Mustaq out? We'll give you one crore to vacate. Fifty lakhs each. Think about it.'

'You're insane,' Bonu tells Samar as they walk back to the main house later. 'That was a highly irresponsible thing to do.'

He turns to face her, clearly excited, his eyes alight. 'But it's such a good idea! We can just cut out Mustaq Khan. He isn't living in the annexe, they are! And clearly, they need the money. If they vacate, well, we'll just knock down the bloody annexe overnight. You should be thanking me.'

But Bonu shakes her head. 'Samar, you don't live here, so maybe you don't get it, but Mustaq is a thug. He runs a massive mafia. You think he'll let these poor Trings get away with their money? They'll be chased down and beaten up, perhaps even hacked to death as a salutary lesson to anybody else who's thinking about being disloyal. The whole thing will end in a mess. And the Trings know this. They'll never agree.'

'They looked pretty excited with the offer,' Samar objects, reluctant to let his brainwave go.

'That's because they hadn't thought it through,' she replies firmly. 'And because they were drunk.'

He doesn't contest this interpretation. But he doesn't look entirely convinced either. His jaw sets, and he makes for the main house, without bothering to see if she's following.

'I'm right about this,' she calls after him. 'We'll have to think of something else!'

No reply.

'Mustaq will *kill* the Tring Trings!'

No reply.

Bonu sits down on the boundary wall, shivering, suddenly thoroughly depressed. Shit, she shouldn't have drunk so much.

A strong hand grabs her elbow, pulling her up.

'Come along.'

'You came back,' she says, faintly surprised.

'You were right,' he admits. 'And I was wrong. We'll think of something else. Now, come on.'

Bonu gives a wide, relieved smile.

'So we're good.'

'Yeah.' She can't see his face in the semi-darkness but there is definitely a smile in his voice. 'We're good.'

'Good!'

She sits back more comfortably upon the low boundary wall, crosses her legs beneath her butt and sighs gustily.

'This whole thing is *balls*.'

She has settled herself down for a while, clearly. Resignedly, Samar sits down beside her.

'What?'

Bonu Singh makes a sweeping gesture.

'Everything! The way the Trings live! All of them cooped up in that little annexe, eating pigeons, so poor and so grateful, obediently doing the bidding of that creepy snake Mustaq. It's sick!' She turns to look at him aggressively. 'Isn't it sick?'

He nods soberly. 'It's sick.'

'They're good people,' she says passionately. 'They deserve better.'

'They do.'

'Can't we do something?'

'We can. We will.'

'Yes, we will. These people are my family. The Trings, my tailors, Gulgul mama and BJ. Except, BJ's gone now. Have you ever been to Bhutan?'

'Yes,' he nods, unfazed by the sudden change of subject. 'Most of my first film was shot there, though we pretended the location was Ladakh. It's lovely.'

'I've never been abroad,' she says.

Samar turns, surprised. 'Really?'

Bonu nods. 'Yes. Mummy-Papa couldn't afford it, of course,

and then, afterwards, BJ and Nani were too old to take me, and there wasn't much money, na… They did write to Eshu mausi and Chandu mausi in the US, asking them to have me for the summer, but one said I was too much of a handful and the other didn't even reply. Cows.'

'Cows,' Samar agrees, finding her hand—which is small and warm and just a little sticky—and squeezing it hard.

'I want to go to Bhutan someday. And the US.'

'You will.'

'What're you so worried about?'

'Huh?' Turning his head, he finds her eyes looking right into his, solemnly and without skittering. Clearly, the alcohol is having its usual effect.

'You. You're worried about something. You've had a nasty scowl on your face all day.'

'I'm fine,' he says shortly. 'It's just…work. My film.'

Bonu rolls her eyes at this idiocy, then leans in, raises one hand to his face and grabs his chin firmly. 'Your film is gonna *rock*. Okay?'

And then she smiles encouragingly.

Her fingers are warm. And small. And shy. As she moves his chin up and down, making him nod, Samar feels like somebody has put a hand inside his chest, grabbed his heart and squeezed it hard. The harsh lines of his face soften.

He smiles back and says, his voice an odd, husky whisper, 'Okay.'

He wakes up the next morning happy for no reason at all. The weather's foul, hot and stagnant, his film's driving him crazy, there's a bloody item song to shoot, and his promise to BJ is still hanging over his head. But Samar is feeling extremely summery. He bounces into the drippy bathroom, bounds out twenty minutes later, whistling, eats three bananas for breakfast, and sits down with his iPad in the verandah, sipping a glass of cold water and smiling to himself.

Soon it will be nine o'clock, he thinks. And Bonu Singh's tailors will walk through the gate and go upstairs and start the machines whirring. At about ten I can drop in and talk her about...uh...about how to evict Mustaq.

He is thinking these happy thoughts and tapping away busily, when he happens to look up and encounters Namgay Tring's beady eye glaring at him meaningfully, and gets a nasty start. The Tring blinks with his one eye, and after a couple of blinks, Samar realizes that he's not blinking, he's actually winking.

'Hi, Namgay Tringji,' he greets him. 'Come sit. What's up?'

N. Tring sidles into the verandah.

'Samar bhaiyya, are you trustworthy?'

Good question, thinks Samar as he sits back to ponder this. *Is* he trustworthy—a boy who once stole sarbanna-status from his sweet little cousin Monu? Who recently got drunk and badmouthed the industry that applauded his talent? Who is in a relationship with one woman but can't stop thinking about another?

'Why, you want to marry me?' he asks lightly.

Namgay Tring titters with disproportionate mirth at this mild joke. Samar waits him out.

'What I mean to ask is, can we trust you?'

'Speak saaf-saaf, Namgay Tringji,' says Samar. 'What's on your mind?'

N. Tring looks here and there, zooms in on the hovering

Lachhu, then leans in closer to Samar and jerks an eyebrow meaningfully.

'Let's go inside,' he hisses.

Samar gets to his feet, his curiosity stirred, and leads the old pahadi into his bedroom.

'So, what is it?'

N. Tring promptly attaches himself to Samar's shirt collar. Samar can feel tobacco-laden breath on his cheek, as the old man speaks hoarsely.

'What you said yesterday, about one crore. We want it. Give it to us and we will melt away like smoke and never come back.'

'Whoa,' Samar says, taken aback. 'But…where will you go once you leave the house? Aren't you afraid of provoking Mustaq bhai's anger? Suppose he comes after you and kidnaps your grandchildren?'

N. Tring smiles, all gummy cunning, and taps the side of his nose meaningfully.

'Villuj.'

'Huh?'

'Bhutan.'

Samar's brow clears.

'Ah, you'll go back to your village in Bhutan? Wow, that's a good idea, that's actually a *great* idea. You'll be safe from Mustaq there. But hang on, won't your father's rich ex-Fancy laugh at you? Or did she just die or something?'

He looks hopefully at the old man, who shakes his head, clearly waiting for Samar to get with the plan.

Samar continues thoughtfully, 'But you won't be rich and famous—wait, what am I saying? Of course you'll be rich! But what about being famous, Namgay Tringji?"

The tiny pahadi leans forward, his single eye agleam.

'Can Anji didi's baby boy be trusted?'

Samar can't quite see what his answer to this elliptically phrased question has to do with anything, but he nods.

'You can trust me.'

'Because we are not so sure we can,' is the frank response. 'But we trust Bonu didi, we have seen her grow up and we love her and we know she loves us. And we trust your pretty mother.' His eyes soften, grow reminiscent. 'She was always very nice to us...'

'Yeah, well, let's not get into all that,' Samar says hastily. He doesn't want to know what his stepmother could've got up to with these two during some long, boring summer vacation back in the seventies, when they were young and unwrinkled. 'What's on your mind?'

N. Tring leans in, eye glittering, and tells him.

'You'll do the item song, but only if it features two ugly old pahadis, one lame and one blind? Are you nuts?'

'Not blind,' Samar corrects his appalled producer. 'One-eyed. And they're not ugly, they're character faces.'

Cougar groans.

'Samar baby, word's out already that our film is shaky. How will two old chinks shaking their booty make it better?'

'It's *not* shaky,' Samar's hackles rise. 'I'm just unsure about how to close it, that's all.'

'Actually, *you're* shaky,' Cougar grouses. 'Your friend Zeeshan has been complaining to everyone that you got out his best performance ever, and now you're sitting on it. AK's sulking too.'

'Tell AK I'm shooting an item number. That'll shut him up. We shoot in five days.'

'We need a song,' Cougar says. 'A lyricist, music director, choreographer, exotic dancers…'

'Leave all that to me,' says his miraculously-converted-to-item-songs director. 'By the way, they want ten lakh hits on YouTube within a day of the song's video release or the deal is off. So—'

'Who's they?' asks Cougar suspiciously. 'And when did *you* start giving a damn about YouTube hits?'

'Everybody gives a damn about YouTube hits, Cougar baby!' Samar says quickly. 'So I've set a target of ten lakh hits within twenty-four hours of the release—that's as much as *Fevicol Se* got, I believe.'

'Samar Vir Singh is going to direct a *Fevicol*-type number?' Cougar wheezes in delight. 'How low the mighty have nose-dived! I'm game.'

Once he agrees to take on the item song, Samar dives into it with full gusto. If a thing's worth doing, it's worth doing well, he thinks, grinning a slightly manic grin as he closets himself in the downstairs bedroom, and with his earphones firmly in place proceeds to Google and watch every item song ever filmed. When the electricity blips briefly at ten in the night, he roars out in fury, but then the generator kicks in, and he goes quiet again. By seven the next morning, he is prowling about in the garden, gesticulating animatedly, unslept and unshaved, as he briefs the harassed lyricist back in Bombay.

'See, I've done a full analysis on this,' he tells her. 'And currently, there seem to be five kinds of item songs. A, based on names—like Sheila, Munni, Chameli, Jalebi, Billo-rani etc. B, based on items of clothing—like chunari, choli, ghoonghat, ghagra, ghughroo, etc. C, based on geographical locations—like UP-Bihar, Agra-Viagra or Dilli-ki-sardi. D, based on slyly horny metaphors. And finally, E, based on pretentious pseudo-Sufi, Urdu porn.'

'Okay,' she says hesitantly. 'I think you're over-simplifying this dreadfully, but okay.'

'I forbid you to do *any* of these,' he tells her crisply. 'Do anything *but* these five. Goodbye.'

Putting away his phone, he walks into the dining room. His aunts eye him curiously.

'What's up with you, Summerwine?' Dabbu asks. 'You've spent the last twenty-four hours on your phone. Your ears will burn to a crisp and fall off.'

Samar ignores this. 'I'm going to Bombay,' he says instead, buttering a toast busily. 'Just now.'

The aunts look alarmed.

'What about Mustaq?' Chandu's voice is sharp. 'You're supposed to fix him.'

'I'm going to Bombay to fix Mustaq.'

'How?' Is Eshu's logical question.

He gets up and looks down at them, bouncing a little on the balls of his feet, his eyes glittering with suppressed excitement.

'That's a secret,' he says finally and strides out of the room.

'Batao!' Exclaims Debjani looking extremely harassed.

'He's lying,' Chandu says with a sniff. 'He's just running back to his glamorous life in Bombay, that's all.'

Keeping this whole thing secret is key, Samar knows. If Mustaq gets even a whiff of what the pahadis are cooking, he'll crack down on them immediately. Samar's already sworn the Trings to secrecy, and, after thinking about it for a while, decided not to say anything to anyone in the house. For the time being, anyway. But two hours later, as he strides across the verandah, his rucksack on his back, his cab at the door, his mind on his shoot, he finds his feet walking him not down the driveway but up the stairs to the tailoring unit.

Bonu is squatting down on the ground with Daulat Master, bales of cloth spread all around them, but she springs up as soon as she sees him. Where has he been since they parted at her bedroom door that night?

'Hi,' she says breathlessly.

Samar stops by the door, leaning on the door jamb. For support, perhaps?

'Hey.'

Long pause.

They hadn't talked much the night before last. They had sat out there, on the boundary wall, for a good half hour, side by side, not even holding hands. Afterwards he had walked her to her room, said goodnight formally, and then walked downstairs to his own room like a man in a dream.

'I, er, like what you're wearing,' he says now.

She glances down at herself in surprise. She is wearing standard summer gear—a pastel salwar kameez with a light dupatta.

'Thanks.'

He waves a hand about vaguely.

'The, um, colours.'

'Yes.'

'Nice and airy,' he continues foolishly.

'Yes,' she agrees.

Are the sweet-faced ladies tailors sniggering? The backs of Samar's ears start to turn red. And not because he's been talking on his phone all night.

'I must get a few stitched for myself,' he finishes with a rueful roll of the eyes. 'Sorry…I'm babbling.'

Bonu laughs. 'That's okay. Where are you going?'

Samar stares at her. She knows he's going away. She can read his mind! Their connection is clearly magical, mystical, meant to be.

'How d'you know I'm going someplace?' he breathes.

Bonu raises her expressive brows. 'Uh, there's a rucksack on your back?'

The ladies tailors are definitely sniggering now. Even Daulat Master is smiling toothily.

Samar says, with as much dignity as he can muster, 'Yes. I'm going to Bombay, brat. C'mon out to the stairs, I have to tell you something.'

Cheeks pink, she follows him out of the unit and shuts the door behind her. They stand on the landing at the top of the stairs, a tiny but totally private space, with sunshine streaming in through the grill in the roshandaan.

'What?' she asks, shaking back her hair and looking up at him inquiringly.

Samar grasps her hands and stares at her face, his brain splitting cleanly into two.

Calm down, you've seen prettier.

No, I haven't.

Dude. Her chin is big.

I like it big.

You like them big, you mean, you horny bastard.

Hello, this is a pure emotion.

Yeah. Pure lust.

Zip it.

You zip it. Seriously. Don't tell her the plan, whatever you do. She'll flip.

Meanwhile, Bonu is looking at him, puzzled.

'*What*, Samar?'

'Huh?' he starts, squeezing her hands. 'Look, something's come up—that item song they wanted? I have to go shoot it. It'll be a few days.'

Does she look disappointed? He'd love to think so. He can't tell, though. Her hair has fallen forward on her face...

'That's too bad,' she says softly.

'Why?'

Her brow wrinkles, she looks up.

'Arrey, you didn't want to shoot it, na. You're a serious film-maker and all.'

'Oh.'

A bulbous little head peeps through the door.

'Maidumbji?' It is Daulat Master. 'Those pyjamas—how many L and how many XL?'

Samar immediately drops Bonu's hands and moves back, red-faced.

'You're busy. So, uh, I'll see you then.'

She nods.

But as he starts to head down the steps, she calls out, 'You'll be back soon, right?'

He turns, really wanting to tell her the plan. Wanting her opinion on it. But he holds himself back.

'Yes.'

In Bombay, he dives into the shoot like a mad man, summoning his band of trusty assistant directors and HODs to his office, barking orders at them at machine-gun speed while they stare at him, lips pursed, stunned and speechless.

'What?' snarls Samar finally. 'What's the problem? Spit it out!'

'Three days prep is insane,' the studious looking 1st AD from Lucknow shakes his head dubiously

'These lyrics are sexist,' sniffs the chesty, feminist 2nd AD from Miranda House.

'I have principles, man,' the fat, south Bombay 3rd AD chimes in virtuously. 'I don't do item numbers. Why can't we just release the film as is?'

'And these pahadis are non-actors,' pipes up the logistics-driven 4th AD. 'The Junior Artists Association may sue because you're bringing in outsiders. I don't think—'

'ADs don't think,' Samar snaps at him, brutally bludgeoning them all into silence. 'ADs *execute*. And the lyrics are not sexist—I have four maternal aunts and one stepmother, so trust me, I can't do sexist without being ostracized. These lyrics are merely raunchy. Get off your pretentious high horses and get cracking on this shot-breakdown before I sack the lot of you. Who's coordinating with the choreographer?'

Galvanized into action, the red-faced ADs scurry off in different directions, and over the next two days, the shoot starts to fall into place. The art department resurrects the sandstone haveli from the main film, the legal department gets permissions for shooting with animals at record speed, Susan's team delivers the loveliest of costumes in jewel-like colours, exotic makeup artists are flown in from LA, dance rehearsals take place round the clock, and the DOP's crew of dour-faced Tamilian camera assistants perfect their lighting and movements. By the end of the second day, Samar is exhausted, but happy. It's going to be a good shoot, he thinks as he glugs down a bottle of cold water and collapses into the back of his car, satisfied. We've thought of everything.

But as usual, they haven't. The one thing he hasn't factored in kicks in with a vengeance on the drive home. His phone rings, and he answers to the voice of his fat, south Bombay 3rd AD, sounding unusually cowed.

'Boss, I'm at the airport.'

'So?' Samar snaps. 'I don't recall telling you to report your precise location to me every minute of the day.'

The reply comes in an agonized whisper.

'There's a chick with the chinks. A real ball-breaker. She's pissed off as hell—breathing fire through her nostrils, practically. She almost hit me on the head with the name placard I was carrying. She wants to speak to you.'

'I'm not speaking to some chi—' Samar starts to protest but the craven AD has already handed the phone over. A hissing voice spits into Samar's ear.

'What the *fuck* d'you think you're playing at?'

Samar holds the phone away. He has never heard her voice on the phone before, but he has no problem recognizing Bonu Singh.

'Who told you?' he asks her, his tone slightly bored. 'Breaking and Entering?'

'Well, of *course*! How *dare* you go behind my back like this! You're endangering their lives, Samar! If *anything* hap—'

'How many people have you told?'

'*Nobody* of course, duh! I've kept it *really* quiet. But—'

'I don't have time for this conversation,' he says crisply and cuts the call.

He sits stock-still for a moment, frowning, then flops back upon the leather seat and smiles, his harsh face transformed, his driver notes with surprise in the rear-view mirror, by a softened, almost boyish expression.

She's here, he thinks. *She couldn't stay away. I'll see her tomorrow.*

He remains in this pleasant daze for almost five minutes, dreamily watching the street lights float by, before sanity reasserts itself. He must take pre-emptive action and placate the Bonster before she stirs up trouble on his set tomorrow. Leaning forward, he taps his driver on the shoulder.

'Dabbu mausi ke ghar chalo.'

Knowing what a cheapskate Bonu is, she is sure to be shacking up there for free.

Taking advantage of Dabbu's prolonged sojourn in Delhi, the Shekhawats—father, daughter and son—are cooking up a sneaky, sinful, non-vegetarian storm in Dabbu's beautiful no-meat-allowed kitchen. The chimney is humming hard, pumping tell-tale odours out onto the Arabian Sea, and their two adopted street dogs are wagging their tails and sniffing hopefully around the pretty mosaic floor. Dylan is preparing Mutton Biryani à la Juliet, his mother's spicy Mangalorean riff on regular mutton biryani, and the two children have been deployed as assistants.

Fifteen-year-old Pasta, nicknamed after her favourite food—a delicately spiced aglio olio—is in charge of the raita. Everything about Pasta is elegant and delicate, not to mention flirtatious. Tall and slender, she has recently started spilling out of her lacy C cups, and is growing up to be very like her aunt Anjini, a development her father regards with mild consternation.

Chubby ten-year-old Pow (his favourite food is vada pow) is chopping up leftover mutton into a feast for the pets, a task he is performing much too conscientiously for his father's liking.

'And that's another choice piece down the ungrateful cur's throat,' Dylan says in disgust. 'Look at the expression on his face—he looks like all his Christmas turkeys have come at once.'

'Don't be mean, Dadda,' Pow protests. 'There's more than enough meat for all of us—and you know if we leave any evidence, Ma'll find it and flip.'

'We are not committing a crime,' Dylan says with great dignity. 'Your Bonu didi is visiting, so naturally we need to be good hosts and feed her well.'

'How come Bonu didi's come to stay?' Pasta asks curiously. 'She's never visited before.'

'Hmm...yes, she has some work in Bombay,' says her father. 'Don't be so stingy with the prawn masala now, Pasta. Chuck it all in.'

'Bonu didi's fun,' Pow muses. 'She used to make bushy mustaches for my face with bits of her hair. And for my armpits also.'

'Eww,' his sister rolls her eyes. 'Gross.'

Bonu emerges from the loo at this point, clad in a long t-shirt nightie, face pink and glowing, hair towelled up on top of her head.

'That smells *divine*,' she smiles. 'Home-cooked food is *such* a treat for me.'

Dylan glances up, his eyes keen. 'How come?'

Bonu's already at the dining table, sitting down cross-legged upon the chair and rubbing her hands in anticipation. 'Well, while Naniji was alive the food was rocking, naturally, but since then it's been just Lachhu, and he usually dished out bland fare for BJ, you know. Now of course, I mostly eat bread and Nutella.'

'I see,' Dylan says. Then his lean dimples flash in an encouraging smile and he shovels large amounts of biryani onto her plate, taking trouble to ensure that the generous portion is studded with not one, not two, but three juicy pieces of meat. 'Eat up, young Bonus!'

'I can't possibly eat all this!' Bonu gasps.

'Nonsense!' he replies firmly, splashing wine into her glass. 'Red meat and red wine! Essential for a growing girl! Eat up, kids!'

Bonu eats. Handsome, successful Dylan mausa, so much more attractive than her own father, has always aroused in her a sort of wary, resentful defensiveness. Besides, she can never quite forget that she almost broke up his rishtaa with Dabbu mausi back when she was a child, four years younger than Pow. She doubts he has quite forgotten this either.

'So what brings you to Bombay, Bonster?' Dylan asks as he sits down at the table, his plate heaped high. 'Work?'

The child's expression grows inscrutable. Studying her as he sips his wine, Dylan thinks that she is indeed, as Debjani says, complicated. But sweet, he decides. There's no malice there— just pain and pride, and a big bruised heart. She's been through so much crap, and both he and his wife have been working too hard running a 24/7 newsroom and attempting to 'save the world', he thinks guiltily, to watch out for her.

Bonu gestures vaguely as she sucks on a marrow bone with concentration, reminding Dylan at once of a particularly independent stray cat that shows up at the office sometimes, snootily begging for scraps.

'Well?' he prompts her.

She shrugs. 'Oh, just some…stuff.'

He's intrigued—and even more intrigued when, halfway

through dinner, his elusive nephew, whom he hasn't seen in months, drops in unannounced.

His arrival is preceded by the dogs barking up a storm, like pageboys announcing a royal personage, before the front door opens to reveal Samar Vir Singh, flashing the sudden boyish smile that softens his strong features and holding his arms out to receive the children, who fall upon him with cries of glee.

'Samar bhaiyaaa!!!'

'Where've you beeeen???'

'Is everybody still mad at you?' Pow demands eagerly, hugging his big, cool cousin. 'That clip of you and Zee went viral, did you know? All the popular class nine kids want to be my friends now!'

'Beware of fair-weather friends,' Samar solemnly tweaks the chubby ear. 'Wow, but you've grown, Pow! You're almost as high as my ankle now. Vada vada vada?'

'Pow-pow-pow!' roars Pow as he launches himself on Samar in ecstatic outrage. They tumble onto the Persian rug, wrestling wildly, while the dogs gather around them, barking hard.

Samar's grey tee gets all rucked up, displaying taut brown muscle, a development Bonu can't help but notice with interest. She coldly turns her eyes away, however, and focuses on her plate of biryani.

Meanwhile, Pasta regards Samar's worn jeans and scruffy sneakers with dissatisfaction. Pointing a beautifully manicured, peppermint-green nail at him, she asks, 'How can Susan let you dress like this?'

'Dump her!' Pow implores, now seated astride Samar and hammering him hard on the chest. 'None of us likes her! She looks like an Adams from *The Addam's Family*.'

Dylan splutters, spilling wine on himself. 'Samar, I'm appalled—Pow, apologize, please.'

But Samar just grabs Pow by the seat of his pants and throws him halfway across the room with practised ease.

'Then I'm the Gomez to her Morticia,' he says lightly. 'Have you kids been bitching out my friends? Wouldja *please* get a life?'

Pasta rolls her eyes, the unbelievably long lashes she has inherited from her father making the gesture even more dramatic. On Dylan those lashes go mostly unnoticed, but on Pasta they are, as her besties in school tell her (far too often, in her parents' opinion), 'smoking hot'.

'We *have* lives,' she says indignantly. 'Fully happening ones.'

'Pow, your apology!' Dylan is on his feet, thundering like an Old Testament prophet. 'That was rude and ungentlemanly!'

But this reminds Pow of something. He slaps his forehead. 'Oh, ya, it would be *ungennelemanly* of you to dump her because she got so badly dumped last year only. Mamma explained. Sorry.'

'That's it.' And Dylan, his face grim, scoops his son up by the collar and marches him out of the room.

'I hope Dadda kills him,' Pasta says dreamily. 'He's a *dog*.'

'Agreed.' Samar sits up and pulls down his t-shirt. 'Uh, hello there, young Bonu Singh. Fancy seeing you here. You look so regal. Like the Maharaja of Patiala.'

She gives him a look that would shrivel plastic plants and turns away. Dylan, re-entering the room and catching this comment, notices with interest that about two minutes later, she removes her towel, hangs it behind her chair and fluffs out her pretty hair.

Samar accepts a plate and cleans up the leftover biryani with gusto, chatting easily with the children as he does so.

'When's your new movie out?' Pasta wants to know.

Soon, he tells her, shovelling rice into his mouth. He goes on to mention, casually, that he has a shoot at Mehboob tomorrow. The children perk up at once.

'I'll come,' announces Pasta, with great condescension, 'with three of my girlfriends.'

'No groupies on my set please,' counters Samar.

Pasta's mouth opens wide in outrage. She sucks in all the air the room possesses, or so it seems to her harassed father, then explodes.

'*Oh. My. God.* I am *so* not a groupie! Groupies are *lame!*'

'Then don't act like one, brat.' Samar's smile is a careless caress.

'I wouldn't be so disappointed, Pasta,' says Bonu with a peculiar, challenging edge to her voice, 'the shoot might get cancelled.'

The three Shekhawats look up, sensing tension at their table.

'Oh, I hardly think so,' Samar replies lightly, but there's an edge to his voice too.

Her chin shoots up. The Shekhawats' eyes swivel to her interestedly.

'Some of the actors may not show up on set,' she retorts.

'They've signed contracts,' he says calmly. 'They have to show.'

The Shekhawats, now feeling like they're at a tennis match, turn to look at Bonu again.

'They could get sick,' she flashes.

Three pairs of Shekhawat eyes turn to Samar. He folds his arms across his chest.

'They'll have to pay for a day's cancellation. That would be about...forty lakhs?'

'Balls!'

'Not balls,' he clarifies politely. 'Rupees. Forty lakh rupees.'

Pow giggles.

'Okay, you two,' Dylan sets his palms down on the table. 'Why don't you take this conversation someplace private, because it's clearly a private conversation, hmmm?'

'Gladly,' says Bonu through gritted teeth, gets to her feet and chhamchhams out to the terrace.

'Sorry,' Samar mutters and follows her.

The trio at the table look at each other, wide-eyed.

'Vibes,' says Pasta knowingly. 'Pheromones. *Tennnn*sion.'

'She'll win,' Pow nods vigorously. 'Like a boss! My money's on her.'

'Pass me the last of the biryani, will you,' says their father practically. 'I doubt those two will be eating any more tonight.'

Out on the beautiful sea-facing terrace, lush with fragrant plants grown lovingly by the homesick-for-Delhi Debjani, Bonu whirls around to glare at Samar.

'How dare you! After I told you what all Mustaq is capable of, you *still* went ahead with this dumb idea!'

Samar throws up his hands peaceably.

'I can explain.'

'Balls!'

He takes a step closer to her.

'Look, they came to *me*. It was their idea. And they have their disappearance to Bhutan all planned.'

She snorts. 'They have as much practical sense as two Smurf dolls! You're taking advantage of their naivety. And you went behind my back! And I don't want you to make them look like clowns in your film for everybody to laugh at!'

'They won't look like clowns,' he says swiftly. 'Trust me on that—I know what I'm doing. They'll be superb, I promise.'

She shakes her head, unconvinced. 'You think you can control everything! Mr Fix-it! BJ's Chosen One to get the house sold and everything settled! There are about fifty loopholes in this dumb plan!'

'Do *you* have a better plan?' he inquires, his tone silky.

She stamps her foot in frustration. 'No, I do not have a plan!'

Silence.

Sneaking a sideways glance, he fancies that she's cooling down somewhat but he can't be sure.

Presently she asks him, 'Do the mausis know?'

He shakes his head. 'I can't do everything by committee. There's too many of them and they argue too much.'

Bonu can't dispute this, so she doesn't.

'So where's the one crore going to come from?' she asks finally.

'I have savings,' he shrugs. 'If my plan works out, everybody can repay me later.'

'And how will you keep this quiet?' she demands after she has absorbed this, her tone more mollified. 'Suppose Mustaq finds out before we can get them out of the country. What then?'

He looks grim.

'The best thing to do would be to get them out now,' he admits. 'Before the video is released. But they're refusing to vacate unless they get ten lakh hits on YouTube in one day.'

'But Mustaq might see the video!' she gasps. 'That's idiotic.'

'They want to be famous. Because the Fancy will laugh at them otherw—'

'I know about the Fancy!' she snaps. 'But…' Her expression grows sceptical. 'Can you even *do* it? Isn't ten lakh hits in twenty-four hours a lot?'

'It is a lot,' he admits. 'But it's doable. And we'll give them sleek little pencil mustaches so they won't be instantly recognizable.'

'That's not enough!'

'Yeah, but I can't disguise them entirely or no one will be able to tell it's them. So it's gonna be pencil mustaches—plus they'll take lots of photos at the shoot while the make-up's being done, and with Zee and Pree and all, in case the Fancy doesn't believe them.'

'This is idiotic,' she repeats hopelessly.

'Maybe,' he admits. 'But it can't be helped. We'll just have to take that punt.'

She stares at him in disbelief. 'Take that *punt*? These are *lives* we're talking about!'

'Now who's being filmi?' Samar demands. 'Mustaq isn't the freaking Godfather. He'll be taken by surprise—he won't be able to rally his goons that fast. As long as we've got the getaway to the airport all planned, we should be fine.'

She looks torn. 'Samar, we have to be very, *very* careful.'

He moves in closer. 'We *will* be careful. I promise.'

'I just want them to be safe,' she says worriedly. 'They think they're so cunning, that they've maxed it. They sat on either side of me on the flight, so excited, and when the airhostess asked them Veg or Non-veg, they flipped open their trays and replied, Yes, please.'

'Bones, they're grown-ups,' Samar tells her firmly. 'You are *not* their mummy. The item number was their idea, after all, *they* came to me, and I'm gonna keep my side of the bargain. Why don't you come for the shoot, by the way? It'll be fun.'

She stares up at him, feeling vaguely manipulated, but not sure how to wrest back control. Perhaps she overreacted. And he's right, there is no other plan, and the Trings are adults—she needn't sheepdog them around.

And she's never been to Bombay. Or to Mehboob Studio—which sounds seriously cool.

'I don't know,' she says dubiously. 'Maybe I'll come.'

9

When Bonu emerges from the bathroom the next morning, she finds Pasta sprawled across the bed on her tummy, chin propped up in her hands.

'Whatchu wearing to the shoot, Bonu didi?'

'Uh, I hadn't thought about it, actually,' Bonu replies untruthfully.

Pasta gives a disbelieving little scream.

'But you have to look good! Zeesh—I mean, everybody will be there! Besides,' she changes gear, 'Ma says it's silly to dress up for other people but there's nothing wrong with dressing up for yourself. It boosts your confidence.'

Bonu opens the door and jerks a stern thumb. 'Git.'

Pasta gives an entreating wriggle and stays put. '*Please* Bonu didi!'

'I'll wear jeans,' Bonu says. 'And a plain t-shirt. And sneakers.'

Pasta pulls a face. 'Then you'll look like Samar bhaiyya with boobs.'

'Okay, that's it,' Bonu says. 'Leave. Now.'

But she comes down for breakfast looking pretty enough to draw a soft sigh of satisfaction from her young cousin—wearing fitted dark slacks, flat canvas shoes and one of BJ's worn, loose-collared shirts for luck. It is thin and beige and semi-transparent, and with the sleeves rolled up, the top two buttons unbuttoned, and the laminated SONIX tag dangling down the front, Bonu hopes it is both flattering and sensible.

'Ooh, boyfriend shirt. Nice,' says Pasta approvingly, jumping up from the dining table. 'But don't leave your hair open, it's covering all your bouncy bits. Make a messy French plait…here, I'll do it…and lay it along one shoulder, the way my mum does. Your eyes need to be smokier, though, and the lipper a tad darker.'

She suits her actions to her words, then stands back and admires her handiwork.

'How does she look, Dadda?'

Dylan looks up from his stack of about thirteen newspapers, some English, some Hindi, some Marathi. 'Lovely,' he says sincerely. 'Like a gorgeous but practical chap. Sleeves rolled up and ready to work! You *are* a practical chap, aren't you, Bonu Singh?'

'Yes,' she nods. 'I'm logical and practical. There isn't a single creative bone in my body!'

Dylan's eyes twinkle behind his reading glasses. 'Practical people and creative people usually make a very effective team. They balance each other out nicely.'

She looks up at him sharply, but the smile he meets her with is very bland. Bonu decides it is safer to just take her leave.

The drive across the Bandra Sea Link is exhilarating and soon she is pulling up outside the gates of Mehboob Studio. It is a major studio, the driver assures her, reeling off names of films that have been shot here. Bonu nods dazedly, steps out of the cab, and walks down the drive, past the straggly front lawn, to Floor No. 3, a huge, warehouse-like building with towering wooden doors. There is a smaller door built into the massive one, guarded by several intimidating men dressed in black. Bonu Singh surveys them doubtfully. Should she just walk in?

Vanity vans are parked in the quadrangle outside, marked with mysterious abbreviations. There are racks of clothes, several sewing machines, ironing boards, and a table loaded down with biscuits and coffee. A scrum of busy-looking people hangs around the area, working and talking.

Bonu can't help going up to the clothes and examining them. They are ghagras in rich jewel-like colours, exquisitely stitched, paired with tiny knotted bralettes.

'Arrey, AKji is so humble that we call his vanity van a *humility* van,' she overhears a man in a bad wig tell a pimply boy with rippling muscles and blond-streaks. 'While your boss is such a harami his make-up van is called a *make-out* van.'

The boy grins lazily. 'Of course he's a humble!' he snickers. 'For every ten scenes Zeeshan Khan has in this movie, AK has one. Has-been, saala. Actor bhi, actor ka dresser bhi.'

The man in the bad wig curses and lunges for the boy, who takes a hasty step backward and bumps into Bonu and the clothes rack.

She staggers, and a hand comes up from behind to steady her.

'Whoa, watch it, Wilson,' says a deep voice and Bonu turns to see Samar, dressed in his usual scruffy clothes, a sheaf of papers tucked under one arm, and a walkie in his hand. He is clearly in shoot mode, all bright-eyed and stubbled, and radiating energy. 'Ah, Bonita,' he grins, his eyes lighting up when he realizes it's her. 'I should've known by the chhamchhamming sound effects. Come!'

And grabbing her hand in a strong grip, he whisks her into the van marked 'PRIMARY CAST'.

Namgay Tring and Biren Tring are inside, pencil mustaches in place, looking remarkably exotic with kohled eyes, wearing white safari hunter outfits vaguely reminiscent of the Raj.

'Wow,' says Bonu, and she means it. 'You guys look great!"

The Trings grin, flashing a newly installed gold tooth each. Then, very stylishly, they draw a pair of golden-handled pistols and point them at Bonu.

She claps, delighted.

Their grins grow wider. Namgay Tring shows her a knotted leather whip. For the panther, he explains.

'There's a *panther*?' Bonu gasps.

'Yeah,' Samar grins. 'And peacocks and a tiger and snakes and, as you can see, guns. We've gone *all* out. This qawwali is right in the beginning of the film. Zeeshan, playing the young Thakur, is having a decadent bachelor's party in the haveli the night before his arranged marriage to his simple village wife.'

'It's an Aur Jee,' Biren Tring explains to her kindly. 'An Aur Jee is a very big, sexy party, in case you didn't knew. The main punch of the quwaali is…'

He trails off, looking expectantly at the fat, south Bombay 3rd AD, who screws up his eyes and reads out, in a slightly pained voice:

Upar waale ne diya hai sab kuch, magar
Dil maangta hai thoda aur jee!
Aur jee, aur jee, aur jee, aur jee!
Aur jee, aur jee, aur jee, aur jee!

'How…how nice,' breathes Bonu, rendered practically speechless.

'And we are the *main*,' the Tring says triumphantly. 'The *main* singers! We will sing, and forty exotic dancers will dance around us!'

Bonu's eyes slide to Samar's in apologetic gratitude. She'd been worried he'd make them look like fools—clearly he had no such intention. But Samar is too busy showing Namgay how to wield the whip to either notice or respond.

'Your father's Fancy will die of jealousy!' she tells the Trings.

Walking onto the set a few minutes later, she enters a whole new world. A starry night sky forms the backdrop to a massive, gothic sandstone haveli, with stained glass windows that gleam like angry jewels. It's placed in the middle of an inky pond dotted with pink lotuses, seemingly squatting above its own perfect reflection. Forty incredibly beautiful women of every skin tone—black, brown, dazzlingly fair—their Benarasi silk ghagras tied scandalously low on their slender waists, are lounging about in the verandahs while their attendants sprinkle gold dust on their swelling bosoms, most of which are on display encased in tiny bralettes. And seated before the monitor, wearing nothing but blue striped pyjama bottoms and a thin moustache, is the hottest young star in the country, Zeeshan Khan. One of the wispy little bralettes the item girls are wearing is flung rakishly around his neck like a trophy. The pimply young boy, Wilson, is daubing at his golden, sculpted chest with a white malmal cloth.

'Super-hit track!' Zeeshan beams, his kohl-rimmed eyes sparkling manically. 'Dad loves it!'

'How reassuring,' Samar bares his teeth in a not-so-pleasant smile. 'Zee, this is Bonita.'

'Bonita!' echoes Zeeshan. 'Err…I love your work. Huge fan.'

'She's my cousin,' Samar says dryly.

'Oh! Bo*nita*,' Zeeshan's eyebrows snap together, and his smile grows significantly wider. '*Hel*-lo.'

'Hi,' Bonu replies rather breathlessly, reeling in the face of so much masculine beauty. Because Zeeshan really is perfect. From his carefully-careless highlighted hair, to his shapely eyebrows, to his super-white teeth, to the rippling lines of muscle across his abdomen, he's so highly maintained that Bonu feels exhausted just looking at him.

Zeeshan continues to drink her in with his kohl-rimmed eyes, beaming from ear to ear.

'Thank God!' he declares finally, which Bonu thinks is a little random. 'Please sit, have a drink, have a fruit, have something!'

'I'm fine,' she smiles at him. 'I love what you're, uh, *not* wearing. Looks great.'

'Not showing too much body na?' he asks anxiously. 'I'm never too sure, you know, one doesn't want to come across as desperate.'

'It's an item number, Zee,' Samar, sprawled in the director's chair with his long legs stretched out before him, says without looking up from his shot breakdown. 'You wanted it, you've got it. Now don't go all convent school girl on me.'

But Zeeshan continues to look worried. Bonu, not knowing quite what to do, accepts a glass of coconut water from a hovering spot-boy and sips from it.

'Don't fret, Zee, you're the Goldilocks of item boys!' an exquisitely pitched voice declares gaily, and Bonu turns to see designer Susan Adams striding up towards them. Dressed for work in a casual tee and tights, and sporting a soft leather tote bag, she still manages to exude an effortless sense of style. Bonu's heart sinks. The woman is an absolute fashionplate.

Susan continues, still pursuing her Goldilocks theme, 'You're revealing not-too-much and not-too-little. You're *just* right!'

But Zeeshan doesn't look convinced. If anything, he looks even gloomier.

'So you're back,' he says with a remarkable lack of enthusiasm. 'And you've brought the beast with you.'

He nods at the large, sloppily-dressed man who has waddled in alongside Susan.

'Too expensive, too expensive,' rues this new entrant, looking like he's suffering from a painful bout of indigestion. 'This set is fuckin' obscene! Is that a Phantom? And why d'you need a motion control rig, for fuck's sake? And a goddamn helicam drone? Are those 24k par can HMIs? Samar baby, you're supposed to nanga karo Zee for this song—why are you nanga-karoing *me*?'

'It's money well spent, Cougar,' Samar pats his producer's beefy shoulder reassuringly, and quickly strolls off to stand with his DOP, closer to the shoot-setup.

'Smooth bastard,' wheezes Cougar feelingly. Then he turns his jaundiced eye on the dancers, sashaying around in their ridiculously ornate ghagras. 'And apparently the ghagra material cost five thousand rupees a metre! Each ghagra is thirty metres and there are forty dancers. Just do the frikkin math!'

'Haha! That's funny!' says Bonu, feeling it is high time she say something and prove she has a tongue.

Everybody turns to look at her.

Susan arches a thin, haughty eyebrow. 'Excuse me?'

And Zeeshan, instead of introducing Bonu, sits back in his chair and lets the scene unfold, with the pleasurable anticipation of somebody watching a Wimbledon final from the best seats, complete with a punnet of strawberries and cream.

Bonu looks confused. 'What you said about the price of Benarasi. That was a joke, right? I mean, *which* Benarasi costs five thousand rupees a metre?'

Susan continues to stare at Bonu like she is a strange object.

'*Genuine* Benarasi,' she says, speaking slowly, as if to an idiot.

Bonu looks back at her, even more confused, and feeling suddenly, extremely gauche.

The fat man sighs gustily. 'I wish it was a joke, but it isn't.'

'But why would you use genuine Benarasi anyway?' Bonu continues, somewhat defensively. 'I mean, one can only tell real Benarasi brocade from faux by flipping it over and looking at the reverse side, so why bother with real for a movie?

Zeeshan smothers a cough. Susan's eyes narrow.

'Perhaps you don't realize, but the Phantom shoots a thousand frames a *second*,' she says in freezing tones. 'Intricate detailing is visible at the speed. We can't get away with *fakes*.'

'Ya, but why shoot with a Phantom in the first place?' Cougar says plaintively. 'This is self-indulgence begetting self-indulgence.'

'Using real Benarasi helps the weavers preserve their traditional *craft*,' Susan continues witheringly.

'I see,' Bonu looks doubtful, then continues with more confidence, 'but you know, the fake Benarasi looks and falls really well, too. And you don't need to buy it by the metre, you can buy it by the thaan in Tank Road—a roll of one hundred metres priced at twenty thou. *You* do the math.'

'Oh my *God*...' Susan mutters.

Zeeshan smothers a smile.

'It's worth every penny of the money we spend,' Susan says passionately. 'When you know you're wearing *real* Benarasi, woven with genuine gold thread on genuine silk, lined with pure satin, there's an arrogance to the way you carry yourself. Your entire body language changes. You move differently, sinuously, voluptuously. We need that khandaani regality in this film.'

'I'm an actor, darling,' Zeeshan drawls. 'I don't need props to feel the part.'

Susan flushes.

'Besides, even the best real Benarasi costs only about eight—' Bonu rushes on to say, but she stops short. The look Susan is giving her is so glitteringly basilisk-like, that it paralyzes Bonu's speech. She shuts up, grateful she hasn't turned to stone.

But the fat man's eyes gleam with interest. 'I'm Kuber Malhotra,' he says, extending a meaty hand to Bonu. 'Very nice to meet you. Er, where is Tank Road?'

'Behind Karol Bagh,' she smiles.

'Oh, you are from Dilli? And your name is...?'

'I'm Bonu Singh.'

'*Bonita*,' corrects Zeeshan, eyes twinkling with enjoyment as he gives the name its Spanish pronunciation, softening it down to a light caress. 'She's Samar's cousin.'

'Step,' Bonu corrects him automatically. 'We're not related by blood.'

Samar, walking back at this exact moment to sit down in the director's chair, overhears and flashes her a lazy, intimate grin. Bonu blushes bright red. Why had she felt the need to make that stupid, unnecessary clarification?

'But you told me Bonu Singh was a man!' Susan blurts out, upset.

The backs of Samar's ears turn a tell-tale red. 'Did I?'

'Yes, you did!'

'Whoops,' he says lightly. 'Maybe you misunderstood.'

'And she's not even your real cousin!'

Samar's lips tighten. He doesn't reply. Instead, he reaches for his mic and switches it on.

'Right, let's do this. Positions, everyone.'

His voice booms out, deep and easy and perfectly relaxed, and the unit responds to it at once. The assistant directors put down their walkies, the choreographer whistles to his dancers, who stop chattering and straighten up, adjusting their cleavages, the camera glides soundlessly and comes to a halt at the end of the trolley track. The floor goes quiet.

Susan gets to her feet and stalks away.

'We'll try one rehearsal,' Samar says. 'Travel Namgay Tringji and Biren Tringji please, I need to brief them.'

A pause follows, during which the ADs speak frantically into their walkies. Namgay Tring and Biren Tring have gone AWOL. Samar shoots Bonu a dirty look, and totally intimidated by his director persona, she forgets to argue and leaps to her feet to hunt for them. They are discovered at the back of the set, giggling and clicking pictures of each other against the impressive bosoms of the exotic dancers.

'Come here, you two!' she hisses and they stump towards her, grinning widely, not at all cowed. At the monitor, they look Zeeshan up and down with frank enjoyment, then turn to Samar.

'What we haf to do?'

'Confiscate their phones,' is Samar's cruel response. 'They can take pictures later. This is a place of work, not freaking Disneyland. Now you two, you know the chorus of the song, right? It's just two words repeated over and over, so it can't be too hard. Get on your knees and belt it out, with full energy, as many times as I tell you to. Roll sound, please.'

'*Aur jee, aur jee, aur jee, aur jee,*

'*Aur jee, aur jee, aur jee, aur jee,*'

blares out the sound system, and the shooting begins.

The songmakers have done their job well: the music is catchy, hypnotic and totally dance-worthy. The camera team swoops down on Namgay Tring and Biren Tring from every angle possible as they clap and sway and give the deathless lyrics everything they've got. The dancers swirl and dip and pout and whirl, Zeeshan Khan plays the slavering lecher with happy abandon, confetti flies, tinsel shimmers, peacocks flutter past, big cats roar. Samar glowers down at the monitor, legs spread wide, hands on his lean hips, watching every movement keenly, and Bonu, sitting a little removed from the action, drains her glass of coconut water, puts it down, and acknowledges, with a sense of utter consternation, that what she feels for her carelessly hot step-cousin is not a long dead attraction rattling about half-heartedly in its grave, nor some random hormonal surge, nor groupie-ish lust. The pathetic but true fact is that she is wholly and irrevocably besotted with him.

Shit shit shit, she thinks, clammy-palmed, nauseous but also profoundly grateful for the fact that nobody has as yet invented a mind-reading device. It means I have shown *no* character progression since I was, what, five years old. I'm exactly where I was all those years ago—all that struggling to forget him, all those self-help books I read, all the boys I dated, the gyaan I gave myself, the work I put into building my business and getting on with my life, all that might as well not have been. I'm just like those poor fat auntiejis who spend years dieting and exercising and undergoing liposuction to get thin, and then hit the grease in a weak moment, bloat up and go right back to square one. What a waste.

But oh, just look at him standing there, staring down at the monitor, so messy, so in-control and so unaware. She loves how intense and how focused he is. She loves the fact that everybody at his set clearly adores him—the bearded DOP, the quartet of ADs, the scrotum-scratching men whose job function she isn't entirely sure of, the forty hot item girls and, of course, his snooty, real-brocade-loving girlfriend. She loves the way his boyish smile flashes out suddenly, when he particularly likes a take, taking years off his face. She loves the fact that he…

'…is directing an item number with the same passion that he would direct, say, a really high-brow artsy scene.'

Huh? Bonu looks around. Petite powerhouse Preetali Shroff, the star of this film, the girl who plays the Pushkarni, is smiling at her, looking about fifteen years old in jeans and a sweatshirt.

'No?' Preetali smiles engagingly. 'Don't you agree?'

'I wouldn't know,' Bonu replies, 'but I can believe it. He's always been a bit of a control freak.'

'Susan said you're his cousin?'

Bonu nods, not bothering to correct her.

'I'm Pree.'

'Hi,' Bonu greets her. 'Are you in this song too?'

Preetali shakes her head. 'Oh no, I just came along to watch, you know, because only the paranoid survive.'

'*Okay*.' Bonu is confused. 'Matlab…?'

Preetali leans in confidingly. 'Matlab I don't want Sonix to cast some really hot chick in this item number, stick her into all the trailers and let her steal the movie from me under my very naak. Like how Ash stole *Bunty aur Babli* from Rani with *Kajraare*, you know.'

'Ah!' says Bonu, enlightened. 'I see what you mean. But there's no main girl here, as far as I can tell.'

'There isn't,' Preetali confirms, satisfied. 'Just those two cute unclejis. *Superb*, they are! Fantastic casting! But then that's Samar for you, he's the *bomb*.'

'Um, yes.'

'Such honesty, you know, and such passion. I simply *screamed* when I saw that vid of him and Zee! *Every*thing they said was true!'

'Okay, who let her in?' a deep lazy voice booms out on the mic behind them. 'Security! Intruder on set! What are all you jokers doing?'

The security guards grin sheepishly and finger their badges. The camera crew exchange indulgent smiles. The spot boys look coy. Preetali pouts appealingly.

'Don't be *mean*, Samar, Susan let me in. I'd have gotten a full report from her anyway, but then I thought, why not drop in? It's *my* movie too, isn't it?'

This last is said in a challenging voice. In response, her director rocks back on his heels and looks down at her sardonically.

'I won't stab you in the back, babe, don't worry.'

She beams.

'Liar. I bet you handpicked each and every one of today's dancers. You did, didn't you?'

His eyebrow rises. 'But of course. I'm a perfectionist, remember? Your words, not mine. And I do go into every minute detail.'

'Oh, I *know*,' Preetali makes a face, waving him away and scooting closer to Bonu. 'Go shoot your silly song now, I want to talk to your cousin.'

Samar shakes his head and walks away.

'I *swear* if he wasn't dating Susan I'd throw myself at him,' Pree says candidly as the music restarts. 'He's so…*himself*. So unshakable. Nobody's opinion bothers him—I can't tell you how rare that is in an industry as fickle as this. Even now, with everybody whispering about how there's trouble with the climax of our film, I know he'll get it right.'

Bonu says, her cheeks feeling hot as she forces the words out, 'Have they been dating long?'

'Almost a year,' Pree replies. 'They're not official-official, but yeah, it's been a pretty steady thing for a while now.'

Zeeshan, coming back from the shot, drops into a vacant seat beside them and pulls on a sweatshirt.

'Are you bitching about Samar?' he grins. 'Cool, I'm in!'

Bonu starts to shake her head in denial but Pree nods. 'Come closer!' she beckons imperiously.

He pulls his chair closer.

'Tell her!' Pree says.

Obediently, Zeeshan pins Bonu with his compelling superstar gaze.

'Look, Bonita. We're worried.'

'Yeah,' Preetali nods feelingly.

'What...what about?' Bonu stares from one to the other, taken aback at this sudden change in mood.

'Samar,' says Zeeshan firmly. 'I don't know if you know, because it's this great big secret, which only I'm supposed to know...' He pauses to look at his co-star. 'Pree, plug in your iPod for the next five minutes...'

'What the hell!' she gasps. 'I'm not a child!'

'You're ten years younger than me,' he says authoritatively. 'Just do it.'

'*Twelve* years younger,' she corrects him. But she listens to him.

'Good,' he says. 'Now I'll crank the volume up real loud...Ya, so, Bonita, d'you know what this film is about?'

He looks at her questioningly and she nods.

'Pushkar and his wife.'

'Exactly!' Zeeshan says. 'So you know. Anyway, Samar's been acting weird ever since that dude came and confessed to him that Pushkar himself ordered the murder. But after your BJ died he's upgraded to a whole *new level* of flipped. Pree, you can listen now—he keeps cutting and recutting the edit, saying it's a fake, glittering turd and that he's going to shelve it, crazy stuff like that. Naturally, Cougar's shitting bricks. One night at After, he leaned on Samar too hard and Samar threatened, actually *threatened*, to delete *all* the footage—the back-up files and everything—if Cougar didn't get off his case. The poor behenchod shat his pants. He backed off so fast he almost rammed his ass on the trophies in the reception, and now he's sitting frozen in horror and gibbering to himself, working up the dum to throw Samar out of his own film.'

'That's insane,' says Bonu, wide-eyed.

Zeeshan shoots her an old-fashioned look. '*Please* do not use that word when talking about Samar. But yes, it's worrying. Sonix is traditionally very strong on upholding the director's vision, but they're losing patience. Talk in the corridors is they're about to sack him. This could ruin his career.'

'And Susan doesn't help,' whispers Pree. 'She keeps telling Samar to be *real* and *true* and *authentic*, you know?'

Bonu snorts contemptuously. 'As if!'

Zeeshan grabs both Bonu's hands.

'Please help us get to the bottom of this. If he knew what really happened, I'm pretty sure he'd move on. *Find out* something!'

She looks at their anxious faces—the impossibly handsome man and the childlike girl—and then across the length of the warehouse-like studio, at the tall, restless figure with the dishevelled hair, deep in conversation with his basilisk of a girlfriend who, she notices, is now chatting prettily with him, all signs of sulkiness magically gone.

Does she give a damn about his stupid career and his stupid

life? Bonu wonders moodily. Wouldn't it be better if he somehow imploded? Then maybe she'd stop finding him so damnably attractive.

'I'll see what I can do,' she says shortly.

'Haan bhaisaab, jahan chhoda tha, wahin se utha lo,' Bonu tells her cabbie wearily that evening as she walks out of the studio after the shoot has wrapped up. And then can't help thinking that these words fully sum up the story of her life—Samar too could pick her up right where he left her, she's still as besotted with him as she was when she was five. God, she is such a loser.

'Bonita, over here, get in. I want to talk to you.'

Samar's long black car, which had been parked next to the vanity vans all day, is nosing its way out of the gate.

Shit shit shit. She really doesn't need this. Her cheeks are hurting from so much polite smiling, the words *aur jee aur jee aur jee aur jee* seem to be looping in her head endlessly, and her hair and skin feel gritty with dirt. She continues to walk.

'Madam, Samar-sir will give lift!' the smiling driver rolls down the window and says.

Damn. Heartbeat accelerating humiliatingly, she yanks open the door closest to her and climbs into the back. The interior of the car is plush, all expensive leather and cool minty air, dimly lit by the twilight outside and the little green lights glowing in the instrument panels.

'Yes?' she says gruffly.

He is leaning forward, ticking off all the shots they've taken, but now he looks up and grins.

'Arrey! How was your day? Your first shoot ever! No girlish

gushings? What did you think of the track? The Trings? Zeeshan Khan?'

These cheerful words are met with a sullen silence.

Finally she shrugs. 'Nice.'

'Nice?' Samar looks insulted.

She nods. 'Yeah, the set was nice, and the song is fun, and the Trings are being looked after well, and your friends were nice, and,' she draws a deep, shuddering breath, 'your girlfriend was nice too, I suppose. Very elegant. I'm going back to Delhi tomorrow.'

Samar stares at her, unreasonably, absurdly disappointed. Why is she leaving? It's a six-day shoot, and it's as glamorous as it gets. She lives in Delhi, for heaven's sake, and talks to tailors.

'Okay,' he manages to say.

In reply, she tosses her head and looks out of the window.

Samar stares at her averted head, frustrated. He's been aware of her presence on his set all day, he admits now. He knew where she sat, what she ate, whom she spoke to, when she laughed, when she took a phone call. This has never happened to him before. He has always been able to focus on his work completely, no matter who is visiting.

'You wanna get a coffee before you go?'

He regrets the words the moment they're out of his mouth. Damn—now he sounds needy as hell. Resentfully, he waits for this impossible girl to turn him down.

'But you don't drink coffee,' Bonu mutters. 'You drink cold water. Whole bottlefuls at one go. Like a camel.'

Samar's heart gives a glad, upward leap.

'You stick your hair up into a Samurai knot with a Natraj pencil whenever you're about to fight with people,' he retorts. 'Like Kung Fu Panda.'

She chokes. 'I do *not*!'

He continues, staring down blindly at the storyboard in his hand, his voice low, his tone confessional, 'And whenever you sit cross-legged, you first pass your hand over the back of your pants to see if you're flashing any butt cleavage. If you are, you spring up immediately, thus cancelling Christmas for millions.'

'Shut up,' she says, flustered.

But Samar can't stop himself now. 'And when the sun hits you, you stretch out and smile. I've never seen anybody enjoy the sun so much—like a sleepy cat, or a well-fed crocodile.'

'Huh?'

'And you're wearing only half your regular stack of silver bangles today, you've left off the big ones with the entwined elephant heads—why, too fancy to wear to a shoot?'

He looks up at her, his smile savage, his eyes ardent. Bonu's heart starts to slam. Hard.

'Er...yes,' she falters. 'Samar...?'

'Go back to Delhi tomorrow,' he says violently. 'Who cares?'

Bonu sits quiet for a while. Samar stares out of the window. The car pulls up at Dabbu mausi's building.

'Bye,' she says awkwardly.

He stares ahead at the road moodily.

'I thought we were getting coffee.'

'No thanks.'

He turns. His eyes are alight.

'A drink, then. Vodka. Your favourite.'

'Go home, Samar.'

'Why are you so mad at me? That day on the wall, I thought we were friends.'

She sighs, fiddling with her hair. 'Look, what is your *problem*?'

He throws up his hands. '*I* don't have a problem, *you're* the one who's ding one day and dong the next.'

She blinks.

'Isn't a dong a penis?'

'Like a *pendulum*,' he says witheringly. 'There's a coffee shop right here with a great sea view.'

'Dabbu mausi's house has a great sea view.'

'Good for Dabbu mausi.'

'And the coffee will be free.'

'Cheapskate. I'm asking you out, Bonita. Are you coming or not?'

She raises her chin.

'Not.'

His face grows harsh.

'Goodnight then,' he says evenly.

Bonu nods, her heart heavy, her mind made up.

'Goodnight.'

⚬

A message from Zeeshan Khan lights up Samar's phone early the next morning.

Bro, she's EPIC. I love her. But you're screwed, you poor bastard. How're you gonna produce a Soojan for Susan when you're clearly nursing a Boner for Bonu?

Samar swears and hurls the phone across the room.

10

Chachiji stumps over to number 16 one fine morning when the dahlias and the dogflowers are in straggly bloom, jowls a-quiver, all beaming, chirpy bonhomie, as though nothing has happened to mar the family peace. She is bearing a bartan of homemade gunjiya and wearing a determined smile. Her nieces, stunned at such brazen cheek, can only gawk wordlessly as they slide a cup of tea towards her along with a slice of Anji's famous Dundee cake.

'So how are you-all?' she inquires genially as she stirs her tea. 'All well?'

'All well,' Debjani manages to say, 'no thanks to *you*.'

Chachiji slurps her tea and opens her beady eyes wide. 'Hai, what did I do?'

Eshwari tries for sarcasm. 'Nothing.'

'Haan, nothing!' Chachiji agrees. 'Achha, now that all of you are here in India, I want to keep a party for you. Call all the neighbours and family and all. Do you eat non-veg, Chandu?'

Chandu can only stare at her. Anjini's clear sweet voice is the one to answer, relaxed and reasonable.

'Chachiji, your husband has branded our father a bastard and he is actively trying to steal our inheritance. Why should we party with you?'

Chachiji spreads out her hands. 'Ladkiyon, this is not a new story! Your uncle filed this case sixteen years ago! Your mother and I still remained friends!'

'Friendship' is not the word the Thakur sisters would have used to describe the relationship between their late mother and her sister-in-law but it is indeed true that Mamtaji continued to dish out tea and sympathy to Chachiji pretty much till the day she died.

'Ya, well maybe if Ma had told us about the case we wouldn't have let her talk to you,' Eshwari says belligerently. 'I feel like such a fool, I was still living at home then—I should have known!'

'This is not a children's business,' Chachiji says virtuously. 'Gulgul also found out now only.'

'Oh God,' Anjini looks up, horrified. 'I just realized something—Ashok chacha filed this case just a few months after Binni *died*? When Ma and BJ were already so shattered?'

Chachiji's face crumples. Tears fill her beady eyes. 'Hai ladkiyon, has your uncle ever listened to me? He only cares for women, and the money needed to buy them! You should have let me finish him off, Dabbu, twenty years ago, when I had my knife at his throat. All this is your and your husband's fault only.'

Debjani chokes. Chachiji slurps her tea and continues, 'Anyway, in big-big families these small-small things keep happening.'

'Small-small things?' Eshwari is furious. 'Excuse me? He called BJ a cuckoo in the nest!'

Chachiji replies, her mouth full of Dundee cake, 'So what if he was cak-koo?'

As she pronounces 'cak' to rhyme with 'suck', everybody is a little confused.

'Arrey bhai, even if they have different fathers, mother is the same, no?' she continues. 'So they are still brothers and we are still family. I love you like daughters—every year on the navrataas didn't I call all five of you to my house and do your pooja as devi-ka-roop? And Gulgul is so fond of all of you! Don't make your hearts so small that you carry this fighting to the next generation.'

'It's *already* in the next generation,' Eshwari says hotly. 'Gulgul bhaisaab is Chachaji's lawyer. He's clearly picked a side.'

Chachiji waves a dismissive hand. 'All that is in the profayssional space. Why should that introod on the personal space? Mature people keep these two separate-separate. That is the correct way.'

'*We* should keep separate-separate,' Debjani tells her bluntly. 'Anything else would be hypocrisy. It's probably illegal for us to even talk, now that the matter is in court. You should go home, Chachiji. Thank you for the gunjiya.'

Gulab Thakur gulps in panic when his cousins bear down on him in his gym that afternoon, their hair a-blowing, their expressions grim, ready for battle.

'Huh…huh…hullo sisters!' he smiles weakly, his bouffant hair bobbing as he puts down his barbell and wipes his sweaty palms on his sweaty t-shirt. 'Come for a workout? It's free for you, of course—no charge! Heh heh.'

'Gulgul, you *worm*…' Eshwari begins scathingly, but Anjini rebukes her.

'Haw, Eshu, you can't just call him Gulgul, call him Gulgul *bhaisaab*.'

'*Worm* bhaisaab,' Eshwari restarts. 'How could you do this? Looting your own sisters? D'you know how angry Hanumanji is gonna be with you?'

'Sorry Anji didi, sorry Dabbu-Eshu,' Gulgul says instantly, tripping on the barbell and sending it rolling. 'Papa made me do it!'

'Your papa's too sick to make you do anything!'

Gulgul gulps again. 'He's much better now, I swear he is! He comes to the gym every evening and lifts weights for twenty minutes! He does cardio also! And walks on the treadmill!'

'You're pathetic,' Eshwari sneers. 'You do all the weight-lifting in the world, but inside that bulky body, you're weak, weak, weak, and *nothing* will ever put steel in your spine.'

Gulgul doesn't bother to defend himself. His bulky shoulders slump and he looks miserable.

'Couldn't you have said no?' Debjani asks gently.

Gulgul shakes his head. 'No. I loved Tauji, he was so kind to me, and you all are like real sisters, and Bonu toh is like my own daughter. To be honest, I thought, theek hai, let me draft the letter to keep Mummy-Papa happy and of course the Judge will never believe it and it will be thrown out of court.'

'You thought right!' Anjini nods vigorously. 'That will is a *joke.*'

Gulgul's gulab jamun eyes grow large and stricken.

'No, Anji didi, it was a joke when Papa filed it back in the early nineties. But this new Judge, he has a grudge against Tauji because Tauji caught him doing some shady samjhauta when he was a young lawyer and shamed him publically. He was thrilled when this case was re-opened and placed before him. He bought drinks for all his friends and he's vowed to let it drag on for as long as he can, and maybe even give an adverse ruling in the end.'

The sisters exchange worried glances.

'Shit,' says Dabbu. 'Now what do we do?'

'Bribe him, too?' Eshwari asks.

'Flirt?' Anjini suggests automatically, then shakes her head. 'No, I'm being stupid…'

'We could talk to Ashok chacha and come to some kind of compromise…' Chandu says doubtfully.

'We *cannot* come to a compromise,' Anjini says hotly. 'BJ was *not* a bastard. We have to get the case thrown out of court. *Help* us, Gulgul!'

'I can't help,' Gulgul says miserably. 'I try so hard to be a good son but I'm not. I took fourteen years to get my law degree and my legal practice is a failure. I have no wife and no children and no achievements. I'm a disappointment to my parents. This is the first time Papa's found me useful and given me something to do. I can't let him down.'

'You *are* a good son,' Dabbu says fiercely. 'You're dutiful and loving, and your gym is a huge success. You make good money!'

'Arrey rehne do, Dabbu,' Gulab sounds resentful for the first time. 'You live a big, successful life in Bombay and come on TV every day—it's not easy being your relation.'

Anjini suppresses a twinge of resentment at this matter-of-fact assumption that Dabbu is the brightest jewel in the family crown.

'I know that other people in the family seem to be more successful than you, Gulgul,' she says sympathetically. 'Like my son Samar, for instance. Such a big star! But family is family. Can't you make your father see reason?'

But Gulab Thakur's fleshy face has started to quiver. His eyes grow liquid, his nose red. He takes a deep breath, stares down at his barbell as if for strength, then looks up and starts to speak, his voice thick with emotion.

'I hate my father. I know it is not correct of me, and I ask Bajrang Bali every day to give me a big enough heart to love him, but until now, He has not obliged. I hate my father because he disrespects my mother and because he gambled away my inheritance. I am his only child, imagine! I would have inherited *whole* of number 14 and I would have been five times as rich as each one of you girls! And all I have, in spite of being the grandson of the so-great Pushkar Narayan Thakur, is one chhota-sa flat in Hailey Court. It makes my blood boil— with anger, with frustration and with jealousy. No, don't shake your head, Dabbu, it really does!'

They hear him out in stunned silence. Nobody has ever seen good-natured Gulgul lose it like this before.

Gulab Thakur sighs, shakes his head and picks up his barbell again. 'I am not your well-wisher, please understand. I try to be but I cannot promise that I am. My heart is not that pure—I am Human, after all, not Hanuman.'

'Gulgul,' Dabbu reaches for him, but he moves back.

'Anyway, even if I was, Papa wouldn't listen to me. All I can suggest you-all to do is read that will we have submitted very carefully. It may contain some clue, some small lead, that could help you.'

❧

'It was honest of him to confess that his heart may be impure,' Debjani says when they're back in the kitchen at number 16. 'No?'

'It shows his conscience still burns within him,' Chandu agrees.

'Please!' Anjini snorts. 'He very honestly told us that he is dishonest. Are we supposed to be grateful for it?'

'He's just weak,' Eshwari says in disgust. 'That's why he over-compensates with the body-building. Poor sod, I'd hate to be him, living with his psycho mom and horny, avaricious dad and having to look to Hanumanji calendar art for clarity.'

'Don't sneer at the spiritual, Eshwari,' Chandu says seriously. 'It's—'

But Eshwari has already reared up, pulled on her sneakers and gone out for a run.

It is a hot, still evening and Hailey Road is fairly empty but for the inevitable huddle of street dogs and the occasional honking bus. Above Eshwari, the amaltas trees are thick with yellow buds, hanging like chandeliers, each one curled up tight inside its light green jacket. Feeling decidedly déjà-vu-ish, Eshwari sets off down the road, fallen leaves crunching beneath her feet. She crosses number 17 and number 18 and the gleaming bevelled glass windows of Gambhir's Bistro, Patisserie, Charcuterie and Delicatessen; she passes the ruins of the old stepwell, scattered with its usual scrum of young lovers, foreigners and balloon-sellers. And when Satish Sridhar falls into step beside her, his feet hitting the ground in perfect synchronicity with her own, she isn't at all surprised. Somehow, it feels right.

'Any breakthrough on your legal troubles?' he asks her after they've jogged awhile, and she remembers how, when they were in school and prone to quarrelling violently, he would casually start talking to her again after weeks of silent warring, like nothing at all had happened in the interim.

She shoots him a sideways glance and says, with a shrug and a smile, 'Nada. If I were you, I'd pick another house to buy. Seriously.'

'*Don't say that.*' His response is so vehement that she stares at him in surprise.

Satish sees her expression and smiles. 'I've harboured this dream of razing down Milord's house for years. How can you steal that from me?'

Eshwari laughs and starts running faster. 'How come your voice is so much deeper than I remember?'

'It hadn't broken then,' he explains with a straight face. 'I hadn't yet hit puberty.'

Eshu's mouth hangs open. 'You hadn't yet hit *puber*...Steesh, if you'd been any more hormonal than you were back then, your scrotum would've probably burst.'

He grins.

'Not true, Bihari, not true. It broke right after you left, along with my heart.'

Eshwari chokes and turns to look at him, jogging steadily beside her. Tall, brown, unshaven, with a twinkle in his eyes. A little wrinkly around the eyes, to be sure, but then, she too is a little thicker around the thighs.

'Idiot!' she says, a little uncomfortably. 'And here I thought you'd become all suave and civilized.'

'Well, I *was* trying hard that day,' he admits. 'Because it was you pricey Thakur girls, you know. But mostly I work with construction crews and low-life politicians—I'm still a dicey mohalla boy.'

She laughs, shakes her head and runs on, suddenly feeling like she could run forever. They reach the end of Hailey Road and turn onto Barakhamba Road.

'Are you in touch with the gang from school?' he asks.

She shakes her head. 'Sort of, but not really. You?'

'Oh, just reunions and all that. You were my best friend from school, anyway.'

'From our batch, you mean,' she says without looking at him. 'You had lots of little *friends* in the batches below us.'

He looks rueful but doesn't reply, and they jog on in silence for a while. Finally they end up back at the Gambhir shop windows.

'Wanna go in?' Satish tilts his head.

'Are we well-dressed enough?' Eshu asks doubtfully. 'In our sweats and all? Gambhir Stores seems to have become really upmarket...Let's come back here when we're dressed posh.'

'But you're scary when you're posh,' Satish tells her. 'That day, in your posh New Yorker clothes with your posh New Yorker shades and your posh New Yorker lipstick, you gave me the fright of my life. Let's just go in like this, c'mon!'

And he grabs her hand and drags her inside.

Eshwari, still arguing and resisting, emerges through the swinging glass doors into an interior that is charmingly country. There are exposed stone walls, very similar to the architecture of the fourteenth-century stepwell close by, wooden tables draped with snowy tablecloths upon which sit green wine bottles with guttering red candles stuck into them. There is a chalkboard displaying the menu of the day, and at the back, perfectly preserved, is the old counter of the original Gambhir Kirana Stores, complete with its row of big candy jars, hanging egg baskets, a portrait of Guru Nanak and twinkling electric lights. Behind this counter, extremely stooped and looking like a mixture of Santa Claus and the Wahi Guru himself, is Old Mr Gambhir.

'Oh!' says Eshu, instantly charmed.

Old Mr Gambhir welcomes her in a voice as quavering as a bird's, and apologizes for not attending her father's funeral. He is too old to get around now, he says, but his family had done the catering. Eshwari hadn't really been involved with those details, she remembers guiltily, Samar and Bonu had seen to all that. Old Mr Gambhir tells her he is approaching his ninety-fifth birthday, and asks her how she likes the new setup. It is the brainchild of Young Mr Gambhir's Amreeka-educated daughter, he says, and was painstakingly and flawlessly executed by the man standing beside her in sweaty tee and tracks—Satish Sridhar himself.

After they have sat down and placed their order, Eshwari turns to look at Satish, eyes glowing.

'This place is the bomb!'

'Thank you.'

'You're so talented!'

'I've built a school or two, too,' he says modestly. 'Some big housing projects also. Save some gush for those.'

'Yeah, but this has been made so much pyaar-se! I thought you were this cold, business-minded construction magnate, but you're not. You're an artist!'

'The two are not necessarily incompatible,' he points out, grabbing a bit of bread and dousing it liberally with olive oil. Eshwari watches him wolf it down and thinks about…well, all kinds of things generally.

'I must confess the letter from your unsavoury uncle came as a total bolt from the blue,' he says presently. 'I haven't had such a nasty shock in a while. None of you knew about this case? Not even the older girls, not even Anji didi?'

Eshwari puts down her wine glass.

'No, none of us knew. We think our parents didn't tell us because it involved BJ's mother, and he was old-fashioned about things like that, and that last day, when he briefed us about his chat with you on Skype, I think it just faded from his mind. He didn't want to think about it, so he sort of…forgot.'

Satish picks up another piece of bread. 'Yeah, that makes sense. But even Ashok kept it very, very quiet—I did a bit of homework before coming to meet your dad and the case never came up.'

She shrugs. 'Well, maybe he respected his mum's memory in some twisted way too. Anyway, it's come up now. Chachaji and family are dishing out a toxic mix of naked greed and emotional blackmail, and none of us really knows how to cope.'

'Welcome to the new Hailey Road,' he replies wryly. 'Honestly, when I think about all the Happy Diwali melas and crazy Holis we used to celebrate down here, it seems like a dream. Kids don't come out to play like that anymore—no cricket, no kite-flying, no going down to Gambhir Stores for an orange bar. Today, if some enthu child went around ringing doorbells the way we used to, to collect chanda for the Blind Society, he'd probably get mauled by a Rottweiler or shot by the security guard or something. This place is rife with security cameras and property disputes. I was my father's only heir, otherwise I bet I'd be embroiled in one too.'

'Why d'you still live here, then?' she asks, bridling. 'You sound so disenchanted with the place.'

He spreads out his hands. 'I'm not a kid anymore, so it works for me. My office is here, so's the house—my folks have moved back to their place in Chennai. And I do have a lovely garden, much better than in other parts of the city, anyway.'

He pauses to sip his wine. Watching him, Eshwari acknowledges that in spite of his screwed-up past, he's still quite a catch—a youngish, landed, construction tycoon with a flat stomach. Good for him.

'Do you still play the drums?' she asks.

Satish laughs. 'Not very often. And you, d'you still play basketball?'

'Sometimes. We have a half court in the office.'

Satish leans in. 'Do you know we've never sat across a table together? Like this? Like two people on a date? Pretty cute, huh?'

'I got laid off,' Eshwari says abruptly.

He drops his bit of bread, startled. 'Oops.'

She looks away, wringing her hands in an awkward, confused gesture. 'I don't know why I'm telling you this. I haven't told anyone. Not my friends, not my sisters—nobody. It happened quite recently.'

'D'you need money?' he asks in a low voice.

She laughs. 'Oh, nothing so dramatic! They gave me a golden handshake and all that. But yeah, it's not a nice feeling to be let go, no matter how nicely they do it.'

She looks at him and notes that he seems to be reeling slightly. Good, she thinks with dark satisfaction. Hadn't bargained for so much unburdening when he offered to buy me a drink, had he?

'But I'm actually pretty excited,' she continues. 'Because with the money from this sale, I'll have the funds to do what I *really* want to do—set up my personalized international trekkers club venture, Make My Trek dot com, and be a happy gypsy for the rest of my life.'

'Sounds like a plan,' he says lightly. 'But that brings us right back to the conundrum with Ashok—what the hell is *wrong* with you?' Because Eshwari has started spluttering and the finest of white wine has ended up splattered across his face.

'Co...conundrum,' she manages. 'You've started using such big words. It's hilarious.'

He cocks his head to one side, invoking her old impression of a shaggy dog that wants to play. 'It's mean to laugh at people,' he says solemnly. 'Did I laugh when you told me you lost your job?'

'No,' she says contritely. 'You were very nice about it.'

'Did I laugh when you told me you lost your virginity?'

'No...wait, shut up, Steesh, I never told you that. What crap you talk!'

He grins. 'But it's *gone*...right?'

'Oh, yes,' she smiles reminiscently. 'Gone in a lovely, enjoyable way too, a very long time ago. And yours?'

'I've been saving myself for you, of course,' he says promptly, and she sits back and groans. He leans in, eyebrow cocked. 'So are you seeing anybody these days?'

'We were talking about the conundrum with Ashok,' she reminds him, bouncing forward and propping her elbows on the table.

He gives her a decidedly nasty look but accepts the change of subject. 'Yes, so...how are you planning to deal with that?'

'Initially we were kind of hoping he'd die,' she admits. 'But he seems to be getting better, by all reports—he's even started gymming.'

'Well, I know a very good lawyer who specializes in stuff like this. Would you ladies like to meet him?'

'I guess so,' Eshwari replies cautiously. 'The dude who handled the case for BJ when this case first came up is dead, anyway.'

'Bihari, you *must* appoint a lawyer. It'll send a solid message to Ashok. But it can't be any lawyer—it has to be a real shark.'

'You know sharks?' She is impressed.

He grins, showing his teeth. 'I *am* a shark, baby.'

She laughs. He is so idiotic—with his messy, just-jogged hair and his badly fitted sweats. It's impossible to take him seriously.

'If you say so,' she tells him.

He pours them more wine.

'I do. You need to let Ashok know you're not backing down, that you have both the appetite *and* the pockets for a fight. Besides, it's always good to get an expert's opinion. This shark is pretty expensive, though. His fees are three lakhs per hour.'

Eshwari almost chokes on her wine.

'Wow!'

'Should've become a lawyer, like Milord wanted,' Satish says sapiently. 'You could've fought your own case.'

'Shut up.'

'Should I set up a meeting?'

She considers this, playing with the stem of her glass. Then she takes a deep breath.

'I guess it couldn't hurt. Well, except financially.'

His big brown hand lands on top of her small sturdy one. 'Don't worry about anything, Bihari,' he says, his voice suddenly gentle. 'Money, your job, the house, Make My Trek dot com. You'll max it all and come out on top, with a fuck-you grin plastered across your face. You always do.'

Ever since she made it, Bonu has been regretting her eminently sensible decision of not going out for coffee with Samar. The virtuous high of doing the 'right' thing fades fast, and again and again, she catches herself wondering *what* that coffee could've led to. Deep, meaningful conversation, mesmerizing eye contact, mind-melting kisses, passionate love-making in the backseat of his fancy car? Surely that's what he had been implying with all those hot things he'd said?

It was all the sort of smooth stuff guys say when they want to get into your pants, she tells herself firmly. Or even worse, stuff guys say when they want you to agree to sell houses you don't want to sell. Thank God you had the strength to come right back to Delhi, instead of lingering needily at his shoot, watching him look hot while he worked.

Determinedly, she puts the little scene in his big car out of her mind and throws herself into work, showing her tailors pictures of the *Aur Jee* ghagras and bralettes and getting them to replicate the design in sizes XS to XXL. But even this petty revenge doesn't provide her with any relief.

Finally, restless and reckless, she decides she might as well try to unearth the truth about the Pushkarni's death. If she finds out something, she will have a perfectly good reason to call Samar up. Not that she admits this motive to herself. Nor does she admit that she may be doing this because two of India's hottest stars have asked her to, which is kind of flattering. She's doing this *only* because she really wants to know, for *herself*, what the real deal is. Her curiosity has been piqued. Why had her great grandfather Pushkar Narayan Thakur ordered his wife's execution if he loved her so much? *Had* he really loved her? Or had he not? Had BJ known all along? Or had he just been feeding himself and Samar, and through Samar the world at large, a synthetic fairy tale? Who would know?

As Samar has already spent a lot of time with Chachiji and come up with zip, zooming into Ashok is her only real option, Bonu decides. She has heard that the rapidly recovering Ashok toils for twenty minutes on the treadmill at Gulgul's gym every evening, so at six that evening, she grits her teeth, changes into her dry fit gear and heads for the gym.

'Hullo hullo!' Gulgul greets her with a slightly shame-faced smile. 'Come come…I was just shutting the place up, but you're always welcome, my favourite niece, after all, heh heh. Lock up the place and leave the keys in the box in front of Hanumanji-ki-murti when you finish, okay?'

Bonu manages to nod, finding it rather surreal that he is talking to her so matter-of-factly and that she is talking back. This is how mature, civilized people must act in the real world, she thinks as she programs her treadmill. Half an hour later, when she is running hard, Ashok shows up.

He slinks up to her so slyly that she doesn't even realize he is there until he wheezes 'Bonu bitiya?' practically inside her ear, giving her the most horrible start.

She whirls around, hair in her eyes, almost falling off, hitting the emergency stop button in her confusion. The treadmill stops with a thump and she lurches forward, cursing.

'Halleeyo,' he says melodiously, clambering onto the treadmill next to hers and smiling his sleazy, I-used-to-be-handsome-once-now-I-am-overdyed-and-underlaid smile.

'Uh, hi,' says Bonu, feeling rather panicky. This is a dumb idea—how on earth is she going to broach the topic of his own mother's death to him? God, his face looks twisted. Is the Bail's palsy back? Or has he become so twisted inside that his internal twistedness has started manifesting itself externally? Is that even possible? She gives herself a stern little shake.

'Khafa ho?' he asks in a baby voice, pouting creepily. 'Angry with your Ashok chacha?'

Bonu wraps her arms tight around her chest.

'A bit,' she manages to say, keeping her voice natural. 'Definitely little bit I'm angry.'

'But *why*, beta?' he asks, his voice all whiny and injured.

She turns her big black eyes full on him.

'Because you never shared your pain,' she says simply. 'You should have told me all this before—I grew up unloved myself, I would have understood.'

He chokes up, tears rising tremulously to his yellowing eyes, and grabs her hand. She gives it a formal little shake—and thus begin their evening interactions. Trudging along on his treadmill, growing more garrulous every day, Ashok manages to cover quite a lot of ground, quite fast. Bonu is given long, elaborately constructed justifications for his various infidelities, which anyway exist, he claims, only in the head of his delusional wife. Never have I cheated on her, *never*, he declares, huffing and puffing and sweating profusely at three km an hour. It is just that the ladies seem to like my company, so I also talk to them in a jolly way and Bhudevi misunderstands.

He admits that in his youth, he had gone into gambling dens, yes! But only to pull out his foolish friends who had become aiyaash and addicted to taash. Always hate the sin, beta, he tells her virtuously, *never* the sinner!

He tells her about how he had received wedding rishtaas from royalty.

He shows her the scar from his prostate surgery.

And Bonu suffers these outpourings stoically, figuring they are like the stuff the ocean spat out during early churnings of the amrit manthan, and waits to hit pay dirt.

Finally, one Sunday evening, a full week from the time they start 'working out' together, Ashok switches off the treadmill, leans upon it heavily and heaves a gusty sigh.

'I am a much misunderstood man.'

'But *I* understand you, Ashok chacha,' Bonu assures him with mechanical glibness. 'You've had such a tough life—not being loved by your own mother, always being made to feel like an outsider in your own home, no?'

He licks his lips.

'You're right,' he says. 'It was very difficult. She hated me, you see, because she hated my father. It was a terrible hate—a passive, chup-chaap but strongly burning hate.'

Bonu digests this version, so different from the one BJ had narrated to Samar. Which one is true?

'Did he know?' she asks as casually as she can. 'Your father, I mean. Did he know she hated him? Is that why she…' She pauses, then takes the plunge. 'Is that why she died the way she did?'

'Hrrrmphh!' Ashok does slow, stiff, torso-twists. 'And how did she die?'

Bonu adjusts the speed of her treadmill, slowing it down a little.

'I heard ki…I could be wrong, of course, because people on this road talk so much rubbish… It's shocking, really. Of course, I denied it immediately.'

'What?' he grunts.

She turns to look at him, limpid-eyed, and says in her most innocent voice, 'Can you imagine, Ashok chacha, they actually had the guts to tell me that your father, uh, had her…um, *finished*.'

She nuances this outrageous remark beautifully, hovering between statement and query, and waits, heart pounding, for his reply.

There is a pause. He restarts his treadmill and they both work in silence, she running, he plodding. Presently, he wheezes out, his voice very low, 'It was never proved.'

Goosebumps rise upon Bonu's arms. As casually as she can, she asks, 'What happened exactly?'

Another long sigh. Much wiping of sweat. At last he speaks, his tone suddenly challenging.

'I don't want to talk about all that bakwaas. Let's get to the main point, shall we?'

Huh?

Bonu almost stops in surprise. She eases her speed to a walk and says, her voice shaking a little, 'Which is?'

He switches off his treadmill again and turns to face her, his lopsided face working strangely.

'You have not started coming here every day to talk to me about that old Pushkarni-ka-bhoot waali kahaani.'

'I haven't?' Bonu falters.

Ashok smirks.

'Of course you haven't. So let me tell you another kahaani. One that none of the neighbours nor those silly, English-speaking women next door know anything about.'

Hello, I speak English too, Bonu thinks, rather miffed. Ashok leans on his treadmill, wipes his forehead, and continues.

'See, in those days, before I filed this case, I was more or less contented with my lot. Theek hai, so Laxmi bhaisaab had a big house and all I had was a small flat, but I had only one son to provide for—not five-five daughters! So I consoled myself and controlled myself and was happy with my son and wife...'

(And Hot Dulari, thinks Bonu privately, wondering what the hell is coming next.)

Ashok leans in.

'Till your mother, my favourite niece, who spent her growing-up years in *my* house and not with her snooty sisters, came weeping and wailing to me, begging me to do something to save her husband's dying business. To somehow help her twist your grandfather's arm and get some money out of him.'

Bonu stares at him, startled.

'Really?'

Ashok nods.

'Yes.'

As she watches his lids dip over his eyes like wrinkled grey shutters over dirty yellow windows, Bonu has a weird sense of foreboding.

'So then I started to think ki how to get money out of Laxmi? Only for poor Binni's sake, of course!'

'Of course,' she echoes numbly.

'I remembered the old whispers. My father's old suspicions. The fact that he'd made a new will which my mother—who loved her paramour's son more than me, the son of a man she was forced to marry—had hidden. I searched—and I found it. And then I filed the case.'

When Bonu speaks her voice is a shaky whisper. 'You did it all for Mummy.'

He nods. 'Yes.'

'Did Mummy know that her whole family would end up with nothing?'

Ashok nods. 'Oh, yes. She knew.'

Bonu's stomach starts to churn. Her head starts to throb. This horrible old man is lying to her. This can't possibly be true.

'And Papa?'

He nods again.

'Papa also.'

Bonu sinks down shakily until she is sitting on the still treadmill.

'Why are you telling me all this?'

Ashok crouches down eagerly, hunching down till he is at level with her face.

'To get you on our side, beta. On the *right* side! Your

mother, she was really more Bhudevi's and my daughter than anyone else's! She grew up in our house! And she wanted this money for Monu and you only! Why should Pushkar Narayan Thakur's money go to Dabbu's Christian brats and Anjini's stepson and Chandu's half-foreign child? *You* are his true heir!'

Bonu blinks. 'But Mummy is also BJ's daughter.'

Ashok clicks his tongue. 'I just now said na, Binni was as good as my daughter—that's all, bas, finished!'

She doesn't reply. He leans in closer.

'I have a proposal for you.'

'No, thanks.' Bonu gets to her feet hastily. 'I'm really not interested!'

'Then why you are coming here every day and running with me?'

She stares at him, helpless and without words. He smiles, his lopsided face sweaty under the tube light.

'Beta, you have lived alone with Laxmi bhaisaab for the last five years. So if *you* testify to the court that Laxmi bhaisaab told you many times about how my father made a new will leaving everything to me, that Laxmi bhaisaab talked about it in his delirium saying he had destroyed it but feared that there may still be another copy out there—then my case will be ironclad.'

Bonu stares at him open-mouthed.

'And *why* would I do that?'

Ashok smooths his overlong hair around his sallow face and flutters his lashes.

'Because then I will give you a big cut—the same cut I promised your Mummy-Papa. *Double* the hissa you're currently getting. Two-fifths of 16 Hailey Road! Because I know how much your grandfather loved you—much more than he loved his daughters, frankly. And I know you loved him too.'

It takes Bonu almost a minute to realize she's staring at him with her mouth hanging open. She shuts it with a snap.

'No!'

She turns to leave, shaking with revulsion. Ashok follows, one foot dragging slightly behind the other.

'They treated your mother so badly. Left her to rot in the village with me and Bhudevi for years. I tell you, *we* were her parents, not them! You owe them nothing!'

Bonu whirls around. 'They left her there because she had asthma! The weather in the city didn't suit her!'

Ashok smirks. 'Those are all just things to say. They *left* her, na? Chalo, maan jao. You'll regret it otherwise. My case is very strong. Sach bolo toh, I was holding back while your grandfather was alive—so as not to distress such an old, sick man—but now, I don't have to hold back anymore. I will win my case.'

'You're a hypocrite!' Bonu spits out. 'Not that I believe a *word* of your story, but even if I did, even if you *were* really fighting this case so you could get some money for my mother, why are you fighting it now? She's dead, isn't she? You're doing it because you're a greedy, immoral man!'

He laughs.

'Maybe I am. But that is not the point, is it? Point is ki do you want double your hissa—or none at all? You've played Diwali teen-patti with me, you know when I'm bluffing and when I'm not. And I know how you think. It's double-or-nothing, Bonu bitiya, and you want to risk it, I know you do. You always do.'

'Teen-patti is different,' she tells him, feeling sick to the stomach. Why couldn't she have played innocent games of kot-piece with BJ, instead of teen-patti at high stakes with bloody Ashok? 'This is real life, in which you're swindling your own brother. Why should I trust *you*?'

She meets his gaze fearlessly. He leans in, his sour old-man breath, heavy with a cocktail of medication, hot on her cheek, and pats her hand.

'Just think it over with a cool head. You're a smart girl—you know who is doing chikni-chupdi baatein and only pretending to care for you, and who *really* has your best interests at heart. Don't you?'

Bonu shuts her eyes tight, opens them again and pushes him out of her way resolutely.

'Not *you*, for sure,' she snarls and makes for the stairs.

He stumbles, recovers, grabs the banisters and shouts, as she blunders away, 'I will wait for your answer! Call me anytime. Remember, this was your dead parents' wish! And the Judge who's hearing the case hated Laxmi bhaisaab—my chances are very strong!'

11

Satish had called Shahrukh Paperwallah a shark, but the lawyer turns out to be more of a smug, silver fox. He is sleek, handsome and clean-shaven with a trick of flicking a lock of exquisitely coiffed grey hair out of his eyes that is positively feminine. He arrives at his office exquisitely dressed, in a silver grey BMW, exuding solicitousness and expensive perfume, and Anjini can almost hear *You're so vain, you probably think this song is about you* playing as he enters his chambers.

Then he starts to speak, pinning them down, one by one, with heavy-lidded, beautiful liquid eyes. His voice is soft, very English public school, and also a little rustly.

Like a girgit crawling through dry grass, Dabbu thinks, hackles rising. Ugh.

'Ladies, ladies, make no bones about it, this is *war*. And it's the worst kind of war—a civil war. You are fighting against your own flesh and blood and things are going to get nasty. If you do not have the stomach for it, I suggest you desist now. There will be no half measures here, no pulling of punches. You are the five Pandavas and Hastinapura is at stake. When you ride into Kurukshetra you will take no prisoners, you will show no mercy. Wars are *not* won by wimps—is that clear?'

Wow, think the Thakur sisters, stunned. Suddenly the serene, beatific picture of Krishna behind the dude's desk, which they had taken to signify a spiritual, God-fearing nature, makes total sense.

Paperwallah continues to speak, now referring cosily to Laxmi Narayan Thakur as 'Daddy', which is disconcerting to say the least.

'You may think Daddy has the moral right here. You may know for sure that Uncle Ashok is a liar, a cheater, a gambler and a whore-monger. By contrast, Daddy was a fine man, a great attorney and judge, and a loyal husband. But these things mean diddly-squat in the eyes of the law. Diddly-*squat*.'

The sisters exchange unsure looks. Could this be true? Paperwallah flicks the lock of hair off his forehead smoothly and continues:

'Now, this case has been languishing in the District Court since 1989. At that time, Daddy's reaction to Uncle Ashok's claims was emotional. Instead of focusing on the single all-important fact that the will was a forgery, he took the rather ill-advised stance, at the very first hearing, to focus on proving that the illegitimacy story was cock-and-bull from the word go. Understandable, considering the personal agony Daddy must have been going through, but not sound legal thinking, not by a long shot. This caused what was a fairly simple case to go off on an unnecessary tangent, and by the time Daddy realized his error it was too late. The "will" that Uncle Ashok had presented had already achieved *locus standi*, and all other judges since have always had the same question—if the will Uncle Ashok presented was a forgery, why didn't you say so in your first rebuttal? Why bring it up only later, after you realized it was difficult to prove legitimacy or illegitimacy one way or the other?'

By the end of this long speech, the sisters look quite depressed.

'So this is real?' Anjini asks. 'It could happen? Chachaji could take away our inheritance right from under our noses?'

Paperwallah nods. 'He could. It's a serious situation, ladies, please do not labour under the illusion that it isn't.'

'Why did he go so quiet on it for all these years, then?' Eshwari asks.

Paperwallah steeples beautifully manicured fingers. 'Oh, I think he must've thought our legal system would be sympathetic to a sick old man who was losing his faculties. But not so sympathetic to a cabal of young, high-profile heirs who've clearly done well for themselves. Also, I think the news of an impending sale has galvanized him. Naturally enough.'

'So what's the plan going forward?' Chandu demands. 'What will you say in court tomorrow?'

Paperwallah flicks the errant silvery lock off his eyes.

'Well, though the signatures on the will Uncle Ashok submitted match your grandfather's signatures all right and tight,' he says, 'my team has managed to dig up something quite useful.'

He pauses, stretching out the tension (and the minutes, thinks Eshu, very conscious of the three lakhs per hour meter ticking away), and then continues: 'When he was young, Uncle Ashok once got arrested for forging his father's signature—and we have the court records to prove it.'

'Excellent!' Chandu exclaims. 'That proves Chachaji could've forged Pushkar's signatures!'

Shahrukh Paperwallah beams at her, liquid eyes agleam. 'Precisely.'

'Goodie!' Eshu is delighted. 'Sleazy old Ashok chacha—I can just see him slinking about, forging cheques in fancy establishments! What did he fake it for? Booze bills?'

'Amongst other things.'

'What else have we got on him?' asks Chandu.

Paperwallah spreads out his hands.

'That's pretty much it as of now, ladies. Tomorrow's hearing will be a sort of testing of the waters, really. We'll both rattle our sabres and talk tough and see where it goes from there.'

'What a player,' Anjini says admiringly on the drive back from Shahrukh Paperwallah's chambers. 'Worth every penny. I liked how he said we're the Pandavas, didn't you? 'Coz I'm so honest and responsible and all. Like Yudhisthir.'

'Uh, Yudi gambled away his family's entire inheritance,' Eshwari reminds her. 'And their spouse.'

'Chalo, you're not married, at any rate,' is Anjini's comforting reply. 'So I can't gamble away your husband.'

'I don't like him,' Dabbu says decisively. 'Do you know, I read that he's been married thrice?'

'That's entirely irrelevant,' Chandu snaps.

'And each time he got widowed, he got richer.'

'You don't like him only because his silver hair is prettier than yours.'

'He's too pretty,' Dabbu says disgusted.

'Unlike your Dylan, who's a bit of a blunt weapon,' sniffs Chandu. 'Anyway, I too, like Anjini, have a very positive feeling about tomorrow…'

But their mood plummets when they reach the District Court the next day. It is a sprawling, seedy building, noisy and smelly and crowded, furnished with the standard sarkari décor of paan-stained corners and desultorily rotating dirty fans.

'It's like Hazrat Nizamuddin railway station without the poopers and the beggars,' Eshu says. 'What a dump.'

Paperwallah and his team hurry towards them, sailing

through the squalid surroundings with the air of Mumbai fashionistas catwalking through slums.

'How lovely you all look,' he greets them gallantly. 'We're in Court No. 22. The sitting Judge has some old grudge against Daddy, apparently. We'll just have to roll with that for now.'

The Judge-with-the-Grudge turns out to be cranky and cadaverous. He is extremely tolerant of Gulgul's fumbling opening speech, helping him along in a manner that is blatantly partisan, sneers openly at Paperwallah when he presents proof that Ashok Narayan Thakur is an incorrigible forger, tells him rudely to his face that it proves *nothing*, and then asks Gulgul what else he has to say.

His face pink, Gulgul Thakur scrambles to his feet and asks to present a witness for the prosecution.

'Yes, yes, of course,' the Judge-with-the-Grudge beams obligingly. 'Bring him on!'

Paperwallah rises to his feet to protest that nobody had informed him about a witness but he might as well have saved his breath. The clerk announces a name that sounds vaguely familiar and, to the consternation of the Pricey Thakur Girls, dour-faced, Doberman-like Lachhu lopes up to the front, dressed in formal trousers and an oversized double-breasted navy blue blazer with shiny silver buttons. He climbs onto the small cement platform in front of the Judge, and in a hoarse, seldom heard voice, takes an oath to speak the truth and nothing but the truth so help him God.

'Your name?'

'Lachhman Kumar.'

'And you were employed by the late L.N. Thakur?'

'Yes, sir.'

'For how many years?'

'It would have been nine years this July, sir.'

'In what capacity were you employed?'

'My duties included bathing, massaging, feeding and changing the patient, pushing his wheelchair, reminding Bonu didi to give his medication, and sitting by his bedside while he slept.'

'And for this you were paid...?'

'It was hard work, sir. I was on call night and day for twenty thousand rupees a month only. It has been two years since I have seen my wife and children.'

Gulgul lets these facts sink in before framing his big ticket question.

'Did the Judge talk to you, Mr Lachhman?'

'All the time. He talked to me, and he talked to himself constantly.'

'What did he say?'

'All sorts of things—he complained about the food being tasteless, he complained that the gardener was a slacker, and he worried that Eshu didi wasn't married.'

There is a titter of laughter around the courtroom. Gulgul looks back sternly and it subsides.

'Did he ever talk about a will?'

'Yes sir, quite often. It was something he seemed to be worried about.'

'What did he say?'

'He talked to his wife about it—even though she is dead.'

'And what did he say to his dead wife?'

Lachhu assumes a voice that is a surprisingly accurate though cruel imitation of the late Judge: 'That good-for-nothing Ashok, my half-brother, has revealed my secret, Mamtaji. He has found the real will which I carefully suppressed. Our girls must not find out that I am a bastard, or that the will on the basis of which I inherited this house is actually null and void!'

'Objection!' roars Paperwallah.

'Overruled,' smirks the Judge-with-the-Grudge.

Lachhu reverts to his normal voice. 'Things like that, sir. He said them all the time.'

'He's lying!' Eshu cries out. 'It's so obviously rehearsed! How can you do this to us, Lachhu! And *you*, Gulgul!'

'Silence!' snaps the Judge.

And there is silence. Lachhu steps off the cement platform composedly, the buttons on his oversized blazer glinting dully in the tube-lit room. Gulgul slaps him on the back, but somewhat mechanically. Unlike his client, he is both sweaty and miserable, and his large soft eyes look haunted.

'So basically, between the bloody Grudge-saab, and that ungrateful snake Lachhu, we got totally bajaaoed.'

Samar yawns and rubs his eyes. His stepmother has been talking for the last half hour. It is late and he is at After, cutting the final edit of the *Aur Jee* video. He has put Anjini on speaker and laid the phone down on the console, making yes, no, and no-shit noises while he works, too glazed over with exhaustion to pay complete attention to what she is saying.

'Relax,' he repeats now. 'It's all good.'

'Arrey, what relax-relax! This is how Lachhu repays my poor father? Who helped him so much all his life? The lying, greedy bastard!'

'Ashok chacha must've paid him off.' Samar leans back into his chair and rakes his hands through his hair. Images of gleaming flesh clad in rich brocade swim sinuously before him on three monitors. He needs to stick in some more shots of the dancers to draw the attention away from the Trings' weirdest takes, where they clap with far too much zeal and mouth the lyrics with far too little precision. It's going to take him another night at least. He could leave it to the editor to do, the man's extremely talented, but Samar always prefers to cut the final-final edit himself.

Anjini laughs bitterly. 'Well, obviously! That's what Mr Paperwallah tried to imply too, but I'm not sure the Grudge-saab bought it. Uff, that man was so blatantly prejudiced!'

'Your lawyer sounds competent,' Samar says encouragingly.

'Ya...' she agrees dubiously. 'He's the best—everybody says so.'

'Everybody can't be wrong.'

'Oh, I don't know about that. Yesterday on *KBC*, one man used the audience poll lifeline and *ninety-three* percent of the audience said the answer was A. So he went with A and lost like, fifty lakh rupees.'

Samar frowns at the monitors, focusing on minimizing the errors in Biren Tring's lip-syncing as far as possible.

'Ma, you've got to stop thinking like this... It's not constructive.'

'Samar, could you please sound more interested? This is *your* inheritance too!'

'I *am* interested! Besides, Dabbu mausi briefed me already. I met her yesterday!'

He doesn't mention that Dabbu mausi had eyed him very speculatively and asked all kinds of pointed questions about Bonu Singh when they'd met. God alone knows what Dylan mausa and his brats have told her.

'This whole item song plan is absurd. I'll be extremely surprised if it works.'

Samar rolls his eyes. 'It'll work, Ma.'

'It had better,' says Anjini darkly. She and the aunts have finally been told about the Tring solution and they aren't too optimistic about it. 'The Trings have started giving interviews left, right and centre.'

Certainly the Trings have acquired a newfound taste for fame. They are constantly giving interviews to random journos, posing for pictures against the weathered walls of the annexe, and glibly mouthing Mustaq's line about how they're being discriminated against and how the Thakurs are throwing them out on the streets so callously.

'But they *have* to do that, Ma,' Samar explains. 'Or Mustaq will suspect they're up to something. Don't take it personally.'

'But suppose they're playing us?' Anjini says apprehensively. 'I mean, suppose they take your money also, and act in the item song also, and don't move out also! What will we do *then*?'

'They won't do that. They're my friends,' Samar assures her. 'And uh…Bonu's friends too. Besides, I'll pay them their money only at the airport. All their tickets have been done, by the way. They're flying to the Bhutan airport with full family exactly twenty-four hours after the song releases.'

'What if we don't get ten lakh hits in one day?'

'We will,' Samar replies. 'Bonu's main worry is that Mustaq might see the song and figure the Trings have been bribed.'

'Oh, he'll be too busy protesting and rallying to notice,' Anjini says. 'You should see all the stuff he's getting up to here…'

Mustaq's Discrimination against the North-East and Discrimination against Handicapable Persons campaign is definitely gathering momentum. It has garnered more than fifty thousand likes on Facebook, and he has called for a dharna in a weedy, disused park close to number 16. The entire staff and student body of Muskaan School for Challenged Children will be there — along with many TV crews, since physically challenged children protesting against rich Lutyens' bungalow owners make for a good photo op. Even the Minority Affairs minister and the HRD minister are rumoured to be attending.

'*When* will your stupid song be ready?' Anjini asks. 'You're too slow.'

Samar, whose entire team has been carping non-stop about how rushed the schedule for the song has been, and how he's going to screw it up by being in too much of a hurry, nobly refrains from snarling.

'It'll be ready when it's ready,' he says soothingly. 'What else did your Mr Paperwallah say?'

'Oh, he said that, on the bright side, the judge's roster will change next month and we may get a new judge, a better judge, somebody neutral.'

'That's a good thing.'

Anjini continues, 'Which is all very well for him to say because naturally, the longer the case drags on, the more money he gets to make.'

'Who's paying for all that, by the way?' Samar asks, bending over the computer to sliver a shot finely.

'We've made a little fund,' Anjini replies. 'Bonu isn't contributing because she doesn't want to sell, and Chandu isn't paying because she has no money. The rest of us are forking it out, but we're keeping tabs — we'll settle it with the others once the sale is done.'

'That makes sense.'

'Mr Paperwallah's bills are mounting, though. He called for an urgent fifteen-minute conference with us outside the courtroom—which put us back by another seventy-five thousand rupees, of course.'

'To say what?'

'To demand a complete list of all the people who might turn against us. Ex-drivers, old nannies, relatives, *everybody*. To stay two steps ahead of Uncle Ashok, he said, we must anticipate, approach and intercept all parties before they reach the court, and arrange for them to be silenced.'

'Silenced? As in *bumped* off?'

Anjini makes an impatient sound. 'No, you stupid boy. Nothing so filmi! Paid off.'

'Aaah, I see,' says Samar wryly. 'So...d'you think there are any turncoats lurking in the wings?'

There is a long pause.

'Ma?'

'Not really,' Anjini says finally. 'I did notice last week, you know, that...'

Samar pricks up his ears.

'What?'

'Nothing,' she says. 'Go cut your song. And don't forget to eat properly. Goodnight.'

Walking along Hailey Road, Eshwari and Satish are discussing Shahrukh Paperwallah's legal advice too.

'So what he *said* was that if we could identify potential turncoats, we could pay them off first,' she tells Satish. 'But I wouldn't be at all surprised if he was suggesting something worse.'

'Murder most foul?' Satish grins. 'That's entirely possible. But the revelation that Ashok's a convicted forger is useful news. Did you know you had forgery in the family?'

She shrugs. 'Well, we have traitors and pimps and gamblers and guns-for-hire, so why not forgers? You know, the more I think about it, the more I feel that maybe BJ really *was* a cakkcoo.'

'Cakkcoo?'

'Cakkcoo in the nest,' Eshwari explains. 'Chachiji's pronunciation.'

'Oh fuckkoo,' replies Satish, looking worried. 'Don't even *say* that out loud, Bihari you idiot.'

They are walking back from Gambhir Bistro, where they've often started going for a beer in the evening. The weather is oppressive, Hailey Road feels hot and airless, even this late in the evening. As Eshwari enters through the gate of number 16, Satish glances up at the windows on the first floor.

'Bonu Singh back?' he raises his eyebrows. 'How's her state of mind now? Is she more in the mood to sell?'

Eshwari rolls her eyes.

'Dude, I have no clue. Anyway, Bonu Singh is hardly a biggie. Getting the annexe vacated and the court case sorted come first.'

Bonu has certainly been in a bit of a daze post Ashok chacha's 'revelations'. She's been lying awake nights, wondering if it could really be true that her mother and father had turned against their family so viciously. The thing doesn't ring true— her mother, never mind how much she moaned about her sisters, had always spoken of her father with the greatest respect and affection. And she had loved her mother, there was no doubt about it.

He's just trying to create a rift, Bonu has been telling herself repeatedly. It's a lie, a cruel, mean lie and I mustn't fall for it. I just wish there was somebody I could *talk* to about this!

But there is nobody. Talking to the aunts is out of the question. Talking to Gulgul mama is impossible too. She doesn't want to discuss family stuff with outsiders. As for Samar, well, perhaps he could be trusted, but he's got enough on his plate at the moment.

Her tailors have noticed the change in her. Ever since Bonu didi started jimming again, they whisper to each other, she has been snarling and snapping constantly. Just yesterday she saw Parveen's eldest daughter—eight years old and bright as a button—threading naada through a consignment of salwars in the workshop, and threw the most hysterical fit. They were all given a blistering lecture on how child labour was illegal and how Parveen's daughter should be in school and did they all want Bonu to be thrown into jail? Parveen tried to explain that the summer vacations were on, the little girl was bored and had accompanied her mother to the workshop so she could watch TV as there was no bijli in their quarter. But Bonu snarled that she wasn't running a bloody crèche, the little girl burst into tears and vomited, and all the tailors could've sworn that Bonu didi, who never cried, was perilously close to tears herself.

'I think-so didi ko love ho gaya hai,' they speculate as they share their lunch at the big worktable. Which is a good thing, everybody agrees, but who can the fellow be?

As the only personable young man who's been around lately is Samar, naturally, the finger of speculation points towards him. Parveen thinks back to the two times she has seen Bonu with Samar, once at her own house and once in Chandni Chowk, and wonders—then she dismisses the idea. The second time, didi had looked like she wanted to do *murder* of Samar bhaiyya. Besides, he was her cousin, no? And Hindus didn't marry their cousins.

'Maybe she is stress because the unit will have to be closed,' the tailors conclude. 'Because the house is to be sold, no? So that must be worrying her... Also, that bald aunt of hers is quite an aafat.'

Certainly Bonu, already heavy-hearted and sleep-deprived due to Ashok Narayan's confidences, is finding Chandu mausi particularly hard to live with. She is always wandering around the house, touching things and muttering to herself, doing weird asanas in the garden or praying in chants, handing out little homilies to Bonu if she sees her wearing shorts, or swearing, or even playing music too loudly. She has also taken to gliding up the steps to Bonu's unit, clutching metres of banana yellow cloth, and asking the ladies tailors to stitch clothes for her for free. When Bonu sees Daulat Master bent over the bright yellow cloth for the first time, she demands to know what the hell it is and he looks quite trapped.

'It's Chandu mausi's,' he snivels finally. 'Her holi robes.'

'And who told you to stitch it, Masterji?'

'*She* did,' Parveen pipes up instantly. 'Your aunt. We told her we don't take orders from anyone but you, but she got around Masterji.'

'She is holi,' Daulat Master mutters in explanation. 'It's a sacred work, stitching her clothes.'

'He's hoping for a tip in dollars, of course,' the ladies tailors snigger.

Daulat Master turns red and says that his family used to stitch the clothes of all the granthis in the gurdwara when they lived in Lahore. We were very big tailors there, he tells them loftily. Rich and respected. And landed, too. We had *acres* of land.

The ladies retort tartily that haan haan, if all the people who had left acres of land behind in Pakistan and come empty-handed to India were to be believed, then Pakistan's area in square kilometres would be bigger than Africa's.

Bonu hushes the women, manages to restore order somehow, and resolves to take slimy Chandu mausi in hand.

'Here are your robes,' she tells her pleasantly that evening, handing her the neatly tailored and ironed garments. 'The bill will be three thousand rupees. If you need any more things stitched, tell me, I'll brief the tailors—I don't want them to make any mistakes with your stuff.'

Chandu's pale eyes glow as she takes the bundle from Bonu.

'So. A *bill*. My own niece is handing me a *bill* for getting a few clothes stitched in her grand business unit! Of course, human beings let us down in a million little ways, but the thing that hurts the most is *ingratitude*. Sharper than a serpent's tooth it is to have a thankless child!'

Bonu thinks this is a bit much. It's not like Chandu mausi has played the NRI aunt role particularly well. She didn't even bring Bonu a stick of Hubba Bubba gum, let alone duty-free perfume, when she came in from the US. On the contrary, her suitcase had been entirely full of things she wanted repaired—shoes, zippers, and two crappy old cell-phones.

'I've given you a discount,' she says as nicely as she can, pointing at the bill. 'Look, twenty percent off.'

Chandu gives her a nasty little smile. 'Twenty percent!' she murmurs. 'If I too had given your mother only twenty percent off, how would she have managed, huh? How?'

'I don't know what you're talking about,' Bonu replies tightly.

'And I would have thought, as you're so holy and honest and all, that you would have come to *me* and told me you wanted something stitched instead of going behind my back and intimidating my tailors into doing it for you for free. We work on very tight deadlines in my unit—and I can't take on small-small jobs and put my delivery dates in jeopardy.'

This isn't strictly true. Bonu does take on small-small jobs—for the Hailey Court aunties, for Dabbu mausi and Pasta, even for Anji mausi. And she often does it for free. But there's something about Chandu mausi and her smug, holier-than-thou attitude that raises Bonu's hackles. Or maybe she just can't handle so much naked, freshly shaved scalp on an empty stomach.

Chandu stares at her in disbelief, her nostrils flaring, and finally gives a scornful laugh. 'Take your three thousand rupees,' she says. 'Anyway, your tailoring is sloppy. I should have known to expect no less from a daughter of Binni's!'

Bonu Singh goes very white.

'What is *that* supposed to mean?'

But Chandu shakes her head in a maddeningly superior fashion. 'My lips are sealed. I will not speak ill of the dead.'

She sidles off, without, of course, giving Bonu the promised three thousand rupees. And drops in on Anjini and Eshu drinking tea in the drawing room.

'Have you noticed how much time Bonu spends with Ashok chacha?'

Eshu looks up, startled, then thoughtful.

'No...not really.'

Chandu nods. 'Yes. She goes to Gulgul's gym every evening and they work out together. I saw them last Sunday. And several times before that too. Strange, no?'

Anjini looks uneasy

'Yes,' she admits.

Chandu gives a delicate cough. 'Remember what Shahrukh Paperwallah said? *I* think working out was just an excuse—they were having talks, and now that they've come to some understanding, she's stopped going there.'

'Maybe she got her chums,' Eshwari suggests. 'I doubt Bonu Singh is plotting against us, Chandu. Sit down and have some tea.'

Sonix reveals title of SVS's new film
Releases party song '*Aur Jee, Aur Jee*'

It is a project that has been mired with controversy, but finally, Sonix's untitled project with director Samar Vir Singh has a name, a release date and a party song.

At the press release last night, Sonix announced that the film, a romance-cum-family drama set in the 1930s, is to be titled *Thakur Saab*.

When queried on this tame title, an Assistant Director on the film had this to say:

'Well, the unofficial name for the film was *Tharki Thakur*, after Zee and AK saab's character, you know. So at first we thought, why not call it that? If we can have *Rowdy Rathore*, why not *Tharki Thakur*? We could shorten it to make it sound more hip. But *TT* sounds like the dude who collects tickets on trains and *T2* sounds like an airport terminal, and then the censor board told us that *Tharki Thakur* was obscene, so we thought chalo, let's just go with *Thakur Saab*.'

Well, we've seen the video and heard the song, and can safely tell you that *Aur Jee, Aur Jee* definitely makes up for the film's prim title. Watch the mind-blowing video here.

The creative team behind the troubled project appeared

both triumphant and united at the press conference last night—
with Zeeshan Khan doing the signature step on stage and
giving the press a flash of his six pack, and studio head Kuber
Malhotra grabbing Samar Vir Singh by the shoulders and
kissing him soundly on both cheeks.

'Soty, soty!' he told the gathered press. 'Sonnng Of The
Yearrrr! Lyrics, choreography, music—all three awards have
our name on them!'

Superstar Zeeshan Khan corrected several journalists who
referred to the track as an 'item number'. 'It's a *party* song,' he
clarified. 'It's intrinsic to the plot and serves as an introduction
to the young Thakur Saab.'

Samar Vir Singh, accompanied by designer Susan Adams,
was even more restrained, and seemed inclined to talk less
about *Aur Jee, Aur Jee* and more about the kind of cinema he
likes to make. 'The kind that is real, that stirs the soul, ignites
the mind, touches the heart—'

'And tickles the private parts!' signed off his jubilant
producer.

Thakur Saab releases on the 15th August weekend.

The morning after the big press release is quiet. Samar wakes
up alone and pads about restlessly in his apartment, chugging
cold water and ignoring the newspapers. The film he had
crafted as a surprise birthday gift and a labour of love for his
grandfather, is actually a fake vapid saga about a romance that
never was—an 'eternal love story' between murderer and
murderee. But he also knows that he can't delay the release any
longer. There's just too much money involved. His mood is
consequently black.

'*Aur Jee* is live on YouTube!' Pasta squeals into his ears
when he answers his first call of the day. 'Oh my God, Samar
bhaiyya, Zeeshan is looking so *hot*, thank you *so much* for

making him take his shirt off! I *love* it, all my girlfriends love it! We're going to play it at all our parties—when's the DJ remix coming out?'

Several calls follow after that, most of which Samar doesn't bother to pick up. The YouTube hits climb through the morning and by ten o'clock, the song is ranked number one on YouTube India's Most Watched list. It's still some eight lakhs short of the one million mark, though.

But there's plenty of time left for that, Samar thinks as he finally sits down to breakfast. Just as he is about to bite into his toast, the phone rings again. A number he has saved but never had the occasion to use before.

Bonu Singh.

Bonu Singh, who charmed his picky best friend in just one meeting. Who fled his car like he had some kind of infectious disease. Who's way too cool to have coffee with him.

He stares at it for a while, feeling alternating waves of exultation and anger wash over him, before snatching it up in one smooth movement.

'Yes?' he says crisply.

'The Trings are on the front page of freakin' *Delhi Times*,' she says without preamble, her tight, calm voice leaking blind panic. 'In all their *Aur Jee* glory.'

Samar frowns. 'Shit, that was fast—must be a grab from the video. How big is the picture?'

'Not too big,' she replies. 'Like there's a much bigger photo of Zee, and the dancing girls, and one of you, but they're *there*—on page *one*—right where Mustaq can see them!'

'What does the caption say?'

There is a pause. He can hear newspapers rustling.

'Famous Farsi Qawwals.'

'Excellent. That's the bullshit I gave the press—it should throw Mustaq off the scent a bit. Plus they've got their pencil mustaches—'

She cuts him off. '*Screw* their pencil mustaches! There's gonna be a dharna today in that grubby park near the house—it starts at eleven. Mustaq's thugs are buzzing around our road! When's your flight? Get your butt here quick!'

'I've organized the money and I'm booked on a four o'clock—' he starts to say but she cuts him off again.

'*Now!*'

By noon Bonu has started to breathe again. There hasn't been a choon or a chaan out of Mustaq yet, and chances of him seeing a newspaper later in the day are relatively small. She starts to think that maybe, just maybe, they can pull this off.

Walking down to the annexe with Eshu mausi, she finds the mood openly jubilant. There is alcohol and chicken and celebration, and the Trings are dressed in their festive best. Suitcases are being packed, the price of a motorcycle is being haggled over fiercely, and the little children are weeping over the street mongrels.

'And Dabbu said they eat dogs,' Eshwari shakes her head. 'If she saw this she would be ashamed of herself.'

The brothers themselves are hunched over a scratchy old PC screen staring at glossy images of themselves in frank, gap-toothed delight. They had been too much in awe of Samar to watch the takes on the monitors during the shoot, but now they can't get enough of seeing themselves gyrate and clap and lip-sync on screen.

'I think half of the hits are coming from their constant rewatching only,' Eshu tells Bonu as they sip glasses of Thums Up while *Aur Jee* plays in a loop behind them. 'But it really is a good song. Samar's smart, he's played to their strengths. I thought they'd come across as fools, wearing dark glasses and over-acting, but they're great—somehow radiating innocence and a sort of native wisdom all at once.'

Bonu thinks back to Samar demanding a whole extra day's shoot to work with just Namgay Tring and Biren Tring, 'Because let's face it, they're no Meryl Streep'. And how mad that had made his producer.

He's a good director, she supposes. And a good person. He watches out for people. He just happens to have a girlfriend, that's all.

Then the Trings start reading the comments thread below the video and get all worked up. While the majority of viewers have talked about the hotness of the item girls, the coolness of Zeeshan Khan and how cute the qawwals are, several disgruntled folk have written things like Chutiya chinkie, Chutiya song, and Get out of India, Hakka Noodle.

'We want twenty lakh hits,' they grumble. 'And more money. We have been insulted on national television.'

'It's not television, it's YouTube,' Bonu tells them bluntly. 'Nasty comments go with the territory. Stop whining.'

They continue to look mutinous, however. Things get even more stressful when two jeepfuls of Mustaq's thugs drive noisily past the 16 Hailey Road gate, but they've just come to oversee the erecting of the shamiana and get the dharna warmed up. The massive tent rises, and then patriotic songs start blaring from loudspeakers, causing siesta-taking auntiejis all along Hailey Road to spring out of bed wild-eyed and cranky. A street theatre troop arrives and puts up a rousing, high energy Hindi play, very stinging and sarcastic, about people who claim to not practise racial discrimination but actually do. One of the actors is a regular from a popular TV show and manages to gather quite a crowd.

The terrace of number 16 provides a clear view of the action in the park so Eshwari and Bonu climb up there to watch.

'It looks really well-organized,' Bonu says, her palms clammy. 'And it's so close to the house!'

'Where's Mustaq?' Eshu wonders. 'When's *he* arriving?'

He doesn't arrive any time soon—but a rock band does: three skinny tattooed boys and two beefy men lugging lots of equipment, clearly excited about landing a 'gig'. 'Hellllooo Hailey Roaddd!' shouts the skinny lead singer after an hour of sound checks, his jeans in imminent danger of slipping off his scrawny backside. 'How are youuuuu?'

The crowd, which has been accumulating steadily, roars back that it is absolutely fine, and the band dives into its first song, the much abused by agitators everywhere *Sadda Haq*.

Mustaq still doesn't show up. The lead singer, clueless about the cause-du-jour, gives a learned little homily on gender sensitization, violence against women and being nice to HIV positive people, until a heckler from the crowd tells him off. He apologizes and switches smoothly to what an abomination the Armed Forces Special Powers Act is, which at least is slightly closer to the issue at hand.

The sweet scent of marijuana smoke drifts down Hailey Road around three in the afternoon, and the crowd quietens down. There's still no sign of Mustaq. Restless and jumpy, Eshwari and Bonu stroll down to the annexe and find the mood tense. The YouTube hits have reached five lakhs and then plateaued out.

'No new hits in the last half an hour,' says one of the pahadi's kids sombrely. 'And the nasty comments are growing. People are calling us Chinese Checkers. This is not what we were promised.'

Bonu wants to say hello, yesterday you didn't have even one hit, and now five lakhs isn't good enough for you, but all she says is, 'Must be because America has gone to sleep. Maximum Zeeshan fans are NRIs, so when it's daytime in the West, it'll jump again.'

'But it's daytime in the Gulf now,' says the kid, who clearly knows his geography. 'I hope so you have not made a flop song, Bonu didi.'

Driving to the house, loaded down with one crore in cash and checking his phone repeatedly for the YouTube hits count, Samar Vir Singh has exactly the same fear on his mind...until his car swings onto Barakhamba Road and brakes sharply, coming face to face with a full-blown rock concert. Samar lurches forward, his face colliding with the ghastly wooden-beaded backrest the cab driver has slipped over the front seat. Sitting up, he sees a massive crowd, OB vans from several news channels, a crew of electricians stringing AHUJA loudspeakers and electric light bulbs along the lamp-posts, and three hopeful looking ice-cream vendors.

'What the hell!'

'It's a big dharna, ji,' his cab driver says, leaning forward and resting his elbows comfortably on the steering wheel. 'Very big public meeting. Full road has been blocked off. Nestle-waalon ne organize kiya hai.'

'Nestle?' repeats Samar blankly.

The driver squints up at the banners strung across the road.

'North-Eastern Students Today want Learning and Education.'

'Superb,' mutters Samar, curiously undisturbed by this news. In fact, as he gets out of the cab and weaves his way through the crowd, breathing in the music and the marijuana, he is feeling lighter and happier than he's felt in a fortnight. Somewhere in this swelling crowd is Bonu Singh, and soon he's going to find her...

12

Bonu and Anjini are sitting in the living room when Eshwari comes hurrying in. 'Okay, don't flip out but somebody just joined the dots between the Trings and *Aur Jee* and Samar and us. Came over to the annexe and asked point blank if they'd been bribed with the song to leave the place.'

Anjini sets down her phone with a thud.

'What did the Trings say?'

'Denied it,' Eshwari replies with a triumphant smile. 'Said quite stolidly that it wasn't them in the song at all and that it was *very* racist to imply that all chinkie people look the same.'

'Wow, and those guys bought it?' asks Bonu nervously.

'I think so,' Eshu says. 'In any case, they left.'

'We should just head for the airport *now*,' Bonu says. 'This is stupid.'

'Well, they're refusing to leave until we cross ten lakh hits,' Eshu says, looking harassed. 'Mulish little shits.'

'But the later it gets the harder it'll be to get them out!' Bonu's voice rises. 'Mustaq will be here soon!'

And now Chandu enters, moving at a fast clip, very different from her usual dignified pace. 'It's over! We've been back-stabbed!'

Everybody whirls to face her.

'What?'

'The Trings! They've switched sides! They've betrayed us!'

'That's impossible,' Bonu says steadily.

'Arrey, I *told* you!' Chandu shrieks. 'I told you those wily pahadis were untrustworthy! They're sitting outside on the dais on either side of Mustaq Khan, bitching about us! Go see for yourself!'

All four women hurry down Hailey Road to find the shamiana in the park packed and buzzing. The first ten rows are filled with children from the Muskaan school. Behind them sit masses of general junta, made up mostly of hiply-dressed Manipuri and Mizo youth with edgy hairstyles, ripped jeans and gorgeous t-shirts. The rock band has lingered, standing at the back, smoking cigarettes and looking suitably intense.

Mustaq Khan, dressed in a crisp white pyjama kurta and looking exactly like a juicy shami kebab wrapped in a white paper napkin, is seated bang in the middle of the dais. The Minority Affairs minister and the Human Resources Development minister of the state of Delhi sit on either side of him. A huge portrait of Mustaq's father, the late freedom fighter Mustafa Khan, festooned with green and gold series lights, glows benignly a little to the right of them. Below this, grinning from ear to ear, sit Namgay Tring and Biren Tring, very distinguished in checked coats, grey trousers and pahadi topis. Their cheeks and noses are red.

'They look drunk,' Bonu whispers, her heart sinking.

'They *are* drunk,' Eshu says, disgusted. 'They've been boozing since the video went live on YouTube.'

As this depressing realization sinks in, the three Thakur sisters and Bonu stand in a line, helplessly watching the action unfold upon the stage.

A bespectacled youth—the president of NESTLE—is giving a speech.

'And so, my dear brothers and sisters, we have come together to battle the grave persecution faced by our brothers Namgay Tring and Biren Tring in this city, this great city, capital of our nation, where all Indians, fair or dark, hillsmen or plainsmen, healthy or handicapable, are meant to be treated as equal!'

This is met with tumultuous applause. 'And addressing us now is Mr Mustaq Khan, philanthropist, social worker, educationalist and tireless fighter for the rights of the downtrodden!'

'Shit.' Bonu sags slightly. Could the Trings really have betrayed her?

'And there's nothing we can do now!' Chandu has worked herself up to quite a despairing high. 'The song's out, they're famous already—we have no hold over them whatsoever!'

A deep voice speaks conversationally into her ear, making her jump.

'We haven't given them the money yet, Chandu mausi. We still hold that card. Relax.'

Chandu gives a little cry and turns around. Bonu, standing next to her, senses her pulse quicken. Blood rushes to her cheeks as she internalizes the fact that Samar is standing tall and steady and scruffy behind them, his arms folded across his chest.

'All this was *your* idea,' she mutters, eyes still on the dais, not bothering to look at him. '*You* only fix it now.'

'Oh I will,' he says calmly.

Appalled at how glad she is to see him, even in this desperate situation, she manages an unimpressed snort.

'Is the money in the bag?' Chandu mausi asks eagerly.

Samar nods. 'Yeah.'

He's looking very pleased with himself, Bonu notes, risking

a quick glance at him. Clearly the fact that his dumb song is a huge hit has gone to his head.

On stage, Mustaq has finally lumbered over to the mike, bent repeatedly in namastes and adaabs, and started to speak. He chooses to begin with a series of lateral questions.

'If anybody does discrimination against our brothers from the North-East, do you know what will happen?' he demands nasally of the crowd.

'No!' everybody shouts.

Mustaq gives a creepy grin, like a shami kebab showing its pink innards, rimmed with sharp little slivers of garlic.

'Mary Kom will give them one good box!'

Everybody applauds. The sound of extra-loud clapping and a familiar happy cackle causes Anjini to look around and she spots Chachiji in the corner seat of the second row. Chachiji waves, pink-cheeked with excitement, and gestures to some empty seats beside her.

'You'd better go sit with her, Ma,' Samar says. 'I'm going closer to the stage. It's imperative I establish eye-contact with the Trings.'

He settles his stepmother and aunts down beside Chachiji, depositing his rucksack at their feet. Then he strides ahead. Bonu follows him, grim-faced. If the Trings really have switched sides, it's imperative she establish eye-contact with them too.

Fifteen feet away from the podium, Samar stops suddenly. Bonu comes up against his back with a bump.

'Let's stop here,' he murmurs, his arm dropping around her shoulders. 'It's a good place to lurk.'

It *is* a good place to lurk. There is a trio of bamboo pillars around them, holding up the shamiana and obscuring them from the people on the dais. Bonu and Samar stick their necks out at a careful angle so that they can gaze accusingly at the Trings while staying hidden from Mustaq.

'Would you look at those honest, open faces,' Samar whispers. 'When will they look our way?'

'They're too ashamed to,' Bonu whispers back, resolutely resisting the urge to snuggle into his shoulder and cry out *I've missed you! I've missed you! Have coffee with me!*

They continue to stare at the Trings steadily. A good three minutes pass. Then,

'Whoa,' Samar breathes in sharply. 'Did Namgay Tring just wink at you?'

'I *think* so,' Bonu sounds uncertain. 'It's hard to tell of course, because you know, he could just be blinking—wait, he did it again!'

She clutches Samar's arm as she says this, and his hand instantly covers hers. She could be imagining it, but he seems very happy to be clutched.

'D'you think they're staring down at their phones to count the YouTube hits?'

She pulls her hand away. 'Hopefully, yes. And when the song hits ten lakhs, maybe they'll sneak out, pretending they have to go to the loo or something…good thing I've told the cabbies to be on standby down the road.'

Samar fishes out his phone, puts it on mute, and gets onto YouTube.

'Nine lakh eight hundred and sixty nine hits,' he murmurs.

'Not *enough*,' she whispers back.

Meanwhile on stage, Mustaq is still asking the audience questions.

'If anybody does discrimination against our brothers from the North-East, do you know what will happen?'

'No!' everybody shouts.

'Baichung Bhutia will give them one good kick!'

Everybody cheers.

Mustaq throws out his arms.

'Danny Denzongpa will take out their supari! Arnab Goswami will grill them! Irom Sharmila will stop their food and drink!'

The crowd roars with laughter.

'Haw, I didn't know Sharmila Tagore was a North-East,' Chachiji says cosily to Anjini. 'Waisey, this is so exciting, no? Like a mela. The rock band was too good! They played all the *Rock On* ke gaane, did you hear? Such a deep nice voice the singer had! But this Mustaq sounds like a mosquito bhinbhinaoing. Still, I toh feel so much for these poor chinkies and handicaps ki I can't tell you! You want chips?'

Her nieces say that no, they don't want chips.

Chachiji continues, munching, her good mood unaffected, 'Gulgul and AN think it will be a good thing if these chowkidars vacate. But I think ki it is too bad. You can't just throw people out of their homes like this! After so many years, too!'

'*You* clearly have no conscience pangs about throwing *us* out, Chachiji,' is Eshwari's sweet reply. 'You shouldn't be preaching to other people, you know.'

Chachiji draws back, hurt.

'All attitude, no gratitude,' she says resignedly, turning her attention back to the stage. 'Same story, every time! And this after I got them a place to sit!'

At that very moment, up in the front, Samar and Bonu hear it. Soty—as Samar's producer had called it—the Song Of The Year, a thumping, happy party track that, heard in this context, sends a chill down their backs and goosebumps up their arms.

Aur jee, aur jee, aur jee, aur jee!
Aur jee, aur jee, aur jee, aur jee!

'Fuck!' says Bonu. 'Why's that playing here?'

'Maybe it's just a coincidence,' he replies, scanning the crowd warily. 'It *is* the most popular thing on YouTube today.'

'Show off,' she mutters.

Luckily, Mustaq decides to crank up his act right then, and his yelling and the cheering from the crowd drown out the song.

'So do *not* take pangas with our mountain lions from the North-East!' he roars. 'Or you will regret all your life!'

The crowd explodes.

'Is not the winner of this year's *Indian Idol* a Nagalander? Is not the momo India's third most popular snack? Is not every beauty parlour and hair salon run by people from the North-East?'

Um, that's racial stereotyping, thinks Bonu as everybody cheers yet again. She looks uneasily around the shamiana—something is definitely brewing. There seems to be a lot of whispering and nudging, especially in the front row. Then she hears it again, louder this time.

Aur jee, aur jee, aur jee, aur jee!
Aur jee, aur jee, aur jee, aur jee!

'It's the kids,' Samar mutters. 'They've got the video playing on their phones. They're giggling and pointing, look!'

Bonu swallows and looks. Sure enough, the children from the Muskaan school are holding up a phone, bobbing to the beat of the song and grinning widely at the Trings.

'Is that you?' calls out one little kid, with hesitant cheekiness.

Bonu's blood turns to ice.

'Singing?' asks the one next to him, in a bolder voice.

'And *dancing* with the *nangi ladies!*' shrieks a third with eardrum-piercing glee.

All three of them giggle convulsively and collapse into a hiccupping little heap upon the ground.

The Trings try and look all lofty and above-it-all, but Bonu can tell that they're cracking. Shit shit shit.

Meanwhile, Mustaq, oblivious to this drama on the side, is ploughing on.

'Thirty years,' he says. 'Thirty long years, these two men have lived in the annexe of this house. They have married here, had children and grandchildren here. When they begged to be allowed to stay, do you know what the diabolical Thakurs, steeped in sin and debauchery, had the guts to say?'

'No!' roars the crowd.

'They said, "Send your pretty teenage granddaughters to warm our beds and you can stay!" Chhee!'

'What lies!' Bonu gasps. 'As if!'

'Not so loud,' Samar mutters. 'Frankly, I wouldn't put it past Ashok chacha.'

Aur jee, aur jee, aur jee, aur jee!
Aur jee, aur jee, aur jee, aur jee!

It's impossible not to hear it this time. Mustaq looks around, displeased.

'Please turn off your cell phones,' he frowns. 'This is very disrespectful to the peoples of the North-East.'

Bonu heaves a sigh of relief. But then,

'Is that them in the song?' the little kid who's got the song playing on his phone stands up and demands, his voice ringing clear as a bell.

Mustaq bends forward a little.

'What song?' he smiles, trying for fatherly playfulness and achieving coyly villainous.

Three Muskaan students struggle to their feet.

'*This* song!'

And Bonu feels her entire stomach heave as the first little kid limps up to the stage and hands the cell-phone to Mustaq Khan.

Mustaq feels about in his stiff white kurta, produces a pair of gold-rimmed spectacles, puts them on and squints down at the phone. An ominous hush falls over the crowd.

Shit, Bonu thinks. Shit shit *shit*.

Then Mustaq gives a dismissive snort and hands the phone back to the kid.

'Of course that isn't them,' he says, jerking his head contemptuously towards the Trings. 'Those are obviously some famous Farsi qawwals, some trained artistes. These fellows are just chowkidars. Now sit down and don't interrupt me again.'

As Bonu and Samar collapse in relieved disbelief, Mustaq returns to his speech, working himself up to a frothy, high-pitched climax.

'Brothers and sisters and friends of the North-East, I appeal to all of you!'

'And we're at nine lakh ninety nine thousand and ninety,' mutters Samar. 'Almost there. Let's hope they just walk out quietly at ten.'

'And to all you Indians—Punjabis, UP-ites or Haryanvis! We have to stop this discrimination! This greed! This flouting of basic human rights, this denial of dignity...we have to decide...'

'Ninety-nine...'

'That we will *not* be crushed...'

'*Ten*,' Samar says softly.

And Bonu hears a phantom temple bell ring a loud, sonorous *dingggg* inside her head.

On the podium, Namgay Tring and Biren Tring put away their phones and get to their feet in one smooth, synchronized move.

'Oh good,' Bonu almost wilts in relief. 'They're coming down! Thank *goodness* they're finally coming down! We'll whisk them away to the cabs and then they can fly off to—what the *fuck?*'

Because, instead of discreetly walking off the dais, the brothers have limped up to the mic and wrested it from Mustaq Khan's nerveless fingers. A confused hush falls over the gathered crowd.

'Chupp, behenchod,' says Namgay Tring in a magnified voice, very lucidly and without heat. 'Be quiet, you ugly little toad. Thirty years we've worked for you and you damn-cared about us.'

'Haw!' says Chachiji, clapping a hand over her open mouth.

She isn't alone. The entire audience joins her in a collective gasp.

Namgay Tring changes gear, going from mild to militant in one sentence flat.

'Not a bonus on Diwali, not a mithai-ka-dabba on Eid, not a holiday on 15th August! Human *rights* ki baat karta hai!'

'Haw *ji*,' says Chachiji decidedly. 'This is toh very bad. But these Muslims are like this only.'

The crowd has started to murmur. Mustaq gestures agitatedly to the organizers at the back of the shamiana to cut the sound on the mics. They get to their feet at once, but the beefy drummer and burly keyboardist envelop them in restraining hugs.

'Freedom of speech, bro,' they say, grinning widely. 'Let the dude have his say.'

'Talks about non-discrimination!' shouts Biren Tring

hoarsely, limping closer to the mic and pushing away his brother. 'This is the same man who told us, when we were children, that God gave us flat faces so everybody could step on us!' He draws a long breath and lets a big gob of spittle fly across the dais. 'I *thooo* upon you!'

The crowd lets out a loud hostile hiss. In reaction, Mustaq's thugs get to their feet, hands balling warningly into fists.

Samar pulls Bonu closer.

'Holy crap.' His voice is grim. 'Bones, you need to get out of here pronto. This sitch is spiralling totally out of control.'

'We need to get those morons out of here pronto,' she replies. 'Or they'll get themselves killed.'

'I'll handle all that,' he says tersely. 'Go *now.*'

Her chin shoots up.

'But—'

'Get the mausis and my mom. And Chachiji. Do it now.'

He gives her a light shove in the relevant direction. Shooting him a mutinous look, she obeys, just as the lead singer from the rock band jumps forward, arms raised.

'Mustaaaaaq Khan…?' he shouts.

His band smoothly provides backing vocals. 'Hai hai!'

'Mustaq Khan?'

'Hai hai!'

Samar bends down towards the Muskaan school kids.

'You guys should leave,' he tells them. 'Make an orderly line. Hold each other's hands. Now, forward march.'

The children obey, but not without reluctance. After all, things are just starting to get exciting. They dawdle, holding hands, their eyes wide and delighted.

'You damn-care about the handicapped!' shouts Biren Tring. ''You damn-care about North-East! You damn-care about SC-ST! You only care about money!'

The children applaud this filmi sentiment.

'That *is* us in the video!' shouts Namgay Tring, capering about wildly. '*We're* the Farsi qawwals in the video! Here's a video of us with Zeeshan Khan! Here's a photo of our make-up being done! Here's a selfie of us and the exotic dancers! Look! Look!'

'Okay, that's it,' Samar growls and makes for the stage, moving fast—but not as fast as Mustaq's thugs. The Muskaan children trip the thugs up, however, and they fall, snarling and muttering curses, onto the muddy ground, and Samar makes it to the podium before them. Grabbing the Trings by the scruff of their fancy coats, he starts to hustle them towards the exit. The brothers, drunk and feisty, wriggle away and run back into the heart of the melee. Feeling like he is caught inside a nightmare, Samar realizes that both of them are laughing. And joyously singing.

Aur jee, aur jee, aur jee, aur jee!
Aur jee, aur jee, aur jee, aur jee!

Meanwhile Bonu has reached her aunts. They're on their feet, their expressions worried, looking oddly vulnerable.

'Come on, mausis, let's go,' she tells them. 'This place is gonna explode.'

'But Samar?' Anjini's voice is high and thready.

They all turn to look for Samar. The milling crowd clears for just a moment and they spot him upon the dais, standing protectively in front of the Trings, grinning and bouncing on the balls of his feet. His nose is bloody and his eyes are sparkling with what looks suspiciously like pure enjoyment.

'Come on, you bastards!' he is yelling. 'Bring it on.'

'Hai dekho toh,' says Chachiji, delighted. 'Poora Thakur nikla! Fighting, shouting, doing so much gunda-gardi. Who would have thought? With that boring banker for a father, always acting so khandaani!'

'Samar will be fine,' Bonu says firmly. 'Let's get out—you too, Chachiji!'

As they rush hand in hand towards the exit, Bonu turns back to see that Mustaq has grabbed hold of a mic.

'They've sold out,' he cries in a high, thin voice, pointing a shaky finger at the Brothers Tring. 'Betrayed the cause! Deserted the fight to be in a cheap item song!'

'It is *not* a cheap item song,' bellows Namgay Tring, hurtling past Samar towards Mustaq, waving a broken Pepsi bottle. 'It is a *party* song!'

A thug leaps forward to protect his master and Namgay crumples, a look of comical surprise on his wizened face. As Bonu watches, sickened, Samar scoops up the tiny pahadi by the collar and starts to run with him towards the shamiana exit.

'Here, here!' Bonu hears Anjini's voice over the cacophony. She's riding shotgun in a Meru cab, honking the horn so hard that several grappling people wince, turn around and exclaim in protest. Dragging Namgay Tring, who is still shouting and cursing, behind him like a sack of potatoes, Samar lurches towards the cab and throws him unceremoniously into the backseat. Then he whirls around, his eyes searching the tottering shamiana for Biren.

'There he is!' Bonu shouts, scampering across the crumpled carpet, thick with children, and attaching herself limpet-like to two thugs who have bundled up Biren and are carrying him away. 'They're trying to get away with him! I *told* you this would happen, Samar, you bastard…I told y—*Help!*'

The men shake her off and she tumbles to the ground, hitting her side against a shamiana pole, hard. When she sits up, winded and in pain, she discovers that Samar is already on the spot. He is no longer looking like he is enjoying himself— he is looking very, very annoyed.

There are more than seven men around Biren Tring now. They're holding him up by the scruff of his neck, while his feet dangle a good ten inches off the ground. The plucky pahadi is still taunting them, though.

'It *is* me in the video!' he gloats, his face sweaty and triumphant. 'It's me, you losers! What have *you* done with your life that's half as cool, huh? Yaaaaah!'

Bonu, sick to the stomach with fear, sees Mustaq walk slowly towards the gamely struggling pahadi, his meaty hands bunching into fists...

She sees Samar sizing up the seven thugs, his eyes narrowed to slits...

Then she sees a streak of banana yellow robes and registers somebody taking a flying leap over her prone body.

'The money, the money, the money!' Chandu is panting and half-sobbing under her breath. She trips on her robes and falls hard on the dusty ground, then raises her chin and screams loudly, 'Samarrr, we forgot your *rucksack*! Your bag! *We need...the...bag!*'

Everybody—the captured Biren Tring, the thugs holding him, Mustaq, who is getting ready to clobber him, Samar who's wondering how to stop this from happening—turns to look at the innocuous-looking rucksack, lying bulky and half-obscured beneath the tumbled seats the aunts had been sitting on.

'What's in the bag?' a thug demands, his voice rough, his eyes darting from the bag to Chandu and back.

Chandu, in an agony of tension, lying on the ground with her face all screwed up, opens her mouth, then shuts it abruptly.

Everybody's eyes swivel back to the bag again.

And then Bonu has a bright, blindingly brilliant idea.

She sits up, sucks in as much air as she possibly can, and screams, her voice exquisitely high-pitched and blood-curdling, her finger pointing straight at Samar's rucksack.

'Bomb! Bag mein bomb hai! Bhaago! *Bhaaaaago!*'

Samar goes to bed very late that night. After Bonu's scream emptied the shamiana, he'd scooped up Biren, chucked him into the cab with his brother, driven to the airport with a cavalcade of four taxis, bought McDonald's Happy Meals for all the Trings and deposited the one crore in cash, not into the old men's hands, but into the calloused palms of their soft-spoken, steely-eyed wives. These ladies had immediately vanished into the loo, divvied the money into smaller bundles, and neatly tucked it away into the various cabin bags of the family of seventeen.

Samar had hung around outside the washroom with the menfolk, who had apologized profusely for their extempore abuse of Mustaq at his own dharna.

'We were planning to leave quietly, chup chaap and shanti-se, but the blood rushed into our heads when he said it wasn't us in the party song, Samar bhaiyya. It was too much insult. We couldn't control.'

Samar had feelingly advised them to please control now, get to their village and lie low for the next twenty years. Then he promised a break to one particularly pretty Tring child who wanted to be an actress one day, a recommendation letter to another, who was applying to Columbia University, kissed everybody soundly and watched them clear immigration. Only after he had seen their plane take off had he hailed a cab and made his way back home.

The next morning, he wakes up late, but finds that there are still birds calling sweetly to one another in the garden. Recollecting the happenings of the previous day, he smiles. And then he winces as the movement causes his bruises to crinkle and twinge. Fingering them gingerly, he gets out of bed.

He has a spectacular black eye, he discovers, and a cut on his jaw. There's not much point shaving, so he just washes his face with cold water and emerges onto the verandah.

Here, he finds that the bird cries in BJ's garden have gotten even louder. Or are they bird cries at all? They seem more guttural and less musical. Perhaps it is a chaat wallah, he muses, or those quaint vendors who go through the city streets asking people to get their names engraved into steel utensils. Or a Rajasthani puppet show, the kind that used to come around when Monu and Bonu and he were kids, and set up a bright tinsel stage in the shade of the back wall. How deliciously old world! Pleasantly relaxed and with not much to do, he strolls outside to investigate.

The first thing he sees is a line-up of expensive cars parked higgledy-piggledy in the back lane. And the first thing he hears is a hoarse voice shouting *Laylo Laylo Laylo Laylo!* Turning the corner, he sees women of every age huddled around a little stall as bright and smart as new paint. They are looking at a large suspended LCD TV on which *Aur Jee* is playing in a loop. In front of it stands a black mannequin wearing a very familiar Benarasi ghagra and bralette. *Get your Aur Jee costume here!* screams a glittery banner in purple and green. The women are examining the outfit, tut-tutting at the price and demanding it in various sizes.

'Replicated from the virginal garment in the song, maidumb!' Samar hears Daulat Master say.

'It's a copy,' one snooty lady, standing at the head of the line with her daughter in tow, sniffs fastidiously. 'Not from the designer's house.'

Daulat Master smiles tolerantly. 'Call it what you like, maidumbji. The fact is, it is out and available! The dejainer will not be able to get it into the market for another month at least! And I know, maidumbji, you can afford dejainer prices, you have everything-God-can-give, but do you really want to wait that long? Be trendy, be now, wear it today! It is same-to-same as the garment in the phillum, with two zeros knocked off the price! And when your bitiya wears it, it will look hundurd percent virginal!'

The daughter glows, the mother looks hesitant.

Daulat makes a weird, revving-up sound inside his sternum, throws out his chest and bellows:

'*Laylo Laylo Laylo Laylo! Three* thoujend! Three *thoujend! Three thoujend!*'

'In one wash the material will go,' murmurs the snooty lady undecidedly.

Daulat Master's expression grows extremely superior. 'Mai-*dumb*, who washes Benarasi? Only dry-clean! You also na, saying such silly things! Achha, do you want me to give bitiya the extra-small or small? In green, purple or red?'

'Three thousand is too much for a fake,' the snooty lady declares. But her voice is uncertain.

Daulat Master pushes back his straggly hair with great shaan, rests his hands on his hips and says, in quite a different tone from the one he's been using so far. 'You want or you don't want?'

'We want,' the lady's daughter, a pretty young thing of about seventeen, says immediately. 'Mom, c'mon, it's a steal.'

It *is* a steal, Samar thinks grimly as he turns on his heel and goes in search of that little snake, Bonu Singh.

He finds her up in her lair, looking half-asleep, reading the papers in bed and sipping chai. She looks up when she sees him, and makes a face.

'God, you look foul.'

So much for sympathy. Not that he's come looking for it.

'What the hell do you mean ripping off the costumes of my song and selling them in the back lane for three thousand each?' he demands.

She looks blank for a moment, then sits backs comfortably, her hands going up languidly to knot and skewer her hair into place. Narrowing her bold black eyes and looking alarmingly warrior-like, she says, 'So what?'

'So *what*?' Samar is livid. 'You claim to be so worried about the Trings but they're not the reason you came to Bombay, are they? You came to spy on my shoot and rip off the outfits so you could sell fakes and make money.'

Her mobile face goes from confused to slightly shame-faced to completely sure of herself in the space of under two minutes.

'No, that isn't why I came to Bombay—but yes, once I was there, I thought it was a good work op, so I took it.'

He throws up his hands.

'And *that* didn't endanger the Trings?'

'No,' she shakes her head firmly. 'I had no intention of selling the outfits until they'd left—and Daulat and my ladies are trained to keep absolutely mum about these things.'

Samar stares at her. 'How can you be so brazen? Don't you have *any* kind of moral compass? What you're doing is piracy, plain and simple.'

'Actually it isn't,' she manages to say calmly. 'What I'm doing is perfectly legal. I'm selling a quality garment, painstakingly stitched with attention to every detail, and priced reasonably. What's wrong with that?'

'You're a cheat!'

She throws down her newspapers and leaps to her feet.

'Who the hell are you to be so judgy? Especially after I practically saved your life yesterday! You would've been bludgeoned to death by Mustaq's thugs if I hadn't yelled about a bomb in the bag and cleared the shamiana in three minutes flat!'

'That's a gross exaggeration,' he says steadily. 'I would've got Biren out somehow. Besides, the fact remains that you're a cheat.'

'I am *not* a cheat. If anybody is a cheat, it's your precious girlfriend.'

'What do you mean?' His voice is icy.

Bonu looks shifty.

'Nothing, let it go,' she mutters.

'Tell me!' He grabs her by the wrist and shakes her. The Natraj pencil slips out of her hair.

'Fine,' she says, snatching her wrist back. 'I didn't want to tell you this, but whatever. The truth is that your girlfriend claims the Benarasi she used in the song costs five thousand rupees a metre. Well, it *doesn't*. I know about Benarasi too and that stuff costs eighteen hundred a metre tops. But she billed that fat man five thousand rupees a metre for it. *That's* cheating.'

There is a long, stunned silence.

'Unbelievable,' says Samar, very white about the mouth. 'You are clearly unable to tell the difference between ripping off somebody's creative design and charging a middleman's fee for sourcing genuine material. Making accusations like that just makes you look foolish.'

'*You're* the fool.'

'She uses genuine Benarasi to help the weavers preserve their art.'

'How?' she snorts. 'She pays them eighteen hundred and pockets three thousand two hundred per metre. That's helpful?'

There's some logic to this. Twisted, Bonu-style logic, of course, but she does have a point. He disregards it.

'And you, of course, share all your profits with your people?'

'Yes!' she blazes. 'I *do!*'

Saying which she blinks hard, and then lunges forward and tries to shut the door in his face.

But he stops her.

'Hold on.'

She folds her arms across her chest, sighs and looks martyred. 'Okay, finish your little rant.'

'I want you to shut down that illegal racket at the back of the house, right *now.*'

'Balls, I will!' Bonu returns defiantly and slams the door in his face.

The Thakur sisters, blissfully oblivious of all this warring upstairs, call a family meeting after breakfast to celebrate the successful execution of the Tring Solution.

'Welcome, welcome!' Eshwari beams as Bonu enters the flowered drawing room. 'Brilliant job yesterday, you kids—and Chandu too, you guys were great!'

Chandu mausi smiles smugly. She has spent the morning

moving her things into the vacated annexe. It is now full of RIGID paraphernalia, mysterious looking crystals and the scent of burnt lavender, with transcendental music playing full blast (to purge the area of any lingering spirits that flourished under the heathen regime).

'I was the only one who remembered the rucksack,' she says proudly. 'Everybody else forgot.'

Because there was money in it, the rest of the sisters think in a moment of perfectly synchronized thought.

'And Mustaq is safely routed,' Anjini says with great satisfaction. 'Paperwallah says he has no *locus standi* whatsoever! It's been quite a coup—and thankfully bloodless too!'

'One down, two to go,' murmurs Chandu with a sly glance at Bonu Singh, who stiffens immediately.

'We'll get to those later,' Eshwari says quickly. 'Let's just be happy for now!' She looks around the little gathering. 'How should we celebrate? Go out for lunch someplace?'

'I'm not in the mood, thanks,' Bonu says, her tone subdued.

'Arrey!' Anjini looks concerned. 'What's up? And you Samar, why're you so quiet? Are you in pain?'

Samar, who has been touching his various bruises gingerly, looks up. 'No, I'm okay—they look more spectacular than they are, actually.'

'Like you,' mutters Bonu so softly that everybody almost doesn't hear her.

So the children are squabbling again, Eshwari thinks, irritated. I wish they'd just sort out their issues or their stupid hormones will run amuck and ruin the house sale for all of us.

'C'mon kids,' she cajoles them. 'That was quite a family triumph, wasn't it?'

Chandu nods, but from the other two all she gets is that weird silence. Anjini changes tack.

'Achha, so we'll get to Bonu Singh's selling or not selling later. On the Ashok front, Paperwallah has warned us that Ashok may try to seduce away more witnesses to testify for him, like he did with Lachhu. So we need to keep our eyes and ears open, okay?'

'Okay,' says Samar perfunctorily, his mind clearly elsewhere.

Bonu murmurs something noncommittal. Chandu leans in and pokes her hard between the ribs with bony fingers.

'We're talking to *you*.'

'Hmmm?' Bonu looks around, eyes vague. 'What, Chandu mausi?'

'Your loyalties lie with *us*. Not with your uncle or your cousin.'

Bonu hears her this time. Her vivid brows snap together at once, and she sits up, hair whipping about everywhere.

'*Why would you say that?*'

Samar looks much more attentive now, Eshwari can't help but notice sourly. Poor fool, he's clearly infatuated.

'Calm down, kiddo,' Eshwari says quickly.

'You're questioning my loyalties?' Bonu's voice is soft and stunned.

'Yes,' Chandu nods doggedly. 'I've seen you—hobnobbing with Ashok chacha. Your mother was the same.'

'Matlab?'

Eshu looks uncomfortable. 'Look, Bones, it's just that…we've noticed—couldn't help noticing, actually—that you've been spending helluva lot of time with Ashok chacha, and that's a little weird, given the sitch…so, you know, we were wondering…'

'I had been spending time with him *because*—' Bonu starts to say hotly, then she stops short. She had been spending time with slimy, mind-fucking Ashok chacha because of Samar, that ungrateful, incompetent *ass*. She had been spending time with *all* the people on this road who were alive in that decade, for heaven's sake, and it had been boring, time-consuming and thankless. She'd been worrying about Samar's so-called 'falling apart' and the state of his mind and his stupid movie, while he'd been busy putting her friends' lives in jeopardy and labelling her a cheat.

For a moment, she can't speak—she needs all her faculties to get her body to stop trembling. She is furious, she realizes, as she gets to her feet with a musical jingle, a tall girl with dark, flowing hair and a strong, dignified stance.

'I can't be on the same team as this asshole.'

Samar doesn't react. Anjini looks bewildered, Chandu gives an enigmatic little smile, while Eshu sits forward.

'*Which* asshole?'

A furious gesticulation, accompanied by the jangling of silver bangles, clears this up.

'Now, look here, young woman,' Anjini instantly sits up to defend her boy. 'What did Samar do except save the day, huh?'

'Yeah man, what's the connection?'

Bonu raises her chin.

'I said I can't be in the same team as this asshole. I told him Mustaq was dangerous, I told him this wasn't a movie set where he had full control, I told him they shouldn't appear in any newspapers. He is over-smart, over-confident and he almost got the Trings killed yesterday. That might be just collateral damage to him and to the rest of you people, but the Trings are my *friends*, practically my family.'

'That's a bit of an exaggeration,' Anjini bridles. 'Samar was quite in control.'

'*We're* your family.' Chandu's voice is sharp.

'Everything would've gone *fine*,' Samar speaks at last, his voice dangerously mild, 'if your darling pahadis hadn't decided to make an extempore speech, abusing their employer from the freaking podium. I hadn't bargained for *that*.'

Besides, you're a cheat. And an opportunist.

He doesn't say this out loud but she can see it in his eyes. She totally can.

'Bones, look at his bruises,' Eshwari says reasonably. 'He got the worst of it—and he paid all the money also…'

'I don't *care!*' Bonu's voice is at the edge of hysteria. She takes a deep breath and says, her tone calmer, 'Look, I promised to help you guys get the Trings out, and I have—but I'm getting off board now.'

'What?'

Bonu nods vigorously.

'I'm just not used to so much…*family*.'

The last word comes out like it's a dirty word. Her aunts flinch. Bonu doesn't notice.

'Besides, I don't agree with you on everything. Please don't take it for granted that I'll side with you in the rest of the dispute.'

There is a shocked silence.

'Are you threatening us?' Chandu asks.

Bonu shrugs. 'Think what you like.'

'Oh, you're such a little brat!' Eshwari springs to her feet, her patience snapping. 'Self-centred, contrary, and always wanting to be the centre of attention. Well, I'm done tiptoeing around your orphaned little feelings. You're grown-up now and though I'm *sorry* for sniggering at your dad, *really really* sorry, please remember that I was just seventeen when I did that, and my head was full of stupid romantic notions of what a man should be! I wouldn't snigger at him now, perhaps, now that I'm older and wiser...' She lapses into silence for a moment, then takes a long breath and continues, 'But that is totally beside the point. The point is that *you*, Bonu Bloody Singh, are going to pull together as family, *irrespective* of whether Samar is an asshole or not. You're going to sign the damn papers and sell your share of the house and get the same money as the rest of us, even if I have to drag you down there myself physically!'

'Eshu, please,' says Chandu, licking her lips and looking rather thrilled at these theatrics.

'Oh, *you* butt out!' Eshwari returns rudely. 'Bonita, are you in or out?'

But Bonu is busy listening to a song in her head. A golden oldie that she hasn't heard for a while, that she'd even started to consider overrated, but suddenly, all at once, she realizes afresh that it is evergreen, a classic, and its lyrics make so much sense.

I'll make them squirm like well-salted earthworms.

I won't sell. Even my jutti won't sell.

And if I die na, then even my gosht won't sell.

Her nostrils flare.

'I'm out,' she says, and suiting her actions to her words, gets up and leaves the room.

'I just don't know what to do about that kid,' sighs Eshwari the next afternoon. Anjini, Chandu and she are huddled around the desk at Shahrukh Paperwallah's office, and Debjani has joined them on a conference call. 'She drives me crazy.'

'You were too harsh on her, Eshu,' Dabbu says, distressed. 'She's had a pretty messed-up life, mostly thanks to all of us—

and she must be still missing BJ, and clearly, she's got feelings for Samar.'

'*You* come and handle everything then!' Eshu snaps. 'I want to push the sale through before Akshaya Tritiya! Then maybe we can all get our lives back!'

'Stop shouting, Eshu, we all want our lives back,' Anjini says testily. 'That's why we've called this meeting. I, too, have to get back to Allahabad tonight. Mr Paperwallah, do something!'

Paperwallah's strategy for the moment, however, seems to be to let them all talk.

'Uh, well, from what I can tell, Anji didi,' Dabbu ventures, 'it's *your* boy who is seriously complicating the mix.'

'Haan, it's too upsetting,' Anjini says, with slightly smug exasperation. 'Girls can't help themselves when he's around—he's so attractive, he gets that from me.'

Eshwari closes her eyes. My family is nuts, she thinks resignedly.

'Yeah, well, tell him to turn up the charm quotient,' she says shortly.

Chandu sniffs a superior little sniff.

'Oh, granted your *adopted* son is a bit of a hit with the ladies, Anjini,' she says maliciously. 'But I think we may be overestimating his attractions here...'

Anjini scowls at her. 'Meaning?'

'Meaning that, Mr Paperwallah, we haven't told you the most important thing yet!' Chandu leans in, her pale, lashless eyes glinting. 'Binni's daughter *threatened* us yesterday.'

'She did?' Eshu asks, looking at her with distaste. 'When?'

'That last sentence she said.' Chandu leans in closer to the listening lawyer, and assumes a 'Bonu' voice. '"Besides, I don't agree with you on everything. Please don't take it for granted that I'll side with you in the rest of the dispute." *Those* words.'

'So?' Eshu looks blank.

Chandu looks at her pityingly.

'What could that mean?' Anjini asks, her voice sharp.

Shahrukh clears his throat. 'I think the concern is that your niece was trying to convey that she might side with your uncle in this dispute.'

'Okay, that's a little far-fetched,' Eshwari shakes her head. 'I really don't think she would.'

'Impossible!' says Anjini. 'She's our niece! BJ's grand-daughter.'

'Yeah, but she's lived next door to them for years, guys, and Gulgul and she are really close,' Dabbu points out. 'We can't assume it's not even a *possibility* that she may throw in her lot with them.'

'Of course she will,' Chandu nods decisively. 'She's really money-minded. She asked me for money for getting clothes stitched in her unit, imagine.'

'She did?' Eshu sounds surprised.

'Let us keep the discussion focused, please!' Shahrukh Paperwallah speaks up. 'In fact, your remarks about your niece bring me to my next point. My team has been digging around and they've heard rumours that Uncle Ashok's witness at the next hearing is going to be Bonita Singh Rajawat.'

Utter consternation around the table.

'What!'

'I *knew* it!'

'That can't be true!'

Shahrukh nods. 'And if she says what we think she'll be paid to say, she could upset our entire case.'

'But this is horrible!' Dabbu's voice is anguished. 'How could we have alienated her so much?'

'It's that Samar,' Chandu says, her tone self-satisfied. 'That—and the greediness of her father, which she's clearly inherited.'

Paperwallah shoots a keen glance at Anjini.

'Your, er, *son*, Ms Anjini, whom she is so upset with—could he not persuade her to, ah, *desist*?'

'Oh, yes!' Anjini says confidently. 'I'll get him to charm her...'

'Anji didi, sorry, but I think it's gone beyond that now,' Eshwari says frankly. 'She was looking at Samar like he was some sort of smelly worm.'

'In *that* case,' the lawyer says delicately, 'I think we may have to move swiftly, and make arrangements to silence her somehow.'

'You mean buy her off?' Dabbu asks knowledgeably. 'I doubt that'll work.'

'Oh no,' Shahrukh Paperwallah shakes his head. 'I don't mean buy her off, Ms Debjani. She is too vital a witness for us to risk something like that—the Judge's own grandchild, a beautiful orphan who loved him and who looked after him in his dotage. I mean quieten her somehow. Intimidate her. Teach her a little lesson. Get her to behave, as it were.'

There is silence.

Then Eshwari says, her tone dangerously mild, 'Uh, could you please explain more *fully*, Mr Paperwallah?'

13

Thakur Saab based on Director's great-grandfather's marriage, which ended in murder

Thakur Saab, one of the year's most anticipated films, set to release on 15th August weekend, is auto-biographical! The tender love story is based on the true life relationship between writer/director Samar Vir Singh's maternal great-grandfather and his wife. They belonged to a big zamindar family of UP and New Delhi and owned a string of bungalows on New Delhi's Hailey Road.

Before you say awww, so sweet, listen to this!

The reason why there has been so much bad blood between the director, the film's lead actor, and the production house Sonix is because when Singh wrote the film, he was under the impression that his great-grandparents, though mismatched in every way, had genuinely loved each other.

But evidence he came across recently has revealed that the couple were estranged and that his great-grandfather had actively been involved in his wife's murder!

A deeply upset Samar Vir Singh wanted to scrap the project but Sonix nixed that idea, saying too much money had been spent and the release was non-negotiable. Singh then asked to make some changes in the edit, but this request too was denied.

Our source, who works at the studio where the film is being edited, has been privy to several extremely ugly spats between producer and director.

Meanwhile, our independent investigation has revealed that Samar Vir Singh's family is locked in a nasty property dispute with his grand-uncle, who alleges that Singh's great-grandmother (on whom Preetali Shah's character in *Thakur Saab* is based) was already pregnant when she married his great-grandfather and therefore none of her elder son's heirs, including Samar Vir Singh) has a right to a share in his Rs 200 crore property on Hailey Road.

We contacted all concerned parties but they refused to comment. However, several industry insiders were quick to dismiss these reports.

'It's the oldest trick in the book. When a film is about to release, producers create a controversy around it and earn millions from the free publicity. This is all rubbish, *Thakur Saab* isn't based on anybody's great-grandfather. Shame on you for falling for such an obvious ploy.'

Naturally, everyone in the family has about forty fits each. Even Ashok shows up, waving his fists, roaring threats and vowing that he will get a stay order on this vile movie based on his father-mother's marriage, while at the same time hinting softly out of the side of his mouth that if Sonix pays him off, he might relent.

Samar deals with Pushkar's loyal son by picking him up bodily in a fireman's lift and depositing him (albeit with great gentleness) outside the green gate of number 16. The brawl with Mustaq's thugs has really revived my inner Thakur, he muses as he strides back to the house afterwards, dusting off his hands, quite satisfied with himself. Pushkar's granddaughters are harder to deal with, their reactions ranging from rhapsodizing (Anjini) to horrified (Dabbu). Samar deals with this by moving back into The Imperial and ducking all their calls after one terse sms advising them to speak to *nobody* and give *no* quotes on the matter.

And of course, Pushkar's eldest great-granddaughter's reaction is one he doesn't need to worry about, as she isn't speaking to him.

For the last two days, Bonu can't shake off the feeling that she is being watched. The house is so empty now, with even Anji mausi having left, but as she goes about her daily routine—her morning workout, her briefing sessions with her tailors, her excursions to the fabric markets—she feels a sinister presence breathing practically behind her.

You're getting paranoid, she tells herself sternly. So many people have died on you, you think you're haunted.

At night, as she is brushing her teeth, she fights the illogical conviction that there is somebody lurking behind the window, hanging off the sewage pipes and watching her bathe. It's just because Namgay Tring and Biren Tring are no longer here, she tells herself. They made me feel safe. But it *is* safe here. This is Hailey Road for God's sake, not some unsafe slum on the fringes of the city!

It is only when she finds herself sitting bolt upright in her bed in the middle of the night, jerked into total wakefulness by the sound of a smothered cough barely ten feet away, that she starts to take the stalker seriously.

There really *is* somebody out there, clinging to the bougainvillea or hanging off the drainpipes—but what can Bonu do about it?

Not being on speaking terms with anybody at number 16, she has no option but to confide once more in Gulgul mama.

'Somebody's following me around,' she tells him the next day. 'Should I complain to the police?'

Gulgul is most upset.

'You are a beautiful girl living all alone, Bonu bitiya!' he tells her. 'Be careful!'

Feeling far bolder in the brightly lit sunshine than she had in the gloom of the night, Bonu manages to laugh airily.

'Arrey nahi nahi, it was probably just indigestion,' she dismisses it. 'Who would want to harm me?'

'Definitely not us,' Gulgul replies smilingly. 'Especially as you've agreed to testify in court on our behalf!'

There is a questioning tone to this statement that makes Bonu feel uncomfortable.

'Er, yes, about that,' she replies. 'I'm still not hundred percent sure I'll be doing that, okay?'

'Okay, okay,' he smiles placatingly. 'Don't worry. Take your time.'

She smiles gratefully, but wonders, was he trying to hint that if somebody wanted her out of the way, it definitely wasn't him? Matlab, it was…*who*?

She spends the rest of the day dithering about undecidedly, and as night approaches, finds she doesn't have the stomach to sleep in her own bedroom. Grabbing her pillow and blanket, she stalks down the stairs and into the flowered drawing room.

'The light's gone upstairs,' she lies to the taken-aback Eshwari. 'I'm sleeping here.'

'*Whatever*, Queen of Sheba,' mutters Eshwari, flicking off the TV and walking out of the room like it's infested with rats. Bonu spends a restless night tossing upon the couch, having unwelcome memory flashes of the night BJ died, and how she and Samar had shared the couch.

She sleeps fitfully and wakes up cranky and claustrophobic. As she staggers upstairs to her bathroom, her phone rings.

'Hullo?'

'Bonu bitiya?' Old Mr Gambhir's voice, always high and musical, has become flute-like in extreme old age. 'Haan, that lady I had mentioned to you, she has come. Her train leaves in two hours time—come and see her *now*.'

Oh God. Bonu rubs her gummy eyes.

'Hullo?'

'Yes, hullo, Gambhir uncle. Uh, could I possibly meet her later?'

'No no *no!*' he warbles forcefully. 'She has to leave soon— and she seldom comes to Dilli. And at our age, bitiya, who knows, hain? Better to meet when you have the chance.'

Why are old people always so bossy?

Bonu sighs.

'Okay, fine, gimme twenty minutes. I'll just—'

'Her train leaves in two hours,' he repeats and hangs up.

Whatever. Twenty minutes later, clad in a loose t-shirt and grey shorts, Bonu walks down the driveway and out onto Hailey Road. It is a hot, still morning, but bearable at this hour.

The street mongrels escort her as she jogs down the road, admiring the way the morning sunlight streams through the bright yellow chandeliers of the amaltas flowers.

And then she hears it.

Thapp thapp thapp. Footsteps behind her, walking at her pace, slowing down when she slows down, speeding up when she speeds up. She stops and stoops to tighten her shoelaces. Silence. She starts to run again, faster this time. Behind her, the footsteps speed up.

She stops. The footsteps stop too. Taking a deep breath, she spreads her arms wide, and under the pretext of doing torso twists, turns to look at the road behind her. And sees him.

A tall, wide figure in a black tracksuit, hoodie pulled low, lurking behind the trunk of an amaltas tree.

Fully freaked out now, her heart thumping hard, Bonu veers off the road and runs into the gate of Agrasen ki Baoli. Her plan is to cut across to the next street, which should be more crowded, and enter Gambhir's from the other side.

She hasn't run more than ten metres before she sees him again, in front of her this time. The man in the black tracksuit. She can make out his face now—he has a beard and blood-shot eyes, and one of his shoulders seems higher than the other. As their eyes make contact, he raises one arm and the knife in his hand glints as it catches the rays of the rising sun.

'Fuck!' Bonu gasps, whirling around to run the other way. Black Tracksuit lets out a hoarse yell and gives chase. She can tell from the sound of his footsteps that he's gaining in on her. And then she can smell his breath. He smells of sweat and alcohol and raw onions and wet earth. She screams, a shrill wordless scream, desperately trying to run faster but unable to. Her lungs are bursting, her every muscle is trembling and she is afraid, more afraid than she's ever been in her life.

Black Tracksuit's hand closes on the collar of her t-shirt. She yelps, and as he spins her around, she rams her knee hard into his crotch.

But he is too quick for her. The flat of his hand, cold and calloused, slams straight into her face, jerking her back and almost snapping her neck. With his other hand he twists her around, and then his knife is at her throat.

'I'm going to kill you now,' he says, his voice hot and hoarse in her ear. 'Remember whichever God you believe in.'

Bonu struggles against him, tears of pain and bewilderment spurting from her eyes. 'I can give you money!' she gasps. 'More money than they are giving you! Let me *go*!'

He twists her hair, wrenching hard, making her cry out in pain. He clearly has practice doing this kind of thing. The knife breaks through her skin. 'Pray!'

Bonu almost gagging, continues to struggle...blood rushes to her head...her vision starts to go black...

And then the grip around her neck loosens, and miraculously, she is free.

She staggers backward and sinks to the ground on her hands and knees, coughing weakly.

When she finally looks up, Black Tracksuit is being hit in the stomach, repeatedly and very precisely. The face of the man who is doing the hitting is set in hard lines. His eyes are blazing. Black Tracksuit starts to droop, grunting with every blow, but his assailant still doesn't stop.

'Would...you...please...stop *beating* up people?' Bonu chokes out, her voice raw and ravaged. 'I think he's pretty much done in, anyway.'

The blazing look goes out of Samar's eyes. He lets Black Tracksuit drop and turns to her, but right then, Gulgul rushes up, his bouffant hair bouncing in pretty agitation.

Samar stops.

'Bonu beta!' Gulgul gasps, dropping down on his knees by her side. 'Are you okay?'

She nods weakly. 'Yuh...yes.'

'Tum theek ho? Bonu! Speak to me!'

Her lashes flutter open.

'I spoke already,' she points out.

Standing over the felled stalker, Samar laughs, slightly out of breath, and then sinks to his knees on the earth, coughing. Gulgul looks at him sharply.

'Samar, *tum* theek ho?'

Samar nods, hitting his chest until his throat clears.

'But I don't get it,' he says. 'What the hell was going on here?'

Bonu coughs, looks at the inert body lying ten feet away, and gives a long shudder. 'He said...he was going to...*kill* me.'

Samar's eyes narrow. He glances at Black Tracksuit.

'*Kill* you?' His voice changes a little. 'He wasn't just, you know, your regular Delhi stalker-rapist?'

She shakes her head. 'He said he was going to kill me because...' She wrinkles her forehead. 'I have *no* idea why.'

'Never mind, beta, don't talk,' says Gulgul, busily dialling a number on his phone. 'And lie back—you're in shock.'

'I feel strange,' Bonu winces. 'Dizzy. Were you following me, Gulgul mama?'

'Bhai, you said ki you felt you were being watched,' Gulgul explains. 'So when I saw you leave the house, I followed you. And I brought Samar also.'

'Has he killed him?' Bonu asks fearfully.

Gulgul gets up and prods the stalker gingerly with his Nike sneaker. 'He's breathing. Just.'

'Hai hai, what has happened?' Chachiji comes stumping down the park, carrying her doodh-ka-dolu, and beating her breast in agitation. 'Arrey, is she dead? Pull her shirt down properly, have you no shame?'

Gulgul at once yanks at Bonu's t-shirt, which is slightly rucked up on one side. Bonu can't control a small giggle. Trust Chachiji to focus on the non-essentials.

'AN!' shrieks Chachiji. 'Come see, Bonu is hurt! Raped! Dead! Who could have done this?'

Bonu hears Ashok Narayan's voice, calm and snide. 'Arrey, why are you asking foolish questions, Bhudevi, saaf-si baat hai. Her aunts have found out that she is testifying in court against them, so they have ordered a supari on her. The killer must have been their man, organized by that thug lawyer Paperwallah and that chor builder Sridhar. They are notorious for such things.'

'Save your wild theories for later,' Samar tells his granduncle curtly. 'There's the attacker, passed out on the grass right there. Pick him up and bring him home and we'll get to the bottom of all this.'

'*You* pick him up,' Ashok says.

But Samar walks, tight-lipped, past Ashok chacha and bends down and scoops up Bonu.

'Put your arms around my neck,' he says shortly.

She does so without demurring. The fact that he's an asshole has somewhat faded from the forefront of her thoughts. What's at the forefront now is the texture of his t-shirt, the warmth of his body, and the steady sound of his heart beating against her cheek. All of which add up to a single, reassuring thought: *Safe now, Bonu Singh. Safe as houses.*

Behind them, she can hear Gulgul mama and Ashok chacha grunting and muttering instructions to each other as they truss up the stalker and half-drag, half-carry him to a corner of the Baoli grounds. A crowd has begun to gather, and two officious-sounding cops are already on the spot, hitting their lathis against the tree trunks and spitting out tambaako, and telling the crowd to get a move on.

As Samar turns into the driveway of number 16, Bonu frowns. 'I need to go to Gambhir Stores. It's—'

'I'm sure somebody can go pick up whatever it is you wanted to buy,' he tells her curtly. 'Be quiet now.'

And Bonu goes quiet, too weak and giddy to object.

Chachiji surges in front of them, looking back at the drooping Bonu and ahead at the house while she beats her breast and calls out loudly and importantly to her nieces.

'Hai, Eshu! Hai Chandu! Aaake dekho—look, look! Your paid assassin tried to kill Bonu, and Gulgul saved her!'

Ashok chacha, showing unusual proactiveness and family feeling, telephones the cops at Minto Bridge Police Station and gives them a colourful account of the morning's happenings.

With the result that, half an hour later, Mamtaji's genteel drawing room is occupied by two pot-bellied, lathi-wielding Haryanvi cops—an old, gap-toothed one and a young, keen-eyed one—crunching biscuits and slurping chai and asking the family invasive questions.

'Thyure ij some court case going on, nahi?' inquires the old cop, his eyes gleaming below bushy grey brows. 'Tu-tu main-main over family property? Paper mein padha tha.'

'Nothing like that,' Eshwari says stiffly.

'Oho, so the newspapers are lying? Well, it's possible—we live in Kalyug after all, a wicked, wicked age!' the old cop returns, stirring more sugar into his tea. 'The thing is ki, don't mind, but your chacha is saying ki you four sisterj are cooking some khichdi and trying to dabao his property, and when your niece went on his side, you tried to get her murdered by the assassin now locked up in awar police thaana.'

'My uncle is mad,' is Eshwari's succinct reply. 'Don't take my word for it, speak to anybody in the neighbourhood—they will tell you the same thing.'

'No respect for elderj,' tut-tuts the old cop. 'Living abroad doej this to you. Where you are from, madum?'

'Hailey Road,' she replies.

'Haan haan, that is virginally. But nowadayj where do you live? Desi toh you don't look—NRI ho? London, Canada?'

'US,' mutters Eshwari.

'But even converted in US dollerj this houje ij worth a lot, no? How much? Newspaper said two hundurd crores?'

Before anyone can reply, the young cop chimes in, 'Bhai, money can't buy happiness!'

'Very true!' agrees the old cop, swilling his tea around inside his mouth luxuriously. 'Just look at this family, split right down the middle like a backside, all becauje of money!'

'Do you have any questions—or is this just a moral science class?' Eshu asks politely, her black eyes sparkling with aggression.

The cops titter and take another biscuit each.

'Very hard biscuit,' says the young cop. 'But tastes good dipped in tea.'

'No chocolate cream?' the old cop enquires, looking around hopefully. 'Oreo, Bourbun, imported, vaghera?'

'That's all we have in the house,' Eshwari tells him shortly.

'Is that because of a wow?' the young cop asks, nodding at Chandu's bald head as she sits still and silent beside Eshwari. 'Or fashion? You are also NRI, madum?'

'Yes,' Chandu replies. She passes a hand over her head. 'But it is not because of fashion. I don't believe in fashion.'

'So it's a wow. Religious?'

She nods. 'Yes.'

'But not so religious that you don't want a share in Papa's property!' guffaws the old cop.

Chandu flushes an unattractive red. 'I am going to donate my hissa to charity,' she says rigidly.

The old cop looks unimpressed. 'Yes, that is a good way to save tax.'

The young cop clears his throat. 'Your chacha is very keen to make this case about how you two and your more famous sisters are trying to shut your niece's mouth so you can get the family property even though your father was not the correct heir. *But!*' He holds up one hand dramatically. 'I don't-think-so this case is about property at all. I think your chacha is just trying to phasao you for his own benefit.'

'Thank you!' says Eshwari emphatically. 'First sensible thing you've said!'

'Please don't interrupt, madam. What *I* think—sir, you also please hear my thyory…'

'Haan haan, I am listening,' says the old cop, looking unimpressed.

'Um…hi,' says Bonu, walking into the room, somewhat dazedly, at this exact moment. 'What's up?'

'Come, Bonu Singh,' Eshu pats the cushion beside her. Bonu, however, chooses to sit down in the armchair a little distance away.

The young cop clears his throat importantly.

'Sir, I think-so this crime is about sex.'

He turns to face Bonu so suddenly that she jumps a little 'Why did you go out alone at that hour in such small-small shorts?'

'Sorry, what?'

The young cop nods. 'Ya. You are not an NRI like these others—you know Dilli parks are not safe.'

'They're not safe because you people don't do your job!' Eshwari starts to say hotly, but the old cop puts his teacup down and interrupts her genially.

'Pleaj forgive him, madum! He is young—for him everything is about sex.'

'Wow,' Bonu looks from one to the other. 'So now what?'

The younger cop frowns terribly.

'Why were you out so early?'

Bonu looks a little cagey. 'Uh…just…for a walk.'

'Why would that man want to attack you?'

'That's what you're supposed to find out,' Eshwari snaps. '*Officer.*'

The young cop presses on doggedly, 'He waj not…an ex-boyfriend? Jealous? Angry? Because you rejected him?'

'Did you *see* him?' Bonu says indignantly. 'He's old and smelly! And…and uncouth!'

'You ladiej are so snob,' sniffs the old cop. 'So he was not good enough for you, eh?'

'He almost killed me!' Bonu exclaims. 'Surely you can understand my not finding him charming!'

'Sir, mujhe toh yeh saaf love-triangle dikhaee de raha hai,' the young cop declares. 'This lady was swinging two men at the same time so they attacked each other.'

'You're mad,' Bonu tells him.

'Yes, I also think ki my young colleague ij barking up the wrong tree,' says the old cop heavily. 'I, however, am an old dog, and I think-so the correct tree ij the family tree. Bitiya, I am very sorry, but your aunts have taken out a supari on you. Ladiej, please accompany us to the police station for qwayshioning.'

For a moment, all Bonu can do is stare in disbelief as Eshu and Chandu are escorted to the police jeep outside. Then she runs out, yelling.

'Eshu mausi, Chandu mausi, wait!'

The aunts turn.

'I don't believe it!' Bonu pants. 'I don't think you guys would want to kill me!'

'Oh spare us the theatrics, wouldjaplease, Bonu Singh?' Eshwari snaps. 'You've organized this whole stunt with Ashok chacha. God knows what he's bribed you with.'

Bonu falls back. 'I *didn't!*'

Such is the passion in her voice that Eshwari looks torn. 'Well, we didn't order supari against you either. Chandu, tell her!'

Chandu immediately assumes a virtuous expression.

'Of course we didn't!' she says. 'In fact, when our lawyer suggested it, we gave him a blistering earful and sacked him on the spot!'

'Yeah, and he was kind of expensive too,' puts in Eshwari. 'We'd got to a point where we couldn't really afford him, anyway.'

'So you *discussed* it?' Bonu's voice is high. 'You actually discussed bumping me off?'

'He was only suggesting beating you up,' Eshwari says. 'But yes, we did. And *you* discussed siding with Ashok chacha, didn't you? Gulgul's asked for permission to produce you as a witness — we know.'

Shit. They know. Do they know what Ashok chacha told her about her parents being involved?

'But I *told* him I wouldn't,' she says out loud. 'Even though he promised a double hissa!'

'But you *discussed* it. You should've shut him up as soon as he broached the topic, no?'

'You're right,' Bonu says miserably. 'Where's Samar?'

'Already at the thana,' Eshu says, tight-lipped. 'They're calling him the second attacker.'

'But he was defending me!'

Eshwari shrugs. 'Try telling the cops that.'

Bonu stares at her for a moment, and then climbs into the jeep.

The police look at her in surprise.

'You are also coming?'

She nods resolutely. 'Yes.'

'Shameful, shameful,' Ashok Narayan says with mournful relish, when the little party of Thakurs blows in through the police station's swing door. 'That they would sink so low, just for property. Do family ties have no meaning anymore?'

'You're a fine one to talk, Ashok chacha!' says Eshwari, her black eyes glinting. 'At least all we've allegedly tried to do is murder a niece. You've cast aspersions on your mother's morals!'

Ashok leaps to his feet, thrilled. 'You have all been arrested!'

'We're assisting the police with their inquiries,' Chandu says haughtily.

'As good as arrested!' he gloats. Then he spots Bonu and his jaw drops. 'Bitiya, why are *you* here?'

'Where's this attacker?' Bonu says, ignoring him, pushing up the sleeves of her t-shirt. 'I want to talk to him!'

'And where's my nephew?' Eshwari demands. 'What have you done with him?'

The cops, clearly intimidated by this posse of strange upper-class women, one bald, one murderous and one clad in tiny shorts, point wordlessly towards an inner door. The eyes of the three women swivel to it immediately, but before they can walk up to it, it opens of its own accord and Samar Vir Singh, now sporting not one but two spectacular black eyes, strides out, smiling.

'Mystery solved!' he announces. 'The identity of the attacker has been revealed.'

Ashok Narayan Thakur leaps to his feet.

'He is Paperwallah's man!' he shouts hoarsely. 'Ordered to murder Bonu to ruin my case!'

'Actually, he *isn't*,' Samar's smile broadens.

'Sridhar's man then!' Ashok persists. 'Satish Sridhar's man, ordered to murder Bonu for objecting to the sale of the house!'

'Satish wouldn't do that!' Eshwari gasps.

'Wrong again, Ashok chacha.' Samar is grinning openly now.

'Susan Adams' man?' hazards Bonu, in a low voice. 'Hired to stop me from copying her clothes?'

Samar's eyes, brimming with laughter, swing to meet hers.

'And…wrong again,' he grins, and his gaze is like a caress. She flushes and looks away.

'His name,' Samar continues, 'is Pervez Khan, and his reasons for murdering Bonu—for that was his confessed intention—are entirely personal.'

'Personal?' Bonu repeats, her head reeling. 'Pervez?'

Samar nods, eyes glinting. 'Yeah. Pervezzzz. Does that name ring a bell?'

She shakes her head, bemused. 'Should it?'

'He wanted to kill Bonu, he says, because *four* sisters told him to.'

Ashok jumps up again, gesturing excitedly. 'Four sisters! Haan, theek to hai, na—Anji, Chandu, Dabbu, Eshu!'

'Wrong!' Samar's shoulders shake with suppressed mirth. 'Four *little* sisters, whose dream of having a brother were dashed the day that evil, *evil* Bonu destroyed their father's life! Or, more specifically, destroyed their father's manhood.'

'What?'

'You're talking rubbish, Samar,' Eshwari looks worriedly at her guffawing, battered nephew.

'He's been beaten up so much something's come loose,' Chandu whispers.

'*He* did all the beating,' Eshu replies. 'He's fine! Summerwine, stop laughing and explain *properly!*'

Samar responds to the anxiety in her voice.

'Fine, okay, sorry,' he holds up his hands. 'It's more tragic than funny, actually. Basically, this little ghoul here,' he nods at Bonu, 'believes in looking after her employees' well-being thoroughly. *Too* thoroughly, in my opinion. At least in the case of her tailor Parveen.'

Bonu stares up at him, open-mouthed.

'Basically, a while ago, Bonu sneakily organized Parveen's husband's vasectomy. But he's found out now. He knows it was Bonu's idea and that she paid for it—he found the hospital bill—and now he wants to kill her. Frankly, I think he's justified.'

For a moment nobody speaks. Then Bonu springs to her feet.

'Parveen's *husband*? That was him? Grabbing me by the throat, beating me up? Who does he think he *is*?'

'Who do you think *you* are, madum?' the Haryanvi cops move in closer, bristling. 'You cannot, without cunsent, without a buy-your-leave, just order a nasbandi! If all the ladies starts doing this heinous thing, then where will we all be? Don't smile, arrey, don't *giggle*. If Bhaijaan inside files an FIR against you, you could end up in jail, madum!'

Tired out by the day's excitement, the denizens of 16 Hailey Road retire to bed early that night. In his improvised bedroom next to the verandah, Samar tosses and turns in the too small bed, unable to sleep. Eshu mausi has given him a blue gel-filled ice-pack to put over his eyes, along with some industrial strength American painkiller, which seems to have the side-effect of keeping him all-worked up and wide awake. He can't watch TV, he can't read, he can't focus on anything. All he can do is lie back with eyes resignedly shut, rueing the wild doings of Bonita Singh Rajawat.

What had she been thinking, going off for a jog when she suspected somebody was stalking her? Stupid, idiotic, shortsighted move. And why had she not come to *him*, in the first place, when she suspected she was being followed? Because they'd fought? Because he hadn't bought her childish logic about Susan being a cheat? And now she is sleeping peacefully upstairs, without even bothering to check if he's doing okay, while he's thinking about her, and about that terrible moment when he thought he was too late and she was dead.

But *is* she sleeping peacefully? She's so used to having the Trings around, doing her odd jobs, guarding the place, and now they have departed, bag and baggage. Heck, even Doberman-faced Lachhu has slunk off. What if she's awake and lonely—or having nightmares?

He rolls over in bed, punching his pillow. When did this girl start mattering to him so much? Why is he so worried that he may have judged her too hastily? A girl who doesn't respect any rules—who picks locks and rips off designers and orders nasbandis without worrying *at all* about what is right and what is wrong?

His phone rings. He winces and reaches for it, eyes still shut.

'Bro, why this cruel and unnatural behaviour towards Susan bhabi?'

Samar almost drops his phone. 'Susan *what*?'

'You heard me,' Zeeshan says virtuously. 'She came to me, very upset—said she was feeling neglected 'coz you've been ducking all her booty calls.'

'I'm trying to finish a film,' Samar growls. 'And I have…family stuff.'

'Yeah, yeah, but this is where it gets *interesting*, see—'coz she said there's been no action since late *January*, which, I think, is around the same time you called me in a fevered condition in the middle of the night and babbled on at length about La Isla Bonita. Isn't that correct?'

Samar rakes his hair off his forehead in exasperation.

'Bastard, don't you read the papers? My family's dirty linen is out there on missmalini.com and you're going on about booty calls?'

'So you *haven't* got it on with the Adam since Jan,' Zeeshan cackles triumphantly. 'I *knew* it!'

Samar swears hard and feelingly. His friend, at the other end, whoops and chortles with glee, then suddenly changes gear.

'So where is this number 16, exactly? I *think* I've found it but I wanna be sure. Does it have a green gate?'

'What?' Samar says in a daze. 'Where are you?'

'Here, only. Where will I go? Does number 16 have a grotty green gate covered with some kind of plant growth? And one broken gate light?'

Samar sits up with a groan. 'That sounds right. But…wait, you're here? What have I done to deserve a house visit?'

'I'm here because of my *role*, bastard. You should be grateful.'

'Which role?'

'Tharki Thakur, obvio,' Zeeshan replies. 'Besides, I'm not a fuckin' gate crasher. Bonita invited me.'

'She what? Hang on, I'm coming to get you.'

'And listen, this abstinence shit you're pulling is fuckin' unhealthy. Two whole months of no action…'

'Three,' Samar corrects him, grimacing.

'*Three!* That's like, hectic, dude. All your juice is gonna back up inside your body, clog your bloodstream and give you gigantic pimples. You could even *burst*, like one gigantic pimple.'

But Samar has already cut the call.

Minutes later, Zeeshan, dressed in the loose anti-fit clothes and dark beanie cap that serve as his 'incognito look', is sitting in the flowered drawing room with Samar, grinning in the gloom.

'Hi,' he says.

Samar grunts distractedly and switches on some lights.

Zeeshan immediately does a double take. 'Bro, what the hell happened to you?'

'Oh, this,' Samar touches his face gingerly. 'It's a long story.'

'You look like an extra in a bad pirate film!'

Samar sighs. 'Like I said, long story.'

Zeeshan looks concerned. 'D'you need help? Can I call anybody? What the fuck is happening here?'

'I'll fill you in on all that stuff later, Zee,' Samar says. 'Tell me why you're here first.'

'Does the other guy look worse than you?'

'The other guy,' Samar tells him wryly, 'can't have kids anymore.'

'Excellent!' Zeeshan punches a fist in the air.

'So now why are you here?' Samar asks patiently.

'Okay, okay!' Zeeshan assumes a dramatic expression. 'I'm here…'

Theatrical pause.

Samar raises a brow.

'Because…'

Another dramatic pause. Samar yawns.

'Bonita has a big clue! To the *real* story behind the Tharki Thakur's romance! She called me and told me!'

He ends with a big flourish and freezes, clearly expecting applause.

Samar looks at him sourly. 'When did you two swap phone numbers and get so cosy?'

Zeeshan drops the pose. 'Stop being such a chut. You're just jealous that you were sitting right here and she didn't tell *you*.'

'Also, please do *not* call him Tharki Thakur here,' Samar says, ignoring this dig. 'My aunts will flip. And did you just say "big clue"? What are we, the, freakin' Secret Seven?'

But Zeeshan isn't listening. He is looking around the room. 'So this is the house our haveli is based on, isn't it? Cool!'

'Thank you.'

'Why're you so upset, man?' Zeeshan wants to know. 'Because I'm seeing your humble beginnings? Relax, it isn't *such* a dump.'

'Thanks, *Chawla*.'

Zeeshan grins. 'Achha, where's Bonita?'

'How come you're so jobless?' Samar responds. 'Aren't all your dates taken?'

Zeeshan assumes a sensitive expression. 'Kat's gynae's advised total bed-rest for the next seven days. For the baby, na. And they can't shoot me getting turned on all alone in a jacuzzi.' His grin flashes again. 'Actually they could, and it would look good, but it'll never make it past the censor board.'

'A love scene in a jacuzzi?' Samar scoffs. 'Why d'you do such fuck-all movies?'

Zeeshan looks indignant. 'Not true! I do *one* fuck-all movie and *one* classy movie every year. That's the way to keep the balance. But *you've* let me down. *TT* is supposed to be my this-year-ka classy release.'

'Whatever.' Samar is dismissive. 'D'you want me to drop you to the Imperial?'

'Already?' Zeeshan looks disappointed. 'But I haven't yet met Boni—'

'Ah, there you are,' says a female voice.

And standing in the doorway, clad in a soft Phineas and Ferb t-shirt nightie, holding a stubby candle that does fabulous things for her waves of inky-black hair, and looking peachy and fragrant and deliciously welcoming, is Bonita Singh Rajawat.

Zeeshan beams and holds out his arms. '*Boniiita!*'

Bonu walks up to him, passing Samar with barely a pause, and hugs him.

'Welcome to our ancestral Thakur home,' she grins.

'Thank you!' Zeeshan looks hugely pleased. He wraps his arms around her and kisses her thoroughly on both cheeks. 'Gimme the guided tour!'

'She would if you'd stop hugging her,' Samar says dryly.

Bonu turns to look at him. He looks right back at her. They haven't done this in a while. Perhaps that is why the air between them seems to crackle with electricity.

'What the hell happened to him?' Zeeshan demands. 'Who's been hitting him in the face?'

She hesitates, glancing sideways at Samar. The only words he has said directly to her today are, 'Put your arms around my neck', which sounds pretty good, but isn't really.

'He's been in a fight,' she tells Zeeshan. '*Two* fights, actually.'

'Bro!' Zeeshan throws out his hands. 'Control! We're barely out of the woods on that chutiyon-ki-baraat incident—pardon my French, Bonita...'

'That's cool,' she assures him.

'...and now you're brawling about like this! Suppose the journos get to know?'

'Well, if you continue hanging around my house, they *will* get to know,' Samar says firmly. 'There's always a few of them on your tail. So get back into your car and *git*. This place is a dump in any case, the loos are a disaster, there's no AC, no electricity and no food, you couldn't possibly live here...'

'That's not true,' Bonu protests indignantly, but Samar has already hustled Zeeshan out of the room. 'We *have* food—and my bathroom is extremely nice...'

'I want to hear the *clue*,' Zeeshan says stubbornly. 'And I'm not your guest anyway—I'm hers.'

'Tomorrow,' Samar tells him firmly. 'Butt out now.'

He says this rather significantly. So significantly that Zeeshan flashes him an understanding man-to-man grin, slaps palms with him and strides out of the room. He turns at the door though, his expression concerned.

'Bro, what I told you, about stuff backing up and clogging the bloodstream. It's scientific *fact*.'

'Goodnight,' Samar says with finality and shuts the door in his face.

Then he turns to look at Bonu. Who immediately wants to run straight up the stairs to her room, bolt the door and cower under the blankets. Which is ridiculous.

Instead she mutters a vague 'so goodnight then' and makes casually for the stairs, moving slowly so as to hide the fact that she is, quite cravenly, doing the non-Thakur thing and fleeing the field.

But it is no use. She can hear his footsteps — purposeful, no-more-bullshit, cut-the-crap footsteps — heading towards her, and then he has taken her by the wrist and spun her around to face him.

This move, complemented by strong, set features and those bruised eyes, is definitely knee-bucklingly hot, and it takes all her will to keep her voice steady and her knees unbuckled.

'What?' she says, trying for unimpressed and achieving squeaky.

Staring down at her, Samar notices that she has shed all her armour tonight. The bangles, the rings, all the various silver bits and baubs. It makes her appear smaller, and more vulnerable somehow.

'What's this clue?'

Bonu feels stupidly let down. So it's the clue he's after. Well, what did she expect?

'Oh. Ya…well…it's a person, actually, the clue. Somebody who knew Pushkar back in the day.'

'And he's still alive?' Samar sounds sceptical.

'She,' Bonu corrects him. 'A Mrs Mumtani. She's a pal of Old Mr Gambhir's and apparently she was a spring chicken when Pushkar and Old Mr G and the rest of the gang were in their forties.'

'Old Mr G!' Samar looks chagrined. 'Why didn't I think of him?'

'Because you're too much of a big shot,' she replies smugly. 'He phoned, asking me to go over and meet her this morning — she was passing through on her way to Amritsar…'

He gives her a little shake.

'So that's why you wandered out and almost got killed! Idiot!'

Bonu shakes him off, frustrated.

'I missed her, and now she's *gone*.'

'To Amritsar, not to her final resting place. We can still meet her, presumably.'

'I guess so.'

They are silent for a while. He continues to hold her wrists. It feels...correct to hold her. There's this strong, confirming sense of rightness, the same sense of rightness he feels when he calls cut on a shot he knows he has absolutely nailed.

'If you felt there was a stalker on your tail, why the hell did you go out of the house alone, so early in the morning, wearing shorts?'

'Oh, please,' she rolls her eyes. 'You sound like that young cop today.'

'I asked you a question.'

'So?'

'So answer me, Bonita.'

'Ask me nicely.'

'Excuse me?'

'Yes,' she nods passionately because, somehow, this is important. 'Ask me nicely. Like how you ask people to do stuff at shoots—all nice and polite and considerate. Why are you so nice to other people and so mean to me?'

He stares at her face for a moment, confused, and then he smiles. *That* smile, the one that softens his face, making nonsense of its harshness, and lights up his eyes, so that looking into them makes the looker feel both stupidly happy and also extremely exposed, as though they're not wearing any clothes.

Samar says, his voice dropping to an intimate caress, '*Why* did you go out alone, so early in the morning, wearing shorts, Bonita?'

She looks away, her cheeks hot. 'I told you, to meet Mrs Mumtani.'

His hands release her wrists and slide smoothly down to rest lightly over her butt.

'Ah, but *why* did you want to meet her?'

'To help you!'

His hands grip her harder, pushing her closer to him. Her hair mantles both their shoulders. It smells of roses.

'And *why* did you want to help me?'

'Because...' She looks here and there, caught out, fidgety. 'Because you're all screwed up about your movie and I felt bad for you!'

'But I'm an asshole,' he reminds her, lightly kissing the side of her neck. 'I almost got the Trings killed. And I called you a cheat.'

Her forehead wrinkles. 'But you saved my life. I owed you.'

'That happened after,' he says against her ear, nipping gently at her earlobe. 'Just saying.'

'It did?' Bonu says faintly, now having lost all capacity to think.

'Yes.'

She can hear the smile in his voice as he lifts her a little and pushes her up against him, even closer. His hands are strong and sure, but also a little unsteady. 'Why have you shed all your chhamchham? I really dig those sound effects.'

'I take my silver off before I bathe,' she explains breathlessly.

'Next time, keep it on,' he whispers against her lips.

She is about to murmur something idiotic in reply when the import of what he's just said sinks in. Her eyes fly open and she pushes him away hard.

'What the hell!' she says.

Samar blinks, his hair all tousled, his eyes slightly glazed. 'What?'

'There isn't going to be a next time! There isn't even going to be a *this* time! I don't randomly have sex with people! Besides, you're taken. You have a girlfriend. You're the Gomez to her Morticia!'

For a moment it looks like he's going to deny this. His lips tighten, his eyes kindle, and he makes a hasty movement towards her, but then he backs away, his eyes lowered, his palms raised.

'Phew. You're right, I apologize. I'm sorry.'

She stares at him, angry and frustrated and absurdly disappointed all at once. He looks away, staring moodily into the garden.

There's silence in the verandah for what feels like a long long time. Finally she draws a long, shuddering breath and eyes him uncertainly.

'Moving on?'

He nods in agreement, his voice slightly strangled.

'Moving on.'

'Okay then,' Bonu shakes back her hair and assumes a commendably business-like tone. 'So after I missed Mrs Mumtani, thanks to Parveen's husband, I called Zee because he's like, a big shot, and I thought he might know how to chase her down in Amritsar.'

She waits for him to nod. He does. She continues, 'I thought he might send a private detective up there or something. But anyway, now maybe both of you can go up there togeth—'

Samar gets to his feet abruptly.

'I can't do this now.'

She stares up at him, confused.

'Can't? Can't do what?'

'*Talk* to you. Function. Think.'

'But why?'

'Because I'm not a goddamn robot,' he snaps. 'And I'm not made of fucking stone. Have a lovely sleep upstairs in your pure, pristine lair. Goodnight.'

14

'Tu chutiya hai,' Zeeshan says resignedly as he unwraps the greasy parantha roll the airhostess has just handed them and peers inside it, his expression dubious. 'Loser. Big fat loser. Er, is this low fat?'

'It's paneer,' the pretty young airhostess smiles at him. 'If you want more, I can get you another portion. This morning flight to Amritsar is always empty.'

'No thanks,' Zeeshan replies, and starts tearing open the yoghurt carton.

She lingers at the aisle. 'Could you...could you please sign the napkin for me later?'

'Sure thing, babe.'

She steals a hopeful look at Samar, who has declined breakfast and is sprawled out in his seat, long legs stretched out in front of him, scruffy t-shirt slightly rucked up, eyemask over his face. '*Both* of you?'

'Sure,' Zeeshan looks up at her, his gaze thoughtful, then rests his elbow on the armrest and adopts a confidential tone. 'Listen, you look like a sensible girl. As it happens, we're in the market for some sensible relationship advice from a neutral, disinterested female party—'

'Cut it out, Zee,' Samar growls, lifting the eyemask just a little.

'Er, for a *script*, of course.'

'Hullo, sir,' the girl addresses Samar breathlessly. 'I loved both your movies. I'm really looking forward to *Thakur Saab*.'

Samar raises the mask further and gives her a polite smile. 'Thank you.' Then he pulls it down again. The girl looks disappointed.

Zeeshan, meanwhile, has been reading her name badge. 'So, Dilreen! Can I call you Dilreen?'

'Of course, sir.'

'Thank you. Dilreen, are you familiar with the phrase friends-with-benefits?'

She turns a little pink. 'Yes, sir.'

'So if you were friends-with-benefits with somebody, Dilreen, and it was very clear that the understanding was exactly that— *friends*, you know, who give you, um, *benefits* of a...sexual nature...'

'Fuck buddies,' says Dilreen knowledgeably.

Zeeshan rears up, scandalized. '*Dilreen!*'

'That's telling you, grandpa,' Samar says sardonically from behind his mask.

'Sorry, sir,' Dilreen falters, red-faced.

'Rubbish!' declares Zeeshan, all outraged, avuncular disapproval. 'This new generation! Chhheeee! Anyway, pay close attention now, Dilreen. So as I said, suppose you were friends-with-benefits with somebody, a relationship that suited you because you were too busy with work to invest in a serious romantic relationship, and suited them because you were a high-profile person and they needed to date someone high-profile after being jilted publically by *another* high-profile person...'

The girl nods, wide-eyed.

'And then you met somebody else, your soulmate, your one true love—what would you do?'

Dilreen knits her beautifully threaded brows.

'Does this new somebody love me back?' she asks practically. 'And is this new somebody single, or also in a relationship?'

'What good questions you ask!' Zeeshan marvels. 'No, the good news is that this new somebody is single, clearly loves you back, is very adorable and perfect in every way.'

Dilreen looks doubtful. She is clearly a girl who's been disappointed in love.

'Are you *sure*?' she asks. 'Soulmates are hard to find nowadays…I'm starting to think they don't exist.'

Zeeshan glances at his slumbering friend, waiting for him to deny this, or make some wisecrack, or react in any manner whatsoever. But Samar remains still, eyes resolutely closed. A tiny pulse jumps at the base of his throat.

'We're sure,' Zeeshan tells the girl.

'I'd break up with the first person,' Dilreen says decisively. 'As kindly as I could, because anyway that relationship is going nowhere. And I'd do it ekdum phataphat—before this second person finds somebody else—there must be a long line waiting, if they're *that* special.'

'Well said!' beams Zeeshan. He prods Samar meaningfully. 'What d'you make of that, bro?'

Samar pulls down his eyemask and sits upright. Pretty little Dilreen gets a start. The famous film-maker looks haunted, ravaged.

'But what if the first person told you they're in love with you now,' he says, his voice rough. 'That they hadn't planned on that happening but it's happened, and to please not break up with them because the trauma and humiliation of being jilted twice in quick succession is more than they can stand? That they might harm themselves?'

'Lies!' says Zeeshan vigorously. 'All lies! Lemme tell you, bro…'

But Dilreen is staring down at Samar, her brandy-brown eyes slowly starting to look as troubled as his own.

'Then…' she hesitates. 'Then you should, I mean, the character in the film should—'

The seatbelt sign comes on with a loud *dinngggg!* Dilreen looks up, startled, murmurs an apology and hurries back to her position at the front of the plane, her expression switching back smoothly to the standard glossy mask of good airhostesses everywhere.

'*Ladies and gentlemen, boys and girls, we have commenced our descent into Amritsar…*'

She speaks to him again as he is exiting the plane. Lays a manicured hand upon on his sleeve as he hands her a napkin signed by both him and Zee.

'Don't let her go,' she whispers. 'Don't.'

Samar's lips tighten. 'I'll tell the scriptwriters,' he says, his voice clipped, and strides away.

Mrs Mumtani turns out to be a formidable, ancient lady who lives in a white Plaster of Paris and marble kothi, the size of Mehboob Studio, in a rather seedy part of the city. She possesses a mammoth, shelf-like uniboob, a long, wispy grey plait, a mole with several stiff hairs growing out of it, and a rolling, sailor-like gait.

Fresh from her morning prayers at the gurdwara and dressed

in white lace, she fails to recognize either Zeeshan or Samar as celebrities but is hospitable enough to offer them a breakfast of freshly squeezed pomegranate juice and freshly fried French toast because 'Gambhir ke munde hain'.

'Old age mein she has become very proper,' Old Mr Gambhir had briefed the boys earlier that morning. 'Goes to the gurdwara regularly, and is class conscious and cunserwaitive. But in her young days, she was a real phuljadi. Twenty years younger than Mr Mumtani! He was crazy for her, crazy, and he told her everything. Husbinds didn't used to tell the janani much those days, we were shy fellows, but Mumtani was frank with his young wife, fully frank. They used to chat all night—he would tell her all the kissas and kahanis and adventures, and later she would tease us by dropping hints. But she never told on us to our wives. Jisse kehte hain one-of-thee-boys! But hundurd percent female! If anybody knows the real story of your great-grandfather and his wife, she will! Bas usko daaru pila dena, Samar beta. Get her drunk, then she'll talk.'

When they ask her about Samar's great-grandfather, the old lady nods. 'Yes, Mumtani was very friendly with Pushkar bhaisaab. He stayed with him whenever he went to Dilli— never took me along, of course, girls didn't travel with their husbands those days, it wasn't considered nice. Very fine family, the Thakurs of Hailey Road, very khandaani. No sons, but. The name will die out now. What do you want to know?'

She is so dignified and so formidably correct that they're stumped. How on earth are they to get her drunk and bring up murders in this prim and proper environment?

'Uh, yes, well,' Samar attempts. 'His eldest granddaughter is my stepmother.'

'Oh?' she says, her old eyes glinting. 'His eldest granddaughter married a Singh from Allahabad. Good family, *very* good family. We went for the wedding. I gave two hundred rupees and a pair of gold earrings. They gave me a sari, chiffon but not the best quality—plain si thi.'

'Anjini Thakur,' Samar murmurs.

'Lovely girl,' the old lady concedes. 'Only pretty one in the family. We had heard a lot about the Thakur sisters, but they were nothing great. You put any five girls together with hair and make-up and all, and people start to say *so pretty, so pretty.* Fools. '

'It's called the Cheerleader Effect,' Zeeshan nods intelligently. 'Fools me every time.'

'Er, yes,' Samar says. 'So Mrs Mumtani, actually, I don't know if Old Mr Gambhir told you, but—'

'And one of them married a phorener,' continues the old lady with a disdainful sniff. 'And one an isaee. Girls marry any aira-gaira nowadays. Nobody checks caste or background. Chalo, theek hai, I suppose, kum-se-kum they're not musalmaan. Or achhoot.'

Zeeshan chokes. So does Samar.

The old lady seems to have reached the end of her reminiscences.

'So what did you want to know, puttar?'

Samar leans forward.

'Er, auntieji, it was a long flight and we're tired. Do you mind if we…?' He produces a quarter bottle of Old Monk from his bag and shakes it suggestively over the pomegranate juice.

The old lady nods, pushing her glass forward.

'Haan haan, vy not?'

Samar pours Old Monk into their glasses until the red of the juice turns dull brown. Everybody sips.

Ten minutes later, old Mrs Mumtani is waxing eloquent. 'Mumtani and Pushkar bhaisaab used to go to this gambling den together. But then Pushkar bhaisaab gave it up. He was mad for his wife, absolutely besotted. He stayed home and pressed her feet and taught his younger son math. Full bore he became! The business of the kothawallahs began to suffer. But I was happy. I told Mumtani to learn something from him. But then Pushkar bhaisaab found out that his simple-si wife had a Yaar.'

'A Yaar?'

'Yes. A Luvver, an Aashiq. He used to hook a rope ladder to the cement jaali of her balcony and climb up every Monday night to be with her. The kothawallas only told him. And then, one Monday night, they *showed* him—a handsome young man clambering up a rope ladder like a saanp on a seedi, smelling of ittar and jasmine and anticipation, to warm his wife's bed! Pushkar bhaisaab loved his wife too much to touch a hair on her head, so he ordered his trusted servant to loosen the jaali next Monday, so that when the Aashiq climbed up, the jaali would break and he would fall and break his neck, like he had broken Pushkar bhaisaab's heart. But the Aashiq didn't come that Monday. When Pushkar bhaisaab, who'd gone to his village to avoid the unpleasantness and also to make an alibi, came back on Tuesday morning, he saw his beloved wife in the balcony, freshly bathed, hair still wet, leaning on the freshly-loosened jaali, throwing birdseed to her white pigeons. *Step back!* he shouted up to her, his blood freezing inside his veins. *What, my love?* she called, leaning forward. *Step back!* he shouted again *What, my heart?* she asked, leaning forward even more. Pushkar bhaisaab cursed and waved and shouted, but it was too late—she leaned more and more forward, the jaali broke away, she fell, screaming out his name and broke her neck. He rushed up to her and she died in his arms. Bas! That's the story.'

She picks up her glass and tosses back the last of the anar and Old Monk. Then she burps, a small, lady-like burp.

'And the Aashiq?' Samar manages to ask, stunned.

She shakes her head, stroking the stiff hairs on her mole rhythmically.

'Nobody knew who he was. Pushkar bhaisaab definitely didn't. We still don't know.'

The next day, Anjini Singh arrives at number 16, ahead of the District Court hearing of Ashok Narayan Thakur *versus* Heirs of Laxmi Narayan Thakur, dressed in the latest sleeveless-long-kurti-paired-with-flouncy-peasant-skirt fashion, hair gorgeously curled and skin dewy fresh. She settles into her parents' bedroom in a business-like manner, not at all disconcerted by the fact that they'd both died in their beds—just getting her maid, a healthy young thing named Asharfi, to beat the mattress hard and place a dainty new set of organic cotton sheets from Anokhi upon it.

'I've come to do full and final of this house,' she tells Eshu and Chandu, over a bracing morning cuppa. 'I'm not leaving till it sells.'

When questioned on how the 'paper is going to cope without her, she airily says, 'Oh, peak summer is a slow season for *Allahabad Buzz*—things will pick up only when the festive season starts. And don't you worry about the housekeeping—Asharfi can do ten times the work that two-faced Lachhu did!

What use are two faces in a servant, anyway? Double the talk, and double the food. Better to have only one face and *four* arms and legs, which I assure you is what Asharfi has.'

The neglected house does start to blossom under the healthy young Asharfi's ministrations. Curtains are washed, rooms are aired, papers are sorted through and dust is banished. Food appears on the table at regular intervals, piping hot and steamingly fragrant and Chandu grows decidedly bubblier.

'How much do you pay Asharfi, Anjini?' she asks, lashless eyes gleaming as she ladles large amounts of fragrant lasagna and five-greens salad onto her plate. 'In the US this kind of service would be prohibitively expensive!'

'Oh, would you like to split the bill for her salary for while she's here?' Anjini says sweetly. 'That's nice of you, Chandu. Thanks.'

Chandu immediately stops looking so happy. Anjini beams around the table. 'Eat, Bonu, eat, Eshu,' she urges with a maternal smile. 'Have some salad, take a napkin. The house is to be sold and demolished soon, yes—but in the meantime, there's no reason for us to live like pigs!'

She's clearly here to assume the mantle of the Eldest, Eshwari thinks, noticing, not for the first time, how much Anjini looks like their father. She has the same oval face and honey skin tone, narrow hands and feet, waves of walnut hair, eyes like aam-papad. And the tendency to be bossy. Bonu and I look more like Ma, she thinks, and Chandu, well, Chandu looks like nobody in particular. If there ever was a cackkoo in a family, it's her.

Chachiji stumps in as they're finishing lunch, iron-grey curls waving like antenna on the alert for 'developments'.

'I heard ki Zeeshan Khan is in Dilli?' she asks eagerly. 'Won't he come to meet Samar?'

'That is all a rumour,' Anjini says with great authority. 'He's shooting in Korea.'

'Achha?' says Chachiji, disappointed. 'Khair, now that I'm here, how about some tea, eh? I've really missed you, Anju beta. I still love you girls like you are my own, you know.'

'And you love our house like it's your own, too,' Eshwari shakes her head. 'Really, Chachiji, how do you sleep at night?'

But rhetorical questions are never the way to tackle Chachiji. She immediately launches into a long detailed description of the sleeping arrangements at number 13. Eshwari rolls her eyes but Anjini nods and smiles and hears her out and plies her with more tea whenever she stops for breath.

'Tea is good,' Chachiji pronounces finally, putting down her third cup with a satisfied sigh. 'Girl is good too. Where is she from—Allahabad only?'

Asharfi steps forward and nods, eyes lowered.

'She gives very good massages, Chachiji,' Anjini says. 'I can send her over sometime, if you like.'

Chachiji glows. 'Hai, such a nice girl you are, Anjini! You understand that none of this is personal. All that court-kachehri should not enter the kitchen! These others are all fools!'

And the two of them hug and part on extremely good terms.

Later in the day, Anjini comes tripping prettily up the steps to bond with Bonu.

'How lovely!' she exclaims as she pops her head into the tailoring unit. 'Hello, everybody!'

The tailors look up, charmed at once. Because this is a talent Anjini possesses, she commands instant adoration from everybody who works for her—tailors, carpenters, beauty parlour attendants, bankers, plumbers—regardless of age and gender.

'Hi, Anji mausi,' Bonu says awkwardly, feeling large and

ungainly and dreadfully at a disadvantage. She wonders what Anji mausi would say if she knew what Bonu and her darling son have been doing recently.

'Hi, Bonu Singh!' Anji's voice is determinedly cheerful.

She looks about the buzzing unit, eyes flitting over every bent, absorbed face, and Bonu wonders if she's trying to identify Parveen. Once he had calmed down, vasectomied Parvez had begged that Parveen not be told about his attempt to murder Bonu, as that would lead to a loud fight in which the entire mohalla would come to know about his surgery, and he preferred to keep that under wraps. Bonu had agreed to stay quiet after extracting a promise that he would never, ever touch any of the women in his house in a manner that wasn't affectionate and also that he would stop hogging the mutton pieces in the Sunday biryani. Parveen is stitching away serenely now (a consignment of little boys' nightsuits, ironically enough) and Bonu doesn't want anything to upset that serenity.

But Anjini clearly has other stuff on her mind.

'Arrey, Bonu, did you ever get around to servicing Ma's old machine?' she asks. 'I guess not, na? You've had so much on your plate recently.'

Chandu sticks her bald head into the unit at exactly this moment, her nose twitching hopefully in anticipation of a squabble.

But Bonu's face lights up.

'Oh no!' she smiles. 'We did pull it out—and I'm so glad we did, it was on the brink of ruin and it's such a lovely old piece. Truly priceless! You're lucky to have it, Anji mausi—here it is, look!'

She points to a place behind the central counter, the kind of space usually reserved for a religious photograph or a Godrej safe. There is a machine sitting there, encased in a crisp cream casement cover, hand-embroidered with pretty pansies, dainty wood roses and fat poppies in pastel Neelam threads. Bonu raises the cover with a flourish and there it is, Mamta Thakur's trusty old sewing machine, beautifully restored, gleaming black and silver and gold on its teakwood stand. The embossed 'Usha' on the glossy black body has been blacked out and replaced with a beautifully calligraphed, hand-painted, old-gold 'Mamta'.

Anjini gives a gasp of pleasure.

'Oh!'

'She's trying to appropriate it,' Chandu hurries in and mutters into Anjini's ear. 'That's why she's kept it hidden away like this—she doesn't want anybody to know Ma left it to *you*.'

'And on the other side it says Anjini,' Bonu continues, turning the machine around. 'Look! Samar…(she turns a little pink when she says his name, but continues composedly enough) mentioned it was going to be in a shoot, so I got them to tart it up a little.'

Anjini stares at the strong, sincere young face, and feels a lump rise in her throat.

Bonu Singh takes a deep breath. 'Look, I'm really sorry I encroached on your hissa, Anji mausi. And one more thing—it was for sixteen months, not twelve. I have the rent cheque ready for the balance amount. Please accept it.'

'Girls, she's a *good* kid,' Anjini tells her sisters with conviction as they huddle around the phone an hour later. 'I really don't think she's going to appear in court as Ashok's witness, especially after everything that happened the other day. I mean, she owes us her life!'

'Hello, I've been saying that from the beginning!' Dabbu's voice protests from the speaker phone. 'Bonu Singh is a good kid!'

'So much love just because she got a machine serviced,' Chandu sniffs. 'Most companies offer the service for free. And embroidery is easy for her to do—she has ten embroidery machines in there!'

'It's the thought that counts,' Dabbu points out. 'Like instead of just giving you a cheque, if somebody hand-knitted a cap for you so you wouldn't feel cold in winter, wouldn't that be really sweet?'

Chandu stares down at the phone like Dabbu is mad. 'No.'

'Never mind,' Eshu sighs. 'Anyway, I realized I was fond of the little brat when Samar carried her home half-conscious in his arms. I suddenly had a vision of her as a scrawny little git with black knees and chapped cheeks, whining at me to teach her basketball.'

'In his *arms*?' Dabbu sounds most interested. 'Achha? Is something cooking there?'

The sisters at this end of the call look at each other.

'*I* think so,' Eshu says decidedly.

'Well, Dyl and the kids are convinced they're in love,' Dabbu says excitedly. 'They said the chemistry when he came home was electrifying. They're pretty pumped about it.'

'It's on *her* side only,' says Chandu. 'He can get anybody. Why would he want *her*?'

'She's nice,' Anjini says decidedly. 'I *like* her. Hopefully her children won't look like Vickyji.'

'I got all excited by Pasta and Dyl's report,' Dabbu continues. 'I almost called you guys up—but then I met Samar at a dinner last week and he *still* had that Addam's family in tow. I hope he isn't taking poor Bones for a ride.'

'Arrey, *she* is taking all of us for a ride,' Chandu says with force. 'And all this fuss about not wanting to sell, you all know where it's coming from, don't you?'

The others look at her blankly.

Eshwari says, 'Uff, she told us na, she doesn't want to sell because we wouldn't sell when Binni didi wanted to sell—and because we thought Vickyji was ugly and weird, which, let's admit it, we *did*.'

'She isn't selling,' Chandu says slowly, like she's talking to a trio of morons, 'because *obviously* her mother has told her about that paper she signed in 1993.'

'The 1993 document?' Dabbu sounds stunned. 'You...you think so?'

'*I* don't think Binni didi would've told her about it,' Eshu shakes her head decisively. 'She was too proud.'

'Girls, why are we even talking about the 1993 document?' Anjini's voice is steely. 'It's irrelevant. All copies of it have been destroyed, right?'

The sisters nod one by one. 'Right.'

'Bonu must *never* know,' Anjini says.

Chandu throws up her hands, amazed at this naivety. 'Bonu already knows! That's why she doesn't want to sell!'

Everybody ignores this. There is a little pause and then Dabbu says brightly, 'So, what about the case? What's our lawyer saying?'

Her sisters at this end sigh. The new lawyer is not somebody they're particularly impressed with.

'Not much,' Anjini replies. 'He's a bit of a glum plum. Keeps tsk-tsking about how grossly mismanaged this case has been. He could've won it in about fifteen minutes back then, he says, but because so many lawyers have botched it up along the way, he can't do much—and therefore we should do compro with Ashok chacha only. His rates are four lakhs per hour, btw.'

'Aise kaise compro kar lo?' Eshu demands. 'He called our father a cackkoo in the nest!'

'I'll make Pasta study law,' Dabbu decides. 'No more SAT and foreign university and all. Law it is! By the way, Eshu, did Satish get hassled because we sacked his recommended lawyer?'

Eshwari shakes her head. 'No.'

'Did you tell him his lawyer suggested we get Bonu beaten up?' Anjini demands.

'Yes, he got upset—quite upset—but not *ho-ji* upset. He said that construction and property are dirty businesses and these things happen all the time, so not to be so judgmental.'

The sisters look at each other.

'He's lost it,' Dabbu says finally. 'How can he hobnob with such people—do business with them?'

'He did do six months in Tihar jail, after all,' says Anjini. 'Maybe it eroded his moral compass. I hope you're not spending too much time with him, Eshwari.'

Eshwari's expression turns rather peculiar.

'Noo…er, uh, yes,' she says clumsily.

Everybody looks at her.

'What what?' demands Dabbu's voice from the phone. 'Tell me! What's happening there?'

'Nothing!' Eshu exclaims. 'God, relax, you guys!'

'Are you *seeing* him?' Debjani asks worriedly. 'Eshu?'

'Well, I thought all of you liked him!' Eshu says crossly. 'That day in his office everybody was pushing him at me, and now suddenly he's evil? I'm not seeing him-seeing him anyway— he's working on this housing project in Haryana for NRI types and he's asked me to come along and give him my opinion, because I'm, you know, an NRI. That's it.'

A sceptical silence greets this explanation.

Anjini sniffs. 'That's the weakest story I've heard in a while. The city is crawling with NRIs wanting to invest—why does he need *you*?'

Eshu opens her mouth to answer, but Chandu is faster.

'How many days is this trip? Where will you be staying?'

'It's a day trip,' Eshwari says. 'We'll be back late on the same day itself.'

'Is he *driving*?' Dabbu asks. 'Surely not! I mean, does he even have a licence?'

'Yes, he does!' Eshwari snaps. 'He hit exactly *one* drunk pedestrian, fifteen years ago—will you guys please relax?'

'Yeah, yeah, okay,' Debjani says, but with worry in her voice.

'Achha, suppose he asks me about Ashok chacha?' Eshwari asks. 'What should I say?'

'Tell him we've got a plan,' Anjini says with a very cat-that-got-the-cream smile.

They eye her, confused.

'We do?'

She nods, her eyes dreamy, faraway. 'It's a long shot. But it might pay off, it just might.'

15

Satish picks Eshwari up in a shiny black Land Cruiser the next morning. Watching her slim athletic figure running lightly down the drive dressed in faded jeans and a bravely pink little kurti, from the window of their parents' bedroom, Anjini can't help feeling uneasy. Now that both Ma and BJ are gone, she is the eldest in the family and therefore responsible for her youngest, unmarried sister. Should she just let Eshu traipse off with this wolf-like ex-charsi with the flashy dark glasses, who is even now grinning at her, showing all his teeth? Not that Eshu would listen to her—she'd just point out that she's a big girl and that she's known Satish practically since the day she was born, and that Anjini's a fine one to talk. And so Anjini mutters a little prayer inside her head and walks across to have tea with Chachiji.

'Your heart is as large as mine, Anjini,' is Chachiji's opening remark. 'You don't mind ki there is a case going on and all. You are still talking to me!'

Anjini opens her aam-papad eyes very wide.

'But you're my aunt,' she says simply. 'It's bad enough that I may lose my house—why should I lose my aunt also?'

Tears well up in Chachiji's beady eyes. She gives a noisy little gulp. 'Such a good girl!'

'I just want you to be happy, Chachiji,' Anjini says sincerely.

'Anyway, my husband has so much property in Allahabad and Samar is doing so well, I don't need anything. *Sachhi.*'

'Love of husband and son is the greatest thing,' Chachiji sniffles.

'And you have that now?' Anjini asks. 'I mean, there was a phase when Ashok chacha, you know…' She pauses delicately.

'Haan haan.' Chachiji blows her nose. 'But you know, beta, I had a very bad meenopause. I imagined all kinds of things! But then I started to take iron ki tablets every day and now I know ki your uncle was always faithful to me. *Always.* It was all my veham, those days.'

Anjini manages to keep a straight face. 'I'm so glad.'

'Your uncle is a *pure*,' Chachiji's expression grows dreamy. 'Of course he used to be good-looking and charming also, but most importantly, he is faithful. That is why, even when he does things that trouble my conscience, like re-open this case against you girls, I put a stone on top of my heart and continue to be a good wife and stand beside him.'

'So faithful,' Anjini says thoughtfully. 'Yes, loyalty is the biggest virtue in a husband… If my husband wasn't faithful then I don't know what I would do!' She tilts her head innocently. 'What would *you* do, Chachiji?'

Chachiji's horny little hands close purposefully into fists. 'I would wring his thin nec—' She comes to an abrupt halt, her beady eyes darting agitatedly around the room, then gives her niece a genteel, serene smile. 'Why are we talking about such bad-bad things? We both-of-us have trustworthy husbands. Have some more tea, beta.'

Anjini matches her smile for smile.

'Thank you, Chachiji.'

'Most people don't get into a car if I'm driving,' Satish tells Eshwari lightly as they drive back home from his construction site. 'They make all kinds of convoluted excuses.'

'Most people are chutiyas,' she replies composedly.

He smiles, glancing away from the road for a second. It's been a long day, but they've made good time, and now the sun is finally setting, a brilliant boiled lozenge against the feathery wheat fields. Eshwari closes her eyes and, totally relaxed with him behind the wheel, goes peacefully to sleep.

When she awakes, it's dark inside the car and the engine is turned off. The driver's seat is empty. She looks out of the window to see trucks lined up bumper-to-bumper along the road, honking and rumbling, and Satish standing at a ramshackle thela, eating masala boiled eggs out of a newspaper square.

She lowers the window.

'What happened?'

'A truck's overturned,' he reports. 'The jam could last all night. Want some?'

'Yes, please. But what shall we do?'

He stares at her as she eats, his expression whimsical. 'Look, I promise I didn't plan this.'

'What?'

With careful off-handedness, he says, 'Well, a friend of mine has a tourist property here—I helped him develop it—we could walk there. He'll send over a man to stay in the car and bring it around to the hotel tomorrow morning.'

Eshwari stares up at him, looming above her on the dark, smoke-scented highway, trucks belching diesel fumes behind him. His construction site was massive, everybody had sucked up to him, he had strapped a yellow helmet onto her head and taken her up on a crane to show her the scale of the operation—

he was clearly very influential. But influential enough to organize a pile-up of trucks two miles long? She doubts it. Besides, she could really do with a cup of tea. Or something stronger.

'Okay.'

An hour later they are partaking of a sumptuous buffet in a star-lit haveli courtyard. The hotel, though built along a ridge of the Haryana Aravallis, is aggressively Rajasthani in theme. There are dainty jharokas in dholpur pink everywhere, Shekhawati paintings of elephants and tigers grace the walls, and the inevitable mustachioed musician in red kurta is scraping out the inevitable *padhaaro mhaare des* on the sarangi.

'Is this song from your part of the world?' he asks. 'You guys are Rajus, right?'

'We're more UP than Rajasthan,' she replies. 'This is from Dylan's dad's area, really.'

'*Dyl*-lan.' Satish's expression grows rueful. 'Romantic, swashbuckling, half-Christian-half-Rajput Dylan. Man, that dude used to give me a complex.'

Eshwari smiles. 'C'mon, Steesh, you're pretty romantic yourself now. The brooding builder with the dark past and the bright present.'

He doesn't smile back.

'That night, after I knocked down the drunk pedestrian, my first instinct was to cut and run.'

'That would've been anybody's first instinct.'

'But then I thought of you. And how disappointed you'd be if I didn't man up.'

'You would've been disappointed in yourself if you hadn't manned up,' she says with conviction.

He shakes his head. 'I really don't think so. Anyway, the point is, I manned up. Or messed up, to use my parents' phrase.

They'd have preferred I cut and run, I think. I went to Tihar and had my life fucked up, and my licence revoked and my passport confiscated so I couldn't even travel to freakin' Nepal — while *you* glammed it up in New York.'

Ab, what to say to him? That she didn't hear about him hitting the pedestrian till a week after it happened? And, as they hadn't spoken in over six months at that point, reaching out to him had felt rather fake? Or should she remind him that she *had* called him, and that he had told his mother he didn't want to speak to her, and that his mother had reported this fact to her with great smugness?

'But all's well that ends well, right?' she says finally. 'You're doing great now.'

His gaze becomes distinctly sardonic. 'No thanks to *you*.'

'Matlab?'

'Matlab since then, every time I've been at a crossroad, I've done exactly the *opposite* of what you'd have told me to do — and look, it's paid off so well.'

'That's just idiotic,' she flares up. 'You're not a mind-reader, you can't possibly guess what I would say in every situation.'

'You'd say the noble, obvious thing,' he mocks her. 'Be honest, don't bribe, don't be a chut.'

'Not true,' she snorts. 'You don't know anything about me! Maybe I'd say *be* a chut.'

His eyes widen.

'Really?'

'This is a stupid conversation,' Eshu mutters.

'Agreed.'

She gets up to refill her plate from the buffet. For a while there is no sound in the courtyard but for the scraping of spoons and the wailing of *padhaaro mhaare des*, but soon a group of

European tourists shows up, fresh from a tiger sighting in the forest close by. They come up to Eshwari and Satish to ask what's good in the buffet and then get talking. Eshwari perks up, chatting with them in a mixture of various languages, discussing holidays she's taken or is planning to take, swapping horror stories featuring lost passports, stolen wallets, dropped cell phones and diarrhoea, bragging volubly of sunsets seen, epiphanies had and disgusting things eaten. Satish, a hard-working man with buildings to build and money to make, is first politely and then openly bored.

'Your boyfriend is bored,' one of the Europeans says finally.

'He's not my boyfriend,' she says dismissively, cheeks not even reddening.

'I'm her *father*,' Satish says grimly, scooping her up by the back of her shirt and marching her away, leaving the group gawping.

'Steesh, what the hell!' she struggles. 'Let me go!'

He turns the corridor and lets her go unceremoniously.

'What the hell?' she repeats, flicking her hair out of her eyes.

'Oh, go back if you like,' he mutters. 'Talk to the druggies instead of me.'

'They're not druggies!' she exclaims, her eyes growing round at the idea.

'They smell of weed. And worse.'

'You're so rude!'

He doesn't reply, just glowers down at her, all big, brown, brooding disapproval.

'And south Indian,' she adds. And then feels about seventeen years old.

'What's wrong with south Indians now?' he demands. 'At least my south Indian grandfather isn't being sued by his brother for being a bastard.'

'Why are you so *angry*?'

He stares down at her, his hands balling into helpless fists, confused. Eshwari Thakur—small, gutsy, unattainable.

'Nothing,' he says finally. 'It's just...' He draws a deep breath. 'I'm not rational on the subject of drugs, okay?'

They stand in the corridor, a corridor strangely reminiscent of the Modern School corridors where they spent over ten years squabbling, making up and then squabbling all over again. Satish stares at her and she stares back, seeing that devastating, puppy-like quality stealing into his hard eyes. Then she walks across the little distance that separates them and hugs him.

'I'm sorry,' she says sincerely, her cheek against his shoulder. 'It's just that...I'm just really excited about Make My Trek. I know it's no big construction firm—or a husband and two fine kids—but it's the only thing keeping me going right now.'

'What did you say?' Satish's voice comes out rather faint. 'I didn't hear a thing you said because you were hugging me.'

Eshwari laughs. 'You're such an idiot!'

He offers to go back and be charming to the alleged druggies and give them the entire sales spiel on Make My Trek dot com, but she stops him.

'It's not that kind of website,' she says. 'It doesn't go chasing people. They come chasing it. At least they will, once I set it up.'

Satish clicks his fingers and grins.

'So lemme fund your start-up. In return for certain um...*benefits*.'

'Fuck off,' she replies sweetly. 'Once the house sells, I won't need any funding.'

She starts to stalk away but he reaches out and grabs her by the waist, his hands locking over her navel and pulling her back against him with a gentle *whummp*.

'You don't need anything from anyone, do you?' he says wistfully. 'You're truly, entirely self-sufficient. It's a very unattractive trait.'

'Yeah, *right*,' she mutters, slightly winded.

They sit on the parapet wall of the star-lit corridor, overlooking the cobbled courtyard, and for the longest time all he does is nuzzle her shiny hair as her slight figure leans against his large one, his arms wrapped tight around her shoulders.

'Bihari,' he whispers.

'Hmm?' Her voice is warm and content.

'This feels right, doesn't it?'

'Yes.'

His arms tighten just a little around her body at that, and his eyes blaze with triumph, but she doesn't see this, for her head is resting upon his chest, and she is listening dreamily to the steady beating of his heart.

'Why did it take you so long to realize this feels right?'

'Because I am an idiot,' she answers.

'No, I'm an idiot. I should've done what you asked. Stayed squeaky clean and innocent, and saved up all my lovin' just for *you*.'

'That would've been nice.'

He kisses the top of her head.

'I'm sorry.'

'It's a bit late in the day for all that, anyway,' she says. 'I'm thirty-seven years old—I've seen seven penises.'

'Wanna see your eighth and last?'

'Yes.'

Satish Sridhar wakes up to the sound of a dreadful caterwauling, a sound he cannot, at first, identify. Sunshine filters in through the brightly coloured stained-glass windows—early morning sunshine—it cannot be more than six o'clock. He sits up, staring blankly across the length of the massive haveli-style suite to the gilt mirror on the opposite wall. His hair is messy, and his torso, he is pleased to note, is a decently sculpted deep brown against the blue and white block-printed sheets.

He feels about for his jeans in the tumbled bedclothes, finds them, pulls them on and gets out of bed. Crossing the room in two long strides, he yanks open the French doors to the filigreed balcony and politely requests the mustachioed sarangi player in the courtyard below to please shut the fuck up.

The musician grins, rubbing his finger and thumb together suggestively.

'Anything!' Satish calls down in reply. 'The biggest tip ever! Just, no more sarangi, okay?'

The musician nods, puts down his bow and strolls away. A blessed peace immediately descends over the scene, punctuated only by the sound of peacocks shrieking to each other in the woods beyond. Satish straddles the balcony wall, assessing the drop to the courtyard below, and decides it can be risked.

He jumps, landing clumsily, then gets to his feet and sets off on a long walk.

This is ancestral Thakur territory, desert scrubland, abounding in kinkily curving keekar trees, with lacy grey leaves and giant bone-white thorns. Muscular armoured lizards crawl about in the dry ground below, there are anthills everywhere, and the air smells like a mix of diesel and goat droppings.

As the sun rises higher over the Aravallis and the world stirs and starts to go about its business, Satish Sridhar takes a deep breath and thinks back to the magical night he has just spent.

For the longest time, ever since he can remember, he has wanted to have the E-for entrancing, E-for elusive Eshwari Thakur. And now he has finally had her.

How, if at all, does that change the plans he has for the house that BJ built?

Back on Hailey Road, healthy young Asharfi is giving Chachiji a foot massage. The two of them have struck up quite a friendship over cups of adrak-ki-chai drunk together on warm afternoons, massages with pots of Charmis cold cream and much reminiscing about the good old days when Hailey Court wasn't a building of flats but a lovely old house with pillared verandahs.

'But we may again have a house with garden and verandah,' Chachiji tells Asharfi cosily, looking about the number 16 compound with a proprietorial eye. 'AN will win his case and then this house will be ours. Not that I will throw the girls out—they can come and stay with us any time they like. Family is family, after all.'

'How kind you are,' Asharfi murmurs in reply as she gingerly eases off the silver toe-rings from Chachiji's hoofish feet by applying lavish amounts of cold cream. 'So large-hearted.'

Chachiji leans back in her chair. 'That's what the doctors say also,' she says proudly. 'My heart is enlarged, na, so I forgive people easily—even people who have done me many many wrongs!'

'It's a cruel world,' rues healthy young Asharfi.

Chachiji heaves a gusty sigh. 'True. Chalo, at least I am blessed with a loyal husband who has eyes only for me!'

'How nice,' murmurs Asharfi dulcetly, lashes lowered.

Presently, Chachiji dozes off, her feet spread wide, carefully painted toes sparkling pink in the sunlight. Healthy young Asharfi pads away and gets busy with her many other chores.

The sisters, hurrying out of the house for the District Court hearing, come upon Chachiji's gently snoring figure in the verandah and do a double take.

'Making herself quite at home, I see,' Anjini sniffs.

'She used to do this when the contractors were getting the flat at Hailey Court ready,' Debjani recalls. 'She'd practically breathe down their necks, tell them to zor lagao and polish the marble well, and think about where-where to put which-which bit of furniture. I bet that's what she's dreaming about. Look, she's smiling.'

'Let's put some chilli powder in her mouth,' Chandu suggests impulsively, then gives a guilty giggle at her sisters' surprised expressions. 'What?'

Dabbu smiles. 'Nothing. Just…nice to hear you talk like that. Now let's leave Chachiji to her dreams—we don't want to be late for court.'

'Wow, this place looks like Hogwarts!' Eshwari exclaims, looking around happily at the seedy atrium of the District Court. 'Look at everybody swanking around stylishly in their billowing black robes!'

Debjani gives her a strange look. 'The last time we came here you said this place was filthy.'

Eshwari looks surprised. 'No, I didn't! And it's quite clean, anyway.'

'Cleaner than *you*, Miss Dirty Weekend,' snorts Anjini, her aam-papad eyes scanning her baby sister penetratingly and missing nothing. 'You're looking extremely *"satish"*fied I must say.'

Eshu grins. 'I am.'

Anjini gives a little scream. 'No!'

'No restraint,' Chandu sniffs. 'No morals. Chhee.'

'Already?' Debjani looks disturbed. 'I hope you were careful?'

'Look hair, ladies! Look hair! Could you please come hair!'

They turn to look at the lawyer who has replaced Shahrukh Paperwallah. He has dirty orange, mehendi-dyed hair, combed over to hide a bald spot, a baby-face, a four-day stubble and a weird desi-American twang. His black robes smell strongly of Benedryl cough syrup.

'Yes, Mr Srivastava,' Anjini says politely. 'Right behind you, Mr Srivastava!'

'Look hair, what's going on?' giggles Eshwari as they hurry along through the atrium behind Mehendi Combover, while he marches ahead, robes billowing. 'Who *is* this dude?'

'He's supposed to be the bomb,' Anjini whispers. 'He fought the number 5 Hailey Road case—got the daughter her rights and defeated the brothers. Is that a *love bite?*'

'Of course not!' Eshwari turns red. 'How old d'you think I am?'

Mehendi Combover pulls up in front of the gents' loo.

'Wait hair,' he says impressively and vanishes inside. The sisters look at each other.

'Why does he have an American accent?' Eshu whispers.

'Only you can go to America or what?' Anji replies. 'He's very good—costs four lakhs an hour.'

'And we thought Paperwallah was expensive!'

'If you're so smart, *you* find the lawyers,' Anjini tells her waspishly.

'Sorry.' Eshu grins amiably. 'But *see* how long he's taking! Look hair, can we deduct money for three minutes 'coz he's pissing on our time?'

'Of course,' chimes in Chandu. 'We have to. That'll be about…' she calculates busily, 'twenty grand less.'

The courthouse is teeming with people, all busy talking and fidgeting and making phone calls, and getting up and shuffling in and out of the various rooms that ring the atrium, each one of which is a different judge's court.

Anjini clutches Dabbu's hand. 'There's Chachaji. And Gulgul! Right across from us!'

'They have so many files,' Eshwari says. 'What could be *in* them?'

'Should we say hi?' Chandu asks doubtfully.

'No,' Anjini says firmly. 'He was horrid to Eshu last time—Dabbu, *don't*.'

'I *will*,' Dabbu insists. 'We should. The Bible says "Blessed are the Peacemakers".'

Saying which she walks over to the twosome, who are busy trying to hide behind their files and pretending they haven't spotted the little huddle of Thakur sisters.

'Aur karo Christian se shaadi,' Eshwari says resignedly.

The sisters watch as Dabbu approaches the duo, her smile warm, her hands held out in greeting.

'*Hiiii!*' says Dabbu. 'How are you?'

Gulgul promptly goes bright red.

'Hullo Dabbu,' he says wretchedly.

Debjani kisses him on both cheeks. Gulgul looks even more miserable. Next Dabbu moves towards her uncle, radiating sweetness and warmth from every pore.

'Namaste, Chachaji.'

But Ashok averts his eyes and picks up his phone and starts to fiddle with it, acting like he hasn't seen his niece.

'Namaste Chachaji,' she repeats.

Still Ashok Narayan looks away and plays with his phone.

Dabbu's nostrils flare.

'I said, *Namaste Chachaji.*'

People have started whispering, some of them have recognized her. Trapped, Ashok has no option but to acknowledge her presence. His weak, once-handsome face grows venomous, and he says, not to her, but more in explanation to the thick crowd of people around them: 'Heh heh, what to do? Illegitimate baap ki madwoman beti.'

Debjani, so elegant and composed and serene, staggers back. The fact that her father's brother, a man who once dangled her on his knee, who spoilt them all so fondly, and whose life her husband once saved, has dismissed her so callously, hurts like a kick to the gut of her soul. Her hands curl instinctively into angry fists to be sure, but at the same time tears also spring to her eyes.

Anjini comes up from behind her, her beautiful face set in grim lines.

'Don't talk to him,' she says fiercely. 'Dabbu, come *here.*'

'Yeah, come back hair,' chimes in Eshwari, looking daggers at her uncle. 'The poor man's a nutcase, clearly the loss of his own house has driven him insane...'

'Yes yes come away, Ms Debjani,' says Mehendi Combover, emerging from the loo. 'They are just nervous because they know we have a good case—all their oversmartness has boomawronged on them.'

'You've hired a lawyer with a fake American accent who says *boomawronged?*' Eshwari is appalled. 'Anji didi, what are you *doing?*'

'I know what I'm doing,' is Anjini's level reply. 'We're going to skewer Ashok chacha, one way or the other.'

Dabbu sits down heavily on her metal chair with none of her usual grace. She's feeling physically sick. We're actually in the *thick* of it, she realizes. Full-on family property dispute. Evil uncles, forged wills, traitorous cousins, et al. Who would've thought? Up until now, she's somehow always felt that they are just one candid, sensible conversation away from resolving the whole issue with Ashok Narayan and Gulgul. But clearly that isn't the case.

A large lady in a nylon suit smiles kindly at her. 'Family dispute?' she asks sympathetically.

Dabbu's chin comes up.

'No no. Our family is very close. Just a small, er, *misunderstanding.*'

Dimly, she is aware that Mehendi Combover has buttonholed somebody against the wall and is talking to him about tennis.

'Djokovich ko chhodo, sir! Best rivalry is between Federer and Nadal! One is all ground work and tuff spirit, other has a fluid all-court game. Myself, I am more in the Nadal style—my ground work is my strength and I am tuff. Enough? Yes of course, see you inside, Your Lordship, sir.'

'Our Judge,' he tells Dabbu in an aside, dabbing carefully around his combover with a damp hanky. 'Big tennis fan. Doesn't hurt to chit-chat little bit, no.'

In the courtroom, which looks much like a slightly run-down classroom, everybody rises with so much respect as a solemn-looking gentleman enters that Eshwari half-expects them to sing out 'Good morning sir' like they used to back in school.

The solemn looking person turns out to be some kind of

minion, however. He is carrying an orthopaedic back cushion, which he instals ceremoniously on the Judge's chair. He exits, walking backwards, and then the Judge enters. A short, irritable person who appears to be in some pain.

'Sit, sit,' he says grumpily. 'Yes, show me, what's the case now?' He spots Mehendi Combover and Gulgul bowing and scraping before him and seems to wince. 'Ah, Srivastava saab and young Thakur,' he says unenthusiastically. 'You two.'

Mehendi Combover starts to argue the case, referring to members of their family as Plaintiff 1 and Plaintiff 2 and Defendant 1, 2, 3, 4 and 5. He tries to establish that Ashok is basically a shady dude who has gambled away his own house and is now trying to grab another house and gamble that away too. But the Judge looks unimpressed. He dismisses Ashok's profligacy as irrelevant and asks Mehendi Combover if he has any proof that the will Ashok has presented is fake, as that had been his client's plea last time. Mehendi Combover has to admit that he doesn't have proof as of now, and instead stresses the fact that all this is ancient history, settled years ago, that Pushkar clearly left one house each to his sons when he died, and therefore Plaintiff 1's application is frivolous, baseless, malafide and trying to invent a new narrative.

'Yeah, that's telling him!' Eshwari mutters as Mehendi Combover winds up his little speech.

They look hopefully at the Judge, who says, 'But that isn't what you argued last time. The record clearly shows that last time you said the will was fake—this time you are saying why rake up issues which are so many years old? Make up your mind, please.'

Mehendi Combover opens and shuts his mouth, blinking rapidly.

'Look hair,' he says weakly. 'Look hair.'

'It's *fake*,' Eshwari whispers fiercely.

All eyes swivel to her. The cranky Judge allows himself a thin smile.

'The point is, Srivastava saab, that you still have not managed to establish what you claimed last time, that this will of—what's-his-name-again?'

'Pushkar Narayan Thakur,' supplies Gulgul, springing up like a jack-in-the-box.

'Yes, that this will of Pushkar Narayan Thakur is fake or invalid.'

Mehendi Combover licks his lips. 'But most honourable Milord, we have clearly established hair that Plaintiff 1 is in the habit of forging his father's signature—'

'Which doesn't necessarily mean that he did it this time,' the Judge points out. 'Do you have any other proof?'

Mehendi Combover mumbles something about it being hard to find proof of something that happened so many years ago, as everybody concerned is dead.

'Milord, counsel is again and again attempting to imply that everything was settled years ago!' Gulgul springs to his feet again. 'The fact of the case is that Pushkar Narayan Thakur, deeply suspicious of this supposedly premature cackkoo in his nest, carried out certain enquiries that cunfirmed his suspicions. Once he had this cunfirmation, he made out a new will leaving all his property to his younger son, my client, Plaintiff 1! Tauji—beg your pardon, Laxmi Narayan Thakur, first suppressed and later contested that will, and being a well-connected man in the legal system, he seemed to prevail. My client, burdened by an ailing wife to whom he is devoted and for whose treatment and medication he got so severely into debt that he had to sell his house, stopped pursuing the case due to financial compulsions. Also, he was tender-hearted, and knowing that Laxmi Narayan Thakur had five daughters of marriageable age, he decided to hold his horse and save them all from social embarrassment. So he very considerately waited for both Laxmi Narayan Thakur and his wife to pass away before bringing the case back to your Judgeshipji's notice.'

Saala Gulgul, Dabbu thinks, numbed by these histrionics. Look at him go. The bugger's on fire! Who would've thought he could be this effective? Must be Hanumanji ki kripa. And what was all that crap about Chachiji's illness? She's as healthy as a horse.

Gulgul takes a deep breath and continues, 'Justice has been delayed, Milord, let it now not be denied! It would make Pushkar Narayan's worst nightmare come true to allow his ancestral property to pass into the hands of his wife's paramour and his heirs! They cannot be allowed to sell this land, which Pushkar Narayan bought with money earned by the sweat of his brow! That would also be a grave miscarriage of justice!'

'Selling?' demands the Judge testily. 'Nobody can sell anything till the court rules. Everything is frozen until then.'

'Shit,' mutters Dabbu.

Gulgul whirls around, his hair bouncing prettily.

'Milord, allow me to say that Defendants 1, 2, 3, 4 and 5 — all of whom are rich NRIs and big media personalities and therefore have scant respect for our esteemed District Court — are attempting to do a quick and secret sale to SteelBird Constructions! They think they can throw dust into the eyes of Lady Justice — but they forget that she is blindfolded!'

'Hmmm,' says the Judge, sifting through the files before him. 'Young Thakur wants to submit some more applications, he says. I'll need those to reach a decision. Anything else?'

The sisters look appealingly at Mehendi Combover, but he just smooths his hair and studies his files, his face rather red. He seems to have shot his bolt.

Eshwari prods him hard and he leaps to his feet.

'Er, Milord, my clients have come hair from America and left their news anchoring and their film-directing to settle this. They need to go back to their jobs, so I would like to request a speedy settlement.'

'I'll give the property to Mr Ashok then,' says the Judge mildly. 'Right here right now. That will settle everything. Shall I?'

Mehendi Combover throws up his hands and grins weakly. 'Heh heh, Your Judgeshipji, you are joke—no, of course we will come back—whenever you say. Heh heh heh.'

The Judge adjusts his spondylosis cushion and drinks a glass of water. 'Come back in a month's time.'

And with that he looks at his clerk, who immediately pings the number of the next case.

⚬

'This could go on for frickin' forever,' Eshwari says gloomily.

'It's costing a *fortune*,' Chandu frets.

'Chachaji *hates* us,' sighs Dabbu numbly.

'It's going to be *fine*!' declares Anjini sunnily. 'Wanna go to the beauty parlour at Malcha Marg and get pedicures?'

'Nooo,' groan the other three in rare unison.

'Fine then, grumpies,' Anjini tosses her hair. '*I'm* going.' She looks again at Eshu. 'Won't you come? We can talk about your long drive and your night stay and all? Please?'

'No!' snaps Eshwari, whose good mood seems to have vanished with a vengeance.

Anjini flounces off and spends the rest of the day pampering herself at the salon. With the result that when Samar walks into the dining room in a foul mood the next morning, he finds his stepmother looking stunningly beautiful and cutting apple slices and putting them into Zeeshan Khan's plate while he gazes upon her besottedly. They've clearly set up a mutual admiration society.

'Don't they serve breakfast at your hotel?' Samar growls.

'A mystery has just been solved!' Zeeshan exclaims, ignoring this. 'I used to wonder why you're never dazzled by physical beauty, an ordinary looking sod like you, now I know!'

'What do you know?' Anjini pouts prettily. 'And don't call my son ordinary looking—he's very attractive!'

'Well, if he had *you* ironing his school shirt every morning, no wonder *Playboy* centrefolds and Miss Universes don't impress him in the least!' says Zeeshan.

'Ironing his *shirts*?' Anjini is appalled. 'We had a *dhobi*. What do you think I am?'

'I think you're gorgeous, Anjini!'

'Auntie,' Samar says repressively as he leans forward and scores some sliced apple too. 'Anjini *auntie*. I call your mother auntie—kindly return the favour.'

'Dude, my mother *looks* like an auntie,' Zeeshan returns. '*You* on the other hand, Auntie A, look like—'

'Never mind what she looks like,' Samar says austerely. 'Flirt with somebody your own age.'

'Where's Bonita?' asks Anjini pertinently with wide-eyed innocence. 'Ah, *here* she is!'

Samar immediately swivels around, almost dropping his plate, to find nobody walking in. Anjini and Zeeshan chuckle.

Samar puts down his plate, his lean cheeks flushed.

'Hey, Bonu Singh,' says Anjini. 'Want some apple?'

'I won't fall for it twice, Ma,' Samar growls.

'Thanks, Anji mausi,' Bonu's voice says from behind him. 'Good morning, you guys.'

Anjini and Zeeshan greet her enthusiastically. Samar focuses on his fruit, glancing up briefly to ask his stepmother, 'So what happened at the hearing?'

'It got pushed again,' Anjini sighs. 'Mehendi Combover pulled a long face, said we had better do an out-of-court compro with Ashok chacha, charged us six lakhs and went off happily.'

'Shit,' says Bonu.

'Good advice,' Samar says grimly, rolling up his sleeves. 'I'd like four aloo paranthas with pickle and dahi please, and as soon as I've eaten them I'll go over to Ashok chacha's and beat the shit out of him. I'll punch him and punch him and punch him until he agrees to do compro and take the case back. And then we'll all be able to sell before Akshaya Tritiya.'

Anjini puts down her knife and stares at her boy, her nostrils flaring ominously, very much in the style of her father.

'He's kidding,' Zeeshan says hastily. 'It was a joke. Joke tha.'

'Be quiet,' Anjini snaps. 'I don't need you to translate what my son says!' She turns to Samar. 'Why is beating up people your only solution to everything nowadays? What is *wrong* with you?'

Zeeshan opens his mouth to speak but receives such nasty looks from both mother and son that he wisely decides to eat his apple instead.

Samar tears into his parantha, saying nothing. Anjini continues to glower at him.

'The Pushkarni had a lover,' he says after a couple of bites. 'Not before she got married—that's all Ashok chacha's bullshit—

but much later, when BJ was twenty-five and Ashok sixteen. Pushkar found out about it and had her murdered.'

'What?' exclaims Bonu. 'That's bizarre. Did Mrs Mumtani tell you that?'

Samar nods and fills them in on Mrs Mumtani's recollections.

Anjini hears him out quietly, then closes her eyes and rests her palms over them.

Samar, Zeeshan and Bonu look at each other apprehensively.

Then Anjini sits up and looks straight at Samar.

'So what?'

He stops, a bite of parantha halfway to his mouth. 'Huh?'

She nods. 'Ya, so what? Big deal! So BJ got it all wrong—his parents weren't madly in love—they clearly hated each other, and cheated on each other—but they're all *dead* now, Samar, so why is it even relevant?'

He stares at her moodily. 'Maybe you're right,' he admits at last. 'I just…wanted my film to be true, I guess.'

'Ego,' says his stepmother, picking up her knife and slicing apples with force. 'That's all it is. Ego. And hubris. And self-centredness. You had better make your *own* love story come true instead of worrying about bloody Pushkar's. Then maybe you'll stop wanting to beat up people.'

Zeeshan nods vigorously in agreement. Bonu gets to her feet, rather red-cheeked, and makes for the door.

'Arrey, eat more, Bonu beta,' Anjini calls out but Bonu shakes her head.

'Busy day,' she smiles politely. 'I'm heading to Nehru Place to source some stuff and the traffic's always murder.'

Her gaze skitters to Samar, almost involuntarily. 'Don't kill Ashok chacha,' she says lightly.

She walks out and silence fills the room. Anjini and Zeeshan stare at Samar reproachfully.

'What?' he snarls.

They shake their heads, saying nothing, their gazes pitying.

He reaches bad-temperedly for the pickle, just as Eshu strolls in.

'There's a fat man looking for you,' she tells Samar, rubbing her eyes sleepily. 'I put him in the living room.'

16

'Why's *he* in such an antsy mood?' Eshwari asks Anjini after Samar and Zeeshan exit the room. 'Bonu Singh again? God, I'm *sick* of their cute, lovey-dovey little skirmishes.'

Anjini shoots her a speculative glance. 'Why?' she asks bluntly. 'You were pretty lovey-dovey yourself a few days ago. Your hickies haven't even faded yet.'

'They're not hickies,' Eshwari snaps. 'I'm not a *teenager* to come home with hickies.'

Anjini looks sympathetic. 'Satish hasn't called?'

Eshwari shakes her head, her bold black eyes vulnerable. 'No,' she whispers. 'Oh God, I cannot *believe* I've put myself in this position! I'm disgusted with myself!'

Anjini hugs her. 'You'll be fine.'

'I *am* fine!' Eshu snarls, shaking her off but not ungently.

Anjini hugs her harder, and says consolingly.

'Here, eat some apple.'

Inside Mamtaji's flowered living room, Samar is eyeing his fat visitor uneasily. Cougar Malhotra is breathing hard, and looking all worked up. It's just the two of them, as Zeeshan had taken one look at the visitor, muttered something about an urgent call, and fled the room.

'What's up, Cougee?' Samar asks. 'How come the visit? All good with the film?'

Cougar nods. 'Oh, yes, everything is good. The background score's done, and they've incorporated almost all your changes. You'll need to come and look at it in about a week's time.'

'Good,' Samar says.

'This is about something *else*.'

Samar is startled. 'Okay.'

'Something far more important.'

'*Okay*.'

Cougar leans forward, jiggling one fat thigh against the sofa. 'Samar, baby, you know I love you.'

Samar knows no such thing but he puts on a sincere expression and nods. 'Sure, bro.'

'I give you good advice, and I've got your back—after all, I'm the one who got you this incredibly sweet deal with Sonix.'

Samar could use other adjectives to describe his deal with Sonix, but he's too curious to know where this is going to argue. So he just nods again.

'Of course.'

Cougar leans forward further. He will topple into Samar's lap if he isn't careful.

'I want you to prepare yourself,' he says earnestly.

'I'm all braced,' Samar assures him, wondering what's coming. Has Sonix gone bankrupt? Have they destroyed all copies of the film by mistake? Don't the distributers want the film anymore?

Cougar locks eyeballs with him, inhales and then exhales so gustily that Samar can feel his breath ruffling the hair on his forehead.

'I've betrayed you, brother. I've stabbed you in the back.'

Samar's sense of foreboding grows. Has the bastard promised AK another item song?

'Um…how?' he asks warily.

Cougar scoots in closer.

'*I* got you the Sonix deal. Remember that.'

'Yeah cool, I remember,' Samar replies, now thoroughly fed-up. 'Just spit it out, Coug, you're killing me.'

Cougar lowers his eyes. And his voice.

'Susan and I have got together, Samar baby.'

Samar's mouth falls open.

'*What?*'

Cougar nods.

Samar stares at him, slack-jawed.

'It's a shock to you, I see.'

Samar blinks. His jaw works, but no words emerge.

'Samar!' Cougar looks seriously alarmed.

'Er…uh…yes,' Samar manages to say, his voice coming out strangled. 'Wow! But when…and why…and *how?*'

Now that the worst is over, Cougar sits back, relieved, rather like a fat dog that's coughed up a bone that was stuck in his throat. 'Well, it all started during the *Aur Jee* schedule. Your cousin got us talking about Benarasi, remember? And how we should be using fake stuff for shoots. Susan and I had a major argument about that later.'

Samar nods, seemingly listening intently, but in fact not a single word has registered in his brain since 'Susan and I have got together'. He is conscious of a deep, strong gladness, a sense of celebration so huge it feels like very expensive firecrackers are shooting up into the skies straight out of his heart.

Cougar continues, 'My team alleged that Susan had been marking up the price of the real Benarasi by about three hundred percent. So I called her and in my usual brash, insensitive producer style, threatened to cancel her contract and stop all her payments. She stayed absolutely cool, and asked me out to dinner to discuss things and sort out the misunderstanding.'

Things are starting to register for Samar again. He leans forward, interested.

'Then?'

Cougar turns a rather unattractive maroon.

'We went out and she explained that though her prices *appear* to be marked up, *all* the profits from the business actually go to help the weavers...'

'They do?' Samar says, reeling. 'How?'

'Well, yes, she explained all that to me in great detail...she had pie charts and everything...and she was wearing this perfume...'

'Thierry Mugler's Angel.'

'Yes! And as she talked, the scales fell from my eyes and I saw what a warm, wonderful person she was, in this hard, money-minded world...and right when I was thinking that, she said she was tired of talking about work and that I really reminded her of an uncle she had a crush on when she was fifteen and kissed me.'

'Wow.' Samar, light-headed with relief, realizes that he should be looking suitably shattered and cunningly adjusts his expression. 'I mean, that's *disgusting*—you could at least spare me the graphic details, you insensitive bastard!'

'I'm so sorry,' Cougar says sincerely. 'Anyway, we have been seeing each other since and now we've decided we want to be together.'

'Disgusting!' Samar snorts, now looking grievously wronged. 'How could you do this to me on the eve of my film's release? Suppose I collapse? Crumple? Fuck up the entire post-prod schedule?'

'Please don't,' Cougar says unhappily.

'Unbelievable!' Samar glares at him. Then he frowns.

'Wait, why are you telling me this now? You're smart—you'd have figured it would be better to wait till the film releases.'

'Yeah, well…' Cougar rests his elbows upon his fat thighs. 'Samar baby, there's been a media leak. The journos already know Susan and I are an item. There are stories breaking as we speak. Or there will be by tonight, at the latest.'

'Tonight! I'm to be made a laughing stock tonight!'

The fat man nods. 'So I felt I must come and tell you. It's only the decent thing to do…'

Samar throws a hand over his eyes dramatically, and collapses back on the couch.

'Get out of my sight!'

Looking suitably shamefaced, Cougar gets up and waddles swiftly out of the room.

Samar drops his hand, then pumps his fists into the air in triumph, and laughs—a delighted, disbelieving laugh.

'Thank God!' he says feelingly. 'Thank *God!*'

'And thank *me*, fucker.'

Zeeshan has re-entered the room, grinning. Samar sits bolt upright.

'What'd you do?'

'He told you he and Susan are an item, right?'

'How d'you know?'

'Yes!' Zeeshan collapses onto a flowered couch, and props his legs up on the coffee table.

'Get your feet off my grandma's table,' Samar tells him. 'And spill.'

Zeeshan obeys both instructions, grinning widely.

'Well, I might have had a cosy little dinner for two with the Adam a while go...'

'And?' Samar's voice is sharp.

'Where I might have had too many drinks and voiced my concerns that this er, film that you've directed—*Thakur Saab*...'

'Yes, I know it's called *Thakur Saab*,' Samar snaps. 'What about it?'

Zeeshan gathers speed. 'I revealed that the producers have stopped calling it *Tharki Thakur* and started calling it *Turkey Thakur*. The thing is an absolute turkey—distributors are predicting it's gonna be a colossal, humiliating flop—and how the item song is a desperate gimmick to somehow make it work.'

'You did,' Samar repeats blankly. 'And then?'

'And then I urged her, with tears in my eyes, to be there for you when it flopped because more than anybody else, you needed *her* by your side. He's going to have a nervous breakdown, I told her. The humiliation will *kill* him. Promise me you'll be there—and she nodded and got all teary-eyed too, and put her hand in mine and *swore* that she'd be there for you.'

Samar nods, his gaze sardonic. 'I bet she did.'

Zeeshan grins. 'And then, just to nail the deal, I showed her multiple newspaper articles saying your granddad's just, you know, a bastard with no legal claim whatsoever over this big-ass house, and that your grand-uncle's gonna inherit it and that you'll end up with zip, zero, nada. And then...' He gives a wickedly unrepentant grin. 'Well, and then I guess she discovered Cougee's meaty charms.'

Samar gets to his feet and clasps his friend in a heartfelt embrace.

'Nice work, Chawla.'

'I know,' Zeeshan grins, clapping him hard on the back. 'Now I've got to go back to Bombay and shoot a love scene in a jacuzzi, bro. You are officially in charge of your own love life. Don't fuck it up.'

Outside, in the verandah, the Pricey Thakur Girls have reached pretty much the end of their tether.

'Why the hell must the courts close for the summer?' Eshu gripes. 'Are they schools or courts? Are we all supposed to just live in limbo till they open again? This whole situation sucks balls.'

'What a disgusting expression,' Chandu frowns. 'Chhee.'

'I'm using it to express disgust,' Eshu snaps. 'That's why it must necessarily be disgusting.'

'Girls, please,' Anjini sighs. 'Let's not bicker.'

'Yeah, well, at least, because the bloody IPL's on, I get a couple of weeks off,' Dabbu says brightly. 'It's so good to be here, at home! Especially since Anji didi made everything so comfy! Achha, where are Bonu and Samar? I'd love to see them together and get some vicarious thrills.'

'Why do you care about them?' Eshu says grumpily. 'Don't you urgently need funding so your channel can stay independent?'

Dabbu subsides, her enthusiasm dampened. 'Yes, I do.'

There is silence.

'So what was Gulgul saying to you?' Chandu asks suspiciously. 'You spent the whole morning with him. I saw.'

'Yes, now please don't order an assassin to bump her off,' Eshu says hastily. 'She just, you know, likes hanging with Gulgul.'

'Mehendi Combover's advice was to keep our lines of communications and negotiations *open*,' Anjini says. 'Ninety-three percent of all family property disputes are resolved by out-of-court settlements, so we must keep *talking*.'

Dabbu grins appreciatively. 'Oh he was just generally being pathetic. Saying he doesn't want to see any more photos of girls to marry because what is the mazaa of getting married when he can't even invite his own sisters to the wedding? To tease him and dress him up and guard his shoes when his sisters-in-law come to steal them...'

'Bas, guarding Gulgul's shoes is the zenith of my ambitions now,' Eshu groans.

'Oh, and he said Chachaji's started test-driving cars recently,' Dabbu continues. 'Range Rovers and Mercedes and BMW...and that yesterday Chachiji put on her orange Benarasi sari and went to the big TBZ showroom to do some pre-Akshaya Tritiya shopping.'

'Fuck, Akshaya Thinggummy's here?' Eshu groans even louder. 'Phir, toh, finished.'

'TBZ's so dead,' Anji sniffs. 'She could've gone to De Beers, at least. Everybody know diamonds are in—only solitaires though, not those cheap clustery things. Sounds like Gulgul will inherit nothing again, at the rate those two will rip through our money.'

'They can't possibly blow up two hundred crores before they die!' Chandu says scandalized. 'They'll have to leave most of it to Gulgul.' She gives a thin smile, her lashless eyes blinking knowingly. '*That's* why you were being so nice to him, Dabbu!'

Dabbu looks at her blankly. 'What?' Then she gets it, and continues hotly, sounding a lot like her teenage daughter, 'Oh my *God*, that is the most *warped* thing I've ever hea—'

'Girls, please,' Anjini sighs again. 'Let's not quarrel.'

'*And* we're right back where we started,' Eshu mutters. 'Man, I've *had* it with this situation. Something's gotta *give*.'

The heat gives out first. Pre-monsoon winds sweep through the garden that afternoon, tossing the trees and scattering gulmohar flowers all over the straggly grass. Samar emerges on the verandah smiley-faced and buoyant, and as thunder rolls and raindrops pelt like running-stitch embroidery across a grey gudari of a sky, he gives a native American-style whoop, whips off his shirt and runs straight into the lawn, arms outstretched.

'This is awesome!' shouts the all-new, suddenly demented Samar. 'Woo-hoo!'

He proceeds to splash madly in the squishy grass, then run up the driveway to lean on the gate, and finishes by swinging from a low-hanging branch of the champa tree, shaking it so that rain, flowers and leaves fall about him in a cold, fragrant mess.

'*Such* a handsome boy,' Anjini says smugly from the upstairs window.

'True,' agrees Dabbu. 'What Pasta would call The Bomb.'

'A+ for the butt,' Eshu decides, leaning forward and squinting hard. 'At least I *think* so—you know what, girls, I may finally have to give in and get my eyes tested.'

'And a good person also,' Chandu provides the deeper quotient pointedly, as a reprimand to her shallower sisters. 'Such a caring nature.'

Samar is now lying in a happy stupor upon a drenched garden bench. His eyes are closed, his lips upturned in a happy smile. As the women in the window look down at him indulgently, an auto-rickshaw wheezes up to the old green gate and Bonu Singh gets off. She hands the unseen driver some money, opens the gate and enters the driveway.

'Uff, don't, *idiot!*' hisses Eshu, for Samar, having noticed Bonu's arrival, has sat up, stopped smiling, and started pulling on his drenched t-shirt.

Bonu advances into the garden. Up in the window, her Dabbu mausi sighs and gets all dewy-eyed, her Eshu mausi rolls her eyes, her Chandu mausi appears mostly unmoved, and her Anji mausi appreciates how deliciously her wet malmal kurti is clinging to her voluptuous form. As the two young people approach each other in approved Bollywood style, music playing from a thousand dipping and rising violin bows in the background, a third figure blooms out of the pelting rain. It is Chachiji, moving fast.

She closes in on the couple and shakes them both violently, turn by turn. She gestures animatedly; Bonu nods and grabs her hand, while Samar runs into the verandah. Three minutes later, he emerges with a big black umbrella and hustles the women under it. The three of them then make for Hailey Court at a smart clip, even as the rain changes into fifth gear with a drumroll of thunder and a sword of silver lightning splits the sky.

'What the hell!' Eshu exclaims at the upstairs window.

'Something's up,' says Dabbu.

'Should we also go there?' Anjini asks.

'Yes!' Chandu nods decisively.

Over at Hailey Court, Chachiji's cheeks are wet with rain. Her iron-grey hair is plastered to her forehead and her beady eyes are blazing with righteous wrath. Wordlessly she pushes Samar and Bonu before her through the over-furnished, glitzy apartment, out onto a balcony, and stops them in front of a bedroom window.

'Yes, Chachiji,' Samar tells her soothingly. 'I have my phone,

I already told you three times that I have my phone. What do you want me to record exactl—holy *fuck.*'

Carefully averting his eyes, and without asking further questions, he raises his phone, points it in the relevant direction and presses record. Bonu has no such scruples—she watches the action in the bedroom unabashedly, mouth open, eyes practically on sticks. Samar's camera rolls for a good thirty seconds.

'And...*cut,*' breathes Samar softly. 'Got it, Chachiji.'

'Pukka?' she wants to know.

'Yeah, I'm sure,' he assures her. 'Here, have a look.'

She scans the footage beadily, tears running silently down her cheeks, then nods, and before they can stop her, flat palms the window and starts banging upon it, hard.

Dhaaam dhaaam dhaaam, go Chachiji's palms upon the bedroom window. Dhaam dhadaaam dhaaaam!

Then she turns around, and snarling purposefully, heads back inside to stand like a pug at bay at the bedroom door. It opens, right on cue, and out drifts healthy young Asharfi, only slightly dishevelled, holding a cloth duster with a long handle and looking like butter wouldn't melt in her mouth.

'Cleaning the fan,' she says dreamily. 'Very dirty all the fans in this house are. I'll do the kitchen fan now.'

'Oh no, you won't!' Chachiji snorts, leaping forward and snatching the mop.

Healthy young Asharfi sighs and wanders away with great dignity, moving faster once she's out of Chachiji's line of vision. As she rounds the corner, she comes upon the four Thakur sisters bunched up near the front door, wide-eyed and bedraggled from their little trek in the rain.

'Well?' asks Anjini breathlessly while the others stare at her, puzzled.

'Done,' responds Asharfi nonchalantly and sashays away. The women hurry into the apartment to hear Bonu's voice pleading, loudly, with not too much sincerity.

'Chachiji, stop it! Chachiji, you'll kill him! Chachiji, please!'

When Chachiji had rushed into the bedroom, wild-eyed and bulldog-like, Ashok Narayan Thakur had greeted her with a weak smile from beneath the covers of their heavy teak double bed.

'Not feeling well today, Bhudevi,' he had said. 'That maid fell off the stool when she was cleaning the fan, right on top of me...my head hurts, my neck too...'

'Your neck hurts, does it?' Chachiji had growled. 'Here, let me press it for you!'

She'd lunged for his throat, and Samar had flung his arms around her plump midriff and hauled her off the defenceless man.

Now, as the sisters tumble into the bedroom, Chachiji shakes Samar off (he had been holding on only half-heartedly, truth be told) and, gripping the long mop, she starts raining blows upon her husband as he rolls about the bed, cowering and yelping and begging her to have mercy.

The blanket pitai continues for a while, until finally, Ashok Narayan Thakur goes still and quiescent. Bhudevi stares down at him, bug-eyed, watchful for the slightest movement. A tiny tentative moan escapes his lips after a space, which she promptly punishes with yet another vicious whack of her mop.

Ashok shudders and lies absolutely still.

Chachiji gives a grunt of satisfaction, flings the mop away and sinks to the floor.

'Enough!' she pants. 'That's quite enough. This man is a *pig*, a *worm*, the crooked tail of a mongrel *dog*. *And* a cheat!

How much I looked after him, nursed him through three sicknesses, changed his dirty diapers, never hiring a Lachhu like you rich girls, and this is how he repays me—canoodling with that chunnt Asharfi in my expensive Season's Furnishings bed sheets.'

Samar gently lifts her up and eases her into an ugly but comfy armchair. With her nieces gathered around her, Chachiji starts to weep, shoulders shaking, tears slipping down her jowly cheeks.

'I'm a fool,' she wails. 'I was always a fool about this man— just because he is so hah...hah...*handsome* and I am so *plain*!'

'You're worth *ten* of him,' says Dabbu fiercely as she plonks herself on the arm of the chair and hugs the old lady hard.

Chachiji shakes her head from side to side dolefully.

'No, I'm ugly! But he is ugly inside. He is mean to my poor Gulgul and makes fun of him, and he flatters me only when he wants something from me.'

Dabbu strokes her hair, and under her niece's worried gaze Chachiji goes quiet for a while. Then she raises her chin.

'But I've had enough. I will destroy him—I will become like that langdi Karishma in *Shastri Sisters* and *plot* and *scheme* and *spoil* all his evil plans and *destroy* him! He'll wish he had never been born!'

She kicks the foot of the bed. Ashok, very wisely, lies quiet.

'No man is worth so much effort,' Eshu thumps her back awkwardly. 'Hush now, Chachiji.'

'No, Eshu, let her talk,' says Anjini in her sweet, calm voice. 'Chachiji, how will you spoil his plans?'

Bhudevi Thakur shudders and gives a massive gulp.

'He's trying to cheat you out of your house, ladkiyon, with that fake will he got made in Chawri Bazaar, and I won't let him do it!'

There is a hoarse, pleading moan from the bed. Everybody ignores it. The heirs of Laxmi Narayan Thakur are too busy looking at each other, their eyes registering shock, then relief, then silent jubilation.

'How do you know it's fake, Chachiji?' Anjini asks in the same calm, sweet voice.

The old lady's eyes kindle.

'Arrey, because I went with him when he made it! We went together! Those days anything he told me, I used to do. So mad for him, I was. Because of his Rajesh Khanna good looks and Shashi Kapoor charm, you know. But now I will go to the court and put my hand on the Gita and swear ki he is evil! *And* I'll wear that nice boat-neck blouse Bonu just-now made for me when I do it.'

'That'll teach him,' says Anjini encouragingly. 'Go for it, Chachiji.'

The old lady's eyes well with tears again. 'Hai hai ladkiyon, I actually thought that *this* time, he has really become good! I thought the prostate and the Bail's Pelsy had taught him a lesson and that he had started focusing on God—like my Gulgul, who is *so* devout! But no, he is still up to his old tricks, the dirty old dog.' She looks around worriedly for Samar. 'Hai beta, you got everything, no?'

'I've got it all, nice and clear,' Samar assures her. 'Don't worry.'

'Show me again!' She snatches the phone from him, finds the clip and looks at it avidly, half-weeping, half-laughing, her pudgy shoulders quivering with emotion. 'His body has become all slack and thall-thall,' she gloats. 'See, so loose and wrinkly. I never noticed before, look!'

'Er...yes,' says Eshu.

'Such thin sticky calves!' cackles Chachiji gleefully. 'Horny old goat! Well, I'll do his Bakra Eid, all right.'

Ashok finally dares to sit up in bed, holding a pillow before him like a shield. Behind it, his dirty white hair is stringy with sweat and his eyes have the cringing, desperate look of a cornered mongrel.

'Bhaagwaan,' he says hoarsely. 'Bhaagwaan, listen, these cunning girls are trying to fool you. You know how gullible you are! That woman fell on me, I swear! I was just lying there! I am innocent. She is Anjini's maid and this is a trick to divide us and create trouble in our paradise.'

Chachiji bounds forward, bats away the pillow, and slaps him across the cheek.

'Achha ji? Is this what an innocent, paralyzed man does when a woman falls onto his bed?' she demands, brandishing Samar's phone at him. 'Is *this* what he does? And this? And *this*?'

Ashok closes his eyes and lies back, moaning weakly. Bonu calms Chachiji, taking the phone away from her.

'Chachiji, I only got Asharfi along to help with the housework,' Anjini says virtuously. 'Because Chachaji bribed Lachhu and he became a hostile witness.'

'Not as hostile as *I'm* going to be,' Chachiji grinds out ominously. 'Wait and see.'

By evening, the mood in the Hailey Court flat has grown decidedly raucous. Chachiji, triumphantly reunited with her nieces, is irrepressible. Their chattering grows louder and louder, as they recall all kinds of old anecdotes, and bond and hug and reminiscence. Samar, rather fed up and unable to get any time with Bonu alone, ends up focusing on Ashok chacha and realizing that the comprehensive thulping he has received that day may merit medical attention.

'Because he may actually, like, die or something otherwise,' he tells the women. 'Chachiji sure wasn't pulling her punches today. And I didn't restrain her as thoroughly as I could've.'

Chachiji sniffs and tosses her head. She's in no mood to let Ashok out of the dog house yet.

'You're right,' Dabbu agrees guiltily. 'I should have thought of that. After all, Asharfi *fell* on him from the fan, and she must weigh a good sixty kgs!'

Anjini rolls her eyes. 'Asharfi never fell from the fan, Dabbu, you idiot! He was lying!'

'Let's call in that nice young Dr Bharadwaj?' Eshu suggests. 'You know, with the pink face?'

'There's no need to call in that clown,' Samar growls instantly. 'Gulgul mama and I will take him to RML and get him a thorough check-up.'

And so that evening Samar and a wooden-faced Gulgul bundle up the still-moaning Ashok Narayan Thaur and drive him to the hospital. The team of doctors who gather to examine his multiple bruises eye both his escorts suspiciously. Samar's twin black eyes still haven't faded away entirely, and Gulgul is so muscle-bound that he always looks, well, rather thuggish.

'What happened, exactly?' they inquire delicately.

'I was carrying him to the toilet and I dropped him,' Gulgul replies, before Samar can get a word in. 'He fell rather hard.'

He then has to endure a long lecture on filial duty, carelessness and the importance of having proper medical help. He sits through it stoically, nodding several times and saying nothing. After the doctor leaves the VIP suite they've checked him into, having administered a painkiller injection and prescribed several tablets, Ashok peers up from his bedclothes, and seeks out his son's eyes, his own unusually tremulous.

'You are a good boy, Gulab,' he says hoarsely. 'A much better son than I ever was.'

Gulgul reddens. 'Please Papa, don't talk, take rest.'

But Ashok shakes his head, making his stringy hair swing this way and that.

'You are fit and disciplined. You don't smoke and drink. You don't womanize. I'm proud of you.'

Gulab's husky shoulders seem to shake a little. Samar puts an arm around them and gives a firm squeeze.

'Yeah. You rock, Gulgul mama.'

'I wanted him to have the big white kothi he deserves,' Ashok addresses Samar now. 'Instead of a small flat. Is there anything wrong with that?'

Samar can think of many reasons why that is wrong.

'Nothing,' he says, straight-faced.

Ashok Narayan sighs. 'You are a good son, Gulab,' he repeats, now really hitting his stride. 'Obedient. Dutiful. I was a bad son. Arrey, I was rotten through and through! Do you know I used to steal money from my own mother?'

'Papa please.' Gulgul looks uncomfortable. 'We don't want to know.'

But Ashok continues. His eyes are now far away and his voice has a dream-like quality.

'I was just sixteen. But fully six feet tall! Tall, fair and handsome. TFH they used to call me! Taller than *you*, Gulgul!'

'Of course, Papa.'

'All the loose-ladies in the party palaces wanted to teach

Pushkar's TFH son pyaar ki ABC. Especially because Laxmi bhaisaab was such a big, boring fail in that department. They begged me to visit them—but they wanted money...' He pauses, laughs fondly. 'They always want money!'

'How materialistic,' Samar murmurs.

'My father used to give my mother house-money every Monday. She kept it in a cupboard, near the balcony door. So every Monday night, I would swarm up to her balcony on a rope ladder I attached to the cement jaali, and skim from her money. Yes! From my own mother! I did it Monday after Monday.'

Samar, who has been patting Gulgul's back, stops abruptly at this.

'One note from the tens pile, one note from the fives pile,' Ashok is saying in a sing-song voice. 'Some coins—never too much—so my mother wouldn't notice—and then down the rope ladder and off to the party palace where the loose-ladies lived!'

The saanp on the seedi, Samar thinks numbly. The snake on the ladder. It was him! Not a lover, but a thieving son. Pushkar saw his own son upon the ladder in the dark and leapt, like a stupid, hot-blooded, chauvinistic Thakur, to the wrong conclusion. The whole thing was just a tragic, grisly misunderstanding.

'It's okay, Papa, never mind,' Gulgul is saying, patting the old man's hand. 'You just take rest now.'

The Pushkarni loved Pushkar, Samar swiftly puts the pieces together in his mind. She never had a lover—she never cheated on him. And he, well, he loved her too and he never wanted her dead. That happened by mistake. My film is not a lie. BJ's version is the actual truth.

He realizes he is almost dizzy with relief. First, freedom from Susan, then the confirmation that the will Ashok submitted is indeed a bona-fide fake, and now this blessed release from worrying, non-stop for months now, that he's made the wrong film. Looking down at Laxmi Narayan's unlovely but repentant brother lying upon his sickbed, suffering agonies of conscience, blissfully ignorant of the fact that he caused his father to murder his mother, he feels nothing but love.

'It's okay, Ashok chacha,' he says sincerely. 'We're family, after all. Your parents would've forgiven you because you're their child. And BJ would've forgiven you because you're his little brother. Not half-brother, *full* brother.'

'Yes yes.' A cunning look now enters Ashok's watery eyes. He glances upwards, passes his tongue over his lips and whispers, 'Waise, thanks for the VIP suite, beta, but the fan here is quite dirty. The dust on it could give me asthma. If that young nurse who was here just now could come in and clean it properly it might help me get better quickly…'

'*Unbelievable!*' Gulgul exclaims under his breath. 'Nothing can be done for this man!' Then louder, more heartily, he says, 'Why nurses, Papa? *We'll* stay the night with you—the room is big enough for all of us!'

Meanwhile, an inebriated Chachiji has finally been put to bed and the action at Hailey Road has shifted to Mamtaji's flowered living room.

'We did it!' Anjini exclaims. 'We *did* it. *We* did it! Asharfi came through, and now everything's settled and we can sell and be rich before Akshaya Tritiya, which is tomorrow, by the way!'

'Should we sign the papers?' Dabbu demands. 'Now? Should we just do it?'

'Let's!' Eshwari grins.

'Yes yes,' says Chandu, licking her lips.

Anjini turns to look questioningly at Bonu.

'Bonu?' she asks with pretty hesitance.

Bonu stays silent.

I'll make them squirm like well-salted earthworms.

I won't sell. Even my jutti won't sell.

And if I die na, then even my gosht won't sell.

Her mother's voice seems to have lost both volume and passion. It sounds tinny and scratchy and worn, like something that's fast running out of battery. And Bonu realizes that she lacks the will to run around creating fresh grievances to recharge it with.

'Samar and Susan broke up, by the way,' Anjini blurts out into the silence. 'He hasn't had anything to do with her in months.' Then she hastily adds, as Bonu looks up, pink-cheeked, 'Not that that has anything to do with anything.'

'I'll do it,' Bonu says abruptly. 'Where do I sign?'

Everybody whoops and claps and closes in on Bonu, hugging her and kissing her and thumping her on the back. She hugs them back wholeheartedly, not holding back anymore, feeling a huge weight lifting from her.

'*Such* a lovely girl…' mumble the aunts incoherently.

'Such a kind heart…'

'Such nice, big boobs—nobody else in the family has…'

'I'm *so sorry* I said your father was ugly…'

'And I'm sorry I was such a cow,' Bonu replies sincerely.

And surrounded by the warm circle of family, she takes the pen Anji is holding out, smiles trustingly, and signs the documents with a flourish—a bold, confident, slanting signature.

Bonita Singh Rajawat

17

'I have broken Samar's heart, and that guilt will be with me forever.'—Susan Adam's penitent email to her sister is leaked on the internet and goes viral overnight!

Darling Jackie,

Well, I've done it. I have broken Samar's heart, and the guilt will remain with me forever. It was horrible—he alternated between begging and threatening, was completely distraught and, for a moment even a little frightening, but I stood firm.

I explained to him that I had no choice. The spark was just NOT THERE for me any longer. I have always believed in honesty and authenticity—both in creative work and in relationships—anything less means that we are only cheating ourselves.

I told him that I have been jilted once, so I understand the pain of being the jilted one. It is a terrible place to be in. But I also told him that eventually, this pain is for the best—it forces you to grow, become a better person and a more creative one.

He heard me out, then quietly asked me, 'Is there anything that could make you reconsider?'

I said no.

His eyes filled with tears. He kissed me on the forehead and said, 'Know then, Susan Adams, that I will always love you. I may move on to other women, because hey, I'm a hot-blooded guy, but nobody will hold my heart in the palm of their hand the way you do, and will continue to do forever.'

END OF EXTRACT

Though Ms Adams denies being in a new relationship, the rumour mills are abuzz with tales of her increasing closeness to producer Kuber Malhotra, head honcho at Sonix Studios.

We tried to contact Ms Adams, Mr Malhotra and Mr Singh but got no reply.

'She's a kutiya,' Anjini says fiercely as the women drive to the lawyer's office together the next day. 'Bloody Addams family! Don't believe a *word* she's written. It's been leaked on purpose. Her publicists only have done it. She's trying to make it look like she's the dumper and he's the dumpee, when we all know it's the other way around!'

'Anji mausi, it's okay,' Bonu says tiredly. 'You don't need to keep explaining it again and again to me.'

Anji draws back, opening her eyes very wide. 'Arrey, who said I'm explaining to *you*? I'm explaining to *everybody*—and especially to *you*,' she turns on Chandu, 'because you were *concerned* enough to show Bonu—and all of us—this stupid article this morning.'

Chandu blinks her lashless eyes. 'I was just worried about Samar, that's all,' she protests. 'He sounded heart-broken in that letter—I was trying to help.'

Liar, thinks Dabbu. Hard as it is for her to dislike anybody, Dabbu is struggling to find any redeeming virtues in her sister Chandu. She had slid forward the article so maliciously, right under Bonu's blissful little nose that morning, and as the child's expression had grown crestfallen, she had sat back and looked extremely well-fed, even though she hadn't eaten a morsel of food for breakfast.

'I have never been dumped in my whole entire life and neither has my son!' Anjini declares indignantly. 'Only losers get dumped!'

'Anji didi!' Dabbu shoots a horrified glance at Eshu. 'Shush!'

Eshu grins. 'It's okay. Seriously Dubz, I'm tougher than *that*.'

'Hai, I didn't mean *you!*' Anjini hastily smothers Eshu in her armpit. 'Getting dumped by druggies doesn't count. They can't help themselves.'

'He's not a druggie anymore!' Eshu groans. 'Can we please just stay on the subject, please?' She nudges Anjini and directs her attention back to the silent Bonu.

Anjini turns to Bonu at once.

'Are you upset?' she asks delicately. 'Bonu Singh?'

Bonu blinks and opens her mouth but Dabbu speaks up faster.

'God, would you please give her some *space*, Anji didi!' she says. Then she turns to Chandu. 'Seriously though, shaking that obscure article under Bonu's nose wasn't a very good idea.'

Chandu bridles.

'I was *concerned* about Samar,' she maintains virtuously. 'I thought the article provided a rare insight into the state of his bleeding mind. And I thought that, as a group, if we had that rare insight, we could all be more *sensitive* towards him.'

The sisters look unconvinced.

'You should write a sequel to *Poor Is the New Rich*,' Eshu says candidly. '*Goody-Goody Is the New Bitch*.'

Anji gasps. Dabbu looks pained. Chandu's eyes narrow. She jerks her naked head to look out of the window. It's ridiculous, she thinks, shooting a resentful glance at Bonu in her sleeveless turquoise ganji, black pyjamas and jingling silver jewellery, how much these women fuss over this underdressed, overfed, oversmart orphan…

Samar leaves the hospital in the morning and comes home to a deserted house. He spends the day in a happy daze, reviewing the final edit of his film and waiting for Bonu Singh to come home from the lawyers.

It finally feels *right*, he thinks, relieved, as he watches the beautifully shot scenes unfold. True. Real. Organic. The word makes him think of Susan and he suppresses a twinge of uneasiness. His stepmother had called him in the morning and warned him that Bonu might be upset about the supposedly 'leaked' email. But Samar doubts it. Surely one conversation with him would set the record straight? I'll *convince* her I love her, he thinks determinedly, his hands clenching into fists. I'll go down on my knees and beg if I have to, and if that doesn't work, he laughs to himself, a heady, exultant laugh, I'll just grab her by that luscious butt, lift her off her feet and kiss her till she shuts up.

He hears the gate swing open at about five in the evening and walks out to the verandah, his heart thumping like he's been running fast on a treadmill. Bonu walks in, alone—the aunts aren't with her, much to Samar's relief.

'Wow, you're late,' he says. 'Whatever took you guys so long?'

She gives a gasp of surprise and backs away, her hands reaching up automatically to strike the Natraj into her hair.

She's mad at me about the Susan email, Samar thinks, watching this militant manoeuvre. But I can fix things. He steps closer to her.

'Bonu, I'm really sorry, I can explain everything...'

Her eyes widen, glittering with fury.

'So you *knew*,' she spits out.

Samar rakes a perplexed hand through his hair.

'Knew? Well, yes, I had a heads up that she was going to say something today—I just didn't know it was going to be this excessive.'

Her vivid brows snap together. 'Excessive?' She laughs bitterly. 'That's one way to put it. Anyway, I've been proved absolutely right in my mistrust of that bunch of cows, my lovely aunts, and in *you*.'

He frowns. 'Hang on, what?'

She gulps hard.

'For a while there, I did buy into it. I wanted it to be true. Instead of being this...this alone, self-sufficient person with no family, I *wanted* to be part of a big happy jing-bang that sat on double beds and giggled and gossiped and drank tea together and ate mathri-achaar and made French plaits with each other's hair!'

'And you *are*,' he assures her instantly. 'Of course you are. What's happened to upset you so much?'

She stamps her foot and looks away, hugging her belly.

'Oh, shut up, will you. I got used and screwed and stabbed in the back, and I don't want to have a long polite conversation about it. I'm clearing out of the house first thing in the morning—you're most welcome to enjoy it with my mother's ugly sisters.'

'Bonu,' his voice is urgent. 'Bonita. Listen, wait. I love you...'

'Don't you get it?' Her voice is tired. 'I've signed everything you guys needed me to sign—you don't have to pretend anymore.'

He grabs her by the shoulders and shakes her.

'Didn't you hear a word I said?'

She pushes him away with so much strength that he stumbles back a little.

'Didn't you hear a word *I* said?' she hisses. 'Back off. And *fuck* off! I never want to see you or any of those accursed bitches again!'

'Would you please watch your language?' His voice is cutting. 'That's my mother you're talking about.'

She stares up at him, furious. He stares back, confused, angry, upset.

Then her face crumples, her shoulders slump, tears tumble down her face. She looks like a broken, bewildered child. Even as he reaches for her, stricken apologetic words on his lips, she spins on her heel and dashes up the stairs.

'In the year 1993 my father and my sister Binni signed an agreement,' Anjini says soberly. 'We called it the 1993 document.'

She is sitting at the grilled window in her half of the upstairs. Samar is standing before her, long legs planted wide apart, arms folded across his chest, listening intently.

'It had been a bad year for Binni's husband Vickyji—his chemist shop business had just gone bankrupt. It was a terrible time for the family. Vickyji was even jailed briefly for income tax evasion, until BJ got him out on bail. Well, once Vickyji was out, he had another grand business idea. God knows what it was, I don't remember. Anyway, Binni again started pressurizing BJ to finance it.

'But this time BJ put his foot down. He'd financed the chemist shop idea by selling the house in Kanpur and loaning the money from the sale to Binni. Now that money was gone. He'd planned to leave an equal portion of it to all of us, so naturally he was pretty upset. The worst part was that Binni had developed a highly convenient amnesia about the Kanpur house money and now she started nagging him to sell 16 Hailey Road and give him her hissa of that, too. But BJ reminded her and he made her sign a document saying that if she failed to return the Kanpur house money, she'd have to compensate her sisters as soon as number 16 was sold.

'He hoped that would get her to shut up about selling number 16, and for a while it did. Binni had huge faith in her husband though, that much I'll say for her, and she was confident he'd be able to return the money very soon. Unfortunately that hope died with the accident.'

Anjini wipes her eyes and continues matter-of-factly, 'BJ felt horribly guilty. They were driving down to meet him, to beg him for more money, which he'd refused to advance over the phone, so naturally he felt it was all his fault. He made us all promise to forget about the '93 document, to never let Bonu know about it, and to tear up our copies of it. And so we did.'

'So then?' Samar's voice is harsh. 'Why bring it up if you'd promised you wouldn't?'

Anjini puts up her hands helplessly.

'It was Chandu. She got into a bad mood in the car because of…well never mind because of what. She went all quiet for a while. But then, right after we all signed the papers, she asked the legal people in this sweet, innocent voice if everything from our side was quite done. They said yes.'

Anjini stops and draws a deep, shaky breath.

'And then?' Samar prompts.

'Then she pulled out the '93 document and slid it across the table like a box of chocolates. And asked, "But what about this?"'

'And what did you people do?' Samar asks curtly. 'Watch?'

'Yes,' Anjini admits bleakly. 'For the first few minutes, yes, that's all we did. We were all confused, you see. We had thought all the copies of that contract had been destroyed. Then Chandu told Bonu, "Do you know, Bonita, that as the price of the Kanpur house would have been exactly forty crores today, your entire hissa should transfer automatically to all of us, now? Funny, na?"'

Samar's face darkens.

'Shit.'

'Bonu froze. She sat silent for almost a minute. Then she snatched up the document and read the main points, which Chandu had highlighted very helpfully. We all watched— frozen, literally, like total fools.

'Chandu kept looking at her with this weird gloating expression. It was so creepy, Samar, I could practically see Bonu become smaller and smaller in that room, and Chandu become fatter and fatter.'

'Kindly spare me the poetic flourishes,' Samar says tightly, 'and stick to the main narrative.'

Anjini shakes her head helplessly.

'Then Bonu said, in this tightly controlled voice, that we'd clearly planned this all along, and used her good equation with the Trings and Chachiji to get our work done...'

'Which is true,' Samar growls. 'We did.'

'And that she didn't want *anything* that didn't legally belong to her, and let nobody say that Vikram Singh Rajawat's daughter didn't pay her debts.'

'Wow,' says Samar. 'She went full-on filmi basically. Idiot.'

'You could say that,' Anjini grimaces. 'And then Chandu tittered and said, oh, I was just joking, we don't really want your money, money is mael. Please keep your hissa, I will tear up this paper in front of you, but I thought you should know that your aunts are doing you a great favour by maaf karoing your mother's debts. This will cultivate a proper spirit of humble gratitude and help in your spiritual growth.'

'She's evil, that woman,' Samar says, very white about the mouth. 'Evil through and through.'

'Yes, but then things got even worse, because before I could tell her to shut up, Eshu rounded on her and said she was a fine one to talk about a spirit of humble gratitude—what about the ten lakhs she borrowed from her in 2001 and never returned, huh?'

'Aha! Good for Eshu mausi!'

'And then Dabbu jumped in and said Chandu had borrowed twenty lakhs from her in 2003 and never returned that either!'

'But I thought money is mael,' Samar smiles savagely.

'Exactly!' Anji laughs too, a rather wild little laugh. 'And then I thought I might as well mention that Chandu borrowed about twenty lakhs from me too, so she really shouldn't be talking. And then we all started yelling and Chandu decided to start doing her weird prayer chant. She rolled her head back, fluttered her lashes and muttered *Yelli Yelli Yelli Yelli Yelli*, and Eshu told her to please shut the fuck up, and we forgot about Bonu for a bit and when we finally remembered and looked around, she was gone.'

'Shit. And that's when I met her—and she thought I knew all about this '93 document thingie—'

'But you didn't!' Anjini's voice is sharp. 'You should've clarified immediately, Samar!'

He shakes his head. 'I didn't know what she was going on about! But what about you guys, Ma? How could you just let her go? I mean, really, you could've had your stupid little dust-up later.'

'Ya ya, I know,' Anjini says crankily. 'The timing was awful. Anyway, you'd better go find her now and tell her to please keep her hissa because we all love her. And that you're both going to get married and share everything anyway.'

'What rubbish you talk,' responds her red-faced son.

Anjini smiles, a careworn, worried smile. 'Just find her quick, baby. I don't want to stress you out, but honestly, she looked capable of *anything*...'

'I said I don't wanna meet him!'

Eshwari's voice is hysterical. She is standing on the bed in her pyjamas and grey tee, her expression panicked, her hands bunched into fists. Her shiny straight black hair is all mussed and sticking up in every direction.

Debjani sighs. 'Eshu, would you please get off the bed? You don't have to do anything you don't want to.'

'I can't face him!' Eshwari continues, like Debjani hasn't spoken at all. 'He's going to have a smug, I-did-you grin plastered all over his face and I will die of mortification! Oh God, how could I sleep with him? And do all those things I did? How *could* I?'

'That all I don't know,' Debjani is quite fed up. 'The point is, *you* did him just as much as *he* did you, okay? Remember that.'

Eshu's chin rises. 'That's true enough.'

'Yeah,' Debjani says encouragingly.

'It was just a one-night thing for me too!'

'Exactly.'

Eshwari shoulders slump. 'But then I phoned him so *many many* times afterwards!' she wails. 'I *can't* meet him!'

'Oh God, don't come if you don't want to,' Dabbu replies worriedly. 'We'll invent some glamorous excuse for you if you insis—'

Anjini pops her head into the room. 'You *have* to come, Eshwari,' she says firmly. 'There are documents you have to sign. Now get off the bed, wear black, and slap on some MAC Russian Red lipper. We leave in twenty.'

'Bossy cow,' Eshwari says feelingly as soon as Anjini has shut the door.

But she does get off the bed and out of her 'jammies.

How happy we could've been today, Dabbu thinks wretchedly as they drive to Satish's office in hostile silence. Chatting, laughing, planning holidays and beauty salon visits. Instead, everything's grim—Chandu's smirking, Bonu's missing, Samar's run off to look for her, we're all worried sick, and Eshu's all screwed up about that animal, Satish bloody Sridhar.

She sneaks a look at her only younger sister. Eshwari seems to be much more in control now, thankfully. Very chic in a black skirt, sleekly fitted coal-grey tee, dark shades and luscious red lipstick, she is the first person to disembark from the car and shake hands composedly with Satish Sridhar.

She was always too good for this idiot and she always will be, decides Dabbu staunchly as she slides out of the car and greets Satish with a cold hello. Good riddance, I guess. Is he looking shifty and shame-faced or is she just imagining it? She looks at him keenly. She's imagining it. What a dog.

Chandu, whom no one is talking to, emerges from the front and beams excessively at Satish, who looks taken aback at this effusive greeting. Anjini, seemingly oblivious to all the undercurrents, smiles serenely.

'Happy Akshaya Tritiya.'

Satish smiles back just as serenely, and escorts them all into the big board room.

They go through the ritual of placing their coffee orders and then it's time to get down to business.

'Here are all the papers,' Anjini says, placing a neat manila envelope upon the table, not without an air of quiet triumph. 'Chachaji's lawsuit, squatting tenants, signatures of all five heirs, *all* sorted out. We made the deadline!'

'That is seriously impressive,' Satish says as his minions scoop up the documents and go through them discreetly. 'At one point, it looked like a hopeless coil—you ladies have done a fantastic job.'

We don't need a certificate of merit from *you*, Dabbu thinks resentfully, taking in his shaggy hair, his wide shoulders, his full, sensual mouth and finding all of it extremely irritating. Smooth, oversmart bastard.

'Sir, everything is in perfect order,' say the minions deferentially. 'Papers are all correct.'

'Perfect, huh.' Satish's expression grows rather shifty suddenly. 'That's, uh, like I said, fantastic.'

Why's he waffling now, Dabbu wonders. She glances towards Eshu, wondering if her sister has noticed, but Eshu seems to have turned into some sort of distant, coffee-drinking statue, a cool New Yorker babe, thinking cool New Yorker thoughts.

'Ya, so let's get this done, then,' Anjini says impatiently. 'And then we'll all go out for a celebratory lunch.'

'What a lovely prospect,' Satish smiles with raffish charm. 'Me and so many charming ladies.'

You're not invited, Dabbu thinks fiercely, her eyes flashing.

He catches both the thought and the flash of anger in her eyes and turns a dull shade of red. Good, she thinks, at least he still has some shame left.

But then he says, 'The *thing* is, Mrs Singh—Anjini didi, I mean—there have been some, uh, developments at our end—at SteelBird, that is. Because of which we've had to do some rethinking.'

Debjani leans in, her gaze steely. 'But *you're* SteelBird, right? So *you've* done some rethinking.'

Satish shakes his head. 'No no, I'm the CEO, sure, but it's a big company—not to sound boastful,' he adds hastily, 'but the board felt, collectively, that because of all the news in the papers about the trouble you were going through in clearing the ownership titles etcetera etcetera, this property, realistically, wasn't available to us anymore. We've actually zoomed in on another property, quite close by—not as good as yours, of course, but where the titles are clear and the paperwork minimal.'

A stunned silence descends on the table. This development is so unexpected that the Pricey Thakur Girls just sit there, open-mouthed and shell-shocked.

'You've bought somewhere *else*?' Anjini's voice is a disbelieving whisper.

'We would've intimated you earlier,' Satish continues regretfully, 'but even until four days ago, things were still in such a legal tangle that we thought you'd never be ready and clear to sell by Akshaya Tritiya anyway. We're *really* sorry this happened.'

More silence. Nobody seems to know what to say.

'We can help you find another builder,' he adds swiftly. 'I mean, now that the deeds are all clear and you are in agreement...'

'That'll take ages and you know it,' Debjani replies.

He spreads out his hands helplessly.

'Yeah, but I'd like to help. You're my neighbours,' he hesitates, '*and* my friends.'

'You've helped enough,' Eshwari says abruptly, getting to her feet.

It seems to Dabbu that Satish goes very still at the sound of her voice. Then he gives the tiniest of shrugs.

'Are we to understand,' Anjini's voice is still bewildered, 'that your offer stands rescinded?'

He turns to face her, his eyes inscrutable, his gaze unflinching.

'Yes,' he says quietly. 'That is exactly what I am trying to say. My sincere apologies for wasting your time.'

A small moan escapes Chandu's lips.

Satish sits there, head bowed, while the sisters stare at him in shocked disgust. Then, tight-lipped and white-faced, Eshwari stalks out of the room. Anjini and Debjani look around, still dazed, then rise, bid a cold but classy farewell to the SteelBird team and walk out too, leaving Satish and his team sitting in the empty conference room, staring at the empty Starbucks cups upon the table, the rim of each one emblazoned with a different shade of lipstick.

And Chandu.

She is still sitting there, clutching her sheaf of documents, the lights from the boardroom ceiling reflecting off her scalp, her eyes darting this way and that.

Satish looks at her and lifts his eyebrows questioningly.

'Yes?'

Chandu nods. Several times. 'I have a business proposition for you. Want to hear it?'

Satish looks startled and then quickly schools his features into polite impassiveness.

'Yes, of course,' he says.

Chandu licks her lips. 'My portion,' she begins, 'is the annexe, you know. It's a clean 1200 gajh square, neatly separated from the portions of the other four girls, which are all piled one on top of the other in the main house. They can't sell one without the other, but *I* can. Now I understand that you've invested elsewhere, and you don't have the funds available to buy all of 16 Hailey Road anymore—but I'm sure you have the funds to buy just one-fifth of it?'

'Well, er, yes,' Satish says slowly. 'But...' He looks at her curiously. 'Are *you* sure you want to do this? Sell, without the others?'

Chandu shrugs indifferently. 'Oh, yes. I don't plan on coming back to India again. My sisters and I, we—well, we don't see eye to eye on most things anyway.'

'But Milord wanted you all to sell toge—' he starts to say, then checks himself and holds out his hand. 'May I see the documents?'

She nods, eyes gleaming. Satish gestures to his grey-haired CEO-type assistant. 'Could you compute the price for Ms Chandralekha's hissa, please?'

The minions get busy and Satish turns back to Chandu. 'Your sisters looked really hassled when they left.'

'Yeah. They all need the money badly, you know. I don't. This will be quite a setback for them.'

She doesn't seem too worried about the prospect, though.

Satish, who's heard a bit about her from Eshwari, is intrigued. He says, 'I believe you're deeply influenced by a book called *Poor Is the New Rich?*'

'Yes,' she nods with evangelical zeal. 'Money is mael, you know.'

'And yet…' he murmurs, his gaze quizzical, 'you seem quite eager to close this sale and, um, scoop up a lot of mael.'

Chandu flushes. 'This is *quite* different,' she says stiffly. 'Most of the money from this sale will go to RIGID's charitable works — to help needy children, orphans, widows and sick people. I won't be keeping it.'

But I bet it will hugely increase your power and standing in your organization, thinks Satish. And I bet you love lording it over widows and orphans, rubbing their nose into who the provider of their largesse is. Maybe that's your kick.

Aloud, he says smoothly, 'That's excellent. We too will feel fulfilled to know that our money is going towards such a good cause.'

Chandu's lashless eyes light up. 'Thank you,' she says. 'So, how soon can I have the money?'

'Right away,' says Satish urbanely. He glances at his team. 'Right, gentlemen?'

They all nod. 'Yes sir, of course sir, ma'am. Right away.'

Chandu sits back and crosses her arms.

God loves *me*, she muses with a cold, satisfied smile. 'Not these Anji and Eshu and Bonu and all. He maketh smooth the paths of the ones He loveth. It's because *I* am his special chosen one that I have got my forty crores and *they* have stumbled at the last block.

18

**MCD approves construction
up to ten floors in
Hailey Road area.
Property prices double.**

People owning property in the central Delhi district of Hailey Road have cause to rejoice today, as the central authorities cleared residential construction of up to ten floors in the area. Earlier, buildings in the area could rise only to a height of five floors.

'Builders in the know would have made a killing if the news had leaked out earlier,' explained a city councillor, 'and owners could have got short-changed. That is why the news was kept absolutely secret. Now, of course, residents can rejoice, as prices have almost doubled, especially in the Hailey Road and Hailey Lane areas.'

Purist city planners and environmentalists decried the move, saying it would lead to a crass uglification of the Lutyens' zone, but original residents of Hailey Road, who have not sold out yet, were ecstatic at the news.

Detailed report on page 7

The black Land Cruiser pulls up outside number 16, three hours after the newspapers have been delivered, on a thundery, monsoony morning. Heavy metal is blaring from the speakers, and Satish Sridhar is behind the wheel, dark glasses in place, white teeth flashing in a wide, wolfish smile.

Eshwari gives a little scream and tears out onto the verandah, splashes through the puddles on the driveway and races out of the old green gate before he's had a chance to honk twice.

He is getting out of the vehicle to greet her when he is knocked backwards by the impact of her weight. She throws herself fully at him, her arms locking around his neck in a fierce, possessive hug.

'Bihari, people are looking at us,' he says with unusual bashfulness. 'Stop *hugging* me.'

'Nobody's looking,' she replies. 'Besides, you're hugging *me*.'

Looking down, he realizes that his hands are indeed locked firmly around her narrow waist.

'You're right,' he says, mildly surprised.

Minutes later, sitting inside the car as rain pelts down hard upon the windows outside, she demands, 'Now explain. Everything. Properly!'

He kisses the top of her head.

'Well, I've been pushing for ten floors on Hailey Road for a few years now, oiling the wheels, greasing the palms. Last summer, I got inside info from the ministry that it was finally gonna come through, on this Akshaya Tritiya. So then I started looking for a property on the road to make a killing with. And I zeroed in on Milord's. His house was more-or-less undisputed and I'd heard he'd gone fully gaga.'

'So you came around bearing chocolates?'

'Yes. The plan was to buy your house before Akshaya Tritiya, before the ten floor announcement came through, and make a killing.'

'And then?'

His expression grows whimsical. 'And then *you* showed up, complicating everything.'

She shakes him. 'Explain properly!'

'It's an ugly story,' he says wryly. 'I wanted to get into your pants—to fulfil an old teenage fantasy, of course, not because I fancied you anymore. After that, I would buy your house cheap, because business is business, so what if you got screwed over?'

'Poor Steesh,' she tweaks his nose. 'Sitting in your big fancy office, thinking such dark, depressing thoughts.'

He bats her hand away. 'You're making fun of me, Bihari, you cold, unfeeling monster, but it really was like that for me.'

She kisses him. 'Poor Steesh. And then?'

He scratches his head. 'And then... I got all mixed up—which is the part where I didn't talk to you or return your calls...'

'Bastard,' she says feelingly.

'Hey, I was really confused!' he protests. 'It was a lot of money okay, please appreciate my sacrifice!'

'Get to the good part,' she tells him.

He sighs, rumples his hair.

'The sitch with your house looked too messy, in any case, so I figured you'd never be able to make the Akshaya Tritiya deadline. I started looking at other properties. But *then* you girls showed up at my office yesterday, with all your papers in order, looking so sweet and gullible, and I just couldn't go through with it. I kept thinking how much you'd despise me the next day, when you found out, and I... I discovered I didn't want you—*or* your sisters—to despise me.'

'Hmmm.' Eshwari, usually so quick with her comebacks, finds she is at a loss for words. So she hugs him instead. Hard.

'And I couldn't say anything to you yesterday,' he says. 'Because I was kind of thinking on my feet. Besides, my team was there, and they need to look up to the boss, not think he's a sentimental fool.'

'So now they don't think you're a sentimental fool?'

He grins.

'I *did* buy some property cheap, yesterday.'

'You did?'

He nods. 'I bought Chandu's hissa. Did you know?'

'Well, we figured something was up when she didn't leave the office with us,' Eshwari says candidly. 'And when she left for the US today, we were sure. It made me hate you even more.'

He scans her face, his expression worried.

'You're not mad at me for cheating your sister?'

Eshu thinks this over for a moment. Then she says decidedly, 'No. She's a cow and she had it coming.' She grins. 'I'd love to see her expression when she lands and switches on her phone. Anjini's already mailed her that piece from today's paper.'

'Ouch,' Satish winces sympathetically. 'Poor Chandu. She's really the cackkoo in the family.'

He drinks in the small, strong face, then takes her hand and holds it between his two large ones. 'Let's get married in Milord's big old house as soon as possible, please?'

'Okay,' she smiles. 'Done.'

He kisses her hand.

'And after we've spent one blissful night in your virginal old bedroom there, I'll bring the bulldozers in.'

'You still want to buy our house?' she asks in surprise. 'At double the price?'

'I got Chandu's hissa really cheap,' Satish points out. 'And I'll be paying *you* only for one more one-fifth. That leaves three-fifths, for which I can afford to pay double — d'you think that'll promote me to the status of No 1 in Milord's Celestial Sons-in-Law Rankings?'

Eshwari hugs him.

'You're this big builder shark and I'm a wannabe travel writer,' she muses, pulling a face. 'I don't think I like the power distribution in this relationship.'

'A little humility is good for the soul.' He smiles down at her mistily, his heart in his eyes. 'Put that in your pipe and smoke it, you pricey Thakur chick.'

Bonu has started waking up very early ever since she came to Chongza. There are two entitled-looking roosters with angry red eyes stationed outside her little cottage, who crow with such gusto every morning that she finds it impossible to lie abed. She has no option but to pull on a sweater, stagger out to the porch and throw them some bird feed, which they peck at with noisy enjoyment even as she glares at them, elbows resting upon the railing, muttering the dire warning *butter chicken butter chicken* under her breath.

The sunrise view from the porch is spectacular, featuring a plump orange segment of sun, rising over a gushing silver river, full of bubble and froth and dancing sunbeams. Massive rounded grey rocks fringe the river, and beyond that are huge humped mountains rising as far as you care to look. Bonu often has her breakfast of toast, apricot jam, yak cheese and tea here.

The cottage is part of a tourist establishment run by a section of the Tring family that had chosen to stay back in Bhutan, and it is extremely well managed. Sitting in her spot, yawning and sipping her tea, and curling and uncurling her toes in the sun, she thinks that she could live here forever.

Because, really, what is there to go back for?

Sweet fuck-all, that's what.

I could start up a desi food joint, she muses. Or export sports shoes to India—they're really cheap here. Or maybe I could send Daulat Master a ticket and get into garment fabrication. There's lots of cheap labour around—he could train them... but sourcing material will be a nightmare, gota patti and tiny mirrors and crystal and all that. No, my hand-knitted sweaters idea is the best. Better to stick with that only. There's a massive variety of wool available here, after all. She's already commissioned ski sweater samples and as soon as they're ready she's going to send them out to her contacts in Europe along with pictures of apple-cheeked ladies knitting in the sun and some guff about the unspoilt dragon kingdom of Bhutan. She's sure to get a lot of orders! But... she's so clueless about wool— what's good quality, what isn't, what kind of pricing to do, what instructions to put on the label, and most importantly, where to raise the capital for this ambitious venture?

Don't think so far ahead, she tells herself firmly as the now familiar, whooshing sensation of blind panic grips her belly. Just focus on the crisp toast and the chunky jam and sip your tea and keep your mind on the present.

The present includes a trip to the big city of Thimpu, to get an export permit for the ski sweater idea, issued by no less a personage than the Queen Mother of Bhutan herself. Namgay Tring is taking her. The Trings have become quite the local celebrities, thanks not only to their hit 'party song' but also to their impromptu speech against 'evil Indian politicians' that had been comprehensively covered in Bhutan.

Bonu has a brisk, woodsmoke-scented bath and gets dressed, choosing a businesswoman-like long, black knit dress and flat shoes. She pauses before putting on her stack of silver bangles—

Next time, keep it on

—and then slides them on, applies minimal make-up, twists her hair into a no-nonsense knot and phones the Tring.

'I'm ready,' she tells him brightly. 'Let's go, let's go, let's *go*!'

Five minutes later, the roosters herald his arrival by crowing up a storm and Bonu runs out to the porch, slaps her forehead and scurries back in to re-emerge clutching the file containing her business ideas and loan application form. She runs down to the little car and gets in, slamming the door shut.

'Sorry,' she says breathlessly as she turns to face Namgay Tringji. 'Forgot the loan paper—'

And then the words die on her lips because the man in the driver's seat is not cheerful, wizened and one-eyed.

The man in the front seat is scruffy, sleep-deprived and two-eyed. And both these eyes hold an expression of grim exasperation.

'Oh!' Bonu says faintly.

'Good morning,' Samar says lightly. 'And where are you going, looking so busy and important?'

Bonu has an insane desire to say, 'I'm going to London to see the queen'. She also has an insane desire to throw her arms around his neck and burst into tears. She does neither.

'To Thimpu,' she says airily.

She puts on her dark glasses (spiffy fake-Ralph Laurens bought from the Tibetan market two days ago), straps on her seat belt, folds her arms across her chest and looks straight ahead with her nose in the air.

'*Balls* you're going to bloody *Blimpu*,' Samar grates out in reply.

Bonu raises her vivid brows. 'There's no need to be rude,' she says. 'I have an important meeting regarding a business venture I want to set up—'

'You're not going *anywhere*,' he replies categorically. 'Now take off those fake sunglasses and look at me.'

'How did you know they were fake?' she asks curiously, momentarily diverted. 'They're really good quality fakes! *I* couldn't tell.'

'I know they're fakes because you're wearing them.'

'And I have a tendency to gravitate toward fakes,' she replies, her voice shaking a little, glasses still firmly in place. 'I realize that now.'

Samar swears under his breath, reaches forward and pulls her glasses off.

'I am *not* a fake.'

'The evidence would suggest otherwise,' she mutters, looking away.

His mouth sets in a straight line.

'Susan and me are over,' he tells her. 'You may have read about it, you may not have. She made it sound like I'm madly in love with her and that she did the dumping, but that's not true.'

'Too much information,' Bonu shrugs. 'Not my problem.'

'And the aunts always meant to give you your hissa.'

She stiffens. 'I don't want anybody's pity-payout. I pay my debts. And my parents' debts too.'

'This isn't about *you*,' Samar says harshly. 'Bauji put *me* in charge of the division of the property—he wanted you to have your hissa so I insist you take it. Give it away to charity for all I care!'

'Maybe I will.'

He gives a short, disbelieving laugh.

'Fat chance of that happening.'

She turns to look at him.

'You think I can't do charity?'

She's looking right at him now, which is a big mistake. His eyes are exasperated, of course, but they are also intense, and very, very ardent. She hastily looks away.

'God knows what I think,' he says ruefully. 'I've lost the capacity to think. What are my chances if I close in for a kiss, now, d'you think?'

'Bad,' she says, her cheeks hot. 'Very bad.'

'Really?' he smiles lazily. 'Are you *sure*? 'Coz I sort of sense my chances are pretty damn good, actually.'

The moment he says it, he knows he's gone too far. Her eyes swivel to look at him scornfully for a moment, and then she unpops her seatbelt, gets the hell out of the car, stalks back to the little cottage and slams the door shut.

Frustrated, Samar leans on the horn. Hard.

Inevitably, the roosters start to crow.

Inside the cottage, Bonu looks at herself in the mirror, her arms wrapped tightly across her chest, her eyes wavering between hope and doubt. Why would he come seeking her out unless he really cares for her? There can be no other reason, surely? Unless... he's come to shove her hissa down her throat because of his promise to BJ.

Fuck. That's it. It's his inflated sense of eldest grandchild responsibility at play. Nothing else.

Outside, Samar's honking has attracted quite a crowd.

Heads are peeking out from the neighbouring cottages. Sweet-faced ladies with many silver piercings. Small children picking their noses. Bold-eyed young men. Gap-toothed old people. Slowly they walk out onto the road and look with frank, silent interest from Samar to the shuttered house.

He gets out of the car and looks at the gathered group.

They look back at him expectantly.

'Here goes everything.' He mutters, then turns on his heel and heads for the front door. Flanked by the curious, suddenly silent roosters, he knocks as loud and hard as he can.

Bonu opens the door.

'I don't want any money that isn't rightfully mine,' she says loftily. 'So buzz off.'

'You opened the door.' Samar's smile is goofy.

'To *explain* something to you. Did you understand?'

'I did.' He steps in smartly and shuts the door behind him. 'But the price of the property just doubled. So even if you clear your papa's debts, which *nobody* wants you to do, by the way, you'll still have forty crores left over.'

She gasps. 'What! When did *that* happen?'

He tells her. She listens, wide-eyed.

'So Steesh and Eshu mausi are getting married!'

'Uh… yes,' Samar replies. 'That's not the main point of this story at all, but then again, maybe it is. Yes, they are.'

A long silence follows. Bonu seems to be working things out in her head. He lets her get there, content to just watch, to be there, in the same space as her.

'How do I know Susan's version isn't true?' she demands finally. 'And that this isn't just a rebound thing for you?'

He leans down and cups her face, his eyes alight, his voice husky.

'Bonita, my love, I haven't had sex with her—hell, with *anybody*—since the night you kissed me by the fire.'

Her eyes soften.

'Really?'

He nods.

'Really.'

Silence. He scans her face, trying to read her expression, uneasily noting that it seems to have grown decidedly smug.

'Why?'

He shrugs. 'Women look like furniture to me now. Or trees. Or men. *Other* women that is—except you.'

She absorbs this.

'Maybe you need to see one of those, what-d'you-call-'em, sex doctors,' she says finally.

'Excuse me?' Samar is startled.

'Yeah.' She nods, face serious, eyes dancing. 'You could have, like a *defect* or something.'

'Is that a challenge?' His voice is light, but he gives her a little shake as he speaks, which makes Bonu decide to drop this line of conversation.

Instead she says, 'Well, *I* haven't had sex with anybody since that night either.'

'So this is a competition?' he inquires, his hands sliding smoothly down her arms and sides to grip her butt. 'What does the winner get?'

She pushes him away a little.

'My *dad*,' she says forcefully, waggling a finger under his nose, 'was just ahead of his time. He was a *genius*. All his business ideas—blue popcorn, Cat-bury chocolates, Dex Jelly— were brilliant.'

Samar's expression grows decidedly peculiar, as though he is going through some sort of internal struggle. Finally, he manages to say, his voice strangled, 'Okay.'

She looks at him suspiciously.

'Are you *laughing* at my dad?'

'No no,' he shakes his head. 'How could I possibly?'

'*Good*,' she says, satisfied. 'Where are we going?'

This, because he has scooped her off her feet and is now carrying her in his arms.

'To the bedroom,' he replies. 'Where we can discuss everything, er, more comfortably.'

'There's lots to discuss,' she agrees as her arms go around his neck. 'It's through there.'

'Thank you.' Samar steps through the doorway and drops her onto a bedspread embroidered with rampant mountain lions. Her hair comes loose as she lands.

As he stares down at her she sits up and says, her voice unsteady, 'Look, I don't know what your understanding with Susan was, but I'm *not* interested in a purely physical relationship.'

Samar nods seriously, his intense eyes gazing into hers. 'Okay. So you're into what, exactly? Because I'm already in a double bed with you, and I'm happy to drink tea and eat mathri-achaar too—but I'm not sure I'll be able to make French plaits with your hair.'

'That's not what I mean,' she says crossly. 'I mean, there's got to be *more*.'

'More,' he agrees. He sinks to his knees before her, places a large warm hand around her ankle, right over the single silver chain that encircles it, and starts to stroke it idly.

Bonu swallows hard.

'Uh-huh.'

Samar tilts his head to one side.

'You were saying?' he asks as his hand slides up her smooth golden calf.

'Not interested in anything physical,' she manages to get out.

'I got that,' he nods as his hand rises even higher, past her knee, vanishing below her long black dress. 'It's quite clear.'

She wriggles upright. 'I want to have my own business! I want a committed relationship!'

'You aren't making any sense, you know,' he whispers, his lips now against her throat. 'Those two things aren't connected at all.'

She frowns and pushes him away hard.

'Damn it, Samar, let me think!'

He sits backs on his heels against the sun-dappled wall, and laughs—the sure, contented laugh of a man who knows he is exactly where he wants to be.

'Take your time,' he says. 'Think it out. I'm not going anywhere. Not now. Not ever.'

EPILOGUE

The massive hall is packed with beautiful people. The air is a potent bouquet of adrenalin and expensive perfume. Industrial strength air-conditioners run full blast, but still much of the audience is perspiring. Massive camera jibs swoop and rise smoothly over their faces, beaming the image to homes all over India. All eyes—some glad, some wistful, some envious, some lusty—are on a lean, tall young man in faded jeans and dark jacket, who is embracing a glowing young woman in a tiny black cocktail dress.

'Who's she?' Preetali Shah's mother, always watchful for competition that may affect her daughter's incredible career graph, prods her. 'In the black frock? Why is she kissing him?'

'Oh God, Ma, that's Pasta, his little cousin,' Pree replies. 'She's only like fifteen or something!'

'Cousin, eh? I don't see any family resemblance,' her mother says sceptically. 'And the one he's bending down to kiss now? Sitting cross-legged like she's come to some maata-ki-chowki? Another *cousin*?'

Pree peers across the row of seats and her face brightens. 'That's his fiancée. She's lovely.'

Mrs Shah gasps in dismay. 'Engaged! But when I told you he was a nice, steady boy, you said he was dating that bhaingi Susan! You have too many scruples, Preetali. Clearly this busty girl has none!'

'He got me a Sparkler, Ma,' Preetali replies distractedly, her eyes on the stage. 'That's enough for me. Shush now!'

Because Samar Vir Singh has reached the stage. He strides up to the presenter, kisses her on both cheeks, and accepts the trophy. Then he walks to the podium, and his deep, pleasant voice, informal and relaxed, rings out across the hall and halts the applause.

'First, I'd like to thank everybody at Sparkler for letting Zeeshan and me into this auditorium again. It's extremely gracious and large-hearted of you, and it has quite turned the tables on us and shown us up for the petty, thankless little whiners we are. So kudos to your PR team for that.'

A ripple of laughter runs through the crowd. Several people cup their hands around their mouths and shout affectionate profanities. Samar grins and digs his hands deeper into the pockets of his jeans.

'Some people would suggest that you did this to shut our mouths up with trophies, so to speak, but that is a motive you cannot be accused of, because this year, the newly introduced judging procedure at the Sparklers has been so transparent.' He looks up, his eyes sincere. 'So thanks again. Really. I'm deeply honoured.'

There are whoops and claps from the crowd, especially from the entire *Thakur Saab* crew, who are sitting together, clutching a large number of Sparklers, looking teary-eyed and rather stunned.

Samar looks around the hall, searching for faces, finding them and acknowledging them as he speaks.

'I've already thanked my brilliant crew and fabulous cast and lovely producers when we accepted the earlier awards, so with this final, most coveted Sparkler in hand, I'd like to get a little personal. This may be a long speech so—'

Several people boo and groan.

Samar grins. 'Listen, I made a crisp hundred-and-forty minute film, not a three-hour snore-fest like you guys, so shut it and let me speak, okay?'

More laughter. More applause. Clearly Samar can do no wrong tonight.

'So, I made this movie for somebody. It was supposed to be a surprise. A big, birthday surprise. But the person in question surprised me before I could surprise him.'

He pauses. Everybody waits for him to continue, upbeat, smiling.

'He died.'

Slightly overdone gasps and murmurs of sympathy rise from the audience. AK, who's got a fixed, ear-to-ear grin on his face, quickly assumes a sombre expression.

Samar's gaze grows sardonic. 'Yeah—but as he was eighty-six years old, that was, you know, no biggie. Besides, he left me something that made the parting easier to bear.'

'Very big house on Hailey Road,' Zeeshan's father Zaffar Khan whispers knowledgeably to his wife. 'Worth hundreds of crores.'

Behind them, Susan Adams flushes an unattractive shade of red, raises her chin and hugs her trophy for best costume design (*Thakur Saab*) a little harder.

On stage, Samar laughs and gestures to the front row. 'He left me...well, basically, he left me *that*.'

And as the live action crew zooms in on his beaming, impossible, incorrigible family, magnifying their images on the giant screens, Samar feels such a fierce surge of pride and affection for them that his chest tightens and he can't speak.

Into the breach leaps AK, wielding a mic of his own.

'Arrey, enough of your blathering, young Samar!' he shouts

with exaggerated bonhomie. 'I played your great-grandfather, so now I order you to *shut up!*'

Samar's eyebrows rise, but he does good-naturedly shut up.

AK swashbuckles creakily down the aisle to the Thakur family.

'Look at that old goat go,' Zaffar Khan mutters to his son. 'Anything to grab the limelight.'

'You must be so proud of your son, mataji,' AK says, radiating his usual, slightly suspect sincerity. '*You* say something!'

And then, because Anjini is looking so impossibly young and beautiful tonight, and because Chachiji is so very distinguished in her soft baby-blue and silver Dhakai sari, personally selected by Pasta, he hands Chachiji the mic.

Bonu looks up at Samar, her big black eyes widening in comic alarm. On stage, Samar facepalms, grins resignedly, and hopes for the best.

Chachiji bounces up to her feet, her bulldoggy face wreathed in smiles.

'Thanks AK!' she says chummily. 'And hullo everybody! Yes, we are very proud of Samar, because he's very talented boy, and he's going to marry Bonu Singh, which is a very good thing, because she's an orphan and all! And we're happy ki whole family is together again with no hard feelings, even Chandu, who has got sense now and returned to her husband, and whose hair is looking so cute, like Anushka in *PK*! Aur haan, if you girls want to marry a nice Thakur boy, *just* like Samar, let me use this apourtunity to show you my son Gulab! Stand up, Gulgul, let everybody see you!'

And as she extols Gulgul's many virtues, while he sinks lower and lower in his seat, and the camera crew hastily turn off their recording button, and the audience watches gob-smacked, the curtain falls, for now, on the house that BJ built.

ACKNOWLEDGEMENTS

This was a tough book for me to write. So much change, so much upheaval, so many traumatized children to transplant! We made the big shift from Gurgaon to 'Bangalore Rural', leaving my eldest behind in Delhi, and pulling the younger two out of a school they loved…

Every day, there would be a different crisis. Plumbing leaks, electricity glitches, dead phone lines, people speaking Kannada. But all is finally well with The House that Choku Built. The kids love the new school, and we're sitting pretty in the Halli, enjoying our garden and 'such a lovely weather!'

Choku (aka Niret), thank you for this home, for your love, and for your unflinching support in all that I do.

Moving on to first readers, many thanks to my gorgeous daughter Nayantara, who rocks this cover just as hard as her sister rocks the cover of 'Pricey'. And whose cryptic, 'Naah, not enough happy gas', as she tossed my laptop back to me, kept me rewriting the romantic scenes time and again.

To my gorgeous daughter Niharika, that eater-of-two-two-Snickers and prolific reader who casually devours Dostoyevsky, Fisk and Tart as she rattles about on the Delhi Metro, and whose feedback is usually, 'Um, don't make too many insane things happen, Anju.'

To my hottie son Daivik John, who took printouts of all my

JWT invoices, occasionally asked, 'How many pages today, mamma?', and very importantly, taught me some 'insane' exercises for my lower abs. And who also graced the cover, along with my darling chatterbox Zoya. Thank you both.

To my friend Shalini Beri, my mum Pushpa Raman, and my Ruhi didi, who read early drafts and kept me going.

To my-about-to-be-married editor Neelini Sarkar, who knows the Hailey Road characters as well as I do. Much love and joy to you in the times ahead!

To my two main 'Bolly sources' who cannot be named here ☺

To V.K. Karthika, whose feedback is always so spot-on and who told me exactly what to do with Steesh.

To my agent Anuj Bahri, for being so worldly and so wise both at the same time. And for being nice about the fact that I don't always return phone calls.

To my publishers at Westland, Gautam, KK, Preeti, Varsha and eagle-eyed Deepthi, for having so much faith in this book.

To Anupama, who always takes time out to do my book covers even though she's so busy being this incredibly creative, much-awarded advertising hot-shot.

To Punya, for the epic pics.

For all my family at 18RR, I love all you guys, and I know we will sell our house as happily and amicably as the Thakurs eventually did!

To you, sweet reader, for reading what I write and giving so much meaning to my life.

And to the Lord Jesus Christ for watching over me and mine.

Anuja Chauhan was born in Meerut and went to school in Meerut, Delhi and Melbourne. She has worked in advertising for over seventeen years and has created many popular ad campaigns for PepsiCo, including 'Nothing Official About it', 'Yeh Dil Maange More', 'Oye Bubbly', 'Darr ke aage jeet hai', and 'Live it Abhi'. Her previous books, all bestsellers, have been optioned by major Bollywood studios. She lives outside Bangalore with her husband Niret Alva, their three teenagers, two dogs, two cats and numerous girgits.